William Longman

The History of the Life and Times of Edward the Third

Vol. II

William Longman

The History of the Life and Times of Edward the Third

Vol. II

Reprint of the original, first published in 1869.

1st Edition 2022 | ISBN: 978-3-37504-706-1

Verlag (Publisher): Salzwasser Verlag GmbH, Zeilweg 44, 60439 Frankfurt, Deutschland
Vertretungsberechtigt (Authorized to represent): E. Roepke, Zeilweg 44, 60439 Frankfurt, Deutschland
Druck (Print): Books on Demand GmbH, In de Tarpen 42, 22848 Norderstedt, Deutschland

THE HISTORY

OF

THE LIFE AND TIMES

OF

EDWARD THE THIRD.

BY

WILLIAM LONGMAN.

IN TWO VOLUMES.

VOL. II.

LONDON:

LONGMANS, GREEN, AND CO.

1869.

CONTENTS

OF

THE SECOND VOLUME.

CHAPTER I.
PAGE

THE ENGLISH RULE IN IRELAND, AND ITS FATALLY MISCHIEVOUS
CHARACTER 1

CHAPTER II.

STATE OF FRANCE AFTER THE BATTLE OF POITIERS . . . 17

CHAPTER III.

EDWARD'S SECOND INVASION OF FRANCE.—THE PEACE OF BRE-
TIGNI, AND RELEASE OF KING JOHN 41

CHAPTER IV.

FROM THE PEACE OF BRETIGNI TO THE CREATION OF THE
DUKE OF AQUITAINE 61

CHAPTER V.

DOMESTIC LEGISLATION 70

CHAPTER VI.

KING JOHN RETURNS TO CAPTIVITY AND DEATH.—APPROACHING
RENEWAL OF WAR WITH FRANCE 88

CHAPTER VII.

THE CAMPAIGN IN SPAIN 107

vi CONTENTS OF THE SECOND VOLUME.

CHAPTER VIII.

PAGE

CONCLUSION OF THE SPANISH WAR.—DECLINE OF ENGLISH RULE
IN FRANCE, AND DECLARATION OF WAR BY THE KING OF
FRANCE 134

CHAPTER IX.

RENEWAL OF THE FRENCH WAR, AND END OF THE BLACK
PRINCE'S RULE IN AQUITAINE 157

CHAPTER X.

THE FIRST PARLIAMENTARY CONTEST, AND PREPARATIONS FOR
THE DECISIVE STRUGGLE WITH FRANCE 180

CHAPTER XI.

THE DISASTROUS CAMPAIGN OF 1372 195

CHAPTER XII.

THE LOSS OF AQUITAINE 215

CHAPTER XIII.

PROCEEDINGS OF THE "GOOD PARLIAMENT," AND DEATH OF THE
BLACK PRINCE 243

CHAPTER XIV.

COUNTER REVOLUTION CONSEQUENT ON THE DEATH OF THE
BLACK PRINCE 266

CHAPTER XV.

PROCEEDINGS IN PARLIAMENT UNDER RICHARD PRINCE OF
WALES.—WYCLIF AND THE DUKE OF LANCASTER.—THE
KING'S DEATH 271

CHAPTER XVI.

CONCLUDING REMARKS 291

APPENDIX.

THE ENGLISH SUCCESSION 299

INDEX 305

ILLUSTRATIONS

TO

THE SECOND VOLUME.

MAPS.

MAP		PAGE
7. FRANCE BEFORE THE TREATY OF BRETIGNI	*To face*	41
8. FRANCE AFTER THE TREATY OF BRETIGNI	. .	55
9. SPAIN	. .	107

PLATES.

EFFIGY OF KING EDWARD III. (From his Monument in Westminster Abbey.) . . . *Frontispiece*

MONUMENT OF THOMAS BEAUCHAMP, EARL OF WARWICK. (In the Choir of St. Mary's Church, Warwick.) . *To face* 1

MONUMENT OF PHILIPPA, THE QUEEN OF EDWARD III. (In Westminster Abbey.) 162

MONUMENT OF EDWARD THE BLACK PRINCE. (In Canterbury Cathedral.) 255

MONUMENT OF WILLIAM OF WYKEHAM, BISHOP OF WINCHESTER. (In Winchester Cathedral.) . . . 267

MONUMENT OF KING EDWARD III. (In Westminster Abbey.) 290

WOODCUTS.

PARIS IN THE 13TH CENTURY. (From Viollet-le-Duc's " Essay on the Military Architecture of the Middle Ages." Oxford and London : J. H. and J. Parker.) . . *To face* 21.

A, The Louvre. B, The Temple. C, Palace of King Robert. D, The Law Courts. E, Notre Dame. F, Saint Geneviève. G, Hôtel de Vauvert. H, Château du Bois. I, House of S. Lazare. K, The Infirmary. L, Palace of the Duke of Brittany. M & N, The Markets. O, The Grand-Châtelet. P, The Petit-Châtelet.

viii   ILLUSTRATIONS TO THE SECOND VOLUME.

PAGE

THE LOUVRE IN THE TIME OF CHARLES V. (From Viollet-
le-Duc's Dict.) 28

BASTILLE ST. ANTOINE, AS CONSTRUCTED BY CHARLES V.,
WITH SUBSEQUENT ADDITIONS (*Ibid.*) 37

> A, The top of the Gate of St. Antoine. B, Walls of Paris. C, Bridge
> over the Seine. D, The Bastillon.

> " Dès le temps du roi Jean, ou même avant cette époque, il existait à
> l'entrée de la rue Saint-Antoine une porte flanquée de deux hautes
> tours ; Charles V résolut de faire de cette porte une forte bas-
> tide. Vers 1369, ce prince donna ordre à Hugues Aubriot, prévôt
> de Paris, d'ajouter à ces deux tours un ouvrage considérable, com-
> posé de six autres tours reliées entre elles par d'épaisses courtines.
> Dès lors il paraîtrait que la Bastille ne fut plus une porte, mais un
> fort protégeant la porte Saint-Antoine construite vers le faubourg
> au nord. La bastille Saint-Antoine conserva toutefois son ancienne
> entrée ; dans la partie neuve, trois autres portes furent percées
> dans les deux axes, afin de pouvoir entrer dans le fort ou en sortir
> par quatre ponts jetés sur les fossés. C'était là un véritable fort
> isolé, fermé à la gorge, commandant la campagne et la ville au
> loin, indépendant de l'enceinte mais l'appuyant. Le nom de
> *bastille* par excellence donné à ce poste indique clairement ce que
> l'on entendait par *bastide* au moyen âge."—*Viollet-le-Duc.*

PLAN OF THE PRECINCTS OF WESTMINSTER ABBEY. (From a
Map of Westminster, undated, but probably of the time
of Queen Elizabeth, in the possession of the Rev. Mackenzie Walcott.) (From Scott's "Gleanings from Westminster Abbey." Second Edition, Parker Oxford.) . 57

> A, Abbey Church. B, Littlington's Bell Tower. C, Cloister. D,
> St. Margaret's Church. E, Tower over the entrance to Little
> Dean's Yard. F, Granary and Brewhouse. G, Gatehouse. H,
> Broad Sanctuary. I, Gate to Palace Yard. K, Almonry. L, Or-
> chard. M, Stream of water. N, Westminster Hall.

CHAUCER. (From a Drawing in the British Museum.) . 73

EDWARD THE BLACK PRINCE (From his Monument in Canterbury Cathedral.) 243

> a, Bassinet. b, Camail of chain mail. c, Epauliers, or shoulder-
> pieces of 4 lames or pieces. d, Rerebraces, or brassarts ; armour
> for the rere-arm. e, Coudes, or elbow-pieces. f, Vambraces ;
> armour for the fore-arm. g, Jupon ; a garment of silk, fitting
> closely on the plastron de fer and hauberk, and on which the royal
> arms were emblazoned. h, Gauntlets, armed with gads or gadlings
> (spikes of iron). i, Lower part of the hauberk appearing from
> under the jupon ; it also appears under the arms, and in the
> spaces left vacant by the epauliers. k, Genouillères, or knee-
> pieces. l, Greaves, or leg armour. m, Sollerèts of six pieces,
> or lames. n, Spurs ; these are rowelled, but do not show in
> this view. o, Baudrick, or horizontal sword-belt. p, Tilting
> Helmet with crest.

MONUMENT OF THOMAS BEAUCHAMP EARL OF WARWICK,

in the Choir of St Mary's Church Warwick

THE

LIFE AND TIMES

OF

EDWARD THE THIRD.

A. D. 1327—77.

CHAPTER I.

THE ENGLISH RULE IN IRELAND, AND ITS FATALLY MISCHIEVOUS CHARACTER.

FOR several years after the release of King David, A.D. 1357. there was peace between England and Scotland, and, therefore, the history of the latter country need not now be pursued any further; but, before returning to the narrative of the events which were occurring in England, it is necessary to give an account of King Edward's government of Ireland, and of the troubles with that country, which about this time sorely vexed England.

The iniquitous laws forbidding marriages between Sketch of the English and Irish, which were passed in 1357, the history of the have been already briefly noticed;[1] but their object, Conquest of Ireland. and the causes which led to their enactment, cannot be clearly understood without a short sketch of the

[1] See chap. xix. vol. i.

VOL. II.   B

LIFE AND TIMES OF EDWARD III. CHAP. I.

A.D. 1357. History of Ireland. This will be little more than an account of conquests, of quarrels among the conquerors, of their treacheries and oppressions, and of their alliances with the "mere Irish," when such alliances seemed useful to them, either in supporting their treasons to their King, or in resisting the feudal tyranny of the Viceroys. Of laws for the benefit of Ireland, of consideration for the welfare of the Irish, there will be no trace.

Contrast between the treatment by the English of the Irish and of the Scots, and the Norman treatment of the Anglo-Saxons. It is impossible to avoid contrasting Edward's treatment of Scotland with that of Ireland, whether by himself or by his predecessors. The government of Scotland, by one King instead of six, and its consequent greater unity, undoubtedly enabled it to resist invaders with greater success than Ireland; but, from the beginning, however desirous the Kings of England may have been to subdue Scotland, no attempt was ever made to exercise over it that tyrannous despotism, which, in early times at least, always characterised the English government of Ireland. The same remarks may be made with reference to the Norman conquest of England. It is true that the Norman conquerors of the English exercised oppression enough, and were sufficiently rapacious in appropriating their lands, yet they ultimately became one people with them. The sons and daughters of the two races intermarried, the Norman conquerors lived with the people whom they had subdued, the Norman Kings stayed in the country, and the Normans at last became Englishmen; whereas in Ireland no greater crime could be committed than for an English conqueror to marry or be friends with the Irish whom he had brought under subjection, and was ordered to enslave, nor might he even

CHAP. I.   HISTORY OF IRELAND.   3

adopt their customs or pastimes, or learn their lan-   A.D. 1357.
guage.

The reason of this, as will be shown, was, that a certain portion of the English, to whom Irish lands were granted, became attached to the people and the country, and then endeavoured to become independent of England. The policy of England, was to make the settlers aliens in the land.

When Ireland was invaded by Henry the Second, it was divided into five provinces, viz. Ulster, Leinster, Connaught, and North and West Munster, each of which was governed by a king; but these five provinces elected a Monarch of all Ireland, who possessed, in virtue of that dignity, the central territory of Meath. As Duke William had received authority from Pope Alexander II. to subdue England, so had Henry II. received a Bull, in 1155, from Adrian IV. directing him to subdue Ireland. The pretext was, "to extend the bounds of the Church, and to teach a rude people the rudiments of the Christian faith," as if the Irish up to that time had been pagans. No opportunity for acting on this Bull offered itself for nearly fifteen years; but at last, Dermod MacMurragh, King of Leinster, quarrelled with Roderick O'Connor, the Monarch of Ireland, who deprived him of his throne. Thus there arose an excuse for England's interference. In an evil moment for Ireland, Dermod sought the aid of Henry the Second. Henry had gone to Aquitaine, to quell some disturbances in his French dominions, and thither Dermod went, and offered to do the King homage for Leinster, on condition of his helping him to recover his sovereignty over it. The feudal system was never established among the native Irish, and this promise of allegiance, therefore, could

Political divisions of Ireland at the time of the invasion of Henry II.

[A.D. 1155.]

Pretext for the invasion.

The King of Leinster seeks help from the King of England against the King of Ireland.

B 2

4   LIFE AND TIMES OF EDWARD III.   CHAP. I.

[A.D. 1155.] neither bind his clan—or sept, as these communities were called in Ireland—nor be of force under the Irish law; but yet Henry accepted Dermod as his liegeman, and thus, according to the feudal law, or principle of commendation, became bound to help him against his enemies.

The King of Leinster obtains help from Earl "Strongbow,"

Having received formal documents from Henry, promising his favour to all Dermod's subjects who should help him, Dermod set out on his return to Ireland; on his way, passing through Bristol (which was then, as now, much frequented by the Irish), he made arrangements with Richard Fitzgilbert, Earl of Pembroke, and Lord of Strigul (now Chepstow), who afterwards became celebrated as Strongbow, for help towards the recovery of his kingdom. This earl therefore went over to Ireland to fight for Dermod,

[A.D. 1171.] who marries his daughter.

and married his daughter Eva. On Dermod's death in 1171 "Strongbow" claimed the kingdom of Leinster; but O'Connor, the King of Ireland, refused to recognise his claim, made war upon him, and besieged him in Dublin. Strongbow defeated O'Connor, and then went over to England, leaving Dublin in the custody of Milun de Cogan. In the autumn, he returned with a large army, accompanied by King Henry, who had now resolved to attempt the conquest of Ireland.

Henry II. invades Ireland.

Henry landed at Waterford on October 18th, 1171, and marched through Leinster to Dublin, where he "kept his Christmas." All the Kings of Ireland, except the King of Connaught,[1] agreed to become tributary to him, and in the following spring, Henry, thinking he had done enough to secure possession of Ireland, returned to England. Before his departure,

[1] Ben. Abb. I. 25.

CHAP. I. THE FIRST VICEROY. 5

however, although he had acquired no power over any part of Ireland but Leinster, and in utter defiance of the laws of Ireland, he executed charters bestowing on ten of his principal followers, according to the Norman law, the entire land of Ireland, with the exception of the towns on the Eastern coast, which he kept under his own control. *[A.D. 1171.] Henry grants Ireland to his barons,*

It is evident, that these intruders could not obtain possession of the lands thus granted to them, unless they were able by force of arms to subdue their native lords. Such indeed was the condition of the grants, and thus were laid the foundations of the struggles between the English and Irish, which have never wholly ceased from the days of Strongbow until now. After a time, as will be seen, the invaders became possessed of a great part of Ireland; they then tried to shake off their dependence on England, to which they became a source of great trouble, and quarrelled with each other. But yet, with the exception of some who became attached to the Irish but were forbidden by law to become their friends, they never amalgamated with the natives of the country. *who seize it by force of arms.*

On leaving Ireland, Henry appointed Hugh de Lacy governor of Dublin and head of the Anglo-Norman colony. He was thus the first Viceroy of Ireland appointed by the King of England. *The first Viceroy.*

In 1177, Henry decided on erecting the English colony in Ireland into a distinct dominion or lordship for his son John, and with the Pope's leave invested him as Lord of Ireland. The English to whom grants of Irish lands had been made, were thus compelled to swear to hold their possessions of John and Henry. Strong castles were now built everywhere as defences against the natives, who opposed the new comers *[A.D. 1177.] Henry's son John invested with the dominion over Ireland.*

6   LIFE AND TIMES OF EDWARD III.   CHAP. I.

[A.D. 1177.]

Enmity between English and Irish encouraged.

unceasingly. Even at this time, it was deemed a wise policy, to prevent any friendly union between the invaders and the natives, lest they should become nearer of kin to Ireland than to England; no stronger evidence of this intention can be needed, than the fact that when, in 1181, Hugh de Lacy, the Viceroy, took for his second wife the daughter of King Roderick O'Connor, Henry immediately dismissed him from his office. Henry soon saw his mistake, and thought it best to reappoint him; but, so utterly had De Lacy shaken Henry's confidence in him, by daring to marry an Irish woman, that he would not restore him to his dignities, without taking securities for his fidelity, and associating with him the Constable of Chester (his kinsman), and a priest to act as a spy upon his actions.

Henry fears lest the Norman Lords of Ireland should become independent of him.

Henry now feared lest the barons, for whom he had despoiled the Irish chiefs, should become strong enough to assert their independence and set him at defiance, and, accordingly, sent his son John over to Ireland in 1185, as chief Governor, to keep them in order; but John was soon obliged to return to England, after disastrous conflicts with the native chiefs.

[A.D. 1186.]

Castles built to protect the settlers.

In 1186, De Lacy was murdered by the foster-son of one of the chiefs whom he had dispossessed, and his death was deemed a serious blow to the English authority. By the advice of Girald de Barri, better known as Giraldus Cambrensis, who had been appointed as a companion and adviser to Prince John, more castles were therefore built, passes were cut through the woods, and even the natives under Anglo-Norman control were forbidden to bear arms of any kind, but above all to use the favourite Irish axe.

The Irish forbidden to bear arms.

The English, as had been feared by Henry, now

CHAP. I.   OPPRESSIONS OF THE VICEROYS.   7

endeavoured to make themselves independent rulers, and shake off their allegiance, not only to the King of England, but also to his Viceroy. Thus John de Courcy, Earl of Ulster, the first foreigner on whom an Irish title had been conferred, coined money in his own name, lived in regal state, waged war against the Viceroy, and defeated him in 1204.

[A.D. 1204.] The settlers try to become indepen- dent.

But even the Viceroys, or Chief Justiciaries as they were usually called after the close of the 12th century, were not free from suspicion, and were obliged—as De Lacy had been—to give hostages to the King for their fidelity. The native chiefs, who entered into engagements with the King, were obliged in like manner to give hostages to the Justiciary.

Even the Viceroys are sus- pected ;

But the Justiciaries did not spare their own coun- trymen, and in 1208, Hugh de Lacy the second, son of the first viceroy to whom the government of the colony had been entrusted, so oppressed the colonists, that they joined with the despised Irish, and fought a battle with De Lacy at Thurles. Two years afterwards, King John thought it needful to go over to Ireland to look after his Viceroy, and, assisted by some of the native chiefs, with whom for his own ends he made friends, actually waged war against him. He overran all the country which had been colonised by the English, De Lacy retreating before him and burning his castles. On John's return to Dublin, he made the English Lords swear obedience to the laws of England, and ordered that all subjects holding land by "knight's service," should, when summoned to the King's aid, furnish for each knight's fee a horse-soldier, well mounted, accoutred with helmet, shirt of mail, spear and sword ; and that tenants by "service of foot-soldiers" should provide

[A.D. 1208.] but still they oppress the settlers.

King John goes to Ireland and makes war on his own Vice- roy,

and makes stringent rules for the defence of Ireland against the Irish.

8   LIFE AND TIMES OF EDWARD III.   Chap. I.

[A.D. 1208.]   men well armed with shields, spears, and long knives, for the defence of the colony.

Henry III. forbids the appointment of native Irish to cathedral preferment.

On the accession of Henry the Third, he ordered the Justiciary, to forbid the admission of any native Irishman to cathedral preferment in Ireland. He was soon obliged to recall this order, but its issue is one of the evidences that the principles on which Ireland was governed, were that the natives should be universally reduced to utter subjection,

The King fears to punish the insubordination of the settler chiefs, lest he should make them Irish.

Insubordination among the settlers, and constant warfare with the septs, were now the unvarying phases of the state of Ireland, and the King feared to punish the treachery of his own creatures, lest he should turn them into friends of the Irish. Thus, when the Earl of Pembroke, Strongbow's grandson, fell in battle with the Viceroy, Henry lost no time in conferring his estates on his brothers, and heaping honours on them, in order to secure their fidelity.

Resistance of the Irish septs to English rule.

For some years, there was no change in the system on which England attempted to subdue Ireland. In 1260 the septs rose and gained important advantages over the colonists, and from 1276 to 1282 the English were hard-pressed by the Irish. Sir Robert Ufford, who was Viceroy at this time, tried to lessen their power, by setting the septs one against another, and on being called to account for this by King Edward the First, who ordered him to come to him in England, he said he thought it expedient to wink at one knave cutting off another; at which the King smiled, and bade him return to Ireland.

Ireland divided into liberties

About the beginning of the fourteenth century those portions of Ireland which were nominally under English dominion were divided into five "Liberties," viz. Connaught and Ulster; Meath;

CHAP. I. FRIENDSHIP WITH THE IRISH FORBIDDEN. 9

Wexford, Carlow and Kilkenny; Thomond or North Munster; and Desmond or West Munster. These were also organised into ten counties, viz. Dublin, Louth, Kildare, Waterford, Tipperary, Cork, Limerick, Kerry, Roscommon, and part of Connaught. The Lords of the Liberties exercised high authority, and lived in the state of princes; but, on most of the Liberties, many native septs still existed, sometimes as friends, sometimes as foes, who were governed according to the Gaelic code, known as the Senchus Mor, administered by their Brehons or judges according to ancient precedents. The borders, called "Marches," between the Anglo-Norman lands and those almost entirely occupied by the Irish, were continually attacked by the native septs, who gave the colonists no peace, and who sometimes advanced to the very gates of Dublin. The landholders near the "Marches" were, therefore, obliged to keep soldiers constantly ready, to repel attacks by day or night. But the colonists suffered also, from the constant quarrels of their resident Lords, and from the absenteeism of the others, whilst they were also continually called on by Edward the Third to furnish soldiers for his wars. Under these circumstances, it cannot be matter of surprise, that many of the settlers thought it would be better, to be independent of England, and to unite themselves with the Irish chiefs. Some of them therefore adopted the native habits and manners, and were consequently sometimes taken for and treated as Irish enemies. Thus sprang up an additional difficulty in the management of Ireland. The policy of the kings of England, from the first, was to treat the natives as a horde of savages, to take their lands wholly from them, and to reduce them to

10 LIFE AND TIMES OF EDWARD III. Chap. I.

[A.D. 1309.] the condition of villein labourers, if not of very slaves, on the demesnes, which were once their own but had become the property of foreign conquerors. But, as already related, on the one hand, the Lords sent to Ireland to carry this policy into effect, could not avoid forming friendships with those whom they subdued, or becoming half Irish by marriage with their daughters; and, on the other, they so constantly quarrelled among themselves, and so uniformly oppressed their English vassals, that the latter often banded themselves together with the Irish against them. The colony therefore was far from flourishing, and in 1309 the Anglo-Irish Parliament ascribed the poverty of the colonists to the oppressions of the English Lords, from whom they dared not ask redress. Parliament therefore gave them a right of appeal to the King.

[A.D. 1314.] *The triumph of Bruce in 1314 encourages the native Irish to resist.* The triumph of Bruce over the English in 1314 gave the Irish great hopes of uprooting the alien rule; the crown of Ireland was, therefore, with this view, offered to Bruce's brother, Edward Earl of Carrick, by O'Neill and other unsubdued Ulster chiefs, with whom the ambitious De Lacys united. Edward Bruce readily accepted the proffered crown, and landed on the Ulster coast with about 6,000 men, in May 1315. He was immediately joined by Donald O'Neill and other Irish allies, and after gaining some important victories over the colonists, was crowned *Edward Bruce crowned King of Ireland.* Monarch of Ireland at Carrickfergus. The next year he defeated the Viceroy. The settlers now became alarmed, and, setting forth in a manifesto that " the Scotch enemy had drawn to them all the Irish, many of the English, and a large number of the great lords, seeking traitorously to wrest Ireland from their Lord ' Monsieur Edward,' King of England," entered

CHAP. I.   SEVERANCE OF ENGLISH AND IRISH.   11

into a solemn league to maintain his rights, and, in [A.D. 1818.] order to prevent breaches of faith among themselves, offered to give hostages for their fidelity to the King. Bruce's reign over Ireland, however, was not of long duration, and produced but little effect on its condition. A large number of settlers were driven out of Ulster, and in that territory, as well as in Connaught and North Munster, many of the Irish regained possession of their lands; but Ireland was not freed from the English invaders.

Death of Bruce without any great result to the Irish.

Soon after the accession of Edward the Third to the throne of England, he issued ordinances for the reformation of Ireland; providing, among other things, that all English proprietors of lands in Ireland, whether lay or ecclesiastical, should either dwell on them or provide soldiers for their defence against the Irish. The English Lords, however, still continued their struggle for independence. The junior branches of the De Burgh family (the senior male line having become extinct by the death of Earl William), fearful lest a new feudal absentee Lord should be thrust upon them, occupied and divided between themselves the entire Lordship of Connaught, comprising the present counties of Galway and Mayo, inclusive of the town of Galway. They confederated themselves with the native septs, adopted Irish dress, language and laws, took Irish names, and renounced their allegiance to England. Simultaneously with this defection, a sept of the O'Neills drove the settlers out of East Ulster, and by about 1341, the Irish had regained more than a third part of the territories which had been brought under English dominion.

Edward III. makes laws against absentees.

The De Burghs set Edward at defiance.

Successes of the Irish.

King Edward now sought to secure greater fidelity among his officers in Ireland by separating them en-

12 LIFE AND TIMES OF EDWARD III. CHAP. I.

A.D. 1341.

Edward tries to govern Ireland by severing the governors entirely from the governed, and revokes recent grants of land;

tirely from Irish interests. In 1341, he ordered that all his officers who were married or who had estates in Ireland and none in England, should be removed, and Englishmen having lands in England put in their place. His next measure was still more fatal to the peace of Ireland; in order to replenish his treasury, emptied by his foreign wars, he declared void every grant of land and tenements in Ireland made from the time of his father, and at the same time annulled all acquittances, except those under the great seal of England, which had at any time been given to its debtors in Ireland by the English Crown. New grants were made of the lands thus resumed by the King.

and thus divides the settlers into English by birth and English by blood.

This introduced a fresh element of discord, for the new comers, termed "English by birth," were naturally the enemies of those whose lands they occupied, and who although of English origin were born in Ireland and were therefore called "English by blood."

So great did the hostility between these two divisions of the settlers soon become, that "the King's land in Ireland was on the point of passing away from the Crown of England,"[1] and a few years afterwards a statute was passed enacting that "Although as well those born in Ireland who are of English lineage, as those born in England and dwelling in Ireland, be true English; yet, divers dissensions and maintenancies by reason of birth, between them that are natives of Ireland and them that are natives of England have arisen, whence many evils have heretofore happened, and it is to be feared that greater will happen, unless

---

[1] *History of the Viceroys of Ireland*, by J. T. Gilbert, Librarian of the Royal Irish Academy, p. 192. From this valuable work the present sketch of the History of Ireland has been condensed.

CHAP. I. DISSENSIONS BETWEEN SETTLERS AND KING. 13

a remedy be applied thereto; we will and stedfastly A.D. 1341. command, that our Justice, concerning such dissensions shall earnestly enquire, and the delinquents, by imprisonment of their bodies and grievous ransoms to be made to us, shall punish and chastise, for that such dissensions have no other end but to produce schism, divisions and treasons among our subjects." (31 Ed. III. statute iv. c. 18.)

The Viceroy, on whom the carrying into effect of these ordinances devolved, summoned a Parliament to meet in Dublin in October 1341; but the Earl of Desmond, and others of the chief Anglo-Norman Lords "English by blood," refused to attend, and convened a meeting at Kilkenny. At this they enquired into the causes of the state of Ireland, and embodied their conclusions in a memorial to the King, declaring that "his Irish enemies had retaken more than one third of the lands and manors, which had yielded large revenues to his predecessors, that they had seized or levelled many castles, once the defence of the English, and that his subjects in Ireland (meaning of course the settlers), were reduced to such a state of poverty, that they could no longer exist unless some remedies were devised." They attributed these evils The "no less to the incessant war waged by the Irish " Settler Lords inthan to the frauds of the King's ministers in Ireland, duce the King to and they added that. "many districts had been revoke his ruined because their proprietors never came thither tion of from England, nor made any expenditure towards lands. their maintenance, but sought, by setting them to farm, to extract all the money they could yield." In conclusion, they prayed that the King would not resume possession of their lands. King Edward complied with their petition.

14 LIFE AND TIMES OF EDWARD III. Chap. I.

A.D. 1344.

Strong measures against the Irish.

In February 1344, Edward, having lost confidence in his ministers, issued a proclamation forbidding any of them to quit Ireland until their conduct had been looked into, and ordered the seizure of ships in which they might attempt to escape. A new Viceroy — Sir Ralph Ufford — was then appointed, who tried to repress the Irish with vigour. Part of Kildare being attacked, he proclaimed it penal to furnish the Irish with horses, victuals, or arms; and also declared, that he would enforce the ordinance that there should be only one war and one peace throughout Ireland; meaning, that he would grant no truce or peace to one sept, if another were at war with the colonists. Ufford died in 1346, and was succeeded by another Viceroy; but the septs would not submit, whoever might be the alien ruler of their land.

A.D. 1353.

The settlers are forbidden to leave Ireland.

At last, some of the chief settlers, forbidden to make themselves Irishmen, and wearied with everlasting strife with the ancient owners of the land, prepared to abandon Ireland; and King Edward, therefore, in 1353, ordered that no man capable of bearing arms should leave the country. Many, however, did not thus give themselves up to despair, but continued to live in amity with the Irish, and intermarried with them. Then was passed that iniquitous law forbidding such practices, of which an account has already been given. But it utterly failed to produce its intended effect.

In the meanwhile, the Irish septs, in districts beyond English control, continued to elect their kings and chiefs according to ancient custom, and obeyed the Brehon law; and those who were mingled with the settlers, so harassed them, that they were often unable to attend the Parliaments, and the King was consequently obliged, in 1359, to allow Parliaments to

CHAP. I.   STATUTE OF KILKENNY.   15

be held in different places.   But the enmity between
the "English by blood" and "English by birth"
still went on, and the former married with the Irish,
adopted their language, laws, and dress, and became
bound to them also by "gossipred" and "fosterage."

A.D. 1361.

English by blood, and English by birth.

In the same year, Edward forbade the election
of any "mere Irish" as mayor, bailiff, or to any
other post in his dominions in Ireland;[1] and thus,
the only policy of England seemed to be, to degrade
the Irish in every way.   This, however, did not
succeed; at length, therefore, the King resolved to
send his son to Ireland, and Lionel, created Duke of
Clarence (to whom he had married Elizabeth, heiress
of William de Burgh, Earl of Ulster), and so called
from his Lordship of Clare in Suffolk, landed in
Ireland in 1361.   Lionel's first step was to forbid
any man born in Ireland to approach his camp, but
he was soon driven to such straits by the Irish that,
on February 10th, 1362, the King issued writs "declaring that his very dear son and his companions
in Ireland were in imminent peril," and ordering the
absentee Lords to repair to Ireland to assist him.
At last, in Lent 1367, there was passed the famous,
or rather infamous, Statute of Kilkenny, which re-
capitulated all former ordinances, again forbade marriages between the English and Irish, ordered the
use of the English language and English customs,
and entered with such minuteness into the habits of
daily life, that the Irish were forbidden to ride on
horseback, except in saddles according to the English
custom.   National games, such as "hurlings and quoit-
ings," were forbidden, the practice of the old Irish
system of law, which had been in use since the con-

Lionel Duke of Clarence goes to Ireland.

A.D. 1367.

Statute of Kilkenny.

[1] Rymer, vol. iii. p. 434.

16 LIFE AND TIMES OF EDWARD III. CHAP. I.

A.D. 1357. version of the people to Christianity in the fifth century,[1] was made unlawful, and all means were taken for the utter subjugation of the country. But the quarrels between the "English by blood" and "English by birth" were not forgotten, and it was ordered that the former should not be called "Irish dogs" nor the latter "English Hobbes."

Of course this statute did not give peace to Ireland, but its history cannot here be further pursued. It is sufficient, to have shown the origin of the extraordinary laws relative to Ireland, passed at this period of the reign of Edward the Third; and to have explained the reason, why the English Kings adopted the policy of forbidding friendship between the English and Irish.

The general result may be thus summarised. It is beyond dispute that the land of Ireland was held, according to the Brehon law, in a way peculiar to that country, by which every Irishman was considered to possess a certain proprietorship in it;[2] that the English settlers, by order of the English kings, systematically disregarded that law, and acted as rapacious conquerors; and, that when they showed symptoms of ceasing to do so, the English kings stepped in, and forbade any approach to friendship with the Irish. Can it be matter of surprise, then, that a nation so imaginative, such a worshipper of tradition, so intensely national as the Irish, refuses to forget these things, cherishes the recollection of oppressions long since past away, and still ignorantly believes that the right of the whole people to the soil is not and never can be extinguished?

[1] Preface to *Ancient Laws of Ireland*, vol. i. (Dublin 1865), p. 5.
[2] See *ante*, vol. i.

CHAPTER II.

STATE OF FRANCE AFTER THE BATTLE OF POITIERS.

THE two years' truce between England and France was badly kept on both sides, but the chief blame of its imperfect observance must be laid on the English. Charles of Blois had been released from prison in England in August 1356,[1] just at the time that the Duke of Lancaster returned to Brittany after his campaign in Normandy. War between him and the Duke had immediately broken out, and it continued on until after the battle of Poitiers. The Duke had laid siege to Rennes on October 3rd, 1356, and during its continuance one of those picturesque incidents, so characteristic of the times and of chivalry, occurred.

John Bolton, one of the besiegers, amused himself with hawking in the neighbourhood of the city, and one day took six partridges. He then put on his complete armour, mounted his horse, and rode up to the gates of the city, saying he wanted to see Bertrand du Guesclin, a man then unknown to fame, but who became eventually the chief support of the French throne. Bertrand did not appear, but Olivier de Maunay, a relation probably of the well-known Sir Walter, came to the gate and asked Bolton whether he would sell his partridges to some ladies in the town. "By my faith," said Bolton, "if you dare to bargain a little nearer to me and come so close that we may

A.D. 1357–59.

Non-observance of the two years' truce.

Siege of Rennes.

Chivalric incident during the siege.

---

[1] Rymer, vol. iii. p. 335.

VOL. II.   C

18 LIFE AND TIMES OF EDWARD III. Chap. II.

A.D.
1357-59.

fight, I will deal with you." "As God will, *ouil*," said Olivier, " wait and I will come and pay you." He then came down from the walls to the moat, which was full of water, and, taking off his gauntlets and leg-armour, jumped in and swam across. Bolton and Olivier were not long in beginning their fight, the Duke of Lancaster and his army looking on on one side, and the ladies in Rennes, " who," as Froissart says, " took great pleasure in watching them," on the other. Bolton was overcome, and Olivier took him and his partridges into the city. They were both wounded, but, before they had been long within the walls, Olivier began to feel that his wounds were serious, and accordingly told his prisoner that if he could procure him a safe-conduct for a month he would set him free. Olivier said he knew of some herbs which would cure him, but which could not be obtained in the town. Bolton set off on his errand, the Duke of Lancaster granted the safe-conduct, and Bolton then returned to Rennes and came back again with his captor. The month was spent in the English camp ; the Frenchman was treated by the English surgeons; and, as soon as he had recovered, returned to Rennes with great expressions of politeness and courtesy on both sides.[1]

Raising of the siege of Rennes.

The siege of Rennes was still going on when the truce was made. At the end of the following month, King Edward wrote to the Duke ordering him to abandon it, according to the conditions of the truce ;

The Duke of Lancaster's vow.

but the Duke had made a vow that he would never leave Rennes until he had planted his standard on its walls, and therefore took no notice of the King's commands. It consequently became necessary for

[1] Buchon's *Froissart*, vol. i. p. 369.

MISERABLE STATE OF FRANCE.

Edward to write again, and in a still more decided manner, on the 4th of July. The Duke then complied. As a matter of form, the garrison allowed his vow to be carried into effect; the English banner floated from the ramparts for a short time, and the siege was then given up.[1]

At the expiration of the truce, war between England and France broke out with greater bitterness than ever. In order, however, to understand the relative positions of the two countries, it is necessary to enter, with some little detail, into the history of the deeply interesting events which took place in France during its continuance.

The state of France was dreadful. No country ever suffered under greater calamities, than France after the battle of Poitiers. The Duke of Normandy and the nobles cared for nothing but luxury and extravagance; the enormous amount of the taxes which were imposed, and the debasement of the coin which was practised to support this wicked folly, spread misery from one end of the kingdom to the other. The released nobles made their vassals pay the ransoms they had promised to their English conquerors, and the disbanded soldiers formed themselves into Free Companies, under English as well as French leaders, and roamed about the country plundering and ravaging.

The States-General, which had vainly endeavoured, in the previous year, to introduce reforms into the administration of the Government of France, met again on October 17th, 1356, just one month after the battle of Poitiers; and though the Assembly was again sum-

[1] Rymer, vol. iii. pp. 353 and 359; and Sismondi, vol. x. p. 505.

20 LIFE AND TIMES OF EDWARD III. CHAP. II.

A.D.
1357--59.

moned only from those speaking the *langue d'oil*, it consisted of more than eight hundred persons, comprising nobles, barons, knights, and traders, the *tiers état* or bourgeois (among whom were two doctors in theology) forming at least one-half of the number. The King's brother the Duke of Orleans, and his uncle the Count of Alençon, were present, but neither of them was chosen president of the Assembly. They

Charles of Blois elected president.

had fled at Poitiers, and were disgraced. Charles of Blois, Duke of Brittany, who had been released from his imprisonment in England in the previous July,[1] on payment of 25,000 nobles as satisfaction for the sum of 50,000 gold florins, the agreed amount of his ransom, was the only Prince who received any consideration, and was elected President.

Etienne Marcel and Robert Lecoq.

The most prominent men in the Assembly were, Etienne Marcel and Robert Lecoq Bishop of Laon. Marcel was a merchant draper in Paris, and Provost of the Merchants. He was a man of remarkable character, and, whatever may have been the ultimate result of his patriotic endeavours to bring about a better government in France, there can be no doubt that at this critical period he rendered

Measures taken to defend Paris.

great services to the State. It seemed probable that King Edward would return to France in the spring and march on Paris, or even that the Black Prince might at once attack the capital, which was in an utterly defenceless state. He therefore practised the inhabitants in the use of arms, the right to which had been restored to them in 1355, and, under the authority of the Duke of Normandy, employed three thousand men in fortifying the city. Robert Lecoq, before becoming a priest, had been the King's

[1] Rymer, vol. iii. p. 360.

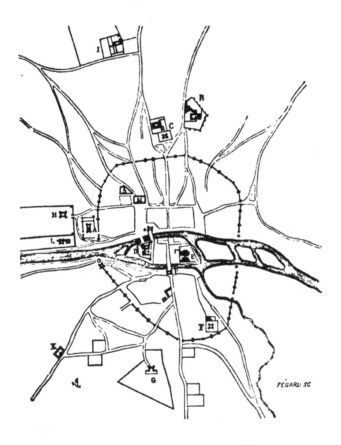

PARIS IN THE THIRTEENTH CENTURY.

From Viollet-le-Duc's Essay on the Military Architecture of the Middle Ages. (For explanation, see List of Illustrations.)

CHAP. II. MEETING OF THE STATES. 21

advocate in the Parliament of Paris, and no one was better acquainted with the abuses under which France suffered, or felt more strongly the necessity of reforming them.

The States met while the fortification of Paris was going on. They were too numerous to debate in full assembly about the measures to be adopted, and a committee of about eighty members was therefore appointed for that purpose. The Committee of Nine, which had been appointed in 1355 for the management of the taxes, having been found an insufficient protection against the royal power, Marcel and Lecoq declared it necessary to go further, to put down the great council of the King, to punish the most guilty of its members, and replace it by a council elected by the States. Proposals to this effect, which amounted indeed to a revolution, were then drawn up by the Eighty and submitted to the States, by whom they were unanimously approved. The States also declared that it would be for the good of the kingdom if the King of Navarre were released from prison. These proposals were to be submitted to the Duke of Normandy on the 31st of October, but their purport transpired before that day, and the Duke, contrary to the advice of Charles of Blois, of the princes of the blood, and of the principal nobles, determined to resist. He said he had received news from his father the King, and his uncle the Emperor, which rendered it desirable to defer the further sitting of the Parliament till the 3rd of November. The States unfortunately consented, and, on the day before the time appointed for their re-assembling, the Duke persuaded them to disperse, under the pretext of giving them an opportunity of consulting their constituents, and

A.D. 1357–59.

Proposals of reform submitted to the States;

but resisted by the Duke of Normandy.

Dispersion of the States.

22   LIFE AND TIMES OF EDWARD III.   CHAP. II.

A.D. 1857–59. of allowing himself time to consult his father. The golden opportunity was lost.

Meeting of the States of the Langue d'Oc. The Duke summoned the States of the Langue d'Oc to assemble at Toulouse about this time, hoping that they would be more submissive; but, although they were quite ready to provide men and means for the defence of the country, they were as determined as the States-General to insist on proper administration.

Their measures of reform They reserved to commissioners appointed by themselves the right of levying and expending the taxes, and declared that they would re-assemble when they pleased, without summonses, to grant subsidies, which they threatened to withhold if the coin were again tampered with. They also forbade all persons, of whatever degree, to wear silver, pearls, or rich furs, and so deep was the depression of the country that they even forbade the minstrels and jongleurs to follow their merry callings for the space of one year, unless in the meantime the King were released.

which are resisted by the Duke of Normandy. The Duke was, however, encouraged in his resistance to the demands of the nation, by the promise of a subsidy, and by the news he received from Normandy of the death of Godfrey of Harcourt, who, together with Philip of Navarre, had, after the battle of Poitiers, begun again to ravage Normandy. The surrender of Pont Audemer was a consequence of Harcourt's death. The Duke tried to levy subsidies by his own officers, in defiance of the appointment of the Committee of Nine; in this he did not succeed, and therefore, glad to escape from the reformers, and hoping that some favourable result would arise from the conference, he set off, on the 5th of December, to visit

Efforts for the King's release. his uncle, the Emperor Charles the Fourth, at Metz. While there, he engaged in fruitless negotiations with

CHAP. II. OPPRESSIONS OF THE FRENCH NOBLES. 23

envoys, both from the Pope and King Edward, for the release of his father; but he spent most of his time in feasting and extravagance, for which, before he set out on his journey, he had endeavoured to find means by debasing the coinage. On the 14th of January, 1357, the Duke returned to Paris without any useful result from his visit. The people were now exasperated, and assembled in the streets in arms. A revolution was evidently at hand; the Duke, becoming frightened, ordered his chief advisers to go away or hide themselves, called Marcel to the palace, promised to stop the issue of base money, gave the deputies of the three orders the right of assembling when they pleased, and consented to bring to justice the seven officers of his Council whom the States had denounced; provided, as he said, he could find out where they were. This was on the 20th of January, 1357.

A.D. 1357–59.

The Duke yields to the demands of the people.

In the meantime, the barons and knights, whom the English had taken prisoners, had been allowed to return to their estates to raise the money for their ransoms, which often amounted to one-half of the value of their whole property. If they had tried to sell their estates, they could not have found buyers; they could not borrow money, for the Jews and Lombard bankers had been driven out of the country; so there was nothing left to them but to squeeze their vassals. They seized their goods; they put them to torture to find money; and thus raised the necessary sums "to buy back," as Sismondi says, "from the English, certain gentlemen who were useless to France." These feudal lords, however, were not content with extorting money from the peasants; they also derided their misery.

The feudal lords raise money for their ransom by oppressive means.

24   LIFE AND TIMES OF EDWARD III.   Chap. II.

A.D.
1357–59.

"*Jacques bon homme* will not pull out his purse unless you beat him, but *Jacques bon homme* will pull out his purse because he will be beaten," was the common talk, and *Jacques bon homme* was thenceforth the contemptuous designation of the French peasant.

The peasants also pillaged by the disbanded soldiery.

But the peasants were tormented with another scourge. The disbanded soldiers of both armies spread themselves over the country, robbing, pillaging, and murdering, " stripping naked those to whom the lords had left a shirt." The bandit bands into which they gathered themselves became, in after times, renowned as " The Companies." One of these, which at first infested Provence, was led by Arnaud de Cervolles, a relation of the Talleyrands of Perigord, who was called the Archpriest on account of a benefice he held, although he was a layman ; but the Pope paid him well to leave Provence, and he then ravaged Burgundy. Another was formed in Normandy, composed of English and Navarrese, under the command of Sir Robert Knolles, a man who had risen from a low origin, but by his marauding activity became at last a great captain ;[1] and a third, of men of various nations, was assembled between the Seine and the Loire, under a Welshman named Griffiths—called by Froissart Ruffin. These companies were sometimes called Navarrese,[2] and sometimes English, although both King Edward and Charles the Bad, King of Navarre, equally disavowed them. The peasants dug ditches round their villages, and fortified the churches, placing sentinels in the

---

[1] Walsingham, p. 286.

[2] The Navarrese mercenaries were infamous, as early as the twelfth century, and condemned by name in the Lateran Council of 1179.—Ben. Abbas, I. 228.

CHAP. II.   THE STATES-GENERAL MEET AGAIN.   25

towers, ready to sound the alarm as soon as they caught sight of an armed man.   At night, in the neighbourhood of the Loire, they sought refuge in the islands in the river, or huddled together, with their flocks and families, in boats which they moored in the stream. Those living near Paris crowded into that city, leaving their lands untilled ; and the monks and nuns, whom the soldiers never spared, also flocked into Paris for protection.   At the same time, Philip of Navarre, finding that the temporary success which had attended the Royal arms on the death of Godfrey of Harcourt had not been followed up, had resumed the offensive.   He established himself at Evreux, which was given up to him by the citizens, who were devotedly attached to his brother the King of Navarre.

It was under these circumstances that the States-General met again on the 5th of February, 1357 ; but the danger of travelling was so great, that the attendance of members was much smaller than at the previous meeting.   The paucity of members was, however, compensated by increased energy.   Marcel and Lecoq were again the leaders.   After a month's deliberation, the Duke was obliged to listen to an eloquent address from Lecoq, setting forth the grievances of the nation.   He said the people could no longer endure them, and demanded that twenty-two of the great officers of the King should be dismissed, and all the others temporarily suspended; that good money should be circulated; that forced loans should cease; that justice, which had sometimes been deferred for twenty years, should be rendered more speedily; that the offices of justice should not be sold ; that the judges should not be allowed to receive money from the great men to shield their crimes ; and that many

A.D. 1357–59.

The States-General meet, Feb. 1357.

Reforms demanded by them ;

26 LIFE AND TIMES OF EDWARD III. Chap. II.

A.D. 1357–59.

to which the Duke consents.

other abuses under which the nation was suffering should be done away with. He then promised to find money for 30,000 soldiers for one year, provided the payment of the men and the carrying into effect of the reforms were entrusted to a commission of thirty-six persons, consisting of twelve prelates, twelve nobles, and twelve citizens, and that the three Estates should be allowed to re-assemble when they pleased. The Duke was obliged to yield, but, as he afterwards declared, did so, hoping at a future time to undo what he then did against his will. The deputies obtained leave to take each six armed men with them, on their return home, for protection against the King's officers, who were ready to waylay and murder them. The only point on which they did not insist, was the release of the King of Navarre.

The Committee of Thirty-six.

The Royal power was now entirely superseded in Paris; the Committee of Thirty-six entered vigorously on their functions, and the revolution seemed complete. One of the first acts of the Committee was, to assemble fleets at the mouths of the Seine and Somme, in order to prevent the Prince of Wales from carrying the King of France off to England. But the Prince escaped with his prisoners, and a truce for two years between England and France was signed on the 23rd of March.

A truce signed.

Opposition of the Duke of Normandy to the Thirty-six.

Before leaving France, King John had forbidden obedience to the decrees of the Estates; and the Duke of Normandy ordered this edict to be proclaimed in Paris, at the same time as the truce. The Parisians were so enraged at this duplicity, as they justly thought it, that the Duke was obliged to revoke the King's orders. He nevertheless easily persuaded the provinces to refuse payment of the taxes proposed by the Com-

Chap. II. MARCEL RELEASES THE KING OF NAVARRE. 27

mittee; and, by sowing dissension between the nobles and the citizens and between the provincial towns and Paris, managed to reduce the Council of Thirty-six to the citizens and to two persons of the other orders, viz., the Bishop of Laon and the Lord of Picquigni. The Duke then ventured, about the middle of August, on the bold step of informing the Committee of Thirty-six, that he intended thenceforth to govern for himself, without their intervention. The Committee were unable to resist, but the Duke could not raise either money or soldiers, and a dead-lock was the result. The Duke was again obliged to yield, and the States-General were convoked for the 7th of November.

A.D. 1357–59.

Marcel now saw that reconciliation with the reigning family was impossible, and resolved to make a friend of the King of Navarre. He therefore delivered him from prison, by main force, on the night of the 8th of November. The Duke did not dare to manifest any anger at this bold step, and gave the King of Navarre leave to enter Paris, where he was received with great joy. He addressed the people, and told them that, if he felt inclined to claim the throne, he could show a better title to it than the King of England. The next morning Marcel, with the consent of the other deputies of the Third Estate who had remained in Paris, presented himself before the Duke of Normandy, and prayed him to restore to the King of Navarre the towns and castles belonging to him, which had been confiscated at the time of his arrest. The Duke was powerless, and, falsely, promised compliance with the request. The King of Navarre then went to Normandy, to enter into the promised possession of his domains; but the governors of the castles refused to deliver them up, without direct orders from

The King of Navarre released by Marcel,

and enters Paris.

28 LIFE AND TIMES OF EDWARD III. CHAP. II.

A.D.
1357–59.
—
Resolves
to retake
his castles.

the King of France. He now saw that he had been deceived, for he could not doubt that the Duke of Normandy was a party to this refusal, and therefore declared he would take possession of his castles by force. His brother Philip, at the head of 1,000 brigands, came to his aid, and ravaged the country up to within a few leagues of Paris.

Paris
fortified
by Marcel.

It was at this time that the peasants living near Paris, harassed by the various "Companies," crowded into the city; and Marcel, fearing lest the brigands should attack it, and equally fearing that the nobles would do the same, redoubled his exertions to complete the fortifications. The Duke of Normandy shut himself up in the Louvre, with 2,000 men in the tower and its immediate neighbourhood, and took no part in preparing for the defence of Paris. The people were enraged at this selfish desertion from his duty to the country; and, by Marcel's orders, all the citizens on his side, preparing for insurrection, adopted a party-coloured cap of red and blue, in order that, in case of need, they might recognise each other.

The
Duke's
charges
against the
Thirty-
six.

Again a revolution seemed at hand. Again the Duke managed to prevent it; but, on this occasion, he adopted different tactics. He pretended to be a friend of the people; asked them to meet him on January 1st, 1358, in their halls; told them he wished to live and die with the Parisians; that, if he gathered soldiers together, it was not to oppress Paris, but to defend them against their enemies; that it was only want of money that had prevented him from leading his troops against the bandits, and insinuated that the Committee of Thirty-six had kept the money from him.

THE LOUVRE IN THE TIME OF CHARLES V.
From Viollet-le-Duc's Dict. de l'Architecture.

CHAP. II. THE FIRST BLOODSHED. 29

Marcel lost not a moment in calling together a counter-assembly, where he refuted the Duke's charges, and the assembly declared, with universal acclamation, that they would support him against all his enemies.

A.D. 1357–59.

Marcel refutes them.

The Duke, notwithstanding, made no change in his proceedings, and acted entirely under the advice of the very counsellors who were most hated by the Parisians, and Marcel and his friends came to the conclusion that it was necessary to put some of them to death.

His resolve.

The red and blue caps were put on; the tocsin of Notre Dame sounded the alarm; and the people gathered together in arms round the palace. The first victim was one of the twenty-two proscribed royal officers, who by accident got entangled in the crowd. After this, Marcel, at the head of 3,000 armed men, entered the palace and confronted the Duke. He called on him to undertake the defence of the kingdom; the Duke answered that that duty devolved on those who received its revenues. Angry words ensued, and Marcel exclaimed, "Sir Duke, be not astonished at anything you may see, for it is necessary." Then, turning to the "bonnets," he said, "Do quickly that for which you came here." The Lord of Conflans Marshal of Champagne, and Robert de Clermont Marshal of Normandy, two of the Duke's confidential advisers, were murdered on the spot, and the Duke was glad to escape under the protection of Marcel, with a red and blue bonnet on his head.

A royal officer executed.

Marcel enters the palace.

Murder of two marshals.

The blood which had been thus shed, and which eventually was the ruin of Marcel's cause, made it necessary to go on with the revolution. Marcel was

Progress of the revolution.

30   LIFE AND TIMES OF EDWARD III.   CHAP. II.

A.D.
1357-59.

master of Paris, but he felt the necessity of a supporter belonging to the nobility, and consequently sent to the King of Navarre to beg him to come to him. Charles the Bad arrived on the 26th of February, and expressed his approval of all that had been done; but Marcel shrunk from placing him on the throne. He wished rather to secure him as a friend, against the ill-will which the nobles and the Duke of Normandy bore against him, than to break finally with the Duke, and commit himself to a complete revolution. He, therefore, contented himself with compelling the Duke to compensate the King of Navarre for his sufferings and his losses. This was a fatal mistake, but it was succeeded by another still more serious. Marcel—who acted throughout with too great a trust in the Duke—allowed him to leave Paris, to preside over a meeting of the Provincial Estates.

The States of Champagne and the Duke.

On the 9th of April, the Duke met the States of Champagne at Provins. They were angry at the murder of their Marshal, and asked the Duke whether he had any cause of complaint against him. The Duke answered that he had none, and the States then promised him their support against the Marshal's murderers. Two Parisian deputies who had attended the meeting of the States, hastened back to Paris to warn Marcel, who wrote a most touching letter of remonstrance to the Duke.[1] This produced no effect, and Marcel, therefore, lost no time in preparing to defend himself;

Marcel seizes the Louvre.

he seized the Louvre, drove out the Duke's supporters, took possession of the artillery and other arms, shut

---

[1] See this most interesting letter in Martin's *France*, vol. v. p. 567.

CHAP. II.   THE JACQUERIE.   31

the gates of the city, barred the river with iron chains, and cleared the ramparts by destroying all the houses built against them.   In order to prevent Paris from being starved out, he wished to seize Meaux and other fortified points on the Seine and Marne, but the Duke was beforehand with him at Meaux.

A.D.
1357–59.

The Duke now prepared for the siege of Paris, and Marcel did the same for its defence.   But a new and terrible danger threatened the kingdom, and, for a time, put an end to all thoughts but those as to the means of averting it.   The *Jacquerie* had begun.

The peasants, oppressed and derided by the nobles, plundered and outraged by "The Companies," while the nobles and gentlemen looked on in security from their castles without moving a finger to protect them, had at last felt their burden too heavy to be borne, and had risen with the ferocity of beasts of prey, to cast it from them.   "Death to all the gentlemen" was the cry of an assemblage of peasants in the neighbourhood of Clermont.   They elected a peasant named Guillaume Callet as their chief, and armed only with knives and iron-shod bludgeons, attacked a neighbouring castle, and killed the castellan and his family. Castle after castle was then attacked in a similar way, and, just as the thatched cottages had been burnt and plundered by the "Companies," so were the castles now treated by the peasants.   The insurrection spread like wild-fire; more than 100,000 peasants cast away their spades, and armed themselves with rude pikes.   No noble sentiment animated the insurgents; they were inspired solely by a fierce desire of vengeance, by a determination to render outrage for outrage, and they acted in conformity with the dictates of their excited passions.

The Jacquerie.
Its origin;

its progress.

32 LIFE AND TIMES OF EDWARD III. Chap. II.

A.D. 1357-59

Surprise of the nobles.

The nobles were stupified. Had the flocks under the charge of the shepherd turned upon him and trampled him to pieces, he could not have been more astonished than were the lords at the uprising of their despised serfs.

The Jacques assisted by Marcel.

Many " rich men " joined the *Jacques* with the intention of moderating and directing them, and Marcel attempted to do the same. He sent 300 Parisians to assist them in taking the castle of Ermonville, and succeeded, for once, in restraining their excesses. Soon, however, this body of the insurgents again began their massacres, and Marcel thought it right to withdraw the Parisians. Paris opened its gates, as a place of refuge, to the nobles who were not notoriously on the side of those who " wished evil to the people;" but at the same time Marcel continued to negotiate with the leaders of the Jacques.[1] The Duchess of Normandy had fled to Meaux with 300 ladies, and Marcel, wishing doubtless to seize so great a prize, determined again to send some Parisians to help the Jacques in attacking it. The Duke had strongly fortified the market-place, and his garrison greatly oppressed the people; the inhabitants therefore entreated the Jacques to come to their rescue. The

They attack Meaux,

mayor opened the gates to the assailants, and nine or ten thousand furious, half-armed, half-starved peasants rushed in, accompanied by the Parisians whom Marcel had sent to their assistance. The citizens first fed the famished multitude, and then led them to the attack.

Marcel was aware that the Duke was not at Meaux, and knew that the garrison was weak; he therefore expected to be able to carry the market-place by

[1] Martin, *Hist. de France*, vol. v. p. 196.

CHAP. II.   THE REVOLUTION PROCEEDS.   33

a *coup de main.* But unlooked-for help arrived at the critical moment. Gaston de Foix, who was one of the most gallant knights of the time, and who soon attained a great renown, was returning, accompanied by the Captal de Buch, from a crusade against the Pagans of Prussia, who, on the cessation of the Crusades against the Turks, had taken their place as enemies to the Christian faith, and whom true believers were bound to extirpate. On reaching Châlons, they heard of the danger which threatened the Duchess, and hastened to her rescue. They reached Meaux in safety, and managed to get into the market-place with a hundred gallant and experienced "lances," as the fully-armed horse-soldiers were then called, before the citizens had begun their attack. The garrison did not wait for the onslaught of the people, but, opening the gates, charged against the half-naked multitude. The poor wretches fought with desperation; but the fight was nothing but a massacre, the peasants were slaughtered by thousands, and a fatal blow was dealt to the *Jacquerie.* Marcel had made a bold, but most unwise, venture, and had failed.

A.D. 1357–59.

which is defended by Gaston de Foix.

Massacre of the peasants at Meaux.

The nobles and gentry now plucked up courage, the insurgent peasants were everywhere attacked, and the revenge of the nobles at least equalled that previously taken by the peasants. "It needed not the English," says an old French chronicler, "to destroy the country, for, in truth, the English, enemies of the kingdom, would not have done what the nobles did."[1]

Revenge taken by the nobles.

Marcel saw, that the time had at length arrived, when he must finally break with the nobles and the Duke of Normandy, and secure another ally, who could

Marcel breaks with the Duke of Normandy and nobles.

[1] As quoted by Martin, vol. i. p. 199.

VOL. II.   D

34   LIFE AND TIMES OF EDWARD III.   CHAP. II.

A.D. 1357–59.

The King of Navarre appointed Captain-General of Paris.

supply him with cavalry, and might even supplant the Duke. He therefore again turned to the King of Navarre, and begged him to come to Paris. It was evident from the speech he made, when previously summoned to Paris, that the King of Navarre aspired to the French throne. With the view therefore of preparing the way for making him a king, Marcel managed to bring about his appointment as Captain-General of Paris as soon as he arrived, and then wrote to all the great towns of France, asking leave to appoint him Captain-General of the whole kingdom. Some consented and some refused; the nobles, who up to that time had been attached to him, and at whose instance the King of Navarre had inflicted a terrible massacre on the *Jacques*, looking on the cause of the Regent as identical with their own, held entirely aloof. Marcel

Marcel loses the confidence of the people.

now made another mistake. He called in the help of the "Companies," and thus forfeited the confidence of the people, who on the one hand had a horror of the bandits, and on the other could not forgive the King of Navarre for his massacre of the *Jacques*. The upper citizens, too, began to fear that they were putting too much power into the hands of the King of Navarre.[1]

The Duke of Normandy besieges Paris.

The King of Navarre was unequal to the occasion. The Duke of Normandy advanced on Paris, and began its siege by cutting off the supply of provisions which came by the Marne and Seine. The King of Navarre, not daring to seize the prize which seemed within his grasp, and wishing to make sure of a friend, negotiated by turns with the King of England and the Regent of France; he ended at last by selling

Charles the Bad agrees

himself to the Regent. This man—who well deserved the name of "The Bad" by which he has

[1] Martin, vol. i. p. 201.

CHAP. II.   TREACHERY OF THE KING OF NAVARRE.   35

descended to posterity—not only agreed, on condition of receiving an immense sum of money, to leave Marcel and the Parisians to their fate, but also bound himself to induce them to pay 600,000 crowns of gold for the ransom of King John, and deepened the profound abyss of his treachery by consenting that Marcel and his chief advisers should be given up to the Duke of Normandy to be done with as he pleased.[1]

The people were furious; they told the King of Navarre that if he deserted them they would do without him, and that they would not pay one penny of the ransom. The wretched creature was frightened, and turned again. He went out, on the 11th of July, to fight the Duke, and had a sharp combat with his troops. He thus managed to retain his office as Captain-General, but did not recover his popularity. The Duke now established a bridge of boats on the Seine, below its junction with the Marne, and by this means entirely prevented provisions from reaching Paris. Famine soon began, and the King of Navarre again opened negotiations with the Duke, agreeing to terms very disadvantageous to the Parisians. Again, and with justice, they raged against Navarre, and Marcel made one more mistake in siding with the King.

An unlucky incident now occurred, which made matters worse. Some of the bandits hired by Marcel had, on their way back to Paris, burnt and pillaged the country up to the very gates of St. Martin, and the people saw the flames from the walls of the city. The Parisians, exasperated at this useless savagery, fell on those who had already entered Paris, murdered twenty or thirty of them, put the rest in prison, and then went

A.D. 1357–59.

to betray Marcel.

The treachery of the King of Navarre.

[1] Buchon's *Froissart*, vol. i. p. 379.

D 2

36 LIFE AND TIMES OF EDWARD III. Chap. II.

A.D. 1357–59.

The Parisians encounter the Companies; but are routed.

to seize their leader at the Hotel de Nesle, where he had been dining with the King of Navarre. On the next day, the 22nd of July, the King of Navarre, again obliged to side with the Parisians, was forced to lead them out against *the English*, as they termed the " Companies," who were encamped in the Bois de Boulogne, close to Paris. By design or accident, they fell into an ambuscade, and were routed with a loss of 600, without receiving any help from Marcel or from the King of Navarre. This entirely put an end to any reliance on the King of Navarre on the part of the Parisians; he did not dare to return to Paris, but retired to St. Denis. Marcel also lost their confidence, by releasing, at the request of the King of Navarre, the bandits who had been put in prison. This was on the 27th of July.

The Duke of Normandy withdraws from Paris.

The Duke of Normandy now stood aloof, and even withdrew his troops from the neighbourhood of Paris. Discord, he well knew, would do more for him than any action of his own. The ground began to tremble under Marcel's feet. He had relied by turns on the revolted peasants, on the plundering bandits, and on the wretched King of Navarre. All had failed him. France was in the greatest danger; at the expiration of the truce Edward was sure to return, and certain to conquer, if unity among the French were not restored. The people began to turn their thoughts to the Duke of Normandy, and Marcel was actually compelled by the Parisians to write to him to entreat his return to Paris to protect them against the Navarrese. The Duke answered that he would never enter Paris so long as the murderer of the Marshals was alive. The letter was put into Marcel's hands.

Fatal conduct of Marcel.

Marcel, abandoned or suspected by all, now took the last fatal step of throwing himself once more into the arms

BASTILLE ST. ANTOINE, AS CONSTRUCTED BY CHARLES V., WITH SUBSEQUENT ADDITIONS
From Viollet-le-Duc's Dictionnaire de l'Architecture. (For explanation, see List of Illustrations.

CHAP. II.   THE REVOLUTION FAILS.   37

of the King of Navarre. He offered to introduce him secretly into Paris on the night of the 31st of July, and proclaim him King of France. It was the final effort of a man who had struggled nobly for the best interests of his country, and who had failed, partly because he was yielding and moderate when he should have been firm and uncompromising, partly because he made use of men from whom he should have shrunk, but mainly because the man, on whom he most relied, was a mercenary traitor and unequal to the part he was called on to perform.

A.D. 1357–59.

In order to secure the entry of the Navarrese, it was necessary to change the guards of the gates, through which they were to pass. On the appointed night, therefore, Marcel, with fifty or sixty companions, all armed, presented themselves at the Porte St. Denis, and told the keeper of the keys to give them up to Josseran de Mâcon, the treasurer of the King of Navarre. This was refused; a quarrel ensued, during which Jean Maillart, guardian of that quarter of Paris, and a partisan of the Duke of Normandy, came up and forbade the delivery of the keys. Maillart then, mounting his horse cried out, "*Montjoie St. Denis for the King and the Duke*," and rode off to the Halls of the people to raise them against Marcel. The Royalists had arranged their plans more perfectly than Marcel, and his plot had been discovered.

His scheme.

The plot discovered.

When Marcel and his party found that their *coup d'état* had failed, they tried to take possession of the Portes St. Martin and St. Honoré. At the former they met with a vigorous resistance. It was midnight. Maillart came up at the moment of their arrival and cried out to Marcel, "Etienne! Etienne! what are you doing here at this time of night?" "John, what is that to thee?" replied Marcel, adding, "I am here to take

38 LIFE AND TIMES OF EDWARD III. CHAP. II.

A.D. 1357-59.

charge of the city, of which I am the governor." "It is not so," said Maillart, "you are here for no good," and, turning to his followers added, "I will prove it to you; see! he has the keys in his hand to betray the town." "John, you lie." "It is you who lie," answered Maillart,

Death of Marcel.

and struck him to the ground. Marcel was murdered; his friends were scattered; many of them, not present at that time with Marcel, but proscribed beforehand, were put to death; and thus ended a badly managed, but, in its outset, a most legitimate and nobly intended effort to free the kingdom from misgovernment and oppression.

The coinage debased.

After executing vengeance on Marcel's friends, the Duke's first act was to debase the coinage; that of the King of Navarre was to sign a treaty with Edward to assist him in conquering France, and then to march off from Paris to join his brother Philip at Nantes.

Treachery of Charles the Bad.

A miserable period of confusion and wretchedness now followed. The King of Navarre, feeling that he had no longer any chance of ascending the throne, made terms with King Edward and took some of the "Companies," among whom were to be found many English who did not hesitate to break the truce, into his pay, and laid waste the country. He paid them with the money raised by Marcel to defend Paris, increased by contributions from Edward. The Duke of Normandy, driven to despair, tried to conciliate the people; but, having no soldiers, he also was forced to have recourse to the "Companies," and, lacking money, continually changed the value of the coinage, altering it within six days to the extent of nine hundred per cent.

Wretched state of the country.

The state of the country was now, if possible, worse than before. Neither corn nor vegetables nor vines were cultivated; burnt houses and churches in ruins everywhere met the eye; desolation universally prevailed, except in some isolated places where

CHAP. II. DUKE OF NORMANDY REGAINS POWER. 39

the peasants resisted the royal bandits, often performing the most heroic deeds of valour in defending themselves against their attacks.

A.D. 1357—59.

Winter increased the sufferings of the people; the price of food became enormous, and famine raged throughout the land.

Sufferings of the people.

At last a ray of hope seemed to brighten the prospect. It was said that a treaty of peace was signed between France and England. Alas! it was but a vain illusion! It was true that John had signed a treaty, but, under such conditions, that the Duke himself could not but prefer to leave his father still a captive, rather than accept them. Calais, Guines, Ponthieu, Normandy, Maine, Touraine, Poitou,—in short, nearly the whole of the western and great part of Central France, with all its ports and harbours and sea-coast,—were to be given up to Edward, and John had actually signed this shameful compact. He valued his own liberty higher than the honour and power of France, but his son set his country's interests above his father's ease. And he was right. He rejected the treaty with scorn, and the people resolved to stand by him. The States-General were called together to assemble on May 19th, 1359. Only a few members came; for such was the danger of travelling along the road infested with brigands, that their lives were not safe. With one voice they declared that the treaty was too hard, and that John must remain in prison. But the Duke did not neglect the opportunity of restoring to their posts the twenty-two officers, whom the States had obliged him to dismiss in 1357.

Treaty signed by King John;

which was rejected by the Duke and by the States-General.

Efforts were made to get rid of the "Companies." The Bishop of Troyes, a warlike prelate, put himself at the head of a large body of the nobles of Cham-

40 LIFE AND TIMES OF EDWARD III. CHAP. II.

A.D. 1357-59. pagne and Lorraine, and drove them out of Champagne; the death of Picquini, one of their leaders, who was assassinated by one of his own men, freed Picardy; the Duke of Normandy attacked Melun, a town occupied by a Navarrese band of these robbers. At this siege the Duke of Normandy availed himself of the services of a man, whom, with rare discrimination, he picked out, against the opinion of almost all the **Bertrand du Guesclin.** lords who accompanied him. He was a person rough in looks, rude in his manners, and unmistakably a peasant in appearance. But the Duke saw the genius of the man, and secured Bertrand du Guesclin to his cause.[1] His value to the Royal arms soon became apparent. Melun however was not taken, and the Duke opened negotiations with the King of Navarre. He succeeded to such an extent, and so suddenly, that his brother Philip of Evreux believed he had been subjected to sorcery. The King himself declared he was inspired by the Holy Ghost, and was resolved to be a good Frenchman and no longer make war on France. His protestations were lies, as his subsequent conduct proved; and it is difficult to imagine what can have induced him thus to pretend a change of policy which he, almost immediately, abandoned. His utter falsity and want of principle is the only solution of the problem. His temporary defection from the opponents of the Duke of Normandy had but little effect, except to induce his mercenary troops to range themselves under the banner of the English. Still, **Edward lands at Calais.** when Edward landed at Calais on October 28th, 1359, France, though unable to offer a successful opposition to the English arms, was yet, not so utterly defenceless, as he would have found it in the previous year.

[1] See Martin's *France*, vol. i. p. 243, for an interesting account of Du Guesclin.

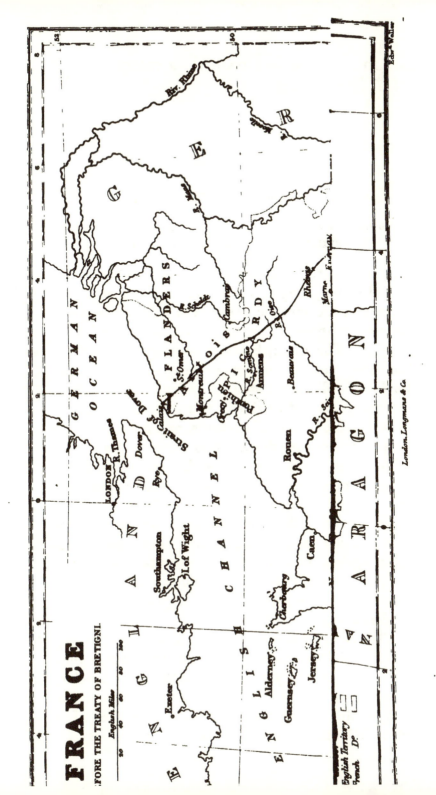

CHAP. III.   THE SECOND INVASION OF FRANCE.   41

CHAPTER III.

EDWARD'S SECOND INVASION OF FRANCE—THE PEACE OF BRETIGNI, AND RELEASE OF KING JOHN.

DURING the two years which elapsed between the arrival of the King of France in England as a prisoner, and the recommencement of the war between the two countries, England was peaceful and prosperous.   The enmity between England and Scotland had been put an end to by the release of King David; the disturbed state of Ireland did not affect the tranquillity of England; and there are no traces to be found of remarkable events, or important legislative enactments, during this period.   Labourers indeed were still striving with employers about the rate of wages—as they have striven to this very day, and will continue to strive to the world's end, unless some master mind should discover the true principle for its settlement—and trade was struggling against vain attempts to regulate its course by governmental action, but during all this time there was nothing to disturb the peaceful progress of the nation.

The royal prisoners were well and courteously treated, and no restraint was put on them beyond what was absolutely necessary for their safe keeping. From the palace of the Savoy where they were first lodged, John and his son Philip were allowed to go to Windsor, where they followed the chase, and

A.D. 1359.

State of England after the battle of Poitiers.

Treatment of King John in England.

42 LIFE AND TIMES OF EDWARD III. Chap. III.

A.D.1359. amused themselves with hawking and other sports, and while there, a great tournament was held, at which they were present. They were afterwards removed to Hertford and from thence to Somerton in Lincolnshire.

Death of of the Dowager Queen Isabella. The only other domestic events of general interest which happened about this time were, the death of the King's mother Queen Isabella, and the marriage of the King's fourth son John. The Queen died at Risings on August 22nd, 1357, after nearly thirty years' confinement in that castle, and was buried in the church of the Grey Friars (now Christ Church) London, on the 27th of September.[1] Such was the state of London at this time that it was necessary to order Bishopsgate Street and Aldgate Street to be cleansed of ordure and other filth for the passage **Marriage of John of Gaunt.** of the body.[2] The marriage of the King's son John, called of Gaunt, from Ghent where he was born, took place on June 14th, 1359. He was then only Earl of Richmond. He married Blanche, daughter and co-heir of Henry Duke of Lancaster, great-grandson of Henry the Third, and thus became the head of the House of Lancaster, and is known to this day as Shakspeare's "John of Gaunt, time-honoured Lancaster."

Negotiations for peace. On January 17th, 1359,[3] Sir Walter de Maunay was sent to France to negotiate for the extension of the truce which was to expire on the 13th of April; on the 18th of March it was prolonged till the 25th of June, in order to give an opportunity for its

---

[1] Sandford's *Genealogical History*, p. 146.

[2] It is singular that the date of this order given in Rymer (vol. iii. p. 411) is November 20, 1358.

[3] Rymer, vol. iii. p. 417.

CHAP. III.   PREPARATIONS FOR WAR.   **43**

conversion into a permanent treaty of peace. As already stated, King Edward and King John had come to an understanding as to the conditions on which the war should cease; the Duke of Normandy rejected these terms at the end of May, and Edward lost not a day in preparing for the renewal of the war. So little confidence indeed had he that the negotiations would succeed, that he had anticipated their failure, by beginning his preparations for war, at the very time that he was negotiating for peace. _A.D.1359._ _Their failure._

As usual, a large number of bows and arrows was the first thing needed, and at the beginning of the year, on the 2nd and 12th of January, and again on the 16th of May, they were ordered to be bought in all parts of the kingdom.[1] About the same time, on the 12th of January, above 1,700 "well-armed" Welshmen were called out; carpenters, and miners were summoned from the Forest of Dean, on the 1st of February; and so early as the 8th of December of the preceding year, ships had been collected for conveying troops; "because, for the carrying on of our war in France, we intend soon to go to foreign parts with our army."[2] Some months subsequently, after the rejection of the offers of peace, nearly 900 sailors were gathered together for the manning of the ships, the largest number for any one ship being 100 for the "New St. Mary." On the 10th of July[3] carpenters, masons, and other artificers were ordered to accompany the army; and indeed the most unusual preparations were made to provide the invaders with everything they could require. Edward knew that, such was the devastated state of France, he _Preparations for war;_ _which are unusually varied and extensive._

---

[1] Rymer, vol. iii. pp. 414, 415, and 426.   [2] Ibid. p. 412.
[3] Ibid. p. 431.

44 LIFE AND TIMES OF EDWARD III. CHAP. III.

A.D. 1359. could not rely on it for any of the necessary supplies. Mills for grinding corn, ovens for baking bread, forges for shoeing horses, and small boats made of jacked leather, each capable of holding three men, to be used for fishing—fish being an indispensable article of food on fast days and in Lent—were among the requisites which they took with them; in addition to all sorts of things which, as Froissart[1] says, "had never before been taken with an army." Eight thousand cars, each drawn by four horses, is the incredible number of carriages stated[2] to have been provided for carrying them. Such, however, was the spirit of pastime which characterised even war in those days, that means and appliances for enjoying the sports of the field were not forgotten. The King took with him thirty falconers on horseback with their falcons, and sixty couples of strong hunting dogs, in addition to as many greyhounds, "with which," as Froissart says, "he went every day to the chase or to the river as he pleased."

Hawks and hounds taken.

The safety of England provided for.

It was as necessary, however, to take measures for the safety of England during the absence of the King with so large an army, as it was to provide for the successful invasion of France. Edward therefore, on October 3rd, 1359, ordered the chief men in their respective counties, to "array" all men between the ages of sixteen and sixty, who were to be ready when summoned by beacon fires on the hills to resist enemies within those districts, and to practise them in the use of their weapons; but they were not to be taken out of their own hundred, except in the case of actual invasion. These men were to be gathered together, the knights under their

All men between 16 and 60 years of age to be arrayed in their respective counties.

---

[1] Buchon's ed. vol. i. p. 417.   [2] Ibid. p. 427.

CHAP. III. PREPARATIONS FOR WAR. 45

constables, who usually had the command of 100 men,[1] and the foot soldiers in hundreds and twenties. Those who possessed land to the value of fifteen pounds a year, and cattle of the annual value of sixteen marks, were to be armed with a haubergeon, which was a shirt of mail smaller than the hauberk.[2] They were also to have an iron helmet, sword, and dagger, and were to be provided with a horse. Those whose land was worth only twenty marks a year were to be armed in the same way, but were to fight on foot. They who held land of the yearly value of 100 shillings were to have a pourpoint, or gambeson, which was "a quilted coat used either alone or with other armour,"[3] an iron helmet, a sword and a dagger. Those again whose holding did not exceed from 80 to 100 shillings in annual value were to be armed with a sword, dagger, and bows and arrows. They who held still less land were to have a spear, hand axe, a dagger and other "minute arms;" but if they had only cattle of less than twenty marks' yearly value, they were to have nothing but a sword, dagger, and other minute arms. All others were to have bows and arrows according to their station; excepting that they who had property exceeding the values thus enumerated were to be armed according to the value of their tenure.[4] In consequence, however, of a supposition that those having land and tenements of more than the annual value of fifteen pounds were excused from service, it was ordered, that all able-bodied men within the specified ages should be arrayed, and that those who were unable to serve on account of infirmity, should find weapons and armour for those who had none of their own.

A.D. 1359.

Directions as to the weapons they were to carry.

[1] Hewitt's *Ancient Armour*, vol. i. p. 215.   [2] Ibid. p. 131.
[3] Ibid. pp. 127 and 239.   [4] Rymer, vol. iii. p. 449.

46 LIFE AND TIMES OF EDWARD III. Chap. III.

A.D. 1359.

Foreign adventurers flock to Calais to join the English army.

The rejection of Edward's overtures for peace soon became widely known. Swarms of adventurers consequently flocked to Calais—from Germany, Flanders, Brabant, and Hainault, and offered their services to the King of England; in order that, under his name, they might pillage the kingdom of France. They would have been equally ready to fight for France against England, if France would have paid them; but the Duke of Normandy was not disposed to avail himself of their services, and indeed made no preparation to resist the English, except that of fortifying Paris. These adventurers began to arrive in August, and were greatly disappointed when they found that Edward had not reached Calais. They were told each week that the King was coming during the next, but the next week came and the King did not arrive. They soon spent all the money they brought with

Their dissatisfaction.

them, and then became so dangerous that Edward, hearing of their discontent, feared they would even attack Calais. They outnumbered the garrison; Edward therefore recalled the Duke of Lancaster

The Duke of Lancaster sent to appease them.

from Brittany, and sent him to Calais with 400 men-at-arms, and 2,000 bowmen and Welshmen, to keep these adventurers in order. On his arrival, the Duke told them it was of no use to idle away their time at Calais, and that they had better join him in a raid in Artois and Picardy. He thus managed to keep them employed until the King landed.

Embarkation of the King, Oct. 28, 1359.

At last, all was ready for the King's departure from England. The troops destined for the invasion were on board the fleet; the safety of the kingdom during the King's absence was provided for, and Edward embarked with his four sons, Edward the Black

CHAP. III.   EDWARD EMBARKS FOR FRANCE.   47

Prince, Lionel Duke of Clarence, John of Gaunt, and A.D. 1359.
Edmund of Langley. Before doing so he appointed
his youngest son, Thomas of Woodstock, then under
five years of age, nominal guardian of the kingdom.
The Queen was left in England. King Edward set
sail from Sandwich on the morning of October 28th,
1359, " between daybreak and sunrise," and reached
Calais the same evening.[1]

According to Matteo Villani,[2] the number of the Number of
King's army exceeded 100,000 men. Froissart does the troops.
not give the total number of the troops, but he does
of some of the " battles."[3] He states that the order
of march was as follows:—First; a body of 500 men
went forward to clear and open out the roads and
cut down thorns and bushes to make way for the
cars; then came the Constable, the Earl of March,
with 500 men-at-arms and 1,000 bowmen; after
these, the " battle " of the marshals, consisting of
3,000 men-at-arms and 5,000 bowmen; then the
King's " battle," the number of which is not given,
and then the cars carrying the baggage, which extended for two leagues in length;[4] and, last of all,
the " battle" of the Prince of Wales and his brothers,
consisting of 2,500 men-at-arms, " nobly mounted and
richly caparisoned." It is remarkable that they were
apparently unprovided with bombards and the other

---

[1] Rymer, vol. iii. p. 452.   [2] Tom. iv. p. 238.
[3] Vol. i. p. 417.
[4] Froissart (vol. i. p. 427) says that there were 8,000 cars, each
drawn by four horses, and (at p. 417) that they extended for two
leagues, that is about six English miles, or under 11,000 yards.
This would give only about four feet for each car and horses,
unless, which is unlikely, they went several abreast. It is evident
therefore that Froissart's two statements are inconsistent, and it is
probable that the error lies in the reckoning up of the numbers of
the cars.

48 LIFE AND TIMES OF EDWARD III. CHAP. III.

A.D. 1359. new engines of war. They marched in close ranks, ready for fighting, " never left even a boy behind without waiting for him," and their rate of march was about three leagues a day. " There was such a multitude that the whole country was covered with them, and they were so richly armed and apparelled that it was a wonder and great pleasure to look at the shining arms, the floating banners, and their array marching in order of battle at a slow pace."

They are met by the Duke of Lancaster. When they had marched about four leagues they were met by the Duke of Lancaster, who, on hearing of the landing of the King, had turned back to Calais, hoping that Edward would be able to satisfy the clamorous demands of his troops of adventurers for money. The raid had been unsuccessful. They had been able to seize food enough to support themselves, but had taken no plunder, either of goods or money. The leaders immediately sought the presence of the King, and represented to him their extreme poverty; they said they had spent almost all their money and been obliged to sell their horses and their harness, and had not even money enough to return to their own

Dispersion of the foreign adventurers. countries. The King, anxious, doubtless, to get rid of such troublesome friends, persuaded them to go to Calais to rest and refresh themselves for a few days, and promised to send them an answer to their entreaties. They followed his advice, and, after a few days, he sent to say that he did not require their services, but that they might join his army, without wages, if they pleased. He, however, told them that they should have a handsome share of the plunder. A portion of them accepted the proposal, although unwillingly, and the King continued his march.[1]

---

[1] Buchon's *Froissart* vol. i. p. 416.

CHAP. III. THE INVASION OF FRANCE. 49

No great army opposed his progress; nor did even flying troops attempt to harass him on his way. The Duke of Normandy shut himself up in Paris. Either he feared to encounter so mighty a host as that which was now marching at its ease, hunting and hawking, through the very heart of the kingdom, or, he thought it his best policy to allow the invaders to exhaust themselves and goad the people to resistance, by wandering like robbers over the poverty-stricken land. Each city prepared to defend itself; but it was only when Edward thought fit to attack a town that he had any fighting. His army suffered dreadfully from the utterly wasted state of the country, which had not been tilled for three years, and from the consequent difficulty of getting provisions. It was supplied with wheat and oats from Hainault and Cambray; although the Flemings—by the orders, doubtless, of their Count—had driven the English merchants out of Brabant, and expelled those citizens of Bruges who, having promised to supply the English army with food,[1] had consequently been taken by Edward under his special protection.[2]

In addition to the sufferings occasioned by the scarcity of food, the weather added to their misery. The rain poured down in ceaseless torrents. It was the end of autumn, and winter was coming on; but Edward was determined not to leave France, until he had either gained the throne, or recovered the ancient possessions of the English Crown, and the difficulties of a winter campaign did not deter him from this object.

His plan was, first to reach the almost holy city of Rheims, where the French kings were always

Side notes:
A.D.1359.

No opposition to the invaders.

Their sufferings from scarcity of food

and bad weather.

Edward's plan to march on

[1] Knighton, col. 2620.   [2] Rymer, vol. iii. p. 452.

VOL. II.   E

50   LIFE AND TIMES OF EDWARD III.   Chap. III.

A.D. 1359.
Rheims and be crowned there.
crowned, and where he too was resolved to be acknowledged the lawful King of France.[1] He marched through Artois, Picardy, and Champagne, following the course of the rivers, with scarcely any fighting, and arrived before Rheims at the end of November. The city was too strongly fortified to be carried by assault, and, as the dreadful state of the

He arrives at Rheims.
weather prevented a regular siege, Edward quartered his troops in the surrounding abbeys and villages, sitting down, as the phrase is, before the town, while small detached parties of his troops, for pastime as well as plunder, attacked first one town and then another in the neighbourhood. The Duke of Nor-

The Duke of Normandy does not attack him.
mandy made no attempt to dislodge him. The policy of inaction, prompted by wisdom or cowardice, or possibly by necessity, was the course he adopted. He had indeed enough to do to hold his own in Paris; but his difficulties arose from the indignation of the people, at having for their ruler a man who would

Conspiracy in Paris.
not raise a finger to defend his country. A conspiracy was set on foot, by those who had been Etienne Marcel's friends, to give up Paris to the King of Navarre. Charles was by no means the man for the occasion, but the people thought he could not be so weak and helpless as the Regent. They therefore resolved to supplant the latter, and, probably, make Charles King of France. The plot was found out; the leader

The King of Navarre declares war against the Duke.
of the conspiracy executed; the King of Navarre fled from Paris and declared war against the Duke; and thus, as Froissart says, " the noble kingdom of France was harassed with war on all sides." [2]

---

[1] Sismondi, vol. x. p. 566.

[2] Buchon's *Froissart*, vol. i. pp. 423 (note), 428; Sismondi, vol. x. p. 566; and Martin, vol. v. p. 224.

CHAP. III. MARCHES INTO BURGUNDY. 51

Edward had hoped that, by threatening Rheims, he would provoke the Duke of Normandy to give him battle. In this he did not succeed, and, being unwilling to lay siege to Rheims in regular force during the winter, at last determined to give up all idea of taking that city, and lay siege to Paris itself, after making a raid through some of the most fertile parts of France. He accordingly broke up his camp at Rheims on January 11th, 1360, and, passing under the walls of Châlons on the Marne, Bar-le-duc, and Troyes without attacking them, entered Burgundy and took Tonnerre and Flavigny by assault. He then retraced his steps, encamped at Guillon on the Serain on the 19th of February, and remained there, on the confines of Burgundy, for about three weeks.

While at Guillon, Edward received offers of peace from the Duke of Burgundy, which he willingly accepted, as it was of great importance to detach the first peer of the kingdom of France from its sovereign. The Duke was induced to take this step, partly by the wish to save his duchy from devastation, and partly by the persuasion of his mother, King John's second wife, who had never loved the Duke of Normandy. The Burgundians promised to pay Edward a large sum, and to give no help to the Duke of Normandy in either arms or money. The treaty was signed on March 10th, 1360.[1]

Although the Duke of Normandy made no effort to drive the English out of France, some of the French, availing themselves of the supposed defenceless state of the country in the King's absence, invaded England. They landed at Winchelsea "in

---

[1] Rymer, vol. iii. p. 478.

52   LIFE AND TIMES OF EDWARD III.   Chap. III.

A.D. 1360.

Invasion of England by the French; they are driven back.

great numbers" [1] on March 15th, 1360,[2] while the people were hearing mass. They broke into the church, and committed the most horrible atrocities; set the town on fire and ravaged the neighbourhood; but, at length, the troops and people round about gathered together, and drove the invaders into the sea with a heavy loss.[3]

Active measures to prevent the French landing again.

As already stated, Edward had made ample preparations for such an event before he left England, and his little son, the guardian of the kingdom, or rather able governors in his name, were not slow in turning them to account. On the 2nd of March[4] a proclamation, issued from Westminster in the Guardian's name, stated that, whereas he had learned that his enemies the French, with a multitude of armed men of all kinds, were at that time actually on board a great fleet, and proposed to land at Southampton, Portsmouth, Sandwich or elsewhere, he ordered the armed men of the maritime counties to go to the coast. On the same day, however, instead of ordering the fleet to sea, a course was adopted which was at once unintelligible, cowardly, and singularly inconsistent with a subsequent order. He directed all the towns on the sea coast, to draw up their ships and boats on land, far from the sea, in order to save them from seizure. On the 15th of March the Government having heard of the landing of the French and the capture of Winchelsea, and roused doubtless by their brutal atrocities, issued an order from

---

[1] Rymer, vol. iii, p. 476.

[2] Idibus Martii, Walsingham, p. 287.

[3] Knighton, col. 2622, and see Nicolas' *Brit. Navy*, vol. ii. p. 125.

[4] Rymer, vol. iii. p. 471.

CHAP. III. MEASURES TO PREVENT FRENCH LANDING. 53

Reading,[1] commanding the northern fleet to go to sea, and join the western fleet. About the same time the castles of Old Sarum, Marlborough, and Pevensey were garrisoned and provisioned. Some of the armed men were ordered up to London either for its defence, or to be in readiness to go to sea and attack the French ships; others to various places on the coast, and these were directed to take their provisions with them when they embarked. The English ships in Flemish harbours were called back to England; all vessels in the harbours on the Southern and Eastern coasts were ordered to be in readiness to go to sea; and "Brother John de Pavely," Prior of the Hospital of St. John in Jerusalem, was appointed "Captain" of the fleets. The collectors of the tenths and fifteenths were urged to greater activity in collecting the taxes, and were ordered to give the men one month's pay in advance;[2] the royal prisoners were removed for greater security from Somerton Castle to Berkhamsted;[3] and the King of France was taken to the Tower of London. These active measures evidently prevented any serious danger to England, for there is no record of any renewal of the attempts at invasion.

A.D. 1360.

---

[1] It seems hardly possible that the invasion can have taken place on the 15th March, as Walsingham states, as the order mentioned in the text is dated from Reading on that very day, and speaks of the invasion as having "lately" taken place "*noviter* invadentes." On the other hand, it seems equally certain that it did not take place on Feb. 24th, as Knighton (col. 2622) states: "Die Sancti Mathiæ Apostoli in Quadragesima Franci applicuerunt apud Winchelse ad summam xx mill. armatorum virorum (!?)," because the Guardian's proclamation of March 2nd speaks of the invasion as a probable *future* event.

[2] Rymer, vol. iii. pp. 477–482.   [3] Ibid. pp. 470 and 485.

54   LIFE AND TIMES OF EDWARD III.   CHAP. III.

A.D. 1360.

Edward marches on Paris.

After signing the treaty with the Duke of Burgundy, Edward began his march on Paris. He descended the Serain, the Yonne, and the Seine, and encamped close to Paris, at Châtillon, a place near Montrouge. The Regent immediately ordered the three suburbs of Paris, St. Germain, St. Marcel, and Notre-Dame-des-Champs, to be burnt, in order to prevent their being seized by the English; but he made no attempt to attack the invaders. Edward then sent heralds to demand of the Duke to give him

The Duke refuses to give battle, or make peace.

battle; but the Duke refused, and even forbade his knights to pass the barriers, when Sir Walter de Maunay came skirmishing up to the very gates of the city. He also rejected, with a confident folly which soon brought its own punishment, all Edward's overtures of peace, notwithstanding that their acceptance was pressed on him by his own subjects. The

Condition of France at this time.

state of France as described by Petrarch, who visited it about this time, was horrible. "I could not believe," he says, "that this was the same kingdom which I had once seen so rich and flourishing. Nothing presented itself to my eyes but a fearful solitude, an extreme poverty, land uncultivated, houses in ruins. Even the neighbourhood of Paris manifested everywhere marks of destruction and conflagration. The streets are deserted; the roads overgrown with weeds; the whole is a vast solitude." [1]

Edward determines to march through France, and besiege Paris in the autumn.

The King of England was not inclined, however, to besiege Paris in regular form at that time; for his army needed rest. It had been encamped or marching for five months at the worst season of the year; the weather during part of the time had

---

[1] Mem. de Petrarque, t. iii. p. 541, as quoted by Hallam, *Middle Ages*, vol. i. p. 54 (note).

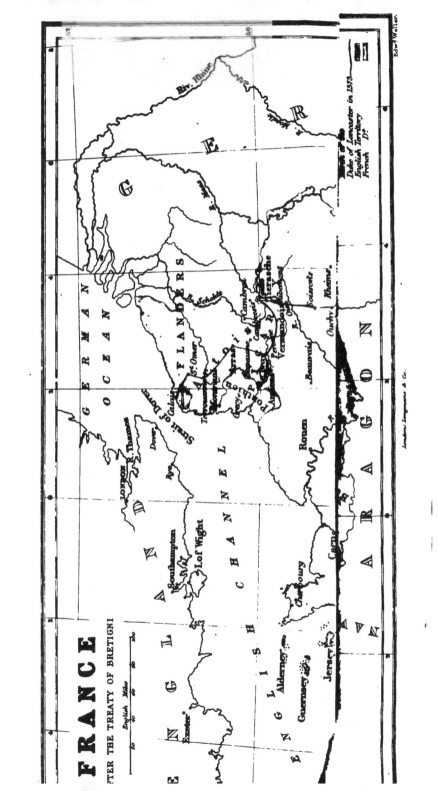

CHAP. III. THE TREATY OF BRETIGNI. 55

been unusually bad; and provisions were scarce. It is therefore hardly to be wondered at that Edward announced his intention of descending the Loire, living on the rich country through which it flowed, of "refreshing himself" on the promising harvests in Brittany, and returning to besiege Paris in the autumn. On the 10th of April he began his march.

A.D. 1360.

The Duke of Normandy now became seriously alarmed; acting under the Pope's advice, he sent negotiators after Edward to treat for peace. They overtook him at Chartres. At first, Edward would listen to nothing except his recognition as King of France; but the Duke of Lancaster persuaded him to moderate his demands, and it is said—with much probability, considering the superstitious spirit of the times—that an awful storm which came on during the negotiations, and during which there fell hailstones so large that men and horses were killed by them, contributed to soften the King's heart. He looked on the storm as a special interposition of Providence to stop the bloodshed and sufferings of the people, and consented to make peace on more moderate terms. A treaty of peace was accordingly signed at Bretigni on the 8th of May.[1]

Alarm of the Dauphin.

Treaty of peace signed at Bretigni.

By this celebrated and most important treaty, it was agreed, that the whole of the ancient duchy of Aquitaine, which Henry the Second acquired on his marriage with Eleanor (the divorced wife of Louis the Seventh of France) in 1152, and part of which had been recovered from King John by Philip Augustus in 1205 and 1206, should be restored, and given up in full sovereignty, to Edward. This comprised, what was then called the Duchy of Guienne, in

Conditions of the treaty.

[1] Rymer, vol. iii. p. 487.

56 LIFE AND TIMES OF EDWARD III. CHAP. III.

A.D. 1360.

Conditions of the treaty of Bretigni.

which the ancient province of Gascony was included; the county of Poitou, which comprehended Saintonge, including Aunix and Rochelle; the viscounty of Limosin; the county of Angoumois; Perigord, including Agenois and Quercy; and the counties of Bigorre and Rouergue.[1] The Counts of Foix, Armagnac, Lille Jourdain and Perigord; the Viscounts of Carmaing and Limoges; and the other Lords, who held fiefs in the counties given up, were to transfer their homage from the King of France to the King of England. In addition to these territories thus surrendered to the King of England in the South of France, a small territory round Calais, composed of the counties of Ponthieu and Guines and of the viscounty of Montreuil, was also to be given up to Edward in full sovereignty. On the other hand, Edward renounced his pretensions to the throne, and gave up all claim or title to the ancient possessions of the Plantagenets north of the Loire, including Normandy, Touraine, Anjou and Maine. Each King renounced his pretensions to the homage of Brittany and Flanders; John of Montfort was to have all the territories held by his father beyond the limits of the Duchy of Brittany; and his claims and those of Charles of Blois, to the Duchy, were to be considered by the two Kings at Calais, where they were to meet at the end of four months for the payment of the first instalment of the ransom of the King of France.[2]

King John's ransom was fixed at three million crowns of gold, of which 600,000 were to be paid before the King could leave Calais, and 400,000 each year till all was paid.

[1] See Spruner's *Hand Atlas*, No. 25.
[2] Rymer, vol. iii. p. 487.

PLAN OF THE PRECINCTS OF WESTMINSTER ABBEY.

From a Map of Westminster, undated, but probably of the time of Queen Elizabeth, in the possession of the Rev. Mackenzie Walcot. (For explanation, see List of Illustrations.)

CHAP. III.   EDWARD RETURNS TO ENGLAND.   57

Among other conditions, it was also provided, that A.D. 1360. intimate alliances should be formed between the two Kings, "notwithstanding any alliances they might have with the Flemings, Scots, or others;[1] and, in order to enable them to get rid of any solemn obligations they might have contracted, the Pope absolved them, on the 2nd of July, from any oaths which were contrary to the articles of peace."[2]

The treaty was signed on the 8th of May; the English army marched for Calais; and the King sailed for England. He landed at Rye in the evening of the 18th of May, and forthwith mounted his horse and rode to the palace of Westminster, where he arrived at about 9 o'clock next morning.[3] His first act was the release of the King of France. Some time however elapsed before King John availed himself of his liberty. He had found his imprisonment in England by no means irksome, and it was not until the 8th of July that he was conducted to Calais by the Prince of Wales and the Duke of Lancaster. The Duke of Normandy came from Paris to St. Omer, at the same time, for the purpose of carrying the treaty into execution. But, in the ruined condition of France, it was impossible to find, within the kingdom, money enough to pay the ransom; the Prince of Wales and the Duke of Lancaster therefore returned to England, leaving the King of France at Calais, in the custody of Sir Walter de Maunay. The ambition of an Italian noble got the French out of their difficulty. Galeazzo Visconti, Lord of Milan, one of the most powerful of those tyrants who, for a century, had been striving to convert the Italian republics into hereditary princi-

King Edward returns to England.

King John is taken to Calais.

Money for ransom cannot be raised.

Obtained in part from Italy by marriage of King's daughter.

[1] Rymer, vol. iii. p. 492.   [2] Ibid. p. 501.
[3] Ibid. p. 494.

58   LIFE AND TIMES OF EDWARD III.   CHAP. III.

A.D.1360.

palities, conceived that it would be an advantage to him to form an alliance with the descendants of St. Louis. He therefore demanded the hand of King John's third daughter Isabella in marriage for his son John Galeazzo,[1] promising to pay 600,000 florins of gold on the marriage taking place. The people of France were indignant at what they considered a mercenary bargain; but the offer was accepted, the money was paid, and the marriage took place about the 8th of October.[2]

Hostages for the rest.

The Italian gold was not sufficient, however, to pay the whole of the ransom, and it was necessary to find hostages for the payment of the remainder. These were, the King's brother the Duke of Orleans; his second and third sons whom he now created Dukes of Anjou and Berri; the Counts of Alençon, Saint Pol, Harcourt, Auvergne; Guy of Blois and other nobles; four citizens of Paris and two from each of the eighteen principal towns of the kingdom.[3] At last all was in readiness, and the King of England landed at Boulogne on the 9th of October in order to be present at the formal release of his royal prisoner. A fortnight was passed in festivities, and in finally settling and signing the treaty of peace and other necessary documents. In a formal deed, dated the 24th of October, Edward again agreed to renounce, among other claims on France, all pretensions to the crown and kingdom, as provided by the 12th article of the original treaty signed at Bretigni in May.[4] In com-

Treaty signed.

---

[1] He became the first Duke of Milan in 1395. His sister Violante married Edward's son, Lionel Duke of Clarence, in 1368.

[2] Cronica di Matteo Villani, t. iv. p. 317

[3] Buchon's *Froissart*, vol. i. p. 451.

[4] Rymer, vol. iii. p. 489.

CHAP. III. KING JOHN SET FREE. 59

pliance with this understanding, Edward did not then   A.D.1360.
call himself King of France, as he had previously done,
but gave that title to King John.[1] It was also provided that King John should also renounce all right
over the ceded provinces. As will be seen in the
sequel, these mutual renunciations were never made.[2]

The affairs of Brittany were almost the only matter
left unsettled. The treaty between the two pretenders
was prolonged; the two kings were to examine into
their respective rights, and endeavour to mediate between them; but, if no settlement could be made in
the course of a year, they were then to be at liberty
to do whatever they pleased; the friends of each were,
under those circumstances, to be free to help them if
they were so inclined, without hindrance from either
king, and this was not to be a case of war between the
two kings; the homage of Brittany was to belong to
the King of France.[3] . Arrangements were made for
the evacuation of the fortresses, held in France by
the kings of France and England, which were respec-
tively to be given up. The ransom was then paid;
the hostages were delivered; and on the 25th of
October the King of France left Calais a free man.   King John
Shortly afterwards, the King of England embarked   set free.
for England, with his sons and the hostages, and
landed at Dover.

Thus ended the first great epoch of the war between England and France; and, deep indeed must
have been the misery and humiliation of the latter
country, to induce it to consent to so disadvantageous
a treaty as that of Bretigni. Almost a third of the

[1] Rymer, vol. iii. p. 521.
[2] Ibid. vol. i, p. 529.
[3] Ibid. vol. iii. p. 516.

60   LIFE AND TIMES OF EDWARD III.   CHAP. III.

A.D. 1360. kingdom was given up to the English; an enormous sum of money was to be paid for the King's ransom; and the very flower of the land went into captivity as hostages for its fulfilment. But the treaty filled France with joy. The King was everywhere received "greatly and nobly;" on his arrival in Paris, on the 13th of December, "beautiful gifts and rich presents" were laid before him; and he was feasted and visited by all the chief prelates and barons of his kingdom.[1]

The prisoners were received in London with the greatest courtesy. During their residence in England they were allowed to amuse themselves with the chase, they visited the lords and ladies as they pleased, and were subject to no restraint, except such as was absolutely necessary to prevent their escape to France.[2]

[1] Buchon's *Froissart*, vol. i. chap. 140.
[2] Ibid. p. 451.

CHAP. IV. UNSTABLE FOUNDATION OF THE PEACE. 61

CHAPTER IV.

FROM THE PEACE OF BRETIGNI, TO THE CREATION OF THE DUKE OF AQUITAINE.

NOTWITHSTANDING the signature of the formal and elaborate treaty of Bretigni, the peace between the two countries rested on no very sure foundation. The King of England was lord over nearly as much of France as the King of France himself. This came, it is true, from the fortune of war; but it was a state of things that could not last, unless unusual wisdom were displayed by the English governor of his foreign people. Beside this, either by accident or design, an important formality in the ratification of the treaty never took place.

A.D. 1360. Peace between France and England on an unstable foundation. —

It was agreed, and confirmed by the Black Prince, that the "renunciations and cessions" should be solemnly made at Bruges on November 30th, 1361; the King of France promised to perform his part, provided the King of England performed his. On November 15th, 1361,[1] King Edward sent commissioners to receive King John's renunciations; but it is very doubtful, whether any ever appeared on John's part, and certain, that the renunciations were never made. When war broke out again between the two countries, the then King of France, Charles the Fifth, alleged that the treaty of Bretigni was consequently null and void.

Mutual renunciations never made.

[1] Rymer, vol. iii. p. 629.

62   LIFE AND TIMES OF EDWARD III.   CHAP. IV.

A.D. 1360.

The ceded towns and castles yielded by the French with difficulty.

Then, again, there were difficulties attending the surrender of the towns, castles and provinces, which were to be given up by each king. Notwithstanding the want of confidence felt by the French nation in either the king or his son, still, as Hallam says, " The French were already knit together as one people, and even those whose feudal duties sometimes led them into, the field against their sovereign, could not endure the feeling of dismemberment from the monarchy." [1] The inhabitants of Rochelle, who had constantly fitted out privateers against the English, and consequently feared their vengeance, were, with reason, especially averse to being placed under their dominion. They prayed the King of France " for God's sake not to release them from their fealty to him ; " and they said, they would pay half their means in taxes every year, rather than fall into the hands of the English. But the King told them they must yield to the conqueror, as the peace would otherwise be broken, and that this would be a great evil to France. Rochelle, therefore, was given up on December 6th, 1360 ; [2] but the Rochellois submitted with gloomy sorrow, saying, " We will obey the English with our lips, but our hearts shall never be moved towards them." The nobles of the south, too, remonstrated against their being dismembered from the monarchy ; they declared that the King had no right to transfer their homage to another ; and that in Gascony they had charters given them by Charlemagne, which showed that this was beyond his legitimate power.

At last, however, all the provinces were surrendered ;

[1] Middle Ages, vol. i. p. 58.
[2] Buchon's *Froissart*, vol. i. p. 452 (note).

CHAP. IV. "THE COMPANIES" RE-APPEAR. 63

and on January 20th, 1361,[1] King Edward appointed his old friend and companion, the gallant John of Chandos, his lieutenant in France.

There were equal difficulties in compelling the mercenaries, who held the French towns for the English, to restore them to their former masters. Most of those that were garrisoned by the English themselves, were given up without difficulty. But there were some, even of the English, who refused to do so, saying falsely that they fought under the banner of the King of Navarre. This excuse, even if true, would, however, have been of no avail, as that King was included in the treaty between England and France. Such of the garrisons as were composed of Germans, Brabanters, Flemings, and even of Bretons, Gascons, and "bad Frenchmen," most of them probably the very men who had formed themselves into "companies" after the battle of Poitiers, also refused. They again gathered themselves together into different "companies," and under various leaders, one of whom called himself "The Friend of God and Enemy of all the World."

Bands of Bretons and Gascons ravaged the country between Paris and Orleans. A "cloud" of Lorrainers, Brabanters, and Germans spread themselves over Champagne and the countries of the Upper Meuse, and these called themselves the "Tard venus," or late comers, "because they had not as yet much pillaged the kingdom of France," and they were determined to make up for lost time. Other bands wasted other parts; but the most formidable, called, par excellence, "The Great Company," and numbering about 16,000 men, devastated Burgundy. They

A.D. 1860.

John of Chandos made Edward's lieutenant in France.

Difficulties in giving up towns and castles by the English.

The "Companies" again begin their devastations.

[1] Rymer, vol. iii. p. 555.

64   LIFE AND TIMES OF EDWARD III.   CHAP. IV.

A.D. 1360. spread themselves over the country, committing such atrocities that prayers were added to the usual divine service, beseeching God " to turn away that scourge," just as had been done in the time of the plague. The King of France forbade his subjects to attack them, lest he should thereby give the English an excuse for renewing the war; he preferred to beg the King of England to put them down. Accordingly on November 18th, 1361, Edward wrote to his lieutenants in France ordering them to punish all those who should continue their depredations;[1] and, on the 18th of the following January, he was obliged to write to John of Chandos, to say, that the King of France had informed him that James de Pipe, Hugh Calverley and other English continued to ravage France, and to order him to put a stop to their outrages.[2]

James of Bourbon sent to put them down. At last, however, the King of France felt it necessary to put them down with his own hand; and he determined to begin with the "Great Company," whose plan was to march through the rich country round Lyons towards Avignon, and rob the Pope and the Cardinals. His cousin, James of Bourbon, was then at Montpellier, whither he had gone to deliver up the castles of Guienne to John of Chandos. He therefore ordered him to gather together an army and attack them, and James consequently assembled all the nobles and knights of the country and marched towards Lyons to meet the "Great Company." The leaders, hearing that the French were preparing to attack them, held counsel together, and settled to wait for them at Brignais near Lyons, among some precipitous hills where they could keep the greater part of

---

[1] Rymer, vol. iii. p. 630.   [2] Ibid. p. 685.

CHAP. IV.   THE ROYALIST ARMY ROUTED.   65

their army hidden from their enemies. James sent
scouts to find out their number, and on their return,
deceived by the cunning tactics of their foes, they
told him that there were only 5,000 or 6,000 of them,
that they were badly armed and quite in his power.
James then turned to Arnaud de Cervolles, "The
Archpriest," who was now on the side of the King
of France, saying, "Archpriest! you told me they
were more than 15,000 fighting men, and you hear
quite the contrary." "Sire!" answered the Archpriest, "still I do not believe they are less; if
they are not there it is God's doing; it is for us;
consider what you will do." "By God!" answered
James of Bourbon, "we will go and fight them in
the name of God and St. George," and made ready
for battle; the Archpriest led the van. The "Great
Company" could see all the arrangements of the
Royalists, but the Royalists could not see them.
They were provided, according to Froissart,[1] with
above 1,000 carts filled with rocks and stones, and,
as the first "battle" of the Royalists approached,
cast the stones down on them, killing and wounding
numbers, and throwing them into such confusion that
they never recovered themselves. Then James of
Bourbon and his son and nephew came on with their
banners flying, and a great host of men "who were
all marching to their deaths." As they neared the
hill, down came the stones on them as they had on
their comrades, and when they were thereby thrown
into utter confusion the robbers came out from their
hiding-places, "thick and serried like brushwood,"
their lances, for easy handling, cut down to six feet
in length, and shouting "St. George! strike at these

_A.D. 1360._

_He is de-
ceived as
to their
number,_

_and pre-
pares to
attack
them;_

_His army
is utterly
routed._

[1] Vol. i. p. 456, Buchon's ed.

VOL. II.   F

66 LIFE AND TIMES OF EDWARD III. CHAP. IV.

A.D. 1360.

Frenchmen." "Why should I make a long story?" says Froissart, the Frenchmen were beaten; James of Bourbon and his son were badly wounded, and were carried with difficulty into Lyons, where the father died on the third day after the battle and his son was soon afterwards carried to the same grave. The battle took place on April 6th, 1362.[1]

The "Companies" spread themselves over the country and prepare to attack the Pope.

After this signal triumph the robbers marched as they pleased through the country. Their success drew to their ranks numbers of vagabond English, Gascons, and Germans; and they now resolved to go to Avignon, and attack the Pope. In order to raise an army for his defence, the Pope proclaimed a crusade against them, offering pardon of sins to all who joined his ranks. Some, who were probably the greatest rascals of the number, accepted the offer; but most, finding they were only to get pardon and no pay, and having consciences as light as their pockets, rejected it. Many even joined the "Companies," where there was plenty of plunder but no chance of pardon, and the "Companies" thus became stronger

The Pope buys them off.

than ever. The Pope was now in despair, when it occurred to him that he might buy off his assailants by getting them employed as regular troops. So he sent for the Marquis of Montferrat, who was then making war on the Lords of Milan, and agreed to give him 60,000 florins to take them into his pay. The Pope thus got rid of 6,000 of his foes.

These incidents, having only an indirect bearing on the History of England, are related in order to furnish some idea of the horrible state of France after the return of King John, and of the difficulty of fulfilling the conditions of the treaty of Bretigni. It

---

[1] See note in Buchon's ed. vol. i. p. 457.

CHAP. IV.   RETURN OF THE PLAGUE.   67

would be easy to add further details, demonstrating A.D. 1361.
the mutual jealousies of nobles and people, the devastated condition of the country, the enormous rate
of interest required for money, and the utterly dis-
organised condition of the kingdom; and to show how
all these miseries produced, and were aggravated by,
the reappearance of the Plague; but enough has been
told to exhibit the state of France in its relation
to England, and it is unnecessary here to pursue
the subject further.

England, on the King's return, was relieved of On the
the vast cost of carrying on the war, and he, be- King's relieving apparently that a permanent peace was now England
established, restored to the " Priors Aliens" their the
houses, lands, and tenements which he had con- "Priories
fiscated to his own use. In the interval, from the
commencement of the war with France, twenty-three
years before, he had let them out to be farmed.

A few months after the war was ended, the Plague The
again broke out in England, as it had also done in Plague
France. The Courts of Law were consequently adjourned on the 10th of May till the 24th of June;
on the 23rd of that month the King again wrote
to the judges, commanding them to adjourn their
courts till the 6th of October.[1] The mortality,
however, was not so great as on the former occasion,
but among its victims was the brave and celebrated
Henry of Lancaster, who died at the end of March, Death of
1361. His daughter, as already stated, had married of Lancas-
the King's son, John of Gaunt, and was the mother ter.
of our Henry IV.

Another event of importance to England happened
during this year, namely, the marriage of the Black

[1] Rymer, vol. iii. pp. 616, 621.

F 2

68 LIFE AND TIMES OF EDWARD III. CHAP. IV.

A.D. 1361.

Marriage of the Black Prince to the Fair Maid of Kent.

Prince to Joan, commonly called the Fair Maid of Kent. She was the grand-daughter of Edward I., her father being Edmund of Woodstock, Earl of Kent, the sixth and youngest son of Edward I. On the death of her brother, John, Earl of Kent, without issue, she became Countess of Kent. The Black Prince was this beautiful lady's third husband; her first was Sir Thomas Holland, Steward of the Household to William Montague, Earl of Salisbury; her second, from whom she was divorced, was Salisbury himself. The Prince and Joan being cousins, a special dispensation to allow of their marriage was obtained from the Pope.

A.D. 1362.

Duke of Aquitaine.

Soon after the marriage of his son, King Edward created him Duke of Aquitaine. It was evident that the large dominions in the south of France of which King Edward was now absolute sovereign, could not be governed by a mere deputy, however wise and personally loved he might be. The English rule was far from popular in France, and nothing but the fact of a king or a king's son dwelling among them was likely to make that rule acceptable. It was for these reasons that King Edward created his son Duke of Aquitaine, and made him ruler over that part of his dominions. But yet, and wisely too, he did not make him absolute sovereign over the country. Such a course would have deprived the King of England of all power over his newly-recovered dominions, and of creating one of his younger sons Duke of Aquitaine at his own death; and would have ended either in the establishment of a line of English Kings of Aquitaine independent of England, or, possibly, of making the King of England subordinate to the King of Aquitaine. The Black Prince would, at his father's

CHAP. IV.   DUKE OF AQUITAINE.   **69**

death, have become King of Aquitaine and England. A.D. 1362.
It was the object of Edward's policy to prevent such but is not
a combination, for the English nation would not have made absolute
submitted to such degradation, and there would pro- Sovereign
over that
bably have risen up a competitor for the English country.
crown. This must have ended, eventually, in the
severance of the two kingdoms.[1] King Edward,
therefore, imposed on his son the annual payment of
an ounce of gold at the palace of Westminster, "as
an open indication and clear demonstration that our
son holds the aforesaid things under us and our
Majesty and by Liege Homage."[2] As remarked by
Mr. Hallam,[3] "so high were the notions of this great
monarch, in an age when the privilege of creating
new kingdoms was deemed to belong to the Pope
and the Emperor," that he added, that he expressly
reserved to himself the right to make Aquitaine into
a kingdom.[4] This was on July 19th, 1362, but it
was not until the following February that the Prince
embarked for his new dominions.

[1] See Sismondi, vol. ii. p. 95.   [2] Rymer, vol. iii. p. 669.
[3] *Middle Ages*, vol. i. p. 57, note.   [4] Ibid. p. 667.

70   LIFE AND TIMES OF EDWARD III.   Chap. V.

CHAPTER V.

DOMESTIC LEGISLATION.

A.D. 1362.
Important
Statutes.

THE importance and interest of the relations between England and France at this juncture can hardly be overrated, but yet there is a more permanent value in the glimpses from time to time obtained of the internal progress of the English nation in civilisation. It was at this moment that various legislative measures were enacted, the effect and interest of which remain at the present day as fresh and important as they were at the time of their enactment, though five centuries have since passed by. The most memorable of these, was that establishing the use of the English language. England had hitherto been almost as much French as English, and, had Edward succeeded in placing himself on the throne of France, would, in all probability, have been merged in France, until, scorning such a position, she again made herself an independent kingdom. But this was not to be. England remained England, and the English language was now to become the language of the nation.

The English language commenced to be used in the Law Courts.

At a Parliament which met on October 13th, 1362, it was ordered that the English instead of the French language should thenceforth be used in pleadings in the Courts of Law. The reason given in the Statute (36 Ed. III. stat. 1. c. 15) for this change, is that "the French tongue is much unknown" in England,

Chap. V. ENGLISH LANGUAGE USED IN LAW COURTS. 71

"so that the people which do implead, or be impleaded, in the King's Court, and in the Courts of other, have no knowledge nor understanding of that which is said for them or against them by their Serjeants and other Pleaders."[1]

A.D. 1362.

It is clear from this, that the English language had already made way, but it is remarkable that this Law itself was written in French. Indeed, although the English language had made so great progress among the nation in general, that the poems of Chaucer, the first and one of the greatest of English poets and the very founder of English literature, may be read with tolerable ease at the present day, yet a bastard kind of French was still the spoken and written language of the upper classes. In the early part of this century, French was the language which the children of gentlemen were taught to speak from their cradle, and it was the only language allowed to be used by boys at school. About a quarter of a century after the passing of this Statute, such was no longer the case. Trevisa, the translator of Higden's Chronicle from Latin into English, says: "This manner was myche yused tofore the first moreyn and is sith the som dele ychaungide—in alle the gramer scoles of England children leveth Frensche and lerneth an Englisch."[2] This change was probably greatly brought about by the

French the language of the upper classes.

[1] *Statutes of the Realm,* folio, vol. i. p. 395, and see also Rot. Parl. vol. ii. p. 273.

[2] Craik's *Hist. Eng. Lit.* vol. i. p. 160, and see the same work p. 98, quoting the original passage from Ralph Higden. "Also gentil mennes children beth ytaught for to speke Frensche from the time that thei both rokked in her cradel, and cunneth speke and playe with a childes brooche; and uplondish men wol likne hem self to gentilmen," &c. &c.

72 LIFE AND TIMES OF EDWARD III. CHAP. V.

A.D. 1362. Statute under consideration. King Edward the Third was hardly able even to speak English,[1] always wrote his despatches in French, and his proclamations were often made in that language; but it was a wretched travestie of it, so much so indeed, that Chaucer writing a few years later, says: "of whyche speche the Frenche men have as good a fantasye as we have in hearing of French mennes Englyshe,"[2] and he expresses the same fact in the well known lines:—

> "After the scole of Stratford atte Bowe.
> For Frenche of Paris was to her unknowe."

But, although the English language was ordered to be used in pleadings in open court, in order that all men might understand what was going on, the pleas and all the proceedings in a cause were ordered to be enrolled in a Latin Record, and "the reports of what

---

[1] "We have no satisfactory proof that any one of the first three Edwards spoke English, and it would appear that Edward III. on some public occasion found it difficult to put together three consecutive words in the national tongue."—Pauli's *Pictures of Old England*, page 208.

[2] Specimen of King Edward's French, taken from a letter to his son. Avesbury, p. 98. "Tresch . . . & tresame filtz nous sauoms bien je vous desviez mult de sauoir bones nouelx de nous & de nre estat vous faceoms assauoir je au partier du cestes nous esteioms heites de corps dieux ensoit loie."

Another, of the language used in proclamations, from Rymer, vol. iii. p. 469; "Come en nostre parlement, pur refriendre la malice des servantz qi furent percionses nient voillantz servire apres la pestilence, saunz trope outrageouses lowers prendre."

Another, of Parliamentary language, from Parliamentary Rolls. "Soit ordeine covenable Remedie, & coment la Ples purra meltz estre gardez & le People de son Roialme vivre en ese . . . & quiete."—Rot. Parl. vol. ii. p. 268.

"Item, que lui plese or deiner plente d'or & d'argent."—Ibid. p. 271.

CHAUCER.
From a Drawing in the British Museum.

CHAP. V.   THE POET CHAUCER.   **73**

passed in court were still taken and published in French, and so continued for hundreds of years after."[1]

It is impossible to quit this account of the first legal recognition and command of the use of the English language without taking some further, though but slight, notice of the "Father of English Poetry." Chaucer was born in 1328, and is believed to have died in 1400. His great poem, "The Canterbury Tales," was not, it is true, written until the middle of the reign of Richard II., and it is to his reign therefore that Chaucer properly belongs. But Chaucer was writing his immortal verse in the English tongue at the time when the Statute commanding its use was enacted. A passing tribute therefore, even if somewhat anticipating time, is due to him, who, in conjunction with his contemporaries Longland, the author of "the Vision of Piers Ploughman," and John Gower, the author of the "Confessio Amantis," was building up the English language; and who is the earliest English poet whose writings can still be read with pleasure, and understood without trouble. He is justly called "The Homer of his country."[2]

Other important laws and regulations relating to trade, and to the manners and customs of the people were made about this time, of which it is desirable to give some account before resuming the narrative of the more public history of the reign; for although many of them were repealed in the following year, they strikingly illustrate the times.

The first of these has reference to that constant interference with trade, either, by protections or restrictions in favour of one or other traffic or ma-

A.D. 1362.

Chaucer the "Father of English Poetry."

Other laws and regulations.

Unwise interference with trade.

---

[1] Reeve's *English Law,* vol. ii. p. 450.
[2] Craik's *Eng. Lit.* vol. i. p. 271.

74 LIFE AND TIMES OF EDWARD III. CHAP. V.

A.D. 1362. nufacture, at the proportionate cost of some other; or, for regulating modes of dealing; or with a view to raising larger revenues for the King personally or for the State, which was so characteristic of this reign. The true principle of trade, viz.: to allow any man to buy and sell as he pleases so long as he does so honestly, was not then understood; but the constant enactments for the regulation of commerce, bear testimony to its growing importance, and to the care with which it was attempted to be fostered, although the foster child ran an imminent risk of being smothered in the process.

Low price of wool

One of the first matters taken into consideration by the Parliament, which met on October 13th, 1362, was the low price of wool, for which a remedy was sought by removing the staple from London to Calais. It is not easy to understand how this could have the desired effect, and it is singular that after the valid reasons given only nine years before (27 Edward III. stat. 2) for the establishment of staples within the kingdom, it should now have been decided that it was better to have them out of it. The effect indeed which staples had on commerce was evidently not clear to the legislators themselves. At the beginning of the reign, however, either sounder views were entertained relative to them, or it had not then become necessary to sacrifice commerce to revenue. They were then said to be contrary to the principles of Magna Charta, and were abolished in order "that all merchants strangers and privy may go and come with their merchandises into England, after the tenor of the Great Charter."[1] The merchants presented a petition to the King, stating that whereas

[1] Stat. 2 Ed. III. c. 9.

Chap. V. EXPORT OF WOOLS AND WOOLFELLS ALLOWED. 75

"the wools of the kingdom are put at little value, as
much because they are taken out of the kingdom into
another Seignory or Power where our Lord the King
has no jurisdiction, as for exchange of money and its
debasement, it would be good to remedy it, and that
the city of Calais, which belongs to the King, would be
a good place for the wools and for the abode of the Merchants to avoid the aforesaid mischiefs and damages,
and by which the price of wools will be amended
and enhanced." In answer to this petition, the King
promised "to show these things more openly to the
Great Men and the Commons and take their advice
thereon,"[1] and the staple was consequently removed
to Calais on the 1st of March following; but before
three years had elapsed this policy was reversed.[2]

In this Parliament, notwithstanding that on the
27th of September the export of wools and woolfells
had been absolutely forbidden,[3] leave was given "that
the merchants denizens may pass with their wools as
well as the Foreigners without being restrained." The
object of this alteration was palpable; for the reason
given for it was, that the King had "regard to the
great subsidy which the Commons have granted, now
in this Parliament, of wools, leather, and woolfells, to
be taken for three years."[4] The duty to be levied was
20s. for each sack of wool, 20s. for each 300 woolfells,
and 40s. for each last of leather exported; in addition
to the ancient duty of a half mark from Denizens and
10s. from Aliens, for each sack of wool, and for each
300 woolfells, and of one mark for each last of leather
from Denizens, and 20s. from Aliens.[5] The export

A.D. 1362.

to be re-
medied by
removal of
staple to
Calais.

Export of
wool, &c.,
because of
subsidy
granted
thereon,

---

[1] Rot. Parl. vol. ii. p. 268.
[2] See Preamble of Stat. 43 Ed. III. [3] Rymer, vol. iii. p. 677.
[4] Stat. 36 Ed. III. c. 11. [5] Rot. Parl. vol. ii. p. 273.

76 LIFE AND TIMES OF EDWARD III. CHAP. V.

A.D. 1362.
but that of manufactured wool forbidden.

of manufactured wool was, however, soon afterwards forbidden; on the 26th of November, among a most miscellaneous list of articles such as corn, lead, sea-coal, cheese, and butter, the export of which was forbidden, "the cloths called worsteds" are included.[1] The forbidding of the export of wool may have had some show of reason, as the object was probably to encourage the home manufacture; but cheese, butter, and the other articles thus prohibited can have been included only in order to keep down their price, to the detriment and discouragement of the producers. This was the frequent object of such legislation, as evidenced by the fact, that the dearness of corn was commonly alleged as the reason for forbidding its export, though, as often, such legislation had for its object, the enhancement of the price.[2]

Export of hawks forbidden,

The minute way in which all details of trade, commerce, and even amusements, were regulated, might be illustrated in various ways. Among these it is interesting to notice, as characteristic of the times, that the price of hawks was fixed,[3] that stealing them subjected a man to the same punishment as stealing a horse,[4] and that their export was constantly forbidden.[5]

Among other singular instances of the minute way in which the Government, through the exercise of royal prerogative, interfered during this era with the daily concerns of domestic life, it may be worth recording that, in 1340, the King endeavoured, by

---

[1] Rymer, vol. iii. p. 683. [2] Ibid. pp. 553 and 603.
[3] Ibid. pp. 709 and 776. The prices of hawks were fixed as follows: A gentle falcon, 20s.; a gentle tercel, 10s.; a lestor, 13s. 4d.; a tercel estor, half a mark; a lanner, half a mark.
[4] Stat. 37 Ed. III. c. 19. [5] Rymer, vol. iii. pp. 613, 694, 724.

CHAP. V.   PRIVILEGES GRANTED TO CALAIS.   77

proclamation, to put down a curious, and, one would think, most unpromising piece of knavery practised by the London butchers. He forbade them to sew the fat of good beef on joints of lean.[1]

A.D. 1363.

The export of horses, and probably of cows also, at any rate without paying duty, was forbidden by the King; but on June 7th, 1363, leave was given to Andrew Destrer of Bruges, the Queen's guitar-player, to take over twenty-five oxen or cows without paying any duty.[2] A few years later, in 1367, one Henry of Halle, a German merchant, obtained leave to import into England from Flanders "eight great horses;" and if he could not sell them in England permission was granted him to take them anywhere else, except to Scotland, whither it was absolutely forbidden to send horses.[3] They were described as of "divers colours, viz.: one black destrere, two red coursers, one black courser with his nostrils cut, one smaller courser of a grey colour, one red courser with his nostrils cut, one bay and another black courser."[4]

and of horses and cows.

Special privileges were granted to Calais, whither the staple was now removed. A corporation of twenty-six English merchants, two of whom were to be mayors, and twenty-four aldermen, was created by an

Special privileges granted to Calais.

[1] "Ex parte communitatis civitatis nostræ London', per petitionem suam coram nobis et concilio nostro exhibitam, nobis est ostensum, quod carnifices qui carnes in Civitate prædictâ vendunt, pinguedinem boum crassorum super carnes boum macelentorum, per fila et spinas de ligno factas, suunt et affigunt, nos igitur, vobis precipimus, &c. &c."—Rymer, voL ii. p. 1120. Until the reign of James the First, legislation by proclamations was frequently resorted to, more particularly in matters of trade, and especially foreign trade, which were considered within the powers of the royal prerogative.

[2] Rymer, vol. iii. p. 704.   [3] Ibid. p. 823.   [4] Ibid. p. 829.

78 LIFE AND TIMES OF EDWARD III. Chap. V.

A.D. 1363. ordinance on March 1st, 1363. This body, "with the consent of the Prelates, Lords, and others of the Council," was allowed to import all sorts of food and provender for the provisioning of Calais, without paying any duty, from England, Wales, Berwick, and Ireland ; provided they were not sold out of the seignory. It was also ordained that no wools, skins, worsteds, cheese, butter, tin, lead, coal, grindstones, and various other English products, should be exported from England, whether by denizens or foreigners, except to Calais. There were some slight exceptions with regard to certain goods which might be sent to Gascony; but, otherwise, the whole export trade of England was compelled to pass through Calais.[1] It is difficult to conceive why the Parliament, which then had and often exercised considerable power, refrained from interfering with regulations so subversive of the commercial interests of England, which were evidently made, by the King in Council, without their consent. It may be however, as indeed is rendered probable by the subsequent agreement of Parliament that such matters should be settled by Ordinance and not by Statute, that they considered the former method less binding and permanent.

It was not easy to enforce these regulations. It became necessary, two months afterwards, to make the collectors of customs, at the various ports of England, answerable that foreign merchants buying wool and other goods in England for export to Flanders or elsewhere should stow them away among the goods of native merchants, and send them

---

[1] Rymer vol. iii. p. 690. "Sachez que nous, par assent des Prelats, Seignurs, et autres de notre conseil, avons ordeigne," &c. &c.

CHAP. V.   PROHIBITIONARY MEASURES.   79

to Calais, instead of shipping them in vessels from A.D. 1364.
foreign ports, as was their custom, and sending them
direct to their destination. A singular proviso was
added to this ordinance, stating that it was "always
provided that no wines, corn, beer, animals whether
flesh or fowl, horses, clergy, foreigners or others, except our merchants," should be allowed to pass out of
the kingdom without special leave.[1] The passage of Regula-
persons out of or into England was carefully watched, tions as to
and not allowed without express permission; and passing
even Scotchmen coming to England for trading pur- ofEngland.
poses required a safe conduct to enable them to do
so.[2] Frequent and numerous parties of rich merchants, with caravans laden with their goods, and
attended by companies of horsemen and squires for
the purposes of defence and security, travelled from
all parts of Scotland into England and the Continent.
They travelled in bodies of fifty or sixty at a time.
On one memorable occasion, a party of sixty-five
merchants obtained safe conducts to travel through
England for the purposes of trade, and their warlike
suite amounted to no less than two hundred and
thirty horsemen.[3]

There was an extraordinary fear of the conse- As to
quences of taking money out of the country, and it taking coin
required a special permission to enable a foreigner kingdom.
selling goods in England to receive money for them.
Thus, on September 30th, 1364, it was proclaimed by
the King that, although he had "lately ordered it to
be proclaimed throughout the kingdom that no one
should be allowed to take gold or silver, in money, or
in any other way out of the kingdom," yet he gave

---

[1] Rymer, vol. iii. p. 698.   [2] Ibid. pp. 646, 647.
[3] Rot. Scot. p. 876 (as quoted by Tytler, vol. ii. p. 53), &c.

80   LIFE AND TIMES OF EDWARD III.   CHAP. V.

A.D. 1362.

Special
leave
required.

leave, to the Flemish and other fishermen, to take their herrings to the fair at Yarmouth, and sell them for money. Similar permission was given to fishermen taking eels and other fish to London, and to others taking herrings and other fish to Sandwich.[1] About the same time, a merchant of Bayonne, who had sold fifty hogsheads of Gascony wine in London, was licensed to export 100 quarters of corn, which he had bought with the money he received for it.[2] That the constant object was to keep money in the kingdom is further confirmed by the statement, in the King's ordinance of July 8th, 1364,[3] that the object of allowing the Gascons to buy herrings in England, with the money they received for their wine, was "in order to retain the money within the kingdom." In a like manner, when William Pernell of Harwich wanted to go in his ship " The Edmund," to La Baye in Brittany to buy salt, it was necessary for him to obtain leave to take money with him to pay for it.[4]

Restrictions on freedom of home trade.

But, it was not merely the foreign trade, that was thus subjected to minute regulations and restrictions of all kinds. The home trade of the country was equally interfered with, the great idea of the period being to keep down prices and prevent the producer from obtaining the natural value of his goods; in short, to protect the buyer against the seller. One motive for this may have been that the King himself, through the " hateful Purveyors," was himself a great buyer. In July 1366, corn was forbidden to be exported because it was dear.[5] In the Parliament held

---

[1] Rymer, vol. iii. p. 748.   [2] Ibid. p. 752.
[3] Ibid. p. 741.   [4] Ibid. p. 739.   [5] Ibid. p. 797.

Chap. V.   RESTRICTIONS ON GOLDSMITHS.   81

in the autumn of 1363, the King ordained "at the request of the Commons and by the assent of the Prelates, Dukes, Earls, Barons, and other Great Men," "for the great mischiefs which have happened, as well to the King, as to the Great Men and Commons, of that that the Merchants, called Grocers, do ingross all manner of Merchandise vendible, and suddenly do inhance the price of such Merchandise within the realm, putting to sale by coin and ordinance made betwixt them, called the Fraternity and Gild of Merchants, the Merchandises which be most dear, and keep in store the other, till the time that dearth or scarcity be of the same," that merchants should deal in one sort of merchandise only, and that each should choose between then and Candlemas what it should be. It was also ordained that "Artificers, Handicraft People, hold them every one to one Mystery, which he will choose between this and the said feast of Candlemas;" but an exception was made in respect of certain workwomen, it being added that "the intent of the King and of his Council is, that Women, that is to say Brewers, Bakers, Carders and Spinners, and Workers as well of Wool as of Linen Cloth and of Silk, Brawdesters, and Breakers of Wool, and all others that do use and work all Handy Works, may freely use and work as they have done before this time." The Goldsmiths, too, were put under great restrictions, it being ordained that "no Goldsmith making White Vessel shall meddle with Gilding, nor they that do gild shall meddle to make white vessel." [1]

In accordance with this statute, in July of the following year, in order to "make the price more

A.D. 1362.

Every merchant to deal in one kind of merchandise only.

Exceptions as to women.

Restrictions on goldsmiths.

Trade in fish interfered with in like manner.

[1] Stat. 37 Ed. III. c. 5, 6, and 7.

VOL. II.   G

82   LIFE AND TIMES OF EDWARD III.   CHAP. V.

A.D. 1363.

reasonable," the King made the following regulations about the sale of fish, viz.: that "no one shall meddle with the mystery of fishmongers except those that belong to it;" and that "the fish shall be sold only in three places, that is Bridge Street, Old Fish Street, and the place called Lestokkes (i.e. 'The Stocks market,' which was held where the Mansion House now stands), except stock-fish which belongs to the mystery of stock-fishmongers." It was also ordered that it should be landed during daylight, and only in particular places, in order that its quantity might be certified, "so that people may know how much fish there is," that it was not to be sold to sell again, excepting in gross, and so forth.

Drapers.

An ordinance for a similar purpose was also made relative to drapers, ordering that "no one shall use this mystery, unless he has been apprenticed to it," and that "those who have drapery to sell shall sell it to no one except to the drapers enfranchised in the mystery, except in gross to the Lords and others who wish to buy them for their own use, and never by retail." The Vintners were subjected to like regulations,[1] and the price of poultry was also regulated by the same ordinance.

It is worthy of notice that in this Parliament the King asked whether "they would have the things agreed to, put by way of ordinance or of statute, and they answered that it was better by ordinance and not by statute, so that if there were anything to amend, it might be amended in the next Parliament."[2] The wisdom of this answer was soon made apparent.

Another matter, taken in hand by this Parliament,

---

[1] Rymer, vol. iii. pp. 741, 742.
[2] Rot. Parl. vol. ii. p. 280.

CHAP. V.   PARTIAL REPEAL OF THE STATUTE.   83

is one which appears even less suited to regulation
by law. It was the dress of the people, and the
reason given was, "the outrageous and excessive apparel of divers people against their estate and degree
to the great destruction and impoverishment of all
the land." A few of the details, selected from the
long and minute regulations embodied in this statute,
are as follows:—All servants were forbidden to wear
cloth of a greater value than two marks for the entire dress, or to wear embroidered gold or silver or
silk, and their wives and daughters were not to
wear veils of above 12d. value. Esquires of a certain income were forbidden to wear furs; but the
wives of those of a higher income might wear fur
turned up with miniver; "carters, ploughmen, oxherds, shepherds and all other keepers of beasts,
threshers of corn, and all manner of people attending to husbandry," not having 40s. worth of goods
or chattels, were not to wear any manner of cloth,
except blanket and russet wool of 12d. a yard, and
girdles of linen according to their estate; and it
was added, "that they come to eat and drink in the
manner as pertaineth to them and not excessively."[1]

Many parts of this statute were repealed in the
following year. The Commons presented petitions
stating that they were "hardly grieved"[2] by the
ordinance of the last Parliament, and prayed that
it might be repealed.[3] Accordingly, after confirming
the "Great Charter and the Charter of the Forest"
for the twelfth time during his reign, the King
ordained "that all People shall be as free as they
were before the said Ordinance, and that all Mer-

A.D. 1363.

Regulations as to dress.

Repeal of parts of the statute.

---

[1] Stat. 37 Ed. III. c. 8, 14.

[2] "Durement grevez."   [3] Rot. Parl. vol. ii. p. 286.

84   LIFE AND TIMES OF EDWARD III.   CHAP. V.

A.D. 1363. chants, as well Aliens as Denizens, may sell and buy all manner of Merchandises, and freely carry them out of the realm, paying the customs and subsidies thereof due; except that the English Merchants shall not pass out of the Realm with Wools or Woolfells, and that none carry out of the Realm Gold nor Silver, in Plate nor in Money, saving the Victuallers of fish that fish for herring and other fish, and they that bring fish within the Realm in small vessels, which meddle not with other Merchandises." [1] By the same statute, the punishment of death, which (as it would seem almost impossible to believe, were not the fact beyond doubt) had been ordered to be inflicted on those who passed out of the country with wools, woolfells and leather without leave,[2] was repealed; the staple was restored to England, and greater freedom was given to the trade in wines.

This statute of repeal is particularly interesting as showing the progress of sound ideas on matters of trade; the impolicy of making enactments contrary to those principles; the power which the Commons had of making themselves heard; and the prudence of the King and his advisers in instantly redressing the grievances against which the Commons presented their petitions.

There was another Royal ordinance promulgated at this time relative to greater perseverance in the use of the bow, which must be here mentioned, as it gives interesting information as to the sports and habits of the people, and possibly shows the effect of the recent introduction of gunpowder.

---

[1] Stat. 38 Ed. III. c. 1, 2.

[2] " Est accorde, q *la forfaiture de vie et de membre* soit ouste de tout en l'estatut de le staple."—*Statutes of the Realm,* vol. i. p. 384.

CHAP. V. PRACTICE IN ARCHERY COMMANDED. 85

On June 1st, 1363, the King, addressed a letter to the sheriffs, ordering that, "Whereas before these times the people of the country, as well noble as ignoble, commonly exercised themselves in the art of archery, and thereby did honour and were of use to the whole kingdom: whereas now, as if entirely putting aside the said art, the same people take to the throwing of stones, wood, and iron ; and some to hand-ball, foot-ball, and stick-play; and to the fighting of dogs and cocks; and some even indulge themselves in dishonest and less useful games: it is to be proclaimed that every man in the county, of able body, on feast days, shall use bows and arrows, or crossbows and bolts, in his games, and shall learn and exercise the art of archery, and shall give up these vain games under pain of imprisonment." [1] This proclamation had, apparently, but little effect, for it became necessary to repeat it two years afterwards.

It is evident that, owing, perhaps, to some extent of demoralisation of the people—which is not unlikely when the habits of the nobles are considered —or, more probably, from a diminishing trust in the value of bows and arrows as weapons of warfare, the practice of archery had become much neglected.

It is not an inopportune moment here to remark that at this time, and indeed for centuries afterwards, the proceedings in Parliament were very different from what they are at present. What is now called "the Cabinet" did not then exist. The King's advisers were what was anciently termed the King's Council, which sprang from the Curia Regis.[2] They "consisted of the Chancellor, Trea-

_A.D. 1363._

The practice of archery commanded.

---

[1] Rymer vol. iii. p. 704 and 770.
[2] Madox, *Exchequer*, vol. i. p. 6.

86　LIFE AND TIMES OF EDWARD III.　Chap. V.

A.D.1363.

General remarks on the Proceedings in Parliament.

surer, Lord Steward, Lord Admiral, Lord Marshal, the Keeper of the Privy Seal, the Chamberlain, Treasurer and Comptroller of the Household, the Chancellor of the Exchequer, and the Master of the Wardrobe; also of the Judges, King's Sergeant and Attorney General, the Master of the Rolls and Justices in Eyre. When all these were called together it was a full council, but where the business was of a more contracted nature those only who were fittest to advise were summoned."[1] There is no evidence that then, or for a long time afterwards, the King's advisers or any member of Parliament brought in what we now call "a Bill." The Commons presented their Petitions for the redress of grievances; it may be presumed that some kind of debate then took place, but there is no trace of this until towards the end of the reign. If the King, or his advisers, thought fit to grant the petition, he either answered " *Il plest au Roi,*" or, as in the present instance, " *Soient si franks come estoient de tout temps auncienement devant les dites Ordinances,* &c. &c.;[2] or, according to the nature of the petition.

Jubilee on the occasion of the King attaining the fiftieth year of his age.

In the autumn of this year a national jubilee was held on account of the King having attained his fiftieth year. There are no records of the way in which it was kept by the nation at large, but the King granted a general pardon, released prisoners, and recalled exiles.[3] He also, on this occasion, created his third son Lionel, who was then in Ireland, Duke of Clarence, which title he took in right of his wife, who was descended from the Lords of the Honour of Clare in Suffolk; his fourth son, John of Gaunt, Duke

---

[1] Hallam's *Middle Ages,* vol. ii. p. 269.
[2] Rot. Parl. vol. ii. p. 286.　　[3] Walsingham, p. 297.

CHAP. V.   THE PRINCE SAILS FOR AQUITAINE.   87

of Lancaster, in right of his wife, daughter of the Earl of Lancaster; and his fifth son, Edmund, Earl of Cambridge.[1]   After this, the King went with a great assembly of the earls and barons of England and all the French hostages, to hunt in the forests of Rockingham, Sherwood, Clun in Shropshire, and various other forests, woods, and parks; he spent, sometimes a hundred pounds, and sometimes a hundred marks a day in these diversions.[2]

The time for the departure of the Prince of Wales to the Duchy of Aquitaine was now approaching; the King therefore went to visit him at the Castle of Berkhamsted, before he left England.   Little indeed was it then expected, that he would return in a very few years, shattered in health, and not untarnished in reputation for high chivalrous feeling, or that the result of his short tenure of the Duchy would be the loss of everything gained by the victory at Poitiers.

A.D. 1363.

Great hunting parties.

The Prince sails for Aquitaine.

[1] Rot. Parl. vol. ii. p. 273.   [2] Knighton, col. 2627.

88 LIFE AND TIMES OF EDWARD III. CHAP. VI.

CHAPTER VI.

KING JOHN RETURNS TO CAPTIVITY AND DEATH—APPROACHING RENEWAL OF WAR WITH FRANCE.

A.D. 1363.

Breach of faith on the part of one of the French hostages.

THE Prince of Wales sailed for Aquitaine in February 1363. He had not been there three months, before one of the French hostages was guilty of a breach of faith, which might easily have put an end to the peace between England and France. They had been treated with the greatest kindness; the utmost practicable freedom had always been granted to them; the King was glad to have them as his companions on his hunting parties; and, in order to indulge in their various diversions, they were constantly allowed leave of absence from the castles, which were called their prisons. Thus—to select two instances, among many, of the liberality with which they were treated, and of the means they took to amuse themselves—on February 16th, 1361, very shortly after their arrival, the King gave the Duke of Orleans leave to go with his hawks, hounds, and friends, as often as he pleased, and wherever he pleased within the kingdom, except in his own preserves;[1] to remain away each time for eight days, returning at sunset on the eighth day; and when the King, on December 14th, 1362, gave certain of them leave to go to Calais, they were permitted to take

[1] Hors des lieux fermez.

CHAP. VI.   FOUR DUKES ON PAROLE.   89

"their greyhounds, other dogs, and falcons" with *A.D. 1362.*
them.[1]

But they became weary of their exile, and were *Four dukes are allowed to go to France on parole.*
half ruined by the cost of living in a foreign land
while their estates were lying in neglect. It was,
however, only the four "Lords of the Fleurs de
Lys," as the Dukes of Orleans, Anjou, Berry, and
Bourbon were called, and a few others, whose desire
for freedom was attended to. On November 13th,
1362, these captives entered into a treaty with King
Edward, subject to King John's approval, by which
leave was granted them to go to Calais, and to travel
three days' distance from thence on condition of
returning by sunset on the fourth day.[2] They
also pledged themselves that, as provided by the treaty
of Bretigni, the territory of Belleville with all its
castles and fortresses, and the county of Gaure,
should be given up; and that the agreed sum of
200,000 florins should be paid to Edward by the 1st
of November following. As a security for the ful- *The conditions on which this leave was granted.*
filment of this pledge, they promised that their own
lands and castles should be delivered to Edward;
and that, if all these conditions of their release were
not fulfilled by the 1st of November of the following
year, they would return as prisoners to England within
one month after that day. Under such circumstances
it was provided, that their lands and castles should
remain the entire property of England. Other arrangements were also made to secure the fulfilment of
all the conditions of the treaty of Bretigni; among
these it was specified that the letters of renunciation,
which were to have been exchanged at Bruges in the

---

[1] Rymer, vol. iii. pp. 603 and 684.
[2] Buchon's *Froissart*, vol. i. p. 465.

90   LIFE AND TIMES OF EDWARD III.   Chap. VI.

A.D. 1363. previous year, should be reciprocally delivered. The giving up of the lands and castles belonging to the Princes was a heavy penalty to pay for their freedom; for, as Sismondi says,[1] "it put the finishing stroke to the surrender of France to the English." Nevertheless, after vainly endeavouring to make some slight changes in the conditions, John agreed to the treaty as proposed by his sons. On its solemn confirmation by the Princes, they were allowed to go to Calais about the end of May.[2]

The Duke of Anjou breaks his parole. It was not long before one of the Princes violated the conditions on which he had obtained his liberty. The French treasury was empty; the ravages of the Companies, the mortality caused by the pestilence, and the universal misery, stopped the payment of all taxes; and, notwithstanding this want of money, King John was running into further expenditure. He had engaged in a new crusade with the King of Cyprus, who had in vain visited the King of England with the object of dragging him also into the scheme; and a war with the King of Navarre relative to the Duchy of Burgundy was imminent. John, on the death of his stepson the Duke, had taken possession of the duchy as the nearest of kin to the late Duke; but the King of Navarre claimed it on the same grounds, being the descendant of Duke Robert of Burgundy by his eldest daughter, while the King of France was descended from the second.

These circumstances rendered it very improbable, that the conditions on which the Princes were set free could be fulfilled. The Duke of Anjou, seeing this, had no hesitation in treacherously breaking those on

---

[1] Vol. x. p. 604.

[2] Rymer, vol. iii. pp. 681, 682, 685, 694, 701.

CHAP. VI. KING JOHN RETURNS TO ENGLAND. 91

which he had obtained his release. He availed himself of the leave granted him to travel four days
from Calais, and never returned. His father, King
John, was deeply distressed at this disgraceful conduct, and, feeling that his own honour was thereby
compromised, resolved, notwithstanding the remonstrances of his nobles, to return to captivity in England, saying " he wished to make excuses for his son."[1]

On December 10th, 1363, only a few days after
the month of grace had expired, King Edward gave
King John a letter of safe conduct, for himself and
200 knights with their attendants, to come into and go
out of England.[2] King John returned to England, but
was not able to avail himself of the leave to go back
to France, for he died about three months after his
landing. During his brief sojourn in England he was
most hospitably entertained. He landed at Dover on
Thursday, January 4th, 1364. When King Edward
heard of his arrival, he sent a body of knights, to welcome him, and escort him to the palace of Eltham, in
Kent, where Edward was then residing. On Saturday morning, the French King and his companions set
out on their journey, and proceeded on that day as
far as Canterbury, where they slept. The next day,
Sunday, they rode on to Eltham, where they arrived
after dinner; "and between that and supper time
there was great dancing and rejoicing, and the young
Lord Ingelram, of Coucy, did his best to dance and
sing well when his turn came; he was gladly seen
by both the French and the English, for it well suited
him to do all that he did;"[3] and indeed he succeeded

A.D. 1363.

King John
determines
to return
to England
as a pri-
soner.

A.D. 1364.

His
arrival in
England.

[1] Buchon's *Froissart,* vol. i. p. 468.
[2] Rymer, vol. iii. p. 718.
[3] Stow's *Survey of London,* vol. i. p. 309.

92   LIFE AND TIMES OF EDWARD III.   CHAP. VI.

A.D. 1364. so well, that he married King Edward's eldest daughter Isabel the next year, and was, afterwards, created Earl of Bedford.

After remaining for nearly two months at Eltham Palace, the King and the other hostages were conducted to London, where they were again lodged at the Savoy Palace. They were most hospitably received by the Lord Mayor and Aldermen. The former, Sir Henry Picard, a merchant Vintner of Gascony, entertained them, together with the Kings of England and Scotland, with great magnificence at his house in the Vintry near St. Martin's Church; after dinner "he kept his hall for all comers that were willing to play at dice and hazard,"[1] "his Lady Margaret at the same time keeping her chamber for the entertainment of the princesses and ladies."[2]

He is hospitably received.

But this pleasant life in England was soon over. King John died at the Savoy Palace on April 8th, 1364, and was succeeded by his son Charles the Fifth.

His death, 8th April, 1364.

For the next five years, until the renewal of the war with France, there were but few events of public importance in England. A strenuous effort was, however, at this time made to bring to a definite issue the important struggle with the Pope, which had been energetically carried on by Edward and his grandfather, relative to his interference with the English Church. It was with reference to this that the "Statute of Provisors" had been passed in 1352.

History of resistance to the Pope's usurpations.

The usurpation complained of (as to some extent already explained) was this, viz. that the Pope claimed the right of appointment to vacant English livings, and even to livings before they became vacant; that,

[1] Barnes's *Edward III.* p. 635.
[2] Buchon's *Froissart*, vol. i. p. 469.

CHAP. VI.   PROCEEDINGS IN PARLIAMENT.   93

he confiscated to himself the first year's income there-   A.D. 1365.
of, and appointed certain persons called "provisors"
to carry these usurpations into effect. It was also
complained, that when these appointments were disputed, the "provisor" carried his complaint into the
Papal courts, and those who resisted were therefore
compelled to defend themselves in the Court of Rome.[1]

At the Parliament which met on January 21st, A.D.   A.D. 1365.
1365, the Bishop of Ely, as Lord Chancellor, opened   Proceedings in
the proceedings in the Painted Chamber. "When a   Parliament.
bishop was Lord Chancellor he took a text of Scrip-
ture, which he repeated in Latin, and discoursed upon
the same; but when a lay judge was Lord Chancellor
he took no text, but in manner of an oration showed
summarily the causes of the Parliament."[2] In accordance with this practice, the bishop took a text from

[1] See Hook's *Lives of the Archbishops of Canterbury*, vol.
iv. pp. 142, 143, 190 and 191; Milman's *Latin Christianity*,
vol. viii. p. 154 (note ‘); and *England and France under the
House of Lancaster*, note 41 (p. 396). It is stated both by Dean
Milman and by the anonymous author of the latter able book, that
it was the Pope's interference with the patronage in the hands of
spiritual persons that was complained of, and the latter gives
elaborate reasons for stating that they "had no relation to lay
patronage." The very plain language of Parliament, "Et aussi des
Impetrations et Provisions faites en mesme la Court de Rome
des Benefices and Offices d'Eglise, appertenantz a la donation pre-
sentation our disposition fire dit Sigñr le Roi et *d'autres patrons
lais* de son Roiaxlme et des Eglises et autres Benefices apropriez
as Eglises Cathedrales" (Rot. Parl. vol. ii. p. 284 g.), seems entirely
inconsistent with this view. The rights of private lay persons,
however, were, probably, not much affected by the Papal Provisions after the great resistance of Sir Robert Thwenge in 1246
(see Lingard), except in such cases of lapse as occurred when a
living was vacated by the promotion of its incumbent to a bishopric, in which case, ordinarily, the crown appointed.

[2] Coke, 4 Inst. 8 (quoted in Campbell's *Chancellors*, post 8vo.
vol. i. p. 223, note).

94　LIFE AND TIMES OF EDWARD III.　Chap. VI.

A.D. 1365.
the Psalms, and applying it to the occasion, stated in general terms, *in the English language*, the reasons why the Parliament was summoned. Then the King, accompanied by the prelates, dukes, earls and barons, repaired to the White Chamber (the Commons remaining in the Painted Chamber),[1] and stated that complaints were constantly made by his subjects to the Pope as to matters which were determinable in the King's own courts; that provisions were made by the court of Rome as to benefices in England belonging to the King and other lay patrons of his kingdom; and that " the laws, usages, ancient customs, and franchises of his kingdom were thereby much hindered, the King's crown degraded, and his person defamed." He therefore asked the advice and counsel of the Lords as to how such things could be prevented.

The Commons were then summoned to the White Chamber, and the substance of the King's address to the Lords was repeated to them.[2] Strong language against the Court of Rome was evidently made use of, for the Act of Parliament (38 Ed. III. stat. 2) founded on the debate, omits " biting words—a mystery not to be known of all men." [3]　The result was that all former statutes were confirmed, and the penalties of the

Statute of Præmunire confirmed, and law ordered to be put in force against Provisors.
" Statute of Præmunire," passed in 1353, were ordered to be put in force against provisors and their agents. According to this statute, offenders after premonition or warning were liable " to be put out of the King's protection," or in other words deprived of the protection of the law.

---

[1] " Les Comunes des Countees, Citees, et Burghs demorantz en Pees en la dit chambre de coffiandement le Roi."—Rot. Parl. vol. ii. p. 283.

[2] Rot. Parl. vol. ii. p. 284.　[3] Cotton's *Abridgement*, p. 100.

CHAP. VI.   THE POPE REVIVES HIS CLAIM OF SUBSIDY.   95

The prelates added to their consent to this statute, that they did not mean to assent to anything which might be, or which might turn to the prejudice of their dignity or estate.[1] They felt they were taking a bold step in thus opposing the Pope. It was a declaration of war against him, and so he considered it. He instantly revived the claim of the annual payment of 1000 marks, promised by King John on receiving back from his hands the English crown, which he had basely surrendered to him. The payment had not been made for thirty-three years. It had been refused by Edward I., but was resumed, and all arrears paid, by his son; and was again refused by Edward III.

A struggle, of the utmost importance to the freedom of England and an evident precursor of the Reformation, then began between the Pope, Urban V., and the King of England. The Pope wrote to the King to demand payment of the arrears, and threatened to take proceedings against him for their recovery; the King called Parliament together to consider what should be done. It met at Westminster on March 30th, 1366; the prelates and great men, as before, in the White Chamber, and the Commons in the Painted Chamber. The Bishop of Ely, as Chancellor, then asked the " prelates, dukes, earls, and barons " their advice on the matter. The prelates asked for a day to consider of it by themselves; the next day they, and afterwards "the other dukes, earls, barons, and great men," answered that " neither King John nor anybody else could put himself, or his kingdom, or his people, under subjection, without their accord and assent." The Commons

A.D. 1366.

The Pope, in his anger, revives the claim of annual subsidy.

A.D. 1366.

Assembly of Parliament.

Parliament rejects the Pope's

[1] Rot. Parl. vol. ii. p. 285.

96 LIFE AND TIMES OF EDWARD III. CHAP. VI.

A.D. 1366.

demand, and settles the question for ever.

answered in the same way; an ordinance was made in accordance with the answer of the two branches of Parliament; and it was added, "it appeared by many evidences, that it (John's submission) was done without their assent and against the coronation oath." The Commons also declared, that, if the Pope attempted to enforce payment, they would resist with all their power.[1] It was not the amount that was galling; it was the degrading thraldom, to which the kingdom had been subjected, by the cowardice of John, for 150 years, that roused the King and the nation to resistance. This was aggravated by the suspicion, that the Pope was instigated to make these demands by the King of France, whose creatures the popes were so long as they lived at Avignon. This solemn resolution set the question at rest for ever.

John Wiclif.

His first appearance as an opponent of the Pope.

This contest is memorable, not only from its own intrinsic importance, but also on account of its being the occasion on which John Wiclif, the first English Reformer, came into public notice. Wiclif had taken part in a controversy between the universities and the friars mendicant, which was brought under the consideration of the Parliament.[2] In reference to the question of the payment of tribute to the Pope, he now came forward, in answer to a challenge from a monk who had written in defence of the Pope's supremacy to defend the refusal of Parliament to submit any longer to its exaction. Wiclif wrote his answer in the form of a report of the debates in parliament on the subject; but there can be no doubt that this was merely the shape in which he thought fit to put his own arguments. It will be necessary, later in the reign, to enter more into Wiclif's history;

---

[1] Rot. Parl. vol. ii. p. 290.   [2] Ibid. p. 290.

CHAP. VI.   DEATH OF BALLIOL.   97

but the first appearance before the world of so great A.D.1364.
a man cannot pass unnoticed.[1]

The only other domestic events of importance
occurring at this time, were the deaths of Edward
Balliol, once King of Scotland, and of Elizabeth,
Duchess of Clarence, both of which took place in
1363.

Death of Balliol and of the Duchess of Clarence, from whom descended the House of York.

The House of York, whose members were the legitimate successors to the throne of England, was descended from this Duchess. Her husband was Lionel,
third son of Edward III. His elder brothers, the Black
Prince and William of Hatfield, died during their
father's lifetime; the latter without issue. Richard, son
of the Black Prince, also died without issue. Henry
the Fourth was son of Edward's *fourth* son, John of
Gaunt. Philippa, the only child of Lionel and Elizabeth, married Edmund Mortimer, Earl of March; his
eldest son Roger was, in 1387,[2] nominated by King
Richard II. as his rightful successor in the kingdom
of England.

By the death of Balliol, David became the undisputed King of Scotland. King Edward had never
thus designated him, but always wrote of him as
"our prisoner;" and indeed after Balliol's death he
refused him that title, and called him simply "our
brother."[3] An attempt was now made by both Edward
and David to bring about a permanent peace between
England and Scotland, and to relieve Scotland from the

[1] See Lewis's *Life of Wiclif*, chap. ii.; Milman's *Latin Christianity*, vol. viii. p. 163, &c.; and *Fasciculi Zizanorum*, edited by
the Rev. W. W. Shirley, M.A., Introduction, p. xix.

[2] See Sandford's *Genealogical History*, pp. 225 and 226.
"This Earl Roger's heirs ought to have preceded the House of
Lancaster to the crown."

[3] See Rymer, vol. iii. pp. 693, 723, 755, &c.

VOL. II.   H

98   LIFE AND TIMES OF EDWARD III.   Chap. VI.

A.D. 1364.

heavy burden of the unpaid ransom, by the amicable union of the two kingdoms. In accordance with this plan David, in March 1363, proposed to his parliament, that, in the event of his death, one of Edward's sons should be chosen to fill the Scottish throne ; and he particularly recommended Lionel, Duke of Clarence, for that purpose. The offer was rejected with scorn ;[1] but David did not give up the project, and even went personally to England to negotiate with Edward for its renewal. The details of the scheme were secretly agreed to between the two kings, and a memorandum (in which, for the first time and for an obvious purpose, Edward designated David as king of Scotland) was drawn up on November 27th, 1363, specifying minutely the terms agreed to between them.[2] David promised to bring the matter under the consideration of his parliament; but it does not appear that this was ever done, and the proposal came to nothing.[3]

Intrigues as to Scotland consequent on Balliol's death.

These were the only domestic events of importance, which occurred, between the death of King John of France and the renewal of the war. During the whole of that interval, the relations between England and France were by no means of a cordial nature. It was hardly possible they could be so. The existence of a kingdom within a kingdom, for such was Aquitaine, must have been most galling to the feelings of every Frenchman, and especially to the royal family; and the necessity of making heavy payments, according

The relations between England and France very unfriendly.

---

[1] Tytler, vol. ii. p. 55, etc.

[2] Ibid. p. 64; and Burton's *Scotland*, vol. iii. p. 39.

[3] See Rymer, vol. iii. p. 715. It seems probable that this curious document, which was entirely unknown to the ancient Scottish historians, is wrongly dated by a year. If it was drawn up before the meeting of the Scottish Parliament, in March 1363, all is quite clear and consistent ; but if afterwards, the whole transaction becomes obscure and improbable.

CHAP. VI.   MISCONDUCT OF THE DUKE OF ANJOU.   99

to the treaty of Bretigni, combined with the disor- A.D. 1364.
ganised state of the kingdom which Edward, however falsely, was supposed to foment, were causes,
amply sufficient, to account for the absence of any
real cordiality between the two kingdoms.

The jealousy which France, not unnaturally, felt Proposed
towards England, and her desire to prevent Edward marriage of the
from establishing alliances which might be detrimen- King's son
tal to her interests, were shown in the successful efforts Edmund and
which Charles made to prevent the marriage of Ed- Margaret of Flan-
ward's fifth son, Edmund Earl of Cambridge (after- ders pre-
wards, in 1385, Duke of York) with Margaret, daughter vented by the Pope.
of Louis Count of Flanders.   This intimate alliance
of the English and the Flemings would have coun-
teracted the long-continued efforts of France to detach them from each other; and the Pope was
easily moved to help his lord and master the King of
France, by finding, in the frequently evaded ground
of consanguinity, an excuse to forbid the marriage.

The Dukes of Orleans, Berri, Bourbon, and many Miscon-
of the hostages, had returned to England with King duct of the Duke
John, but the Duke of Anjou and various others of Anjou and other
did not do so.   Edward therefore wrote to the King hostages.
of France on November 20th, 1364, to complain,
and to demand that he should compel them to come
back.   On the same day he wrote to the Duke of
Anjou himself, telling him that by his treachery
" he had tarnished the honour of himself and all his
lineage," and calling on him to return to England
within twenty days.   Similar letters were written to
other hostages,[1] but it does not appear that they
had any effect.   So completely was King Charles
devoid of those feelings of honour, which had insti-

[1] Rymer, vol. iii. pp. 755, 756, 757.

H 2

100   LIFE AND TIMES OF EDWARD III.   Chap. VI.

A.D. 1364. gated his father to resume his captivity in atonement for his son's treachery, that on the 18th of November,[1] he appointed the Duke of Anjou his lieutenant-general in Languedoc, thus sanctioning his brother's breach of faith, and even shamelessly placing him in the immediate neighbourhood of Edward's son, the Duke of Aquitaine.

While the King of England was thus complaining of Anjou's dishonourable proceedings, the King of France was accusing the King of England of fomenting discord in France; and Edward was obliged to issue orders to his lieutenants to use all their power to put down the "Companies," which had never ceased to ravage France. On November 14th, 1364, Edward wrote to the Lords of his Seignories in France, to the Prince of Wales, and to John of Chandos, Viscount of St. Sauveur, desiring them to do their utmost to repress them. But these letters had, seemingly, no effect; again and again he had to repeat his orders.[2] The "Companies" were too strong to be conquered without a regular campaign, and at last the King of France begged Edward to help him in attacking them; but, the necessary preparations made by Edward so alarmed the King of France, that he

Events in France involving English interests after the death of King John.

entreated him to desist.[3] It was not long after this that the King of France availed himself of the complaints against the Prince of Wales of encouraging the "Companies," to break the treaty of peace, and war between the two countries again began. During the interval which elapsed before the actual renewal of fighting, the whole of France was in a

[1] Sismondi, tom. xi. p. 15.
[2] Rymer, vol. iii. pp. 754, 808, 834 and 835.
[3] Walsingham, p. 302.

CHAP. VI. BERTRAND DU GUESCLIN. 101

constant ferment. No part of it was quiet; and so intimately were England and France then connected together, that a battle in any part of France might easily have rekindled the flames of war. Charles V., not unaptly called "The Wise," writhed under the treaty of Bretigni; and his brother the Duke of Anjou, above all others, hated the English, having behaved as a traitor to them, and having been told so by their King. But Charles was resolved not to precipitate a rupture with England; Normandy and Brittany were as yet by no means certain to support him, and the "Companies" might side with Edward.

A.D. 1364.

Charles "The Wise" wishes to settle France before renewing war with England.

When the King of Navarre retired to his own kingdom, after abandoning his just claim to the Duchy of Burgundy in 1361, he left those parts of Normandy which belonged to him under the charge of his brother Philip. On the death of Philip at Evreux, on August 29th, 1363, the Duke of Normandy, then Regent of the kingdom, endeavoured to recover possession of Normandy. He sent for Bertrand du Guesclin, whose high military qualities, as already related, he had discovered at the siege of Melun in 1359. Du Guesclin carried on war after his own fashion, and disregarded the principles on which it was then usually conducted. He cared more for victory, than for obeying the scrupulous laws of honour which chivalry dictated to combatants, and may therefore be considered, as one of those who materially contributed to the decline of chivalry, which began about this time.[1] Du Guesclin immediately obeyed the Duke's summons; and, in concert with Bouci-

Affairs of Normandy.

Bertrand du Guesclin.

[1] See Martin, *Hist. France,* vol. v. pp. 243, 244; and Sismondi, ii. p. 17.

102 LIFE AND TIMES OF EDWARD III. Chap. VI.

A.D. 1364. cault, Marshal of France, who had just arrived from England with the news of the death of King John, obtained possession of Nantes by means of a stratagem which might without injustice be designated as treachery. The fall of Meulan immediately followed. The free navigation of the Seine, which was of such vital importance to the provisioning of Paris, was thus secured, and Du Guesclin then proceeded to attempt the recovery of the rest of Normandy.

The Captal appointed by the King of Navarre to defend Normandy. After the fall of Meulan, Du Guesclin advanced from Pacy to attack Evreux. The Captal de Buch, to whom the defence of Normandy had been entrusted by the King of Navarre on the death of his brother Philip, posted himself in an advantageous position at Cocherel between those towns, and waited his attack. The forces on each side were about equal; but the French had suffered from marching under a hot sun and from hunger, the country being still in such a devastated state that they had not been able to obtain sufficient provisions; they were therefore anxious that the fight should not be unnecessarily delayed. But the Captal would not leave his position, and Du Guesclin consequently feigned a hurried retreat, hoping by this means to induce him to descend into the plain. The Captal was not to be deceived, but, in spite of his remonstrances, John Jewel, an English adventurer who had joined the Captal's little army, rushed down to attack the French, crying out "Forward! St. George! let him that loves me follow me!" The French at once turned, and attacked him with the war cry of "Our

Battle of Cocherel and defeat of the Captal. Lady! Guesclin!" The Captal, who gallantly took his part in the battle when he saw that it could not be avoided, was taken prisoner by a body of thirty

CHAP. VI.　　SUCCESS OF THE FRENCH.　　103

knights, who were ordered to devote themselves to this object only. Jewel was killed, as were others of the Navarrese captains. The soldiers were consequently left wholly without a leader, and a complete defeat of the Navarrese was the result. This battle took place on May 16th, 1364.

A.D. 1364.

The news of the victory at Cocherel reached Charles V. the day before his coronation at Rheims, the prevention of which had been one of the main objects of the Captal.[1] On his return to Paris, Charles bestowed the earldom of Longueville, the heritage of Philip of Navarre, on Du Guesclin as a reward for his victory. Soon after this terrible defeat of the Navarrese, Louis, younger brother of the King of Navarre, arrived in France, and with a small army of English, Gascon, and German adventurers ravaged the country between the Loire and the Allier.[2] Charles therefore placed Du Guesclin, Boucicault and others, under the orders of his brother the Duke of Burgundy, and ordered them to attack the Navarrese either on the borders of the Loire or in Normandy. In the latter, especially, the French troops had great success, and treated all the Normans and French who fought against them with great severity; but they spared the adventurers, wishing to enlist them on their side to fight for Charles of Blois in Brittany.

The brother of the King of Navarre comes to Normandy.

Success of the French.

The treaty of Bretigni had not put an end to the struggle between the two, competitors for the duchy. The Kings of England and France had in vain tried to mediate between them; and Jeanne of Penthièvre, the wife of Charles of Blois, persuaded her husband to break a treaty which he had signed on July 12th, 1363, agreeing to the partition of the duchy. War,

The affairs of Brittany.

---

[1] Buchon's *Froissart*, vol. i. p. 473.　　[2] Ibid. p. 485.

104   LIFE AND TIMES OF EDWARD III.   CHAP. VI.

A.D. 1364.

The competitors apply for help to England and France.

therefore, between the claimants again broke out, and John of Montfort laid siege to Auray. As before stated, it had been arranged in the treaty of Bretigni, that the Kings of England and France, might each take part in the war in Brittany, without involving their own kingdoms in the strife. Charles of Blois therefore at once appealed to the King of France, who sent Du Guesclin to his aid; and John of Montfort applied in like manner to the Prince of Wales, who was then, as Duke of Aquitaine, holding his court at Bordeaux.[1] The Prince sent the gallant old John of Chandos to help him, and numbers of English, under Sir Robert Knolles and Sir Hugh de Calverley, also flocked to his standard.

Battle of Auray, Sept. 29, 1364,

So soon as Du Guesclin had united his troops with those of Blois at Nantes, he advanced to the relief of Auray, and at the end of September, about four months after the battle of Cocherel, was face to face with the army of Bretons and English under John of Montfort. Montfort's forces were inferior in numbers to those of Blois, and he therefore posted them on a hill behind Auray, where he resolved to wait for the enemy.

Day after day vain efforts were made by the Lord of Beaumanoir, on the part of Charles of Blois, to renew negotiations between the two parties, till at last John of Chandos told him it was quite useless to persevere in his attempt; that his people were resolved to lose all, or gain all by a battle; and that if Beaumanoir did not take care, they would certainly

gained by John of Montfort,

kill him. On the 29th of September the battle took place, and on this occasion fortune turned against Du Guesclin. The French were routed; Charles of

[1] Buchon's *Froissart*, vol. i. p. 489.

CHAP. VI. THE AFFAIRS OF BRITTANY AND NAVARRE. 105

Blois was killed, and Du Guesclin taken prisoner; and thus was settled the succession to the Duchy of Brittany, after twenty-five years of war. The Duke of Anjou, who had married the daughter of Charles, and who hated the English with all the bitterness of a traitor, wished still to fight for the duchy; but his brother, with greater wisdom, restrained him, and the Kings of France and England once more mediated. At last, on April 11th, 1365, a treaty was signed between the widow of Charles of Blois and John of Montfort, by which the latter was secured in possession of the duchy, and the county of Penthièvre was granted to Charles's widow. Five months afterwards Montfort entered into a treaty with the Prince of Wales, and married the daughter of the Princess by her first husband.[1] In December of the following year he did homage to the King of France for Brittany.

About the same time that King Charles thus settled the affairs of Brittany, his quarrel with the King of Navarre was also brought to a conclusion. Perplexed with the intrigues and crimes of the Kings of Castile and Aragon, in which, on his return to Navarre, each by turns had tried to involve him, the King of Navarre thought it would be well to bring his war with France to an end. He therefore gave instructions to the Captal de Buch, who was then a prisoner in France, to enter into negotiations with the King. A treaty between them was signed on March 6th, 1365,[2] by which the King of Navarre recovered all he had lost in the county of Evreux, and received the Lordship of Montpellier in exchange for Lon-

A.D. 1364.

Count of Blois killed, and Du Guesclin taken prisoner.

Settlement of the affairs of Brittany.

Settlement of the affairs of Navarre.

---

[1] Buchon's *Froissart*, vol. i. p. 501.　　[2] Ibid.

106　　LIFE AND TIMES OF EDWARD III.　CHAP. VI.

A.D. 1365. gueville (which had been granted to Du Guesclin), Mantes, and Meulan.

Nevertheless the pacification of Brittany and Normandy, however advantageous to France in general, did not put an end to the "Companies;" but, on the contrary, rather increased their numbers. These were now estimated at 50,000 or 60,000. The soldiers who had been employed in those parts of France, found themselves without occupation; they had too long led a wild life to betake themselves to any peaceful pursuit, and therefore joined the "Companies." Even the soldiers of Du Guesclin could not be restrained from pillage, and he himself was not free from suspicion of encouraging them.[1] Some of the freebooters invaded Aquitaine, but the Prince of Wales drove them back into the centre of France, which they called their "chamber." King Charles tried in vain to engage them in the crusade against the Turks, which the King of Cyprus had undertaken; but the Archpriest, Arnaud de Cervolles, was killed by the Germans while attempting to cross the Rhine, and the "Companies" then refused to have anything to do with it. At length Du Guesclin managed to employ them in Spain. The history of their doings in that country is so intimately connected with those of the Prince of Wales, that, in order to understand them, it is necessary now to give an account of the events in Spain which led to the unfortunate interference of the Prince of Wales in its affairs.

[1] See Martin, tome v. p. 254.

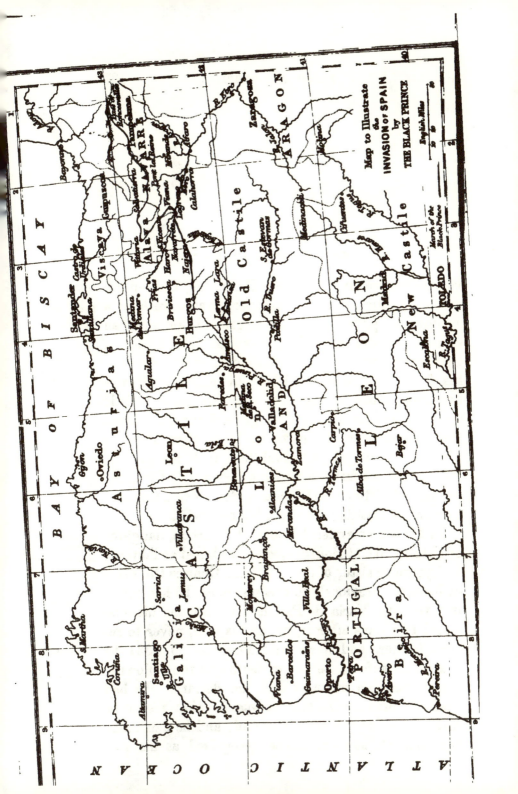

CHAPTER VII.

THE CAMPAIGN IN SPAIN.

PEDRO, known in history as The Cruel, and—if re- morseless murders repeatedly perpetrated without a shadow of pretext furnish a ground for such an epithet — justly so called, ascended the throne of Castile, at the early age of sixteen, on the death of his father Alphonso the Eleventh in 1350. It was not long before he began to earn his characteristic epithet. He commenced his reign with three murders: the first, done in the name of his mother, Princess Maria of Portugal, but doubtless with his privity, was that of his father's mistress Leonora de Guzman; his second victim, was Garcilasso de la Vega, Captain-General of Castile; his next, his own wife.

In 1353 he married Blanche of Bourbon, daughter of Peter, Duke of Bourbon, who was killed at Poitiers, and younger sister of Jane, wife of Charles the Fifth of France. Previously to this marriage, he had fallen in love with Maria de Padilla, who became his mistress; two days after it, he left his wife, never to return to her, and lived with Padilla. In 1361 he caused his wife to be put to death; in the following year, when his mistress died, he declared she had been his lawful wife, that it was for that reason he had refused to live with Blanche; and he demanded that Maria's son should be recognised as his suc-

108 LIFE AND TIMES OF EDWARD III. Chap. VII.

A.D. 1365. cessor. It is obvious that no weight could be attached to the declaration of such a monster; but, even if true, the crime committed against Blanche of Bourbon became only so much the more enormous, as it added heartless treachery to adultery. The indignation of her brother-in-law the King of France was justly great, and decided him to support a rival to the throne of Castile whom Pedro's crimes had

The King of France supports a rival to the throne, raised up. This was Henry of Trastamare, son of Alphonso the Eleventh by his mistress Leonora de Guzman, whom Pedro had murdered on his accession to the throne. Henry had already made Pedro his enemy, by taking the part of the nobles in resisting his tyranny; on their defeat in 1356, he had taken refuge in France.[1]

Pedro had made another enemy beside the King of France. In addition to his other crimes he was accused of oppressing the Church, and allying himself with the Mohammedan Kings of Granada. This was thought a heinous sin. For these offences, Pope Urban summoned Pedro to appear before him. Pedro treated the summons with contempt;

and the Pope also supports Henry of Trastamare. the Pope consequently excommunicated him, and encouraged Henry to aspire to the throne. The Pope now legitimised Henry in order to give him a show of legal claim to the throne; and, in conjunction with the King of France, resolved to make use of the "Companies" to drive Pedro from his kingdom. It was no difficult matter to induce the King of France to espouse the cause of Henry of Trastamare; for, independently of the opportunity thus afforded him of getting rid of the "Companies," he thereby struck a blow at England.

[1] Buchon's *Froissart*, vol. i. p. 503, note.

Chap. VII.   DU GUESCLIN COMMANDS THE FRENCH.   109

Pedro was Edward's ally; he had been affianced to his second daughter Joan in 1344, and the fulfilment of the marriage contract was rendered void only by her death in 1348.   In addition to this, a formal treaty of alliance, offensive and defensive, was entered into between him and Edward in 1362, and had been confirmed in the autumn of 1364.[1] There was, therefore, ample reason why the French jealousy of England which, not unnaturally, never slumbered, should be gratified by the opportunity of attacking her intimate ally without breaking the treaty of peace between the two countries.   The part which the Prince of Wales subsequently took in supporting such a monster as Pedro, may be somewhat palliated by the intimate relations which thus subsisted between the two countries, and by the friendly feelings which must have sprung up between the intended brothers-in-law.   But it was a fatal mistake.

A.D. 1365.

France displeased to attack Pedro as England's ally.

The command of the French expedition against Pedro was given nominally to John of Bourbon, Count of La Marche, cousin of the murdered Queen of Castile, and son of Count James, who was killed by the " Companies " at Brignais; but he was a mere youth; the real commander was Bertrand du Guesclin.   Du Guesclin had been the prisoner of John of Chandos since the battle of Auray, and the price demanded for his release was 100,000 francs.   This was an enormous sum; but so great was the reputation of Du Guesclin, that it was thought indispensable to secure him as Commander-in-Chief, and the sum was therefore paid jointly by the King of France, the Pope, and Henry.

Du Guesclin commander of the French troops;

[1] Rymer, vol. ii. pp. 20, 656, and 753.

110 LIFE AND TIMES OF EDWARD III. CHAP. VII.

A D. 1365.

The next step was to secure the consent of the "Companies" to engage in the expedition, and no sooner was Du Guesclin set at liberty, than he opened negotiations with their leaders. He sent his herald to their headquarters at Chalons-on-the-Saone, to demand a safe conduct, and on its receipt set out on his errand. Du

he secures the services of the "Companies."

Guesclin was well received and hospitably treated by the brother of the Count of Auxerre, one of the captains who had fought at Cocherel, and who went by the name of "the green knight." Sir Hugh Calverley, the Englishman who had commanded the rear guard of De Montfort at Auray, and other leaders of the "Companies" were also present. Du Guesclin declared that the object of the expedition was to attack the infidels in Granada; but he also said, that if he could meet with Don Pedro, he would do all in his power to harass and anger him. The "Companies" had been excommunicated by the Pope, and Du Guesclin therefore promised to obtain absolution for them, which, of course, they did not reject; but this spiritual favour was of little value in their eyes compared with the offer of 400,000 florins, to be paid half by the King of France and half by the Pope, and with the hopes of rich booty which were put pro-

Sir Hugh Calverley agrees conditionally.

minently before them. Du Guesclin's proposals were accepted by a large number of the captains, including Sir Hugh Calverley, who, however, made the stipulation, that he would serve only so long as there was no war between England and France, because, as he said, he was liegeman to the Prince of Wales. Twenty-five of these captains entered into a solemn agreement with Du Guesclin, and promised to give up to the King of France the fortresses, of which they had taken possession in their marauding forays.

CHAP. VII.   DIFFICULTIES WITH THE POPE.   111

These matters being arranged, the "Companies" marched to Avignon. On their arrival, Du Guesclin demanded of the Pope his share of the promised payment; but the Pope made difficulties, saying that it was always the custom to pay for absolution, and that it was hard to ask him not only to grant it without payment, but also to pay the sinners. However, Du Guesclin refused to listen to such excuses, and the Pope paid the agreed sum. Still, Du Guesclin was not satisfied, for he had reason to believe that the Pope had raised the money by taxing the people of Avignon, instead of taking it out of his own treasury. When he had ascertained that this was the case, he returned him the money he had handed over to him, and made him refund it out of his own resources. The Pope indemnified himself by taxing the French clergy.

The invading forces then marched for Spain, and the King of Navarre associated himself with the invaders. John of Chandos refused to have anything to do with them.

In the meantime the King of England, anxious to prevent the breaking of the solemn treaty he had made with Pedro, immediately that he heard of the intended invasion of Spain, wrote (on December 6th, 1365) to John of Chandos, Sir Hugh Calverley, Sir Nicolas Dagworth, and others who had been leaders of the "Companies," ordering them on no account to engage in the expedition. But it was too late; for, as already stated, Calverley and some others, delighted at the opportunity of engaging in war, and of giving employment to the soldiers who had become a burden to them, had actually joined the invading forces.

A.D. 1365.

The "Companies" march to Avignon.

Difficulties with the Pope.

They march for Spain.

Edward tries in vain to prevent the English in Aquitaine from joining the expedition.

112   LIFE AND TIMES OF EDWARD III.   Chap. VII.

A.D. 1365.

The invaders enter Spain,
A.D. 1366.

After leaving Avignon, the allies, about 30,000 in number, marched to Montpellier, where they arrived on the 20th of November. They remained there till the 3rd of December; then, passing through Roussillon, entered Catalonia, a part of the kingdom of Aragon, and reached Barcelona on January 1st, 1366.

The expedition could not be considered as national. The invasion was not preceded by any declaration of war on the part of the King of France; the flag displayed.was not that of France, but that of Castile, for Henry of Trastamare, although a bastard, assumed the title of King; and the forces consisted of mercenaries of various nations, including many English. The army was gathered together with the object of placing Henry on the throne. For this, however, but few cared; it was Du Guesclin's spirit and well-known character for courage and military skill, and the hope of plunder, that attracted the adventurers, and kept the medley mass in a state of cohesion. At Barcelona they were well received by the King of Aragon, and were there joined by Henry. Messengers were sent to Don Pedro by the invaders, to inform him of their approach, and to say, that they intended " to open the roads and passes of his kingdom to the pilgrims of God, who, with great devotion, had undertaken to enter the kingdom of Granada; to avenge the sufferings of our Lord, to destroy the infidels, and exalt the true faith."

Pedro laughed the messengers to scorn; and said, he would not listen to such a set of vagrants.[1] He soon found, however, that the vagabonds were not to be despised; for, when he called on the barons and knights of Spain to gather their troops together and

[1] Froissart, vol. i. p. 505.

CHAP. VII.   CORONATION OF HENRY.   113

flock to his standard, his summons was obeyed by one A.D. 1366.
alone, Fernand de Castro, brother of Inez Queen of
Portugal, whose tragic history, in after times, inspired
the muse of the poet Camoens. The invaders soon
recovered the strong places in Aragon, which Don Their easy
Pedro had previously taken, and restored them to success.
Henry. They then crossed the Ebro, which divided
Aragon from Castile, at Alfaro, and marched to Cala-
horra, where Henry was proclaimed King of Castile.
Meeting with no opposition, they soon took possession
of the whole of Castile; and, on April 5th, 1366,
Henry was crowned at the monastery of Las Huelgas, Corona-
near Burgos, becoming thus the acknowledged King tion of
of Castile. Henry on
April 5th.

This revolution was accomplished by the Castilians
themselves, without other help from the foreign armies
than the mere fact of their presence. In case of need
Du Guesclin would have led the "Companies" to the
field of battle; but no enemy appeared, not a blow
was struck, and they soon began to be weary of inaction. Henry, however, foresaw that, in all probability, he should again have need of them; in
order, therefore, to give them something to do, he
amused them with a proposal of attacking the King
of Granada. This expedition never took place, and,
at the beginning of June 1366,[1] he found it neces- Most of
sary to let the greater part of the "Companies" de- the troops
part. Du Guesclin and most of the commanders soon France.
followed them; but some, including probably several
of the English leaders, remained in Spain, until summoned by the Prince of Wales to join his troops.

In the meantime, Pedro, deserted by his subjects, Flight of
was unable to strike a single blow to save his king- DonPedro:

[1] Buchon's *Froissart*, vol. i. p. 507, note.

VOL. II.   I

114 LIFE AND TIMES OF EDWARD III. CHAP. VII.

A.D. 1366. dom. At the end of March he fled to the south, and took refuge in Seville; but, even there, he found neither help nor shelter, for the inhabitants rose in insurrection, and compelled him to leave their city.

His object was now, apparently, to escape to the north in order to open communications with the Prince of Wales, on whose friendship he had reason to rely. In answer, doubtless, to his appeal, King Edward, as already related, had written in the previous December to John of Chandos, Sir Hugh Calverley and others, ordering them not to take up arms against "the noble prince the King of Spain."[1] This injunction was too late, but it showed the disposition of the King of England to help Pedro; in his need, therefore, Pedro turned for help to Edward's son. But he did not dare to pass through Estremadura, and consequently obtained leave from the King of Portugal to pass through his dominions. He thus escaped *he reaches* to Santiago in Gallicia, and fled thence to the sea-*Corunna,* coast at Corunna. He was accompanied by his only friend Fernand de Castro and his own daughters Constance and Isabella; the former of whom afterwards married John of Gaunt Duke of Lancaster, and the latter Edmund Duke of York, sons of Edward the Third, from whom descended the rival Houses of York and Lancaster—the White and Red Roses. On his arrival at Corunna, Pedro sent Don Lopez de Cordova, Grand Master of the order of Alcantara, with two knights, to the Prince of Wales at Bordeaux, to *and goes* inform him of his misfortunes; he then fled on to *on to* *Bayonne.* Bayonne,[2] where he entered Aquitaine, and at length felt himself on safe ground.

[1] Rymer, vol. iii. p. 779.
[2] "Une cité qui se tient du roi d'Angleterre."—Buchon's *Froissart,* vol. i. p. 507.

CHAP. VII. PEDRO GOES TO BORDEAUX. 115

On their arrival at Bordeaux, Pedro's messengers were well received by the Prince of Wales; who, after consultation with his trusty friend John of Chandos, decided to send twelve armed vessels to Corunna, to bring Don Pedro in safety to Bordeaux. The little fleet set sail, and on its way touched at Bayonne, at a most opportune moment, for Pedro had just reached that port. He was therefore immediately informed that the Prince of Wales had sent him friends to take him safely to Bordeaux, and Pedro joyfully began his journey. The Prince of Wales, wishing to do him all the honour which he thought was due to a King in misfortune, advanced from Bordeaux to meet him, received him with great courtesy, and on his arrival at Bordeaux lodged him in the Abbey of St. Andrew, where he and the Princess dwelt. At first, nothing was thought of but feasting and rejoicing; but, after a time, the lords of Aquitaine, both English and Gascon, began seriously to consider the policy of taking up the cause of a dethroned monarch, so bitterly and so justly detested by his subjects, and one who had no money to pay them for their services. They therefore presented themselves to the Prince, and repeated to him, as indeed they had told him before the arrival of Don Pedro, how grieved they were to hear that he had consented to help the Spanish Prince; that he was a bad man and a tyrant, and that the evil which had befallen him, was God's punishment to chastise him, and to give an example to other Kings through him. These were bold but wise words, and, if the Prince of Wales had listened to them, he would have been saved from a policy, which, though for a time crowned with success, tarnished his fame, lost

A.D. 1366.

The Prince of Wales sends to meet him.

Pedro goes to Bordeaux.

The Gascon nobles are unwilling to give him help.

I 2

116 LIFE AND TIMES OF EDWARD III. CHAP. VII.

A.D. 1366. a kingdom to him and to England, ruined his fortune, broke his health, and caused his early death.

But the remonstrances of the Prince's advisers had no effect. He could see Henry of Trastamare in no other light than that of a usurper, and Pedro in that of a dethroned King whom it was his duty to support; but it must not be forgotten that Pedro had been betrothed to the Prince's sister, and that her death alone had prevented him from becoming the

The Prince declares he is in honour bound to help him. Prince's brother-in-law. Edward declared he had promised to help Pedro and must be as good as his word. "It is not a right thing, nor reasonable," he said, "that a bastard should hold a kingdom, and thrust out of it, and out of his heritage, a brother and heir of the land by legal marriage; and all Kings and sons of Kings should never agree nor consent to it, for it is a great blow at the Royal State." [1]

Pedro promises to pay them well, which alters their views. The Prince's resolute words may perhaps have produced some effect on the Gascon lords; but Pedro's assertion, made without delay, that he had great hidden treasure in Castile, and that he would divide it among them, must have been much more persuasive; for, as Froissart takes every opportunity of saying, "the English and the Gascons are by their nature greedy." They therefore agreed to attend a Parliament, which the Prince promised to call together to consider what course should be taken.

Gaston de Foix. It is worthy of remark that Gaston de Foix, called Phœbus from his youthful beauty, was absent from this gathering. He was one of those Gascon lords who withheld their allegiance from the Prince of Wales as long as they could; and King Edward had found it necessary, at the end of the previous year,

---

[1] Buchon's *Froissart*, vol. i. p. 510.

CHAP. VII. MEETING OF THE GASCON PARLIAMENT. 117

December 6th, 1365, to write to the King of France, requesting him to compel the Count to do him homage, according to the treaty of Bretigni.[1] Gaston, therefore, naturally took the side of Henry rather than that of Pedro.

A.D. 1366.

The Gascon Parliament assembled in Bordeaux. After three days' debate, during the whole of which Don Pedro was present, it was agreed to send messengers to the King of England to ask his advice, and to ascertain what course he wished his son to take.

The Gascon Parliament meets and decides to ask advice of King Edward.

Four knights, with their horses, their harness, and their attendants, were accordingly at once despatched to England. Two ships carried them to Southampton. After taking a day to refresh themselves and disembark their horses, they rode to London, when, finding that the King was at Windsor, they followed him there. Edward received them graciously, and read the letters they brought with them; he then desired them to return to London, promising, that he would take the advice of the members of his Council, as to the weighty matter about which they had come, and let them know the result.

Messengers are sent to England.

The King soon proceeded to London, and called together his son John of Gaunt, the Earls of Arundel and Salisbury, the Bishops of Winchester, Ely, and London, and the other members of his Council, in order to lay before them the letters sent him by the Prince of Wales. After a long deliberation, during which there can be no doubt that the King urged that his son should be allowed to carry out a plan so consonant to the spirit of both father and son, it was agreed that it was right that the Prince should support Don Pedro, because he had been wrongfully

King Edward agrees to support Don Pedro,

[1] Rymer, vol. iii. p. 779.

118   LIFE AND TIMES OF EDWARD III.   Chap. VII.

A.D. 1366. thrust out of his kingdom.   It was added, that the King was much moved to take this course, by the fact that he had already entered into treaties with him to help him in case of need.

but the Gascons hesitate, The messengers returned with these glad tidings, and the Prince at once assembled another Parliament to communicate them to the nobles.   The money difficulty again came in the way.   " My Lord," answered the barons, " we will obey the orders of the King our Lord and your father, as is quite right, and we will help you in this journey and Don Pedro also, but we want to know who will pay us our wages, for men at *and do not consent till they are guranteed their pay.* arms are never thus taken out of their houses to fight in strange countries without being paid and retained.[1] If it were for the needs of our dear Lord your father or for your own, or for your honour, or for the honour of our country, we would say nothing about it."   The Prince then turned to Don Pedro, saying, " You have heard what our people say, it is for you to answer." The throneless King promised them, that so far as all his own money and treasure would go, he would give it them.   This promise was of but little value ; it con-

[1] It is probable that this is a correct translation of the French word *délivrés* although it is not satisfactory. It would rather seem in the present instance to mean a release or *deliverance* from the feudal services which a vassal owed to his lord, in order to enable him to take other service. Buchon, in his glossary to Froissart, explains *délivrance* as " suite, livrée, gens dont un seigneur paie les despenses ; " and our term, " liveried servants," although now applied only to those wearing a particular costume, meant at first, without doubt, those who received pay, *livrée*, and were consequently distinguished by some badge, which we now call livery. The difficulty of considering the word *délivrés* to mean payment is, that the prefix must alter the sense of the original word *livrée*. *Delivered* would seem to be the best translation, but it would not be intelligible, without explanation.

CHAP. VII. PYRENEAN DIFFICULTIES. 119

sequently became necessary for the Prince of Wales A.D. 1366.
to agree to pay any deficiency, and he even consented
to lend Don Pedro what money he wanted until his
arrival in Castile. The meshes of the net, in which
the Prince was eventually to be entangled, were thus
already beginning to be tied. But the Prince had
some semblance of security for his money. Don
Pedro placed his daughters in the Prince's hands; he
agreed to put him in possession of the province of
Biscay and the town of Castro de Urdialès; and he
engaged to pay the Prince's captains 550,000 florins
of Florence before the 6th of February, 1367, and
56,000 more before the 24th of June.[1] Not one of
these promises (except the first) was kept.

Another difficulty now arose. The passes across Difficulty
the Pyrenean mountains were in the hands of the crossing
King of Navarre. Independently of the impolicy the
of converting a concealed and wavering enemy into Pyrenees.
an open foe by forcing the passes, such a course would
have been hazardous in the extreme. The Parliament
was therefore adjourned to Bayonne, in order to secure,
if possible, the attendance of the King of Navarre.
Old John of Chandos was selected to negotiate with
the King, and set out, accompanied by Sir Thomas
Felton, for Pampeluna, where Charles then was.
Their mission was attended with such success, that
they soon persuaded him to attend the Parliament.

The Parliament met; and, at the end of five days, The King
the terms on which the King of Navarre should open promises
the Pyrenean passes were settled, and a treaty was to permit
entered into, by which it was agreed that Charles the passage.
should receive 200,000 golden florins, in addition to
certain territories, and to 56,000 golden florins which

[1] Buchon's *Froissart*, vol. i. p. 512 note.

120   LIFE AND TIMES OF EDWARD III.   Chap. VII.

A.D. 1366. the Prince of Wales had paid him on account of Pedro, and which, as we have already seen, Pedro promised to repay the Prince on the 24th June following.[1] This treaty was signed at Libourne on September 23rd, 1366. Charles had shortly before signed a treaty with Henry at Santa Cruz de Campezco, agreeing to close the passes against Don Pedro; but the treacherous monarch, feeling uncertain as to the side on which success would rest, thought it advisable to make friends with both.[2] The Prince made himself answerable for all the payments promised to the King of Navarre, and for the money which Pedro was obliged to pay to the troops.

After signing the treaty, the King of Navarre returned to his kingdom; the barons went back to their own lands, and the Prince of Wales to Bordeaux.

The Prince of Wales summons Calverley and the "Companies" from Spain.
From thence, the Prince sent to Sir Hugh Calverley and the other leaders of the "Companies" who had fought for Henry of Trastamare against Pedro, telling them he had need of their services. As liegemen to the Prince of Wales, they were bound to obey his orders; they consequently quitted Henry's service without hesitation, taking leave of him, but without informing him of their reason for departure. As soon, however, as Henry discovered that they were on their way to join the Prince of Wales, he took measures to prevent

Their difficulties in getting out of Spain.
their getting out of Spain, by sending Du Guesclin to his friend the King of Aragon to ask him to close the passes. The King immediately ordered his soldiers to guard them; but the "Companies" managed to cross by another route—probably through Navarre. When, however, they arrived in Bearn, Gaston de

---

[1] Rymer, vol. iii. pp. 799 and 800.

[2] Buchon's *Froissart*, vol. i. p. 512, note.

CHAP. VII. CHANDOS AND FELTON. 121

Foix, who had hardly, if at all, acknowledged the A.D. 1366. sovereignty of the Prince of Wales, and who naturally dreaded the presence in his dominions of a horde of mercenary troops, 12,000 in number, refused to allow them passage. When the Prince heard of this, he sent his ever-ready friend John of Chandos to negotiate with De Foix; and Chandos soon obtained his leave for part of the troops to march between Aragon and Foix, while the others were to go, some between Foix and Bearn, and some between Catalonia and Armagnac.[1] Chandos then Chandos and Felton returned to Bordeaux, and he and Sir Thomas Felton try to dissuade the again brought the difficulties and cost of the enterprise Prince before the Prince. They represented to him, that from the enterprise, it would be much more difficult for him to reinstate but in vain. Don Pedro, than it had been for Henry to drive him out; for Pedro was universally hated, and had been deserted by all at the very time he needed their help; and they added, that the Prince would require plenty of men and money to accomplish his object. Finding, however, that the Prince was resolved to proceed, they advised him to melt down the greater part of his vessels of gold and silver and coin them into money, and to write to his father to ask him to let him have the 500,000 francs then nearly due from the King of France. The Prince acted on both these suggestions, and his father granted him the instalment of the French King's ransom, according to his request.[2]

[1] Buchon's *Froissart*, vol. i. p. 516.

[2] This is Froissart's account, and there seems to be no reason to doubt its truth, except that in Rymer, where most of the payments of the ransom are mentioned, no trace is to be found of this payment to the Prince of Wales.

122   LIFE AND TIMES OF EDWARD III.   Chap. VII.

A.D. 1366.

In accordance with the agreement made with De Foix, one division of the " Companies," about 3,000 in number, passed between Aragon and Foix; but they had, and not without reason, earned so bad a reputation that they soon became involved in troubles, and were attacked by the Seneschal of Toulouse on their way to Montauban. They defeated him, however,

The "Companies" reach the Prince of Wales.

with great loss, and then pursued their way to join the Prince of Wales, who quartered them at a place called Bascle among the mountains.[1]

Preparations in England to support the Prince.

In the meantime, preparations had been going on in England to support the Prince of Wales with troops. During the summer and autumn of 1366, orders were constantly issued for the assemblage of archers and others, and for securing ships to convey them to Gascony. In the beginning of November the Duke of Lancaster was ready to set sail ;[2] but he did not leave England till the following February.

The Prince finds he has too many soldiers.

The Prince now found that he had gathered together a larger army than he could conveniently pay, and wrote to the Lord of Albret, ordering him to reduce the soldiers, which he had agreed to supply, from 1,000 to 200. This caused a great quarrel, which was made up for the time, but which, eventually, had serious results on the fate of the Prince of Wales and on the English rule over Aquitaine.

The troops

All was now in readiness for the invasion of Spain,

---

[1] Froissart (vol. i. p. 518) states that this skirmish took place on the Vigil of Our Lady in August 1366, but this appears to be an error. The troops must have passed out of Spain after the treaty with the King of Navarre, and the treaty was not signed until September 23rd. It is true that there are no means of ascertaining exactly when it was entered into, but it is improbable that it was before August.

[2] Rymer, vol. iii. p. 812.

CHAP. VII.   CHARLES THE BAD.   123

and the Prince of Wales sent his troops forward; but he delayed his own journey, until the Princess had gone through the troubles of childbirth.   This event took place in February 1367, when Richard, the future King of England, was born at Bordeaux.   The Prince of Wales then followed his troops without further delay, and overtook them at Dax, on the Adour; he was soon joined, at that place, by his brother the Duke of Lancaster.[1]   While he remained there, the Count de Foix, who had hesitated so much in transferring his allegiance to the Prince of Wales, came to pay him his respects, and, after a friendly reception, returned to his territory, with instructions from the Prince to keep it quiet until his return from Spain.

A.D. 1366.

march for Spain, and the Prince follows them after the birth of his son.

Reports now reached the Prince that the faithless King of Navarre had again allied himself with Henry. He therefore sent Sir Hugh Calverley forward to take possession of Miranda and Puente de la Reyna, two frontier towns of Navarre, in order to bring the King to his senses.   This policy had the desired effect, and the King promised faithfully to keep the passes open for the Prince; but Edward wisely took care, that the King's own person should be a security for the fulfilment of his promise, and made him accompany the army, to guide it across the mountains.

Attempted treachery of Charles the Bad;

defeated by the Prince.

The news, that the allies were about to advance, soon spread far and near; and, while on the one side, the Prince's friends—the faithful Captal de Buch, the Lord of Clisson, the Lord of Albret with his 200 lances, and others—flocked to the Prince's standard, Du Guesclin, on the other, advanced to join the reigning King of Castile with the troops he had collected in France.   The King of France and his vindictive

The Prince's friends flock round him,

---

[1] Buchon's *Froissart*, vol. i. p. 521.

124 LIFE AND TIMES OF EDWARD III. Chap. VII.

A.D. 1366.

and Du Guesclin prepares to support Henry.

brother, the Duke of Anjou, had willingly listened to Du Guesclin's requests, and had allowed him to raise troops for the support of Henry, as the King of England had done in support of Don Pedro; but this conduct was no infraction of the treaty of Bretigni, and war did not in consequence of it ensue between the two nations.

The English cross the Pyrenees,

At last, in the middle of February 1367, the Prince of Wales and his allies set forth to cross the Pyrenees. The passes are so difficult, that a small body of men could easily defend them against a large army; they were covered with snow and the cold was extreme. It was well, therefore, that the Prince had allied himself with the King of Navarre, and had secured himself against treachery by keeping him with the army. The pass, chosen for the passage of the troops, was Roncesvalles, celebrated as the spot where the rear-guard of Charlemagne was defeated, and where Roland died. It was settled that the army should march in three divisions, and that one only should cross on each day. Accordingly, on Monday, the 20th of February, the first division, under the Duke of Lancaster and John of Chandos, went over the mountain with 10,000 horse; the next day, the Prince of Wales and Pedro, accompanied by the King of Navarre, followed them with 7,000 horse in a frightful storm of wind and snow; and, on Wednesday, the last division, with about 10,000 horse, accompanied by the King of Majorca, the Captal de Buch, the Lord of Albret and others, got over safely. The whole body of the troops assembled together in the mountains round Pampeluna.

and muster at Pampeluna.

Henry of Trastamare, hearing of the arrival of the invaders, anxiously expected Du Guesclin with the

CHAP. VII. PREPARATION FOR BATTLE. 125

French troops; but with that singular mixture of courtesy and cool effrontery which marked the age of chivalry, he wrote a courteous letter to the Prince of Wales, saying that he had no doubt the Prince had come to fight a battle with him, and asking him by what road he meant to enter Castile, in order that he might be there to defend himself. The Prince received the messenger with great politeness, and expressed his admiration of Henry, saying, " Truly this bastard Henry is a valiant knight and of great prowess;" but, nevertheless, he did not answer his letter, nor allow his herald to return.

A.D. 1366.

Sir William Felton, and other leaders of the Prince's army, were now sent forward with 160 lances, and 300 horse-archers to reconnoitre.[1] They crossed the Ebro at Logroño, and then advanced as far as Navarrete, where they halted. Shortly after their departure the treacherous King of Navarre, who had hitherto accompanied Edward and acted as his guide, was taken prisoner, under circumstances which roused grave suspicions that his capture was planned in order to afford him an opportunity of escape from the invaders. A knight named Martin de la Carra, however, offered his services to supply the King's place, and guided the rest of the army through the difficult passes which led to Salvatierra, where they arrived in safety. This city yielded to the invaders without resistance, and the garrison were admitted to mercy at the earnest desire of the Prince of Wales, who prevented Don Pedro from carrying out his cruel intention of putting them all to death.

Felton sent forward to reconnoitre.

The Prince of Wales takes Salvatierra.

Meanwhile, Henry of Trastamare, wondering that his herald had not returned, advanced to the frontiers

Felton discovers the position of

[1] Buchon's *Froissart*, vol. i. p. 526.

126   LIFE AND TIMES OF EDWARD III.   Chap. VII.

A.D. 1367.

the Spaniards,

of Castile, and sent out his advanced guard in the direction of Navarrete, to discover the position of the invaders. It soon came in sight of Sir William Felton's troops, and a slight encounter ensued, which revealed the position of both parties to each other. Felton, who had kept up his communications with the Prince of Wales, immediately sent off to inform him of the position of his enemies; and Henry determined to cross the Ebro and attack them at once. Both armies, therefore, marched towards Vittoria as the expected battle-field. Felton's object in doing

and returns to the Prince.

so was to effect a junction with the Prince's troops. This was accomplished, and the Prince and Felton held a conference. While it was going on, the Prince's scouts came in, with news as to the movements of the Spanish army, which led him to believe that an immediate attack was intended. The Prince therefore prepared for battle; but the report was premature, for Henry was waiting for Du Guesclin.

The Spaniards surprise the English.

When the armies retired to rest at night, Don Tello obtained leave from his brother Henry of Trastamare to attempt a surprise of the English on the following morning. During the night, Du Guesclin arrived with about 3,000 French and Aragonese; but it was thought best that he should take no part in Tello's enterprise. At daybreak, Tello led 6,000 men towards the English camp, and on his way met and defeated a small body of soldiers under Sir Hugh Calverley. He then proceeded to the Duke of Lancaster's division, and attacked it with nearly equal success; but the Duke got his troops together, on the top of a hill, and kept the Spaniards at bay. Tello, therefore, left a part of his soldiers to continue the attack, while he

CHAP. VII.   THE ENGLISH SURPRISED.   **127**

and his brother went to seek adventures elsewhere. A.D. 1367.
On their way they came across Sir William Felton
with a small detachment. Felton defended himself
valiantly, charging, with chivalrous rashness, alone
among the Spanish ranks. Defeat and death under
such circumstances were certain; Felton paid the
penalty of his temerity. Tello then returned to continue the attack on the Duke of Lancaster's division,
and, after a desperate struggle, succeeded in over-
coming it; all were slain, except a few who escaped
to carry the evil tidings to the Prince of Wales, who
then, for the first time, became aware of Tello's attempt.[1] It was now too late for further fighting.
Tello and his brother Sancho, who had accompanied   Tello re-
him through the day, returned, therefore, to their   turns to
                                                      theSpanish
brother's camp carrying with them the news of their   camp.
success. They were received with great honour and
exultation; but, after relating their exploits, Sir
Arnold of Andreghen, one of his marshals and a
tried and valiant knight, advanced to the King, and
told him he would find that his enemies were the
flower of all the chivalry of the world; that they
would fight well, and would die rather than yield. He
therefore counselled him to guard the passes, so that   Henry is
no provisions could reach Edward's troops, and thus   advised to
                                                        reduce the
reduce them to surrender by starvation. Henry was   English by
                                                        starvation,
too much impressed with feelings of chivalry, and too   but he re-
confident in the number of his troops, to listen to such   solves to
                                                        fight.
prudent advice, and answered, "By the soul of my
father, Marshal, I so long to see the Prince and to

---

[1] Froissart's account is inconsistent with itself. On p. 529
(vol. i. Buchon's ed.) he says: "Et après vinrent le prince et
le Roi Dam Piètre," and on p. 530: "Bien les eut le prince de
Galles envoyé secourir, si il l'eut sçu, mais rien n'en savait."

128   LIFE AND TIMES OF EDWARD III.   CHAP. VII.

A.D. 1367.   try my power against his, that we cannot part without fighting, and, thank God! I have the means. I
have, first of all, 7,000 men at arms, each mounted
on a good horse and all covered with iron who will
care neither for dart nor bow; then I have 20,000
other men-at-arms mounted on light horses and
armed cap-à-pied; besides which I have a good 60,000
men with lances and javelins, darts and shields,
who will do good service, and they have all sworn to
fight till death."   So the Spaniards resolved to fight,
wines and spices were brought, and they then retired
to rest.

The English advance, but cannot bring on a battle. The next morning, the English forces were ready to
engage, notwithstanding their losses of the previous
day, and the Prince advanced to Vittoria, hoping
to bring on a battle. He did not know exactly where
the Spaniards were, but had heard they were not
far off. The Spaniards were not to be induced to
begin the fight. The English remained at Vittoria
for six days; during the whole time, storms of wind,
snow and rain added to the distress they were already
suffering from hunger. At the end of this time,
they again broke up their camp; either to search
The English march towards Navarrete, for their enemy, or to get into better quarters.
They marched towards Navarrete, through la Guar-
dia, and halted for two days at Viana, a little
town on the left bank of the Ebro. They then
crossed that river at Logroño, and, after a halt of a
few days, took up their quarters at Navarrete.[1]

When Henry heard of the movements of his enemy,

[1] Froissart (vol. i. p. 532) states that the Prince of Wales left
Logroño and went to Navarrete on Friday, April 2nd. This is
evidently an error, as the Prince wrote a letter from Navarrete
dated on the previous day.

CHAP. VII. BATTLE OF NAVARRETE. 129

he too broke up his camp at San Vicente, which was A.D. 1367.
higher up on the Ebro, and, after crossing that river, and the
marched to Najera on the river Najarilla, which now Spaniards
separated the two armies. The Prince of Wales soon to Najera.
heard of the advance of the Spaniards, and was
rejoiced at the renewed chance of coming to an
engagement with them. His position was getting
very serious. Hunger, and inclement weather, would
soon have rendered him an easy prey to his enemy;
but, as on former occasions, his enemies' blunders
saved him from destruction. " By St. George," he
cried, " this bastard is a valiant knight, and it seems
he wants to fight us." He then called his council
together, and, on April 1st, 1367,[1] wrote a letter
from Navarrete to Henry, telling him he had invaded
Spain because Henry had usurped the throne, but
offering to mediate between him and Don Pedro.
He added, however, that he was ready to fight if his
mediation were not accepted. The next day, Henry
wrote in answer from his " palace near Najera,"
saying that Pedro's cruelties had turned everyone
against him, that the people had come of their own
accord to offer him the crown, and that he was quite
ready for the conflict.

Both sides now prepared for battle. The Prince The battle
of Wales sent out scouts, mounted on horseback, rete.
of Navar-
to ascertain exactly where the Spaniards lay; on
their return, having obtained the information required, he ordered his troops to rise up the following
morning at the sound of the trumpet. At the first
blast, they were to rouse themselves and dress; at the
second, to arm themselves; at the third, to mount
their horses, and be ready to march.

[1] Rymer, vol. iii. p. 824.

VOL. II. K

130   LIFE AND TIMES OF EDWARD III.   CHAP. VII.

A.D. 1367.

Don Henry, in like manner, sent messengers to find out the position of the English, and, on their return, ordered his army to be ready by midnight. Both armies then retired to rest. The Spaniards were well provided with food; but the English had only scanty fare. Directly after midnight, Henry's trumpets sounded, and his army was quickly arranged in order of battle. The first division, consisting of 4,000 knights and squires heavily armed, was put under the command of Du Guesclin; the second, comprising 16,000 light-armed horsemen, under that of Tello and his brother Sancho; the third, and by far the largest, consisting of 7,000 horse and 40,000 foot soldiers, was led by Henry himself. The Spanish forces, if Froissart's numbers are not exaggerated, thus consisted of nearly 70,000 men. The English numbered only 27,000.

April 3rd.
Battle of
Navarrete.

At daybreak on Saturday, April 3rd, the Spaniards advanced towards Navarrete; the English marched in the same direction, till they saw the Spaniards in the plain. Then both armies halted. The battle began between the divisions of the Duke of Lancaster and John of Chandos, and that commanded by Du Guesclin. Shortly afterwards, the Prince of Wales, accompanied by Don Pedro, advanced to attack Tello and Sancho. But Tello, notwithstanding the courage displayed by him a few days previously, so soon as he saw the Prince of Wales advancing, imitated the example of the Duke of Normandy at Poitiers. Accompanied by 2,000 horse, he fled, without striking a blow. The Captal de Buch, seeing this, made an onslaught on the foot belonging to Tello's division, and routed them with great slaughter. The Prince of Wales, and Don Pedro, attacked the main division of the

CHAP. VII.   DEFEAT OF THE SPANIARDS.   **131**

Spanish army under Henry; they were received with A.D. 1367.
a storm of stones, thrown from the Spanish slings,
with a skill for which they were as famous as the
English were for their bows.   This at first produced
a great effect.   But the English rallied quickly;
the bowmen poured down flights of arrows into the
Spanish ranks, and turned the tide against them.
In the meantime, Lancaster and Chandos were fighting hard against Du Guesclin; Chandos was thrown
to the ground by a gigantic Castilian, who lay upon
him, and was about to kill him, when Chandos
drew a dagger from his breast and plunged it into
his adversary with a deadly blow.   The escape of
Chandos was of the greatest importance to the
English; for he had great skill and experience in
addition to his valour, and, as Froissart says, " he
advised and governed the Duke of Lancaster this day,
as he had formerly advised his brother the Prince of
Wales at Poitiers."   The great struggle lay between
these two divisions ; at last, the English overcame
the Spaniards and took Du Guesclin prisoner, besides
others of the leaders.

Chandos and the Duke of Lancaster now turned
towards the main division of the Spanish army, under
Henry, which had been gallantly attacked by the
Prince of Wales with a far inferior force.   This now
became the centre of the fight; and here, in addition
to the Prince of Wales, the Duke of Lancaster, and
John of Chandos, might be seen the Captal de Buch,
Sir Hugh Calverley, the Lord of Clisson, and many
other English and Gascon lords, leading and rally-
ing their gallant troops, in a battle in which no
easy victory was gained.   Three times was Henry
driven back; three times did the brave king rally

K 2

132   LIFE AND TIMES OF EDWARD III.   CHAP. VII.

A.D. 1367. his troops, and lead them again to the combat. But it was all in vain. Tello's flight was known and discouraged them; Du Guesclin was a prisoner; at last the Spaniards yielded. Henry galloped from the field, and escaped into France, where he soon found sympathy and aid from the faithless Duke of Anjou.[1] His soldiers fled to Najares, hotly followed by the English, who drove them out of the town to the banks of the Ebro, and there slew them in such numbers, that the stream ran red with blood. The savage cruelty of the infamous Pedro displayed itself after the battle. He at once put to death many of the Castilian nobles, who had had the misfortune to fall into his hands, and then demanded that the

Defeat of the Spaniards. Prince of Wales should give up his own prisoners (including Pedro's half-brother Sancho) for the same purpose. The Prince refused, and Pedro's butchery was stayed, until he was freed from the presence of Edward and his soldiers.

At night the English occupied the Spanish camp, which they found well filled with welcome food; and all supped, relieved from fear of hunger or defeat. It is worthy of remark that no cannons were used on either side.

Thus ended the third, and last but one, great battle fought by the Prince of Wales; it is remarkable that, in every one of them, the escape of his army from utter destruction was little short of miraculous. At Creçy, he was saved from imminent defeat by the good fortune of finding a ford through a tidal river, and being able to cross it, just before the advancing waves rendered its passage impossible and pre-

---

[1] Buchon's *Froissart*, vol. i. p. 541, note.

CHAP. VII.   DEFEAT OF THE SPANIARDS.   133

vented pursuit; and, both at Poitiers and at Navarrete, A.D. 1367.
the folly of his enemies in fighting instead of leaving
him to starve, saved him from the probable necessity
of surrender, and gave him the opportunity of gaining an important and decisive victory.

134 LIFE AND TIMES OF EDWARD III. CHAP. VIII.

CHAPTER VIII.

CONCLUSION OF THE SPANISH WAR; DECLINE OF ENGLISH RULE IN FRANCE; AND DECLARATION OF WAR BY THE KING OF FRANCE.

A.D. 1367.

The Spanish campaign continued.

BEFORE returning to the domestic history of England, it is necessary to continue that of the Castilian revolutions and counter-revolutions, until their consistent end in the brutally savage murder of one brother by the other; and then to pursue that of the Black Prince for a few short years, until his return to England, broken in health, and deeply mortified by defeat.

Prospective view of the conclusion of Edward's reign.

A melancholy period in English annals now begins. It becomes necessary to relate events whose history is a record of the treachery of the tyrant, whom the Black Prince unwisely helped back to a throne, and of the disastrous consequences of his interference; of the illness of the Prince; of the failure of his energies, and of his untimely death; of old and noble warriors and counsellors dying, or retiring from their sphere of action; of jealousies among the commanders, and want of rapid decision in their movements; of a threatened invasion of England; of the loss of Aquitaine; of the death of the excellent Queen; and, last of all, of the death of the King himself, tarnished in fame by the unworthy termination of an eventful reign.

This anticipatory glance presents to view, a sad contrast to the retrospect of forty years; especially if the events are regarded from the usual point of

CHAP. VIII. CONSEQUENCES OF THE VICTORY. 135

view, which attributes glory to military success and gallant courage alone, and takes no account, on the one hand, of the misery inflicted by constant warfare, nor, on the other, of the progressive civilisation, general happiness, and prosperity which usually characterise a period of peace. From this last point of view, England's loss of her French possessions was indeed a mighty gain; from the former, it appears as a clouded spot on her history.

After the victory of Navarrete, Burgos opened its gates to Pedro, who entered that city within two days after the battle, and the Prince of Wales followed him almost immediately. For three weeks, the Prince held tournaments and passed his time in rejoicings, but at last, finding that Pedro never troubled himself about the payment of the money, for which the Prince had made himself responsible, he reminded him of his engagements. Pedro, on whom such obligations sat lightly, made excuses, saying, that if the Prince would go to Valladolid, he would go to Seville, to collect the necessary funds. The Prince unfortunately consented, and allowed the faithless monarch to place himself at such a distance, that all power over him was lost. Months passed away without a florin being repaid. Sickness broke out in the English camp, and the mortality was so great that hardly one-fifth of the army survived.[1] The Prince himself fell ill, and it was even suspected that he had been poisoned; but, whether this crime was attempted or not, it is certain that he suffered to such an extent, that he never recovered his health during the remainder of his life.[2] Remonstrances with Pedro were utterly vain. At last, on hearing

A.D. 1367.

Sad contrast to retrospect.

Consequences of the victory of Navarrete.

Pedro in his prosperity neglects to pay his debts.

The English suffer from sickness.

---

[1] Knighton, col. 2629.   [2] Walsingham, p. 305.

136 LIFE AND TIMES OF EDWARD III. Chap. VIII.

A.D. 1367.

The Prince and the army return to Aquitaine.

from his wife that Henry of Trastamare had invaded Aquitaine,[1] the Prince yielded to the advice of his companions in arms, and determined to return to his duchy. He accordingly marched towards the frontiers of Navarre and Aragon, where he waited a month, for leave from the King of Aragon to cross the passes. At length, wearied with this vexatious delay, he sent messengers to the King, and they negotiated so well, that they not only obtained leave for the passage of Edward and the greater part of his troops, but brought about a treaty of alliance between the King and Pedro. On hearing this, the King of Navarre gave the Prince, his brother the Duke of Lancaster, and his chief companions, leave to cross by Roncesvalles. This was a more convenient route than that through Aragon, and the offer therefore was accepted ; but the main body of the troops went by the latter way.[2] In the course of a few days, the Prince reached Bordeaux in safety, though in ruined health. There he remained, but his brother the Duke of Lancaster, who had come back from Spain with him, returned at once to England.

Henry of Trastamare ravages Aquitaine in the Prince's absence,

In the meantime, Henry of Trastamare had fled from Spain to Toulouse. From thence he proceeded to Montpellier, in order to meet and concert measures with the Duke of Anjou, whose hatred of the English never slept. Disregarding the conditions of the treaty of Bretigni, the Duke entered into engagements with Henry, which were directed as much against the English as against Pedro, and were barely consistent with the conditions of peace between England and France.[3] By these means Henry was enabled to

[1] Sismondi, vol. ii. p. 79.   [2] Buchon's *Froissart*, vol. i. p. 544.
[3] Ibid. vol. i. p. 542, note.

CHAP. VIII.   HENRY RETURNS TO SPAIN.   137

collect together about 300 men at the castle of Roquemaure, on the frontiers of Aquitaine, and to ravage the district of Montauban. When the Princess of Wales heard of this, she not only wrote to her husband, as already related, but appealed to the King of France, who, being most anxious to preserve the appearance of friendship with the English, until it suited him to throw off the mask, at once ordered Henry to desist. But Henry knew too well what were the King's real wishes, and, disregarding his orders, continued his advance into Aquitaine.

On the Prince of Wales coming back to Aquitaine, Henry returned to Spain at the head of 3,000 horse and 6,000 foot soldiers, and found the Spaniards so disgusted with Pedro's cruelties, that all who dared to do so at once opened the gates of their cities to him.[1] Burgos received him gladly, and in the spring of 1368 he laid siege to Leon, and took it on the 30th of April. Henry then marched on Toledo, which, however, held out for Pedro, because he had in his hand hostages for its fidelity.

Early in 1369 Henry was joined by Du Guesclin, who had been ransomed at the end of 1367 for the sum of 100,000 francs, and had been engaged with the Duke of Anjou, in the spring of 1368, in the invasion of Provence.[2] Du Guesclin brought with him about 2,000 soldiers, enlisted, at the request of the Duke of Anjou, from the Companies in Languedoc; he was also accompanied by a number of French knights and squires, who were restless when not engaged in fighting.

When Pedro heard of Henry's entry into Spain,

A.D. 1367 to 1369.

but returns to Spain when the Prince comes back.

A.D. 1368.

He is well received, and marches on Toledo.

---

[1] Buchon's *Froissart*, vol. i. p. 545.
[2] Ibid. p. 549, 550, note 2.

138   LIFE AND TIMES OF EDWARD III.   CHAP. VIII.

A.D. 1369. and of the general defection of his subjects, he turned for advice to the Moor Benahatin, grand astrologer or philosopher, and adviser of the King of Granada.[1] By his assistance he was enabled, in March 1369, to put himself at the head of 20,000 Moors, and of about the same number of Spaniards, whom he had raised in Andalusia. This was the only part of his dominions where he retained any influence. With this army he marched to raise the siege of Toledo. His troops, however, consisted almost entirely of foot-soldiers, only 3,000 being cavalry.

Trastamare and Du Guesclin march out to meet him. Henry was well informed of Pedro's movements, although the latter knew nothing of his, and, after a consultation with Du Guesclin, determined to march out and give him battle, rather than wait his attack. He therefore left a part of his troops to continue the siege, and advanced towards Seville. On the 14th of March,[2] Henry met Pedro near the castle of Montiel, with his army marching in utter disorder, and instantly attacked him with great fury. Henry's soldiers believed that Pedro's army consisted of nothing but Jews and Mahometans, against whom they felt a bitter hatred; Pedro's, on their part, were equally furious against the Christians. Pedro's troops came

Battle of Montiel, March 14, 1369. up in succession, and each body was defeated, in its turn, before its support could come to its aid. Pedro himself fought for a time with the desperate

Defeat of Pedro. courage of a wild beast at bay; but at length his army was utterly routed, and, yielding therefore to the advice of the faithful Fernand de Castro, who had remained his constant and almost only friend, he fled from the field. He escaped to the castle of

[1] Buchon's *Froissart*, vol. i. p. 550, note 1.
[2] Ibid. p. 552, note.

CHAP. VIII. PEDRO KILLED BY HIS BROTHER. 139

Montiel, but it was not provided with food enough A.D. 1369. to stand a siege; at midnight, therefore, he endeavoured to escape from it. The castle, however, was so well watched that his flight was discovered, and he was seized and carried off to the tent of one of Du Guesclin's attendants. Thither Henry went to confront him, and the brothers instantly broke out in bitter recriminations, but soon came to blows and Pedro rushed at each other with deadly hatred. They struggled, and Pedro, being the stronger, got his brother Henry. under him, and was about to plunge his dagger into his breast, when Du Guesclin, coming up, seized him by the leg, threw him over, and Henry then stabbed him to death. Thus ends the miserable history of the Black Prince's villanous ally; and it is unnecessary to pursue the Spanish history any further.

While these events were going on in Spain, the A.D. 1368. King of France and his brother, the Duke of Anjou, were continually plotting against the English dominion in France; and everything seemed to conspire to help them in their evident endeavours to bring about war between the two countries.

On the return of the Prince of Wales to Bordeaux, The the "Companies" who had fought under his banners "Companies" dein Spain demanded their wages. He told them he mand their would never allow them to lose their money, but that pay; as Pedro had not discharged the debts due to him, he but the could not then pay them in full; but he melted down Prince, his plate to satisfy their demands as far as he could, pay them, and also gave them the sums he had received for the ransom of his prisoners. This, however, was far from enough, and he could not restrain them from pillaging Aquitaine. The outcry of his subjects became consequently so great, that he was obliged to order the

140 LIFE AND TIMES OF EDWARD III. CHAP. VIII.

A.D. 1368.
tells them to ravage France.

"Companies" to depart from his duchy, and tell them they might gain their livelihood in France. They passed the Loire in the beginning of February 1368,[1] and gave out publicly that they were sent by the Prince of Wales. It is evident, however, that, for some months previously, they had not confined their ravages to Aquitaine; for, in the previous November, King Edward had written to his son saying that the King of France had complained to him of the invasion of his kingdom by the Prince's people, and enjoining him strictly to prevent such infractions of the treaty between the two countries.[2] It was agreeable enough to the King of France thus to have an opportunity of making plausible charges against the English; for he thereby cast discredit on statements of the same nature, made by the Black Prince against the French, and induced King Edward to listen to the counsels of those "who said that the Prince was rash and impatient of quiet, and desired nothing so much as war,"[3] and that his only object was to induce the King to support him in making war on France. These councillors, in fact, advised Edward

The King of France keeps up an appearance of friendship with Edward,

to pay no attention to the Prince's letters. The King of France took care that the payments due for the ransom of his father were punctually made, and so completely was King Edward thereby deceived, that, a few months afterwards, when his son Lionel Duke of Clarence was on his way to Italy to marry a daughter of Galeazzo Visconti, attended by a retinue of nearly 500 men who, with the enormous number of 1,280 horses,[4] were carried in thirty-nine ships and

[1] Buchon's *Froissart*, vol. i. p. 546, note.
[2] Rymer, vol. iii. p. 835.   [3] Walsingham, p. 307.
[4] Rymer, vol. iii. p. 845, May 10, 1368.

Chap. VIII. THE KING OF FRANCE PREPARES FOR WAR. 141

thirteen small vessels, he allowed him to make a pro- A.D. 1368.
longed visit to the King of France in Paris. Lionel
was received with such outward marks of friendship as
seemed to demonstrate, to those who knew no better,
that the most cordial relations existed between the
two countries.

All the while, however, that the King of France *but all the*
was thus deceiving King Edward, he was secretly *while pre-*
pares for
preparing for war. The Duke of Anjou, as already *war.*
stated, had taken Du Guesclin into his pay immediately on his release. A few months afterwards,
on July 19, 1368,[1] at the time that Henry of Trastamare, as King of Castile, was besieging Toledo, the
King of France made an alliance with him against
Edward. He also lost no opportunity of cultiva- *He courts*
the friend-
ting a friendship with those nobles who were dis- *ship of the*
satisfied with the English, and thus attached to him- *Gascon*
nobles.
self Olivier de Clisson, whose father had been put to
death by Philip of Valois in 1343. Olivier had distinguished himself in the wars of Brittany on the
side of Jane of Montfort, and had fought in the
English ranks at the battle of Navarrete ; but he was
dissatisfied with the recompense he had received, and
consequently had conceived a violent hatred against
the English. In the same way, the King of France
also attached to himself the Lord of Albret, who had
never forgotten the insult which he thought had been
put on him by the Prince of Wales, when the latter
asked him to reduce the number of soldiers he was to
bring with him for the Spanish expedition. In order
to cement a friendship with him Charles gave him
in marriage his sister-in-law, Margaret of Bourbon.[2]

[1] Rymer, vol. iii. p. 850.
[2] Buchon's *Froissart*, vol. i. p. 547, note.

142   LIFE AND TIMES OF EDWARD III.   CHAP. VIII.

A.D. 1368. The important families of Albret and Armagnac were thus detached from the English.

While the King of France was thus making ready for a rupture with England, the Prince of Wales was almost inevitably compelled, by the natural results of foregone events, to take steps, which could not fail to promote the object for which the King of France was striving. As already stated, the Prince was unable, because of Pedro's want of good faith, to pay in full the soldiers who had formed his army of Spanish invasion. It was not to be expected that these mercenary soldiers, whose trade was war, would be satisfied without their wages, although the Prince had managed to persuade many of them to recompense themselves by pillaging France. In order, therefore, to raise enough money to stave off their demands, he was compelled to levy a new tax on his subjects in Aquitaine; and on the advice of his Chancellor, the Bishop of Bath, the one proposed was a tax on hearths—that is, on the fire which the peasant lit to cook his scanty meal. This was to be one franc a-year on each hearth for five years. The amount seems trifling, but the tax was eminently unpopular, which, probably, any tax would have been that pressed on the mass of the people. It is singular, however, that the principal opposition to this tax was made by the nobles. As the Duchy of Aquitaine was governed through Parliaments, it was necessary to obtain their consent in order to impose the tax. One was accordingly assembled at Niort for that purpose, and, although the nobles and representatives of many districts made no opposition, yet others, including of course the Lord of Albret, Olivier de Clisson, and the Count of Armagnac, opposed it

Prince of Wales, being pressed for money, proposes a hearth-tax,

which is unpopular.

CHAP. VIII.   THE HEARTH TAX.   143

A.D. 1368.

vehemently. All that could be obtained from them was, a promise to consult their neighbours and attend another Parliament afterwards. While the Prince was thus asking for money to pay his soldiers, his Court at Bordeaux was kept up with profuse extravagance; the opponents of the tax therefore naturally said, that if he wanted money he should begin by spending less. Malcontents were encouraged by the Lord of Albret, who hinted that, if they persevered in their opposition, they would soon be supported by a powerful protector. Parliament consequently was in vain reassembled, first at one place and then at another, to consider the proposed impost. No consent to the tax could be obtained. Even the Prince's own friends advised him not to persevere; but he rejected their advice, and, in consequence of his obstinacy, even his old and dear friend John of Chandos, finding his advice disregarded, left the Court, and retired to his domain of St. Sauveur in Normandy.

Chandos in vain opposes the tax, and retires to Normandy.

The next step taken in the progress of this fatal story was an important one. On June 30th and again on October 25th, 1368,[1] the Lords of Albret and Armagnac appealed to the King of France, as their suzerain, against the right of the Duke of Aquitaine to tax them. This was a bold and unjustifiable defiance of the Duke. His rights of sovereignty over Aquitaine were indisputable. The King of France had no more right to interfere between him and his subjects, than the King of Castile, or any sovereign on the face of Europe. The King of France of course knew this perfectly well; but he thought it politic to pretend to this right, and actually summoned the Prince

Gascon Lords appeal to the King of France against the tax,

---

[1] Buchon's *Froissart*, vol. i. p. 548, note.

144 LIFE AND TIMES OF EDWARD III. Chap. VIII.

A.D. 1368.

who summons the Prince to Paris to answer their appeal, of Wales to appear before him, to answer the complaints of his own subjects. The anger of the Prince, whose temper was doubtless not improved by his rapidly increasing sickness which had now turned into dropsy, may be easily conceived.

Before venturing on this serious step, the King of France had taken great pains to ascertain, whether he could depend on the inhabitants of Aquitaine and Guienne, in the event of a war with England. These provinces had always been to a great extent independent of France, and spoke almost a different language; they were separated from the seat of the French government by a vast distance; and Guienne had been for more than two centuries under the rule of the English, whose government had contrasted favourably with that of France. But, notwithstanding this, Charles found the people weary of the English yoke. The manners of the English were then, as now, unsocial towards the foreigners among whom they had settled. There are no better colonists on the face of the earth than the English, when the only friend they have to cultivate, and the only enemy they have to fear, is nature and not man; but, when union with the natives of a country as friends and equals is required, there is no nation less capable of adapting its habits to such circumstances. So it was in Aquitaine. The rule of the English was just; but the barons of England had made no friends of the barons of France, and Charles found he need not fear lest they should **having satisfied himself that he might depend on the Gascons.** fight heart and soul for the English. He therefore entered into a solemn agreement with the Count of Armagnac and with the other nobles of Guienne, not to renounce the sovereignty over Guienne, as he was bound to have done long before by the

Chap. VIII. INDIGNATION OF THE PRINCE OF WALES. 145

treaty of Bretigni; and they, on their part, bound A.D. 1369. themselves not to enter into any treaty of peace with England except with his consent.[1]

Charles, accordingly, sent three seneschals to Languedoc as protectors of any persons who might appeal to them; he allowed the Duke of Anjou to enrol *gens d'armes* secretly against the English; and on January 25th, 1369,[2] sent messengers to the Prince, with a letter expressed in the most haughty terms, commanding him to appear before him at Paris.

This affront took the Prince by surprise. It was impossible for him to imagine, that, after signing the treaty of Bretigni, the King of France could claim sovereignty over Aquitaine. He looked at the messengers with astonishment; then gazed at his surrounding vassals; and at last said, "Willingly, we will go to the Court of Paris, as the King of France orders it; but it shall be with helmet on head and 60,000 men with us." The old spirit of the Prince was roused; but his increasing illness had depressed his ancient vigour, and these bold words were hardly followed by corresponding deeds. Indeed it was not until he was really attacked, and war had begun, that he fully roused himself to action. Before the fatal invasion of Spain, he would have sounded the alarm throughout his duchy, and, at the head of an army used to victory, would have marched into the very heart of France. But now, his failing energies, the inevitable accompaniment of his fatal dropsy, made him far from equal to the requirements of his dangerous position.

[1] Buchon's *Froissart*, vol. i. p. 558, note.
[2] Ibid. i. p. 560.

VOL. II.   L

146 LIFE AND TIMES OF EDWARD III. Chap. VIII.

A.D. 1369.

He arrests the messengers.

The messengers were allowed to depart in peace; but, before they were far on their way, the Prince changed his mind, sent after them and arrested them. This roused the anger of the Gascon lords. They determined on revenge; and lay in ambuscade for Edward's seneschal of Rouergue and attacked him, slaying many of his men. Indignant at this outrage, the Prince

Edward recalls Chandos.

at once summoned his old friend John of Chandos to return to him. Chandos, seeing the danger of the Prince, and casting aside all difference of opinion as to the impolitic tax which had produced such fatally momentous results, immediately responded to the summons, and took up his head-quarters at Montauban to support the seneschal. Frequent skirmishes occurred between the English and French; but the Duke of Anjou took great care not to interfere openly, for his brother had strictly forbidden him to make war on the Prince without his orders. For a time therefore no serious hostilities broke out.

The King of France, justly called Charles " The Wise," (unless indeed " The Crafty " would have been a more correct designation,) having thus made the Prince of Wales his irreconcilable enemy, lost no opportunity or means of preparing secretly for

The King of France continues to try to blind the King of England;

the intended struggle. Even while raising troops and getting ready for war, he tried to blind the King of England to his intentions. With this view, on the one hand, he told the hostages who were in France on parole, not to hurry themselves to return to England, because war would soon relieve them from their promises; and on the other, he tried to convince the King of England of the warmth of his friendship, by sending him a present of fifty pipes of wine. But King Edward had now begun to

CHAP. VIII.   EDWARD PREPARES FOR WAR.   147

suspect his treachery, and, on April 26th, 1369,[1] he A.D. 1369.
sent the wine back to him.   It is worthy of mention
however, that, at the very time that he thus showed
his suspicion of France, he ordered that the French
hostages in England should not be molested.[2]

During the autumn of the previous year, King
Edward had been preparing for the possible outbreak
of hostilities.   Early in that year, at the end of
March, the return of the Prince of Wales to England
on account of his illness was seriously contemplated;[3]
but this measure was not carried into effect.   It was
not that any improvement in his health had taken
place, for his disease was getting worse and worse, but
a perception of the fatal results to English dominion,
which were sure to follow from so ill-omened a step,
that led to its abandonment.   The King of England
could not fail to see, that, although the King of
France still ostentatiously professed to be his friend,
he would ere long be his declared enemy, and that the
necessity of sending more troops to support his son
would soon arise.   Accordingly, in September 1368,[4] but
he had ordered ships to be in readiness for the con- Edward
veyance of soldiers to Aquitaine.   Still, it was not prepares
until the following year, that the King of France was for war.
ready to spring his mine on the King of England.
Early in that year, at the very time that he summoned
the Prince of Wales to appear before him in France,
Charles sent ambassadors, the Count of Saarbruck
and William de Dormans, Chancellor of Dauphiné
(made Chancellor of France in 1371) to treat with
Edward as to the difficulties between the two crowns.
This too was evidently an attempt to blind the King

[1] Rymer, vol. iii. p. 864.   [2] Ibid.
[3] Ibid. p. 845.   [4] Ibid. pp. 848, 849.

L 2

148 LIFE AND TIMES OF EDWARD III. Chap. VIII.

A.D. 1369. as to his real intentions. The ambassadors remained in England for two months, amusing Edward with pretended consultations, until the time arrived when Charles had satisfied himself that the inhabitants of Ponthieu and of Gascony were ready to support him, and that his troops were all prepared.[1] When this was ascertained, the ambassadors set out on their way back to France; and, by a most suspicious coincidence, were met at Dover, on the 29th of April, at the very moment of their embarkation, by a messenger from the King of France, declaring war against England. The man selected for this purpose by the King of France, in order to make the communication insulting as well as hostile, was a mere scullion.[2]

The King of France declares war against England, on April 29, 1369.

Though the suddenness of this step may have caused some surprise, the King could hardly have been without expectation of it. In fact, he had been making some preparations for war during the previous autumn, and early in the year he had taken more active measures, not only for the invasion of France by himself, but also against the possible invasion of his own kingdom by the French.

Even as early as January 23rd, 1369,[3] he had ordered ships to be got in readiness to resist "the malice of our enemies the French, already on the seas;" and on the 24th of the following month,[4] had directed that they should assemble, some at Southampton, others at Dartmouth, Weymouth and Plymouth. It was at the same time proposed that the

---

[1] Buchon's *Froissart*, vol. i. p. 564.

[2] "Un de ses varlets de cuisine."—Buchon's *Froissart*, vol. i. p. 564.

[3] Rymer, vol. iii. p. 858. [4] Ibid. p. 861.

CHAP. VIII. PREVIOUS PREPARATIONS. 149

King's son, the Earl of Cambridge, should go with the troops to Aquitaine; but it does not appear that he actually did so, until after the declaration of war.[1] Next month, Calais, the castles of Guines and other places in France, were manned and victualled;[2] and, on the 20th of March, even while the French ambassadors were still in England pretending to treat for peace, Edward had so little confidence in the pretences of France, that he ordered an array of all fighting men throughout the kingdom, in order to resist an apprehended invasion. On the 15th of April, bowmen from various parts of the kingdom were summoned to Southampton, so as to be ready to embark for Aquitaine; and, on the 3rd of May, were warned to be in readiness to obey the King's orders. On the 7th of the same month[3] sailors were to be taken, wherever they could be found, to man the ships; and, indeed, instructions to the same effect were continually repeated. About the same time, it was proclaimed that no man was to absent himself, or remove his goods or chattels, from Southampton, Hereford, Winchester, and Shrewsbury,[4] apparently to prevent those towns from being left without defenders; and corn, flesh, salt fish, and other victuals were bought for the provisioning even of the castles in North Wales.

The French, however, were beforehand with Edward; and no further proof is needed of the sagacity or cunning of the King of France, as his character may be designated according to the side from which his actions are regarded, than the fact, that on the very day that his messengers conveying the declaration

A.D. 1369.

Account of Edward's previous preparations for war.

The French beforehand with the English.

---

[1] Rymer, vol. iii. p. 862. [2] Ibid. p. 863.
[3] Ibid. p. 865. [4] Ibid. p. 866.

150   LIFE AND TIMES OF EDWARD III   Chap. VIII.

A.D. 1869. of war set foot in England, a body of French troops, commanded by Count Guy of St. Pol and Hugh of Châtillon, entered Ponthieu, and, within a week, wrested the whole of it from the English. There had been marauding expeditions for some time previously. The "Companies," as already stated, had left Aquitaine to pillage France in the previous year, nor had the French abstained very strictly from petty warfare, although Charles had forbidden his brother the Duke of Anjou, who was eager for war, to pass the frontier, and had written to the inhabitants of Montauban, who had made an attack on the English seneschal of Rouergue, that he intended to observe the treaty of Bretigni. These little incidents, however, were considered by neither side as a decided infraction of the treaty, or as a beginning of actual war. But now there was no longer any room for doubt. War was declared; the statements made long before by the Prince of Wales were verified; the tardy suspicions of the King of England were confirmed; the struggle was destined to begin, and there could be no doubt of its severity, nor of the spirit of hatred in which it would be conducted.

Charles's messenger delivers the declaration of war. .

When the messenger bringing the declaration of war arrived in London, so well instructed was he as to the way in which he should fulfil his mission in the most insulting manner, that he presented himself unceremoniously at the Palace of Westminster, where the Parliament was sitting, and said, that he was a "varlet" of the household of the King of France, that he was sent by him, and had brought letters addressed to the King of England. But, he added, he was ignorant of their contents, and that it did not behove him to know or say anything. When the

CHAP. VIII. CAPTURE OF PONTHIEU. 151

A.D. 1369.

King opened the letters sent him in so singular a fashion, he and all to whom they were read were amazed, and examined the seals carefully, to ascertain whether the letters were really genuine. Of this however they were soon convinced, and the messenger was quickly sent about his business without an answer.[1]

Parliament instantly proceeded to consider what course should be adopted; and, in the expectation that the county of Ponthieu and especially the town of Abbeville would be at once attacked, decided to lose no time in sending over a body of 300 men-at-arms and 1,000 bowmen for their defence. But, as already related, the French had anticipated these measures; and before the English troops had crossed the sea, news arrived of the conquest of the whole of Ponthieu. Edward's first impulse was to vent his anger on the hostages still in his hands; but a moment's reflexion showed him the cruelty of such a measure, and he contented himself with removing them to safer custody. The preparations for sending troops to France were continued, and the Earl of Hereford was appointed the King's lieutenant in Calais, Guines, and the neighbourhood.[2] He held this appointment for a very short time, as the King nominated his son the Duke of Lancaster to that office only a month afterwards, on the 12th June.[3] Bowmen were still the force on which the greatest reliance was placed; but cannon were now beginning to come into more common use. On the 28th of May orders were sent to dig out 1,200 stones "for our engines" and send them without delay to the

Parliament meets and agrees to send troops to France; but before they depart news arrives of capture of Ponthieu.

Edward's preparations for war are increased.

---

[1] Buchon's *Froissart*, vol. i. pp. 565, 566.
[2] Rymer, vol. iii. p. 866.   [3] Ibid. p. 871.

152   LIFE AND TIMES OF EDWARD III.   Chap. VIII.

A.D. 1369.

Tower of London;[1] but it is not certain that these were for cannons, and indeed, from their number, it is perhaps more probable that they were for *perrières* or stone-bows. The most important step was taken a few days afterwards. On the 3rd of June, Parliament with complete unanimity agreed with the King, that, "inasmuch as Charles, son of John, late King of France," had taken possession of various castles belonging to the English in Ponthieu, and had collected a fleet for the invasion of England, in contravention of the peace between Edward and John, the King of England should resume the title of King of England and France, just as he had it before the peace.[2] Edward immediately gave orders that a new seal should be made, and from that time till the latter part of the reign of George the Third, the kings of England continued to quarter their arms with those of France.

Edward resumes title of King of France on June 3rd, 1369.

Subsidy granted.

The next day, to enable the King to carry on the war, a subsidy for three years beginning at the following Michaelmas was granted. This was an export duty of 43s. 4d. on every sack of wool going out of the kingdom, the same on every dozen score of woolfells, and 4l. on every last of leather. These imposts were in addition to the ancient customs of half a mark on each of the above quantities levied from denizens, and of four marks (except the last of leather on which eight marks was to be levied) from strangers. Shortly afterwards, Edward seized the revenues of the Priories Alien in England, as another means of raising money for the war.[3] He then wrote, on the 19th of June, to his son, informing him that he

[1] Rymer, vol. iii. p. 868.
[2] Rymer, Rot. Parl. 43 Ed. III. m. 2.   [3] Ibid. vol. iii. p. 875.

CHAP. VIII. EXTENSION OF TRUCE WITH SCOTLAND. 153

had resumed the title of King of France; that he intended to make war on France to recover his rights to the crown; and he desired him to make known, that all who assisted him should have hereditary possession of all the lands, castles, cities, and other places, of which they made themselves masters.[1]

Both sides now began to cast about for alliances, and the first necessity of England was to take care that Scotland should not side with France. Scotland was then, as before, a sharp thorn in the side of England. No time, therefore, was lost in making peace with her ; and, on July 20th, 1369, the truce between the two countries was renewed for four-teen years.[2] But, nevertheless, only two years after-wards, on October 28th, 1371, Robert the Second, (son of Walter the High Steward of Scotland, and the first of the royal family of Stuart,) who on the death of his uncle David the Second in February 1371 had succeeded to the throne of Scotland, pre-suming on the gathering troubles of England, entered into a solemn treaty, offensive and defensive, with France. This, it is clear, was especially directed against England. Among other conditions it was provided that in the event of a disputed succession to the throne of Scotland, the King of France was not to interfere; but was to consider, as his ally, whom-soever the Scottish Parliament should choose as King, and, in case of need, defend him against the King of England. It was further agreed, that if the Pope should absolve either of the contracting Kings from his oath relative to this treaty, he should not avail himself of it.[3] The King of France also

A.D. 1369.

Edward extends the truce with Scotland,

---

[1] Rymer, vol. iii. p. 874.   [2] Ibid. p. 877.
[3] Ibid. p. 926.

154   LIFE AND TIMES OF EDWARD III.   CHAP. VIII.

A.D. 1369. proposed certain secret articles, by which he engaged
to invade England, and to persuade the Pope to
annul the treaty between England and Scotland; but
these do not seem to have been ratified by King
Robert.[1]

and tries in vain to make an alliance with Flanders, About the same time that King Edward entered
into the truce with Scotland, he sent (on the 12th of
June) ambassadors to Count Louis of Flanders, and
to the burgomasters of Bruges, Ghent, and Ypres, to
confirm their alliance with England.[2]   But the King
of France was endeavouring, at the same moment, to
attach Flanders to himself. For five years it had been
Edward's object to bring about an intimate connexion
with the Count of Flanders by marrying his son Edmund, Earl of Cambridge, to Margaret, the Count's
daughter and heiress of Flanders, and widow of the
late Duke of Burgundy. The Pope, however, who
was a creature of France, refused, on the ground of
consanguinity, to grant dispensation for this marriage. Nevertheless, disregarding similar grounds
of objection, he granted it for the marriage of Margaret with Philip Duke of Burgundy, brother of the
King of France, which was solemnised on June
19th, 1369.

The Count of Flanders thus became bound to
France; but his subjects knew the value of friendship with England, and the Flemings remained neutral. In the following year, on August 4th, 1370,
a treaty was concluded with them by Edward's
ambassadors, the object of which was, to provide for
the safe carrying on of commerce between the two
nations during the war. Among other conditions of

[1] Tytler's *Scotland*, vol. ii. p. 328.
[2] Rymer, vol. iii. p. 871.

CHAP. VIII.   EDWARD'S FOREIGN ALLIANCES.   155

this treaty, it was provided that, in order to avoid A.D. 1369.
hindrance and loss to the Flemings, no goods of the but secures
enemies of England, that is to say, of France or its neu-
Spain, should be carried in Flemish vessels; that trality.
care should be taken that the goods received into
the vessels really belonged to the parties to whom
they were consigned, and not to the enemy; and it
was also particularly ordained that the Flemings
should not convey any " armour, artillery, or victuals "
in their ships to the enemies of England.[1]

Edward succeeded in securing the friendship of the Other
Duke of Juliers and of his own nephew the Duke of alliances.
Gueldres, who agreed each to bring 1,000 lances to
the field, and were consequently to be " delivered "
for one year.[2] He was not equally successful with
Albert of Bavaria, who then governed Hainault, or
with the Duchess of Brabant, both of whom sided
with France.[3]

The fickle King of Navarre hesitated as to which
side he should take, and consequently bore no part in
the war. The King of Castile of course remained the
ally of France; but the King of Aragon was at least
neutral, for a treaty had been made between England and Aragon on January 10th, 1369, which,
although entirely one-sided, was based on the supposition of complete friendship between the two countries. In it, Edward and his son bound themselves
not to invade or molest Aragon; but the King of
Aragon promised no help in return. Long negotia-

---

[1] Rymer, vol. iii. p. 898.
[2] Buchon's *Froissart*, vol. i. p. 572, "roi d'Angleterre, qui
avoit envoyé devers eux qu'ils retinssent gens . . . et ils seroient
délivrés," &c.
[3] Ibid.

156   LIFE AND TIMES OF EDWARD III. CHAP. VIII.

A.D. 1369. tions, not concluded till February 6th 1371, took place between England and Genoa, which resulted in an agreement, that the Genoese should enter into no confederation against England with her enemies of France or Spain, nor should help them with mercenary troops.[1]

The French bishops preach against the English,

While the two Kings were thus strengthening their hands by human means, they did not neglect to call in spiritual aid. The King of France, having great influence over the Pope although he had left France in 1367, had found no difficulty in nominating priests devoted to his interests in the provinces yielded to the English, who were therefore ready to maintain his cause. Thus the Archbishop of Toulouse went preaching over the country, and turned away more than sixty cities and castles from their English allegiance. In like manner, the priests in Picardy made use of their pulpits to beat up recruits for the King of France, and the King himself, accompanied by his Queen, headed barefooted processions of the clergy, who went about supplicating God to have mercy on the kingdom.

and the English bishops preach against the French.

The King of England was not to be outdone by the King of France in making use of spiritual weapons; and the Bishop of London thundered from his pulpit on the justice of war with France.[2]

[1] Rymer, vol. iii. p. 910.
[2] Tyrrell's *England*, vol. iii. p. 690.

CHAP. IX.   WAR BEGINS.   157

CHAPTER IX.

RENEWAL OF THE FRENCH WAR, AND END OF THE BLACK PRINCE'S RULE IN AQUITAINE.

WAR began in earnest immediately on its declara- A.D. 1369. tion. On the part of the French, as already related, the first step was the seizure of Ponthieu; but, simultaneously with this, the Duke of Berri, who had returned from England on parole in 1367,[1] collected together considerable forces in Auvergne, and the Duke of Anjou did the same in Languedoc. But the frontiers of Poitou and Aquitaine were too well guarded by English troops, for the French Dukes to undertake any great operations. On the part of the English, Edward had gathered together a body of soldiers for the support of his son, the command of which was given to the Earls of Cambridge and Pembroke. Brittany was selected as the most con- War venient part of France for their landing; it was begins. therefore necessary to ask the consent of the Duke, for the passage of the troops through his duchy. He was so intimate an ally of England that there Earls of was no difficulty in obtaining it. On the landing Cambridge and Pem- of the soldiers at St. Malo he sent to meet them, broke got received them hospitably, and, with the consent of the barons and knights of his duchy, granted them leave to go through Brittany into Poitou. While

---

[1] Froissart, vol. i. p. 562, note.

158   LIFE AND TIMES OF EDWARD III.   CHAP. IX.

A.D. 1369.

the English were at St. Malo, they treated with the "Companies" who were at Chateau Gontier and Vire in Maine, and, with the consent of the Duke of Brittany, arranged that they should cross the Loire and meet them at Nantes.[1] The old leaders of the Prince's armies also came forward to take their respective commands.

It has been already related, how that noble warrior John of Chandos had answered to the Prince's call, when Rouergue was attacked, and had taken up his head-quarters at Montauban. The Captal de Buch also came; and Sir Hugh Calverley hastened from Spain, as soon as he heard that the French were about to make war on the Prince, and joined him at Angoulême, where he waited till the "Companies" had arrived from Normandy. The Prince put Calverley at their head; and the forces under his command, amounting to about 2,000 men, marched to attack the Count of Armagnac and the Lord of Albret.[2]

The English troops gather together at Angoulême.

When the Earls of Cambridge and Pembroke, with their English troops, had joined the "Companies" at Nantes, they also marched to Angoulême, and their united forces numbered about 3,000 men. By the Prince's orders they entered Perigord, and overran it; after which, they laid siege to the castle of Bourdeille on the Drome, which they took after nine weeks' operations. They then returned to Angoulême.[3] After this the Prince sent them and Chandos, who had returned to Angoulême from Rouergue, to attack Roche-sur-Yon in Poitou, which surrendered after a month's siege. The conquerors then again returned to Angoulême.[4]

They ravage Perigord and Poitou.

Shortly after this, James Audley, who had been

---

[1] Froissart, vol. i. p. 568.   [2] Ibid. p. 568.
[3] Ibid. p. 582.   [4] Ibid. p. 586.

CHAP. IX.　　CHANDOS AND PEMBROKE.　　159

appointed seneschal of Poitou, retired from his command, and John of Chandos succeeded him. Chandos was not a man to remain long idle, and he accordingly planned a foray into Anjou, in which he invited the Earl of Pembroke, who was then at Mortagne-sur-mer, to join him. Pembroke, however, weakly yielded to the advice of his companions, who persuaded him that Chandos would reap all the honour of the campaign, and that it was beneath his dignity to serve under him. He, therefore, refused, and Chandos set out without him.[1] After some successes in Anjou and Poitou, hearing that the Marshal of France, Louis de Sancerre, was at La Haye in Touraine, Chandos proposed to attack him, and again sent to the Earl of Pembroke, who was still at Mortagne, to join him in the expedition. The Earl again declined, and Chandos was obliged to disband his troops and return to Poitiers.

No sooner did Pembroke hear of Chandos having given up the expedition than, inspired with the vain desire of reaping all the glory for himself, he marched through Poitou into Touraine. The French, however, who were in garrisons on the borders of Poitou, Touraine, and Anjou, looked on Pembroke as a far less formidable enemy than Chandos, and determined to lie in wait for and attack him. The place they chose for their ambush was La Roche-Posay in Touraine, on the borders of Poitou. The English, having made a successful foray in Touraine, were marching back into Poitou, laden with booty and utterly unsuspecting the presence of an enemy. They halted at Puirenon, a village near La Roche-Posay, and while preparing for their mid-day meal, were

A.D. 1369.

Chandos appointed seneschal of Poitou in place of Audley.

Pembroke refuses to join Chandos in an expedition.

and endeavours to carry it out himself,

[1] Froissart, pp. 588, 589.

160 LIFE AND TIMES OF EDWARD III. Chap. IX.

A.D. 1369.

but is surprised by theFrench,

and appeals to Chandos for help.

Chandos at first refuses,

but afterwards marches to relieve Pembroke.

attacked by Sancerre. After hard fighting, they were enabled to secure themselves within the village for the night; but the French made certain of compelling them to surrender in the morning. During the night, however, Pembroke was glad to ask Chandos to render him, in his need, that assistance which he had refused to Chandos. Profiting by a foggy night, he managed to get a messenger out of the village without being seen by the French sentinels, and sent him off to Poitiers to beg that Chandos would come to help him. The night was dark, the messenger lost his way, and it was daylight before he could make out the road to Poitiers. It was late before he could communicate with Chandos, for Chandos was hearing mass when he arrived, and was in no humour to put himself out of his way to listen to anyone coming from Pembroke. The only answer he vouchsafed was, "We could hardly get there in time;" and he sat down to dine. In the meantime, the French had resumed their attack on Puirenon; but the English, hoping every moment that the expected help would arrive, held out bravely, and kept the French at bay. At last, after some hours of hard fighting, Pembroke began to fear he could not hold out much longer; he therefore sent another messenger, mounted on his fleetest horse, to entreat Chandos to hasten to his help, and gave him his ring, as a token of his need and sign of authority. The man found Chandos at dinner, and again the answer was "it is now too late;" but suddenly his generous feelings overcame his anger, and calling his companions to horse, Chandos set out with 200 lances to relieve the Earl. The French were informed of his coming, and dared not wait

CHAP. IX.   PROPOSED INVASION OF ENGLAND.   161

for him; they retreated without delay. The Eng- A.D. 1369.
lish then felt sure that help was on its way, and,
having now no enemy to stop them, marched out to
meet Chandos, some on foot, some on horseback, and
some mounted two on one horse. They had not proceeded far before they met him, and told him how the
French had decamped the moment they heard he was
coming. Chandos then marched back to Poitiers, and
Pembroke to Mortagne.

While fighting, now here now there, was thus
going on in a desultory way in Aquitaine, and the
English troops were no longer massed together and
led as formerly by the gallant Prince, the King of
France, believing that the English had enough to do
to hold their own in the South, was carefully planning a bolder course in the North. This was no less
than the invasion of England itself.

All the summer he had been collecting ships at The King
Harfleur, and gathering soldiers together to such an of France prepares to
extent that, as Froissart says, "it rained down" men. England.
His brother, Philip Duke of Burgundy, was appointed to command the invasion; the King himself
abode at Rouen, in order to be near the fleet, and
every now and then went to Harfleur to look after
the preparations.

The proposed invasion could not be kept secret
from the King of England. Edward therefore, on
becoming acquainted with his danger, roused the
whole country and fortified his seaports against the
attacks of the French, although, as will be seen,
with less speed than was needful. On the 26th
of October, in accordance with the well devised
custom, he summoned a kind of special Parliament,
sending to all the ports and commanding them

VOL. II.   M

162   LIFE AND TIMES OF EDWARD III.   Chap. IX.

A.D. 1369. each to select two persons well informed respecting shipping, merchants, and merchandise. They were ordered to appear before him at Westminster, on the 18th of November, to advise on the best measures to be adopted "in consequence of the French having collected numerous ships and men for the destruction of the English shipping and trade."[1] In addition to these preparations for the defence of England, Edward determined on making a diversion by sending his son, John of Gaunt, Duke of Lancaster, to invade France.

Edward sends Lancaster to invade France.

While these preparations were in progress, a grievous calamity befell England, in the death of Queen Philippa, who expired on August 15th, 1369.

The Duke landed at Calais about the middle of August with 600 men-at-arms and 1,500 bowmen, and was quickly joined by Robert of Namur at the head of another body of troops. They began at once to ravage the country, and after each foray carried their plunder to Calais. When the King of France heard of the Duke's landing and harrying the country, he began to think he had better fight the English on his own side of the water, instead of seeking them across the sea. The invasion of England was therefore suddenly given up; a small number of vessels however were sent to attack and burn Portsmouth in September,[2] and this was accomplished before sufficient preparations had been made for its defence.

The invasion of England given up.

The English were encamped in a strong position at Terouanne, and the Duke of Burgundy was ordered to lead his army to attack them. It was not long

---

[1] Rymer, vol. iii. p. 880.   [2] Ibid.

CHAP. IX.   THE FRENCH ARMY BROKEN UP.   163

before the French army was posted face to face against the English, whom it outnumbered many times over, but yet, notwithstanding this superiority, the Duke made no attack. Skirmishes between small bodies of each army were constantly taking place. One morning the French penetrated into the English camp, and were driven back only by the ready courage of Sir Robert of Namur. But still, neither one side nor the other was inclined to begin a general battle. There was no reason why the English should do so; they were strongly posted, well supplied with food, in free communication with Calais, and were quite ready to receive an attack. To the French, a battle seemed to offer every advantage; but the Duke of Burgundy was bound to wait for the orders of his brother the King, and such orders, notwithstanding perpetual requests from the Duke, the King, most unaccountably, never gave. At last the Duke told his brother that he thought he had better disband his army if he was not allowed to fight. To this the King agreed, and at midnight on the 12th of September the whole army broke up, first lighting their fires to deceive the English.

When the sentinel who was guarding the tent of Sir Robert saw the fires blaze up, one after another, he thought the French were preparing an attack, and sent at once to awaken him. Sir Robert rose instantly, and commanded his soldiers to put on their arms and set themselves in order. The Duke of Lancaster did the same, and all the army, in the darkness of night, for no fires were lit in the English camp, was silently ranged in battle-array, the bowmen being placed where the Duke thought the French would make their attack. For two hours

A D. 1369.

Lancaster and the Duke of Burgundy encamped face to face,

but the French retreat without fighting.

The English are deceived, and do not know of their retreat till too late.

M 2

164   LIFE AND TIMES OF EDWARD III.   CHAP. IX.

A.D. 1369. they waited, but not a man advanced from the French camp. At length, the Duke called a council together, and Sir Walter de Maunay advised that the army should advance little by little, feeling their way, for he said "it will soon be day." One recommended one thing and another another; and at last, it was decided to send thirty horsemen towards the French camp, to ascertain what was going on. When they had set out, De Maunay said to the Duke, "Sire! sire! never believe me again if the French have not fled. Mount and follow them, and you will have a good day." The Duke could not believe that the French would take such a dastardly course, and answered that he would wait the return of his messengers. While they were speaking, the messengers came back, and confirmed De Maunay's

Lancaster returns to Calais. opinion; but it was then too late, so the Duke and his soldiers supped and lodged for one night in the French camp, and then returned to Calais.

After remaining a few days at Calais to recruit his troops, Lancaster again took the field with the

Lancaster ravages the north of France, and then returns to England. intention of destroying the French fleet at Harfleur. He ravaged Artois, Picardy, and Ponthieu on his route, but finding Harfleur too well defended, went back to Calais. Shortly afterwards, about the middle of November, he dismissed his foreign troops and embarked for England, promising to return next year in great force.

Winter was now coming on, and there was but little more fighting till the following year. Before

Death of Chandos. its opening, the Prince of Wales suffered an irreparable loss, in the death of his dear old friend, the gallant, joyous, John of Chandos. Chandos had been appointed seneschal of Poitou on the retire-

Chap. IX.   THE LAST EXPLOIT OF CHANDOS.   165

ment of James Audley,[1] and had been greatly vexed at the capture, a few months previously, of the Abbey of St. Savin. It was about ten leagues from Poitiers, and was taken by Louis de St. Julien and Kerauloet "the Breton," who had afterwards put the fortifications in a complete state for defence.[2] Chandos was determined to retake it, and on the night of the 30th of December set out with that intention, accompanied by Guichard d'Angle and about 300 lances. They took scaling ladders with them, but none except the leaders knew what was the object of the expedition. About midnight they arrived at St. Savin, when they were informed that Chandos' object was to regain possession of the Abbey. They then dismounted, each knight gave his horse to his squire, and got into the ditch, when suddenly the sound of a horn was heard. A small body of French, under Kerauloet, had arrived just at that moment from La Roche Posay, and summoned the warder to let them in, as they wished to persuade St. Julien and some of his garrison to go with them on a foray. Chandos, thinking he had been discovered, and greatly disappointed, retired to Chauvigny, on the Creuse, about two leagues off.

A.D. 1369.

He attempts to retake St. Savin,

but gives up the plan, and retires to Chauvigny.

On his arrival, he dismissed the greater part of his men. He then went into a house, and ordered a fire to be lit, for it was very cold. Sir Thomas Percy, who had remained with him with about 100 lances, asked him whether he intended to stay at Chauvigny. "Why do you ask?" said Chandos. "Because," said Percy, "if you do not intend to march, I beg you to

He allows part of his troops to depart.

[1] James Audley did not die, as stated by Froissart, till 1386. (See Barnes, p. 440.)

[2] Buchon's *Froissart*, vol. i. p. 596.

166   LIFE AND TIMES OF EDWARD III.   Chap. IX.

A.D. 1369.

let me, to see if I cannot meet with some adventure." "Go, in the name of God!" said Chandos, and Percy set off with about thirty lances. He crossed the bridge over the river Vienne, at Chauvigny, and took a circuitous road to Poitiers.

Chandos was greatly out of spirits, and went into the kitchen to warm himself and chat with his companions. After a time he was preparing to go to sleep, and asked whether it was near daybreak; but at this moment a man entered, saying, "My Lord, the French are marching." "How do you know it?"

The French pass by.

said Chandos. "I came from St. Savin with them." "Which way are they going?" "Towards Poitiers, I think." "Who are these Frenchmen?" "Louis de St. Julien and Kerauloet 'the Breton.'" "Never mind,"

Chandos at first refuses to attack them,

said Chandos, "I have no wish to march to-day; they will find some one to fight them without me." But the gallant old knight, though oppressed with unwonted gloom, could not bear such idleness, and presently exclaimed, "Notwithstanding what I have said, it is good that I should keep marching; I must get back to Poitiers; it will soon be day." So he buckled on his armour and set forth on his way to Poitiers, taking the direct road by the side of the river.

but at length pursues them.

He saw the hoof-marks of horses, and concluded that either Sir Thomas Percy, or the French, were before him. It was now about daybreak; and Percy and the French, who were indeed both in advance though Percy was on the other side of the water, caught sight of each other, when they were about a league from the bridge of Lussac, a town on the river Vienne. Both now hastened on at their utmost speed to gain possession of the bridge. Percy and his men arrived first, and, remaining on the same side by which they

CHAP. IX.   DEATH OF CHANDOS.   . 167

had come, dismounted from their horses to guard it. A.D. 1369.
When the French arrived, they also dismounted, and
prepared to attack the English, whom they greatly outnumbered.   The boys who were holding the Frenchmen's horses now saw Chandos coming, and seized
with sudden fright, shouted out "Here is Chandos!
let us save ourselves;" then, mounting their masters'
horses, they fled with utmost speed.   Chandos now
approached the French and began to defy them, telling
them he was Chandos, that he had long wished to fight
them, and they would now see which were the best
men.   The English were on the other side of the bridge,
which, being very high and steep, prevented them from
seeing Chandos, and advancing to his support.   One He attacks
of the Frenchmen now rushed at an English knight, the French,
and struck him to the ground, whereupon Chandos
called out, "How! will you let this man be killed
thus? To foot! To foot!" and they all dismounted.
Chandos wore, under his armour, a long dress of
white samite, which reached to the ground.   The
grass was slippery with a frosty dew; he got entangled in his long robes; his feet slid from under
him, and he stumbled.   He had lost an eye, five
years before, while hunting a stag in the Landes,
near Bordeaux, and therefore did not see a knight
approaching him on his blind side.   This man, profiting by Chandos' helpless position, attacked him before he could recover himself, and struck him on the
forehead with his sword, inflicting a severe wound. and is
Chandos wore no vizor, and the blow was mortal, killed.
though not at the moment; but it deprived him of
his senses, he fell, and the French and English fought
for his body.   Sir Thomas Percy, being on the other
side of the river, neither saw nor heard anything of

168   . LIFE AND TIMES OF EDWARD III.   CHAP. IX.

A.D. 1369. the fighting, and, concluding that the French had retreated, pursued his way to Poitiers.

Chandos' party were greatly outnumbered by the
French, and after hard fighting were obliged to yield
and give themselves up as prisoners; but neither
they nor their captors had horses, as the boys who
held them had galloped off with them all.

The French, unable to carry off their prisoners, There was no fortress within several leagues, they
were exhausted by hard fighting, and were thus in
the singular position, the one of gaining a victory
without being able to profit by it, and the other of
suffering defeat without being in a much worse condition than their conquerors.

The French disarmed two of the Breton soldiers
to enable them to walk, and then sent them to scour
the country to find the horses; but in the meantime
Guichard d'Angle and other Poitevin knights friendly
to the English, who were roaming about seeking for
adventures, came up. When the French saw them
approaching, they knew by their banners that they
were their enemies, and, choosing rather to be in
are made prisoners them-selves. the hands of Chandos' party than in those of their
new assailants, gave themselves up as prisoners to
the men who, the minute before, had been their own
prisoners.

When the Poitevins were told of the mortal wounds
of Chandos, their grief knew no bounds; they wrung
their hands, they tore their hair, and uttered cries of
deepest anguish. They did not however forget that
loud lamentation would not recall to life their trusted
and beloved leader, but gently took off his armour,
laid him softly on their shields, and thus, with
mournful steps, carried him to Mortemer, the nearest
fortress. After one day and night, on January 2nd,
1370, Chandos died; and thus, struck down in a

CHAP. IX. GASCONS RELIEVED FROM HEARTH-TAX 169

chance mêlée, ended the life of as gallant and true-hearted a knight as ever put on armour. *A.D. 1369.*

During all this time the French undertook no active operations; their armies were paralysed by the orders of Charles, called the Wise, who commanded that they should not fight, at the very moment that fighting would, probably, have given them important victories. He had thus prevented the French from attacking the Duke of Lancaster at Terouanne, and had disbanded the armies of the Dukes of Anjou and Berri, which he had destined to occupy Auvergne and Aquitaine, just when their activity might have been decisive.[1] The warfare was only a desultory one, carried on between the revolted barons of Aquitaine and the English, with varying but unimportant successes on either side; and thus at the end of 1369, although the English had lost Ponthieu, they had suffered but little other loss of territory. *No great battles, because the French are ordered to avoid them.*

The English power was however greatly weakened; disaffection was widely spread; the illness of the Black Prince, which prevented him taking the field in person, deprived the armies of a leader who had never been beaten, and whose very name was a tower of strength, and there was no longer the gallant Chandos to take his place.

Two months previously, the King of England had taken an unwise step, which could hardly fail to injure the cause of his son in Aquitaine. On the 5th of November, he ordered him to desist from levying the hearth-tax, and even to restore the money to those who had paid; and he offered a pardon to all who had revolted, provided they returned to their obedience within one month. It is difficult to imagine what can have induced Edward to take this course. *Edward orders his son to give up the hearth-tax, in the vain hope of conciliating the Gascons.*

---

[1] Sismondi, vol. ii. pp. 116, 126.

170 LIFE AND TIMES OF EDWARD III. CHAP. IX.

A.D. 1369. Had he supported Chandos in his opposition to the tax when it was first proposed, he would have acted judiciously; but it was now too late, and, so open a withdrawal of confidence from his son could only weaken his authority without attaining the desired end. The Duke of Lancaster was a witness to the order, and may. have prompted it. The King had lost the counsel of his noble wife, who had always loved her first-born son, and it is not improbable that the Duke of Lancaster was, as subsequent events tend to show, actuated by a jealous wish to supplant his dying brother. A few months afterwards, on July 1st, 1370,[1] his father sent him to Aquitaine with powers which, although granted nominally to enable him to assist his brother, seemed almost intended to supersede him. Be the cause of this proceeding, however, what it may, it utterly failed of its intended effect. Not a man availed himself of the offer of pardon, but more and more Frenchmen daily turned away from the Prince of Wales to serve the King of France.[2]

A.D. 1370.

The year opens with desultory warfare;

The new year (1370) opened with as varying success as before. Sir Thomas Percy had been appointed seneschal of Poitou on the death of Chandos; but before he had received the acknowledgments of the whole province, the French took Châtelherault. On the other hand, the Duke of Bourbon advanced into the Bourbonnais, to lay siege to Belleperche, and deliver his mother, the Dowager Duchess of Bourbon, who was a prisoner to the English in her own castle. The Earls of Cambridge and Pembroke, and Eustace d'Aubrecicourt marched to its relief, and, so strict were the orders of the King of France to his generals to avoid any risk, (the French, according to Froissart,[3] never attacking the English, unless they were three

[1] Rymer, vol. iii. p. 894.   [2] Ibid.   [3] Vol. i. p. 608.

CHAP. IX. FRENCH PREPARE TO RENEW THE WAR. 171

to one,) that they entered the castle without being **A.D. 1370.** attacked by Bourbon. Although their forces were far inferior in numbers to the French, they carried off the Duchess under the very eyes of her son. She was soon afterwards exchanged and set at liberty. The English then evacuated Belleperche, which was taken possession of by the Duke of Bourbon; the Earl of Cambridge went to his brother, the Prince, at Angoulême; the Earl of Pembroke to Mortagne, and Sir Robert Knolles to his castle of Derval in Brittany, from whence, however, he was soon called to England by the King.[1]

The year was not far advanced, however, before *but the King of France* the King of France began to take more active *France* measures for carrying on the war. At the end of *soon begins* the previous year, in December, the Parliament of *great pre-* Paris had had the effrontery to pass a sentence of con- *parations.* fiscation on the Duchy of Aquitaine, on the ground that the Prince of Wales had not appeared in Paris to answer the citation of the King of France, although the sovereignty over Aquitaine was most distinctly given up by the treaty of Bretigni. Charles lost no time after this act in asking for a subsidy, which was instantly granted, with a liberality which showed the national desire for war.

In the following spring the King of France made ready for action. Towards April, he summoned his three brothers, the Dukes of Anjou, Berri, and Burgundy, to Paris, to hold a council of war. It was *He sets on* settled that two great armies should march into *foot two great* Aquitaine, one, commanded by the Duke of Anjou, *armies,* entering Guienne by La Réole and Bergerac; the other, commanded by the Duke of Berri, attacking Querci and Limoges; and that then these two armies

[1] Buchon's *Froissart*, vol. i. p. 608.

172   LIFE AND TIMES OF EDWARD III.   CHAP. IX.

A.D. 1370. and an army of reserve. should unite before Angoulême and besiege the Prince of Wales.[1] The Duke of Burgundy was to command the army of reserve. It was also resolved to send to Spain for Du Guesclin, who was then in the service of the King of Aragon. On receiving this summons from the King of France, Du Guesclin immediately gave up his Spanish command, and joined the Duke of Anjou at Toulouse in July.

The Prince of Wales also makes ready. The English on their side were not idle. The Prince of Wales, to whom danger gave a temporary strength, roused himself, and declared that his enemies should find him neither in town nor castle, but that he would take the field against them, and he issued orders to his subjects and vassals to meet him at Cognac. The King of England supported him by sending the Duke of Lancaster to Bordeaux, in July, with 400 men-at-arms, and as many archers; and the Prince received him with perfect cordiality, notwithstanding the slight that had been put on him

His forces gather together at Cognac. both by his father and by the Duke. Lancaster marched at once towards Cognac, joining the Earl of Pembroke on his way; and a considerable army was soon collected under the banners of the Prince. Sir

Knolles ordered to Calais. Robert Knolles sailed at the same time for Calais, with orders to invade Picardy.

The French begin the campaign. As soon as Du Guesclin had joined the Duke of Anjou, the latter appointed him commander of his forces, and at once began the campaign. The French army consisted of 2,000 horse-lances, and 6,000 footsoldiers, armed with lances and shields. They marched

Anjou invades Agénois. towards the Agénois, and were joined on their route by 1,000 men belonging to the " Companies," who had long been waiting for them. Their success was marvellous. City after city fell, including even

---

[1] Buchon's *Froissart*, vol. i. p. 608.

CHAP. IX. THE FRENCH TAKE LIMOGES. 173

Aiguillon, which Sir Walter de Maunay had held against 100,000 men during the whole summer of 1346. The little town of La Linde, on the Dordogne, a league from Bergerac, was saved from capture by the activity of the Captal de Buch, who, having with the assistance of Sir Thomas Felton, fortified it strongly, placed it under the command of Sir Thomas de Batefol, and then proceeded to Bergerac. The town held out for some time; but the Duke of Anjou bribed Batefol to betray the castle, and all was arranged for the entry of the Duke the following morning. Fortunately, however, information of the intended treachery reached Bergerac that evening, and the Captal and Felton set off about midnight for La Linde. They reached it at daybreak; entered the town, and marched straight through to the opposite gate, through which the French, as they had learned, were to enter. The French were ready to come in, and Batefol was waiting for them. When the Captal arrived, he accused him of his treachery, struck him dead, and the French at once retreated. There was, however, on the part of the garrison of the town, either great disaffection from the English, or the latter were ill prepared to pursue the French, and Du Guesclin, consequently, marched off triumphantly, and without opposition, to within five leagues of Bordeaux.

While these events were going on, the Duke of Berri had entered the Limousin with 1,200 lances and 3,000 foot-soldiers, and laid siege to Limoges, where he was joined by the Duke of Anjou and Du Guesclin, who marched there after their retreat from La Linde. Limoges was soon given up to the French through the treachery of the bishop, who was the governor of the city. Du Guesclin remained with about 200 lances in the Limousin, but the Dukes of Berri and

Side notes: A.D. 1370. They take Aiguillon, and approach Bordeaux. Berri takes Limoges.

174   LIFE AND TIMES OF EDWARD III.   CHAP. IX.

A.D. 1370. Bourbon returned to their own duchies; the rest of the leaders retired into their own countries, to defend them against Sir Robert Knolles.

Knolles' operations in the north of France. Knolles had landed at Calais about the middle of July; at the end of the month he set out, at the head of 1,500 lances and 4,000 Welsh archers, to ravage Artois, Picardy, and Champagne, sparing the cities which were willing to pay black mail for their safety, plundering and burning the others, but all the while continually watched by the French, who fell on any of his stragglers. He was unable to bring any large body of the enemy to a pitched battle. When the English arrived before Noyon, a singular incident occurred which is curiously illustrative of the manners of the times. Sir John Seton, a Scotch knight, one of a hundred lances who had entered into the pay of King Edward according to the terms of the treaty of August 24th, 1369,[1] rode to the barrier of the city, accompanied only by his page. He then dismounted, and telling the page not to move from the spot, entered the city sword in hand. He was soon surrounded by about a dozen knights, whom he addressed in the most courteous terms, saying that, as they did not deign to come out from their barriers, he had come in to prove his chivalry against theirs. He then fell upon them with his sword, killing several, while the people of the town, who had gathered round, looked on with delight at the courage of the Scot, and were restrained by the French knights from attacking him. At last his page came near the barrier and shouted out to him, in English, " Sire! it is time to be off! our people are going away!" He could not refrain from striking a few

---

[1] Froissart (p. 612) states that this was one of the conditions of the treaty, but it is not in the printed document. See Rymer, vol. iii. pp. 877, 878.

CHAP. IX.   SIR JOHN KNOLLES BEFORE PARIS.   175

more blows, and then, jumping on the horse behind
his page, and saying, "Adieu! adieu! gentlemen,
many thanks," galloped away unhurt.

On the 23rd of September,[1] Knolles appeared before
Paris itself. The King, who had 1,200 lances with
him in addition to the citizens, could see the smoke
of the villages burnt by the invaders from his palace,
the Hôtel St.-Pol, in the Faubourg St.-Antoine, but
he would not allow his troops to attack. The next
morning, Knolles, having no intention of assaulting
Paris itself, and being in command of an army whose
leaders were jealous of him, retired to Maine.

Charles, however, had become seriously alarmed by
the victorious career of Knolles, and had sent for Du
Guesclin from the Limousin. He arrived almost immediately after the departure of Knolles, and on the
20th of October Charles appointed him Constable of
France. Du Guesclin was not a man to remain long
inactive, and, accompanied by his former enemy,
Olivier de Clisson, at once set out in pursuit of Knolles.
As already stated, the leaders of Knolles' army submitted to him unwillingly. They looked on him as an
adventurer (which indeed he might well be termed,
as he had risen by commanding some of the "Companies"), and after leaving Paris, they broke out into
open insubordination. Sir John Menstreworth was
the leader of the malcontents, and, placing himself
at the head of about 200 lances, separated himself
from Knolles, whom he followed at the distance of a
day's march. When they had reached the frontiers of
Anjou, Knolles called on the English captains to join
him in giving battle to Du Guesclin, and at the same
time summoned Menstreworth to do the same. The
latter was about to comply, when he was surprised

_A.D. 1370._

He ravages
the coun-
try up to
gates of
Paris.

[1] Froissart, vol. i. p. 618.

176 LIFE AND TIMES OF EDWARD III. CHAP. IX.

A.D. 1370.

by Du Guesclin and utterly routed. This defeat discouraged Knolles, and he therefore dismissed his troops and retired to his castle of Derval in Brittany. Du Guesclin returned to Paris with his prisoners.

The Prince of Wales determines to retake Limoges, and is carried in a litter.

While Knolles was ravaging the North of France, the Prince of Wales had taken measures to avenge the fall of Limoges, and swore " by the soul of his father" that he would retake it. He was unable to ride on horseback, but was carried in a litter, at the head of 1,200 lances, 1,000 bowmen, and 3,000 foot-soldiers. He was accompanied by his brothers, the Duke of Lancaster and the Earl of Cambridge, by the Earl of Pembroke, Guichard d'Angle, and a large number of Gascon knights. The Captal de Buch and Sir Thomas Felton remained at Bergerac, to guard the frontiers against the French and the " Companies." The garrison of Limoges were well provided with cannons, and felt confident that they could prevent the city from being taken by assault; the Prince therefore, who well knew in what way the place was fortified, determined to take it by mining. For a month his miners were at work, the garrison vainly endeavouring to defeat their purpose by counter-mining; at last, at the end of October, the Prince was told that the mine was ready to be sprung whenever he pleased, and he consequently gave orders for the explosion of the gunpowder on the following day. At the appointed hour the train was sprung; a great breach was made in the walls; the soldiers entered and took the garrison entirely by surprise. A scene now ensued which casts indelible disgrace on the memory of the Black Prince. He was broken in health, and had been betrayed by those whom he had every right to trust; but these are no excuses for the savage cruelty of which he was now guilty, and which even Froissart

CHAP. IX.   FALL OF LIMOGES.   **177**

cannot defend.   The soldiers had orders to plunder
and murder, sparing neither man, woman, nor child.
"It was great pity;" says Froissart, "for men, women
and children threw themselves on their knees before
the Prince, crying, 'Mercy! mercy! gentle Sire!'
He would not listen to their cries; and," continues
Froissart, "there is no man so hard of heart that if
he had then been in the city of Limoges, and had
thought of God, he would not have wept tenderly
over the great mischief which was there; for more
than 3,000 persons, men, women and children, were
killed that day.   God have mercy on their souls! for
they were truly martyrs."[1]

This melancholy story of unresisted slaughter, is
relieved by the gallant courage of the three captains
of the city, John de Villemar, Hugh de la Roche, and
Roger de Beaufort. "We are all dead men;" they said,
"but we will sell our lives dearly as becomes knights."
Then said Villemar to De Beaufort, who had not been
dubbed a knight, "Roger, you must be knighted;"
but Roger answered, "Sire, I am not yet worthy,
but I thank you for your offer."   They gathered together about eighty men, planted themselves in one
of the squares in the city, with their backs against a

A.D. 1370.

Fall of
Limoges,
and brutal
massacre
of the in-
habitants.

---

[1] Buchon's *Froissart*, vol. i. p. 620.   An attempt has lately been
made by M. H. Ducourtieux, a French gentleman and a Limousin,
to disprove Froissart's story.   His generosity and impartiality cannot be doubted, and it would be a great satisfaction if this dark
stain on the memory of the Black Prince could be wiped out. But
it seems to me that all that is accomplished by M. Ducourtieux is,
to prove that the numbers of the killed are exaggerated.   The
statement that the Prince ordered the massacre is not disproved.
See *Bulletin de la Société archéologique et historique du Limousin*,
No. 3. t. xi., as quoted in the *United Service Magazine*, Sept.
1862.

VOL. II.   N

178 LIFE AND TIMES OF EDWARD III. CHAP. IX.

A.D. 1370. wall, and with banners displayed waited the attack of the English. The English soon came up and speedily conquered the gallant band; but the Duke of Lancaster and the Earls of Cambridge and Pembroke had each singled out one of the three captains, and was engaged in single combat with his opponent. At this moment the Black Prince arrived in his litter, and his savage rage was softened as he watched the gallant fight. No one interfered, and, says Froissart, "bad would it have been for them who had then advanced." At last the Frenchmen yielded. But still the work of destruction and pillage went on; the city was set on fire, till at last the fury of the Prince was satiated, and, carrying off his prisoners and plunder, he marched to Cognac and dismissed his troops, determining to fight no more that year.

The Prince refuses the terms of alliance with the King of Navarre. The Prince now was guilty of a ruinous error. His father had for months negotiated with the King of Navarre,[1] whose friendship was important to the English, on account of the ports he held in Normandy. With his characteristic duplicity, the latter had negotiated with the King of France at the same time that he was treating with the King of England, but had finally broken off with Charles, suspecting his good faith. He therefore went to England in August, 1370, to treat with Edward personally; on the 2nd of December[2] the two kings signed a treaty of alliance, which, however, required the consent of the Black Prince, as the cession of Limoges to the King of Navarre was one of the conditions. To this the Prince refused to consent,[3] and King

---

[1] Rymer, vol. iii. p. 879, Aug. 29, 1369. Ibid. p. 893, June 16, 1370.

[2] Ibid. pp. 899, 903, 904, 905.   [3] Ibid. p. 907.

CHAP. IX. PRINCE OF WALES RETURNS TO ENGLAND. 179

Edward was therefore compelled to write to the King of Navarre on January 22nd, 1371, to inform him of his son's refusal. The King of Navarre was thus thrown back into the hands of the King of France, and England lost a valuable ally.

A.D. 1370.

After the sacking of Limoges, the Black Prince proceeded to Cognac to join his wife, but was soon obliged, by his failing health, to return to his headquarters at Bordeaux. He so rapidly declined, that his surgeons advised his immediate removal to England. Before he was able to embark, another heavy calamity fell on him. His eldest son, Edward, was taken ill and died; and his own illness had so greatly increased, that he was obliged to hurry away, without waiting till his son was buried. He summoned the barons of Aquitaine, and told them he was forced to go away from them; he represented to them that he had governed them prosperously; and he begged them to obey his brother, the Duke of Lancaster, whom he appointed in his place. To this they agreed without hesitation, and swore fealty to him on the spot. Then, leaving his son to be buried by the Duke, and after an eight years' possession of sovereignty, nearly one-half of which was made miserable by illness and disappointment, he embarked at the beginning of January, 1371, with 500 soldiers, besides a body of archers, and set sail, accompanied by his wife, his remaining child Richard of Bordeaux, and the Earl of Pembroke. They landed at Plymouth, and, after visiting the King at Windsor, the Prince retired to his castle at Berkhamsted. So completely was his health broken, that, except for a short time in Parliament just before his death, he never again took any active part in public life.

He returns to Bordeaux.

Death of his eldest son. His own illness increases.

A.D. 1371.

He returns to England.

N 2

180 LIFE AND TIMES OF EDWARD III. CHAP. X.

CHAPTER X.

THE FIRST PARLIAMENTARY CONTEST, AND PREPARATIONS FOR THE DECISIVE STRUGGLE WITH FRANCE.

A.D. 1371.

The results of the campaign of 1370.

THE results of the campaign of 1370 were of no great importance. England had not lost much that she had held at the beginning of the year : some towns in the Agenois had been wrested from her ; Limoges had been taken, but recovered back ; and Knolles had overrun Picardy and the Isle of France up to the very gates of Paris, although he was subsequently defeated. But still no marked success had attended the arms of either England or France. Charles continued his vexatious but successful policy of avoiding great battles ; the English had now no great leader capable of devising a bold plan, which would compel a decisive measuring of England's strength against that of France. The death of Chandos was a great loss to the English. Had the Black Prince been in full vigour, he would have sorely missed his friend ; but, beaten down by sorrow and ill-health, he doubly felt the want of him ; and now, his own sickness and retirement to England seemed to put the finishing stroke to the misfortunes of the English in Aquitaine.

Edward prepares to renew the war, and sum-

King Edward had for some time seen that it would need all his might to retain his hold on France ; and, on January 8th, 1371, before the Black Prince re-

CHAP. X. EDWARD CONSULTS HIS PARLIAMENT. 181

turned to England, he had summoned a Parliament to meet on the 24th of February to consider the serious state of affairs. Before that day, on the 26th of January, he had ordered a fleet to collect at Lynn, in Norfolk, with the intention, apparently, of again attempting the preservation of Aquitaine. But, so determined had the French now become to harass England with constant warfare, that it was necessary to protect even the shores of England from attack, and, on the 3rd of February, Edward gave directions for the defence of the Isle of Wight against invasion.[1] On the 14th of the same month, about 8,000 sheaves of arrows, "made of good and dry wood," were ordered to be supplied by the 15th of June, preparatory doubtless to another invasion of France.[2]

A.D. 1371.

mons a Parliament.

"Edward, Prince of Aquitaine and Wales," was summoned to the Parliament which was about to meet.[3] On its assembling in the Painted Chamber in Westminster, the King's Chancellor, William of Wykeham, Bishop of Winchester, stated the reasons why it had been called together. He reminded the members, that the King had taken the title of King of France by the consent of the last Parliament, because the peace between them had been broken by his adversary. He then went on to say, that, as he now heard, the King's enemy was making greater preparations than ever; that he had raised a number of men sufficient to oust him from all his possessions beyond the seas; had so many galleys, flutes, lynes, and other ships with castles ready for sea, as seemed to him enough to destroy the whole English navy; and that

Bishop Wykeham states the reasons for requiring a subsidy.

---

[1] Rymer, vol. iii. p. 909.   [2] Ibid. p. 911.
[3] Parry's *Parliaments and Councils of England*, p. 131.

182   LIFE AND TIMES OF EDWARD III.   CHAP. X.

A.D. 1371.
———

he intended to invade England and destroy it. He therefore requested Parliament to advise him how his realm might be preserved and his fleet saved from the malice of his enemies.

A constitutional struggle now began, which had important effects towards the end of the reign, and which may fairly be considered the very first occasion on which the despotic authority of our kings was fairly grappled with. It would hardly be too much to say that, from this period, the modern political history of England begins. A feudal party, whose object was to maintain the power of the barons against that of the King and the Church, and to protest against the monopoly of the great posts of honour and profit in the State by the clergy, had now been formed. Of this party John of Gaunt was one of the principal leaders.[1] It had the support of Parliament, and contributed in no small degree to the increase of its power.

Subsidy granted.

Thorp chancellor instead of Wykeham.

Parliament had been adjourned to the 28th of March, in order to give full opportunity for the consideration of the King's demands. On its reassembling it granted a subsidy of 50,000l. to be levied from every parish at an average of 22s. 3d. from each. It was then once more adjourned, by Sir Robert Thorp, who had, on the 26th of March,[2] been made Chancellor in place of the Bishop of Winchester, in consequence of the general dissatisfaction which had begun to be felt, and which found a voice in the feudal party, at the appointment of ecclesiastics to great offices in the State. Wiclif, who was a close friend of John of Gaunt, wrote against this abuse. "Neither prelates nor doctors, priests nor deacons," said he, "should

---

[1] See Lowth's *Life of Wykeham*, pp. 60, &c.

[2] Foss's *Judges*, vol. iii. p. 526.

CHAP. X.   THE FIRST PARLIAMENTARY STRUGGLE.   183

hold secular offices;" and in another passage there is   A.D. 1371.
a manifest and bitter allusion to the late Chancellor
William of Wykeham, and his skill in architecture.
"Benefices," he said, "instead of being bestowed on
poor clerks, are heaped on a kitchen clerk, or one wise
in building castles, or in worldly business." The
popular feeling in this matter was expressed by Piers
Ploughman the poet.   He says:—

Some serven the King, and his selver tellen,
In the checkhere and the chauncelrie, chalengynge his dettes,
Of wardes and of wardmotes, wayves and strayes.[1]

The Earls, Barons, and Commons, at the first meet-   Petition
ing of this Parliament, had presented a petition   against
against the holding of political offices by ecclesiastics,   clergy
in which the Prelates, naturally, did not join. It stated   holding
that " the Government of the Kingdom had long been   secular
carried on by men of the Holy Church, who are not   offices.
justiciable (i.e. capable of being brought to justice)
in all cases, from which great mischiefs and damages
have come in times past, and more may happen in
times to come;" they therefore prayed, that "laymen
being able and sufficient, none others should be made
Chancellors, Barons of the Exchequer, or appointed
to other great offices of the State for the future."[2]
This petition produced an immediate effect, which
shows how grievous must have been the evil complained of, and how powerful Parliament had now
become. The day after Sir Robert Thorpe had taken
the place of the Bishop of Winchester, Sir Richard
le Scrope was appointed Treasurer in lieu of the
Bishop of Exeter.[3]

The movement however was premature, for the

[1] See Milman's *Latin Christianity*, vol. viii. p. 166.
[2] Rot. Parl. 45 Ed. III. m. 2. 15.
[3] Foss' *Judges*, vol. iv. p. 81.

184 LIFE AND TIMES OF EDWARD III. Chap. X.

A.D. 1371. ecclesiastics were still educated too much in advance of the laity in general for their services to be dispensed with;—after a few years, therefore, they were again appointed as chancellors, and continued to be so till the promotion of Sir Thomas More in 1530.[1]

Petition as to the state of the navy. Another petition was also presented, from which it appears that the navy was by no means in a satisfactory condition, and that Parliament was determined to lay the cause of its disgraceful state plainly before the King. It stated, that, in consequence of the franchises of many cities, ports and boroughs having been taken away, they were ruined and uninhabited, and the shipping nearly annihilated; and they further complained of the way in which vessels were seized for the King's use, long before they were wanted. They also alleged that merchants were so interfered with in their affairs by various ordinances of the King, that they had no employment for their ships, and consequently hauled them up on shore, where they left them to rot; and, that when the masters of the King's ships were ordered on any voyage, they took the masters and ablest men of other vessels, which were thus left without persons to manage them, so that many of them were lost, and their owners ruined.[2] The King promised that he would take advice of his Council how these evils might be remedied; but the crushing defeat of the English by the Spanish fleet in June of the following year shows that no effective remedy was provided.

Singular error in counting parishes. After the granting of the subsidy, it was discovered that a most singular and unaccountable mistake had been made in reckoning the number of parishes in

---

[1] See Hook's *Lives of the Archbishops of Canterbury*, vol. iv. p. 233.

[2] Rot. Parl. 45 Ed. III. m. 2. 31, 32.

CHAP. X.   ERROR IN NUMBERING THE PARISHES.   185

England, and it became necessary, therefore, to set A.D. 1371.
that right.   A Council[1] was accordingly held on the
8th of June, at which " it was shown that the grant
made to the King of 22s. 3d. from each parish would
not produce 50,000l., because there were not so many
parishes in the land as had been supposed, and this The first
they could see and know by the certificates of all the the Lay
Archbishops, Bishops, and Earls of all the land of Chancellor.
England, made and returned to Chancery by com-
mand of the King."   The payment from each parish
was therefore raised to 116s.[2]   It is difficult to understand how the parishes can have been set down
at about five times their actual number, but of the
fact there can be no doubt.   In this tax, all small
livings " which had never before been taxed," were
included;[3] and, in consequence of infringements of
the Statutes of Mortmain (which had been enacted in
the reign of Edward the First and renewed under
Edward the Third), all lands which had passed into
mortmain since the eighteenth year of Edward the
First were also taxed.[4]

It is remarkable that, notwithstanding these grants
of money, preparation of ships, and collecting of ar- Notwith-
rows, no great expedition was sent from England that the great
year to support the English in Aquitaine.   The King preparations, the
war not
¹ Parry (Parliaments and Councils of England, p. 132) states carried
that this was not a Council properly so called, which would have vigour by
no power to alter a tax, but a committee of the last Parliament. England;
(Cf. Hallam on this illegal proceeding.)
² Rot. Parl. 45 Ed. III. m. 1. 10, 11.
³ Walsingham, p. 313.
⁴ Hook's Lives, vol. iv. pp. 235, 236.   Lands in mortmain
were those belonging to corporations—chiefly ecclesiastical—and
held in perpetual succession, unalienable, and yielding no feudal
personal services, nor subject to forfeiture for crimes.   They were
therefore said to be in a dead hand (mort main).

186 LIFE AND TIMES OF EDWARD III. Chap. X.

A.D. 1371. was getting old; and his attention, it is to be feared, was too much occupied with Alice Perrers, a lady of the bedchamber of his late Queen, whose charms exercised a baneful influence over the rest of his life. Froissart gives, it is true, an account of a sea-fight off the coast of Brittany with the Flemings, in which the English were victorious; but it is very doubtful whether this fight took place in that or in the following year. It seems also that, whatever may be the date, it was rather a piratical seizure of twenty-five Flemish vessels laden with salt, than an engagement between the fleets of the two countries.[1] In any case, it was the only part which England herself took in the war during the whole of 1371.

Local warfare in France itself, however, never ceased. Those amongst the Barons of Aquitaine who were favourable to the English, and those who were their enemies, were so mixed together, that their quarrels never came to an end. As Froissart says, " So matters were thus woven together there, and the Lords and the Knights one against another; and there the strong trampled down the weak, and neither right nor law nor reason was meted out to any man, and the towns and the castles were interlaced one within the other, some English, some French, who ran and ransomed and pillaged one the other without ceasing."[2] It is difficult therefore, and hardly important, to un-

but did not cease in Aquitaine.

---

[1] See Nicholas' *British Navy*, vol. ii. p. 139, where good reasons are to be found for doubting the accuracy of Froissart's statements, in addition to which it may be remarked that it is improbable that there was any hostile encounter between the fleets of the two nations in 1371, as stated by Froissart, inasmuch as treaties of peace and for the regulation of trade between the two countries were concluded in April and May of that year. See Rymer, vol. iii. pp. 913, 914, 917, 920, 921.

[2] Vol. i. p. 629.

CHAP. X. CAPTURE OF MONTPAON CASTLE. 187

ravel the history and effect of every little skirmish or A.D. 1371.
to relate the attack on or fall of every fortress; but
still, a notice of the most important of these minor
battles is necessary to explain their general bearing
on the position of the English in France.

The first operation, after the winter, was the taking
of Montpaon, a castle between Perigueux and Bordeaux,[1] by the French, and its recovery by the
English. A body of 200 Bretons whom the Duke of
Anjou had sent to Perigueux, presuming doubtless
on the absence of the Black Prince, set out from that
town to seize this castle; they had no difficulty in
accomplishing this, as the governor, William de Mont
Paon, whose heart was more French than English, instantly surrendered. When the Duke of Lancaster
heard of this piece of treachery, he set out to retake the castle, at the head of 700 lances and 500
bowmen. He was accompanied by Guichard d'Angle,
the Captal de Buch, and a great many other Lords
of Gascony, Poitou, and Saintonge, besides Sir
Thomas Percy, Sir Thomas Felton, and other English leaders. That part of Aquitaine was better
provided with English soldiers than were some others,
but the force thus gathered together was very small,
and, although sufficient for its present purpose, quite
unequal to any great operations.

As soon as Mont Paon heard of the approach of
the Duke of Lancaster, he fled to Perigueux, knowing
that if the castle he had betrayed fell into the hands
of the English, he would be put to death for his
treachery. The siege began, and, during its progress,

The Duke of Lancaster retakes Montpaon.

Treachery of William de Mont Paon.

---

[1] Buchon (p. 626) appears unable to identify this place; but,
with due deference to so great an authority, I cannot doubt that
it is Monpont, near Mucidan, on the L'Isle, a tributary of the
Dordogne.

188   LIFE AND TIMES OF EDWARD III.   CHAP. X.

A.D. 1371. there occurred one of those incidents which, as before remarked, were so characteristic of the warfare of feudal times. Two Breton leaders, occupying a neighbouring town with some troops, heard that there was fighting going on, and were, as usual, anxious to take part in it. They felt, however, that they could not both leave their post, and, consequently, drew lots with straws for the privilege. The one who drew the longest marched off with great glee, and was received with equal delight by the garrison. Montpaon was well prepared to stand a siege, and it was not until after eleven weeks, occupied principally in filling up the ditches with wood and faggots, in order to enable the besiegers to batter the walls, that the Duke's soldiers were enabled to effect a breach and take the castle by assault.

Lancaster dismisses his troops and returns to Bordeaux. After the recovery of Montpaon, the Duke dismissed his soldiers and all the leaders, and he himself returned to Bordeaux. He remained here for the rest of the year, making love to Pedro's daughter, and in a state of inactivity which may be best accounted for by a want of military capacity. It is not improbable, however, that he may have had some difficulty in raising men and in providing money to pay them.

Continuance of desultory warfare. After Lancaster had dismissed his troops, which had been partly recruited from the "Companies," they spread themselves over the country, ravaging and pillaging. In this, they were encouraged by the Duke, but the partisans of the French were not behindhand in pursuing a like mode of carrying on the war. The garrison of Montcontour, a castle on the borders of Anjou and Poitou, four leagues from Thouars and six from Poitiers, and the garrisons of La Roche Posay and St. Savin, were all so constantly moving about, fighting and pillaging, that the

CHAP. X.   SIR THOMAS PERCY TAKES MONTCONTOUR.   189

Poitevin barons favourable to the English were scarce A.D. 1871. able to stir from their castles.[1]

At length the annoyance caused by these tribes of hornets issuing forth from their strongholds and worrying the country, became so great that Sir Thomas Percy, the seneschal of Poitou, resolved to Sir Thos. attack Montcontour, which was the most important Percy takes castle in the neighbourhood held by the French. He Montcon- accordingly gave orders for the assemblage of troops for this purpose, and there were soon gathered toge- ther at Poitiers a body of 500 lances and 2,000 foot soldiers, led on by both Gascon and English leaders, and in the month of September they marched upon Montcontour.   The besiegers brought " great en- gines," probably cannons and mangonels, with which they battered the castle by day and by night, and at last, after nine days' hard fighting, the garrison gave in, and all were slain except the two leaders and five or six men whom " the Companies took to mercy.[2]" Percy then garrisoned the town, in order to guard and then the frontiers against the French in Anjou and Maine, returns to and afterwards returned to Poitiers.

Sir John Devereux, the English seneschal of the Limousin, was equally on the alert in his department. Early in the year he entered Auvergne and took Usson, a town to the north of Brioude, which soon brought down Du Guesclin upon him.   As soon as Bertrand heard of these misadventures, he set off from Paris, Sir John accompanied by the Dukes of Berri and Bourbon and reux's the Count of Alençon, to recover the town of which operations they had lost possession.   They arrived at the end of Limousin, March or beginning of April,[3] but finding Usson was strongly defended, first took possession of some other

[1] Buchon's *Froissart*, vol. i. p. 628.
- Ibid. p. 680.   [3] Ibid. p. 680, n~

190   LIFE AND TIMES OF EDWARD III.   CHAP. X.

A.D. 1371. towns, in Rouergue and on the borders of the Limousin, which were likely to give it help, and then began the siege. Usson soon yielded, but on honourable terms, and the garrison were allowed to retire to St. Sévère in the Limousin. Du Guesclin then returned to France, and no other warlike operations of any magnitude took place during the year.

Pope Urban the Fifth died on December 19th, 1370, at Avignon, whither he had voluntarily returned on the 24th of the previous September, after three years' absence in Italy. He was a Frenchman by birth, and felt himself more at home in the centre of the great theatres of war than in his Holy City; moreover the spirit of liberty which pervaded the republics of Italy was very distasteful to him. His successor, Gregory the Eleventh, now endeavoured to bring about a peace, and in the month of November

The Pope tries to arrange a peace, but fails. sent two legates to England to effect that purpose.[1] The King of England could not refuse to open negotiations with this object,[2] but they naturally failed.[3] England was not yet sufficiently humiliated to make the requisite concessions, and France had not yet gained sufficiently great advantages over England to justify her in demanding hard conditions.

The English and French seek alliances. Both court that of Brittany. Each monarch now again endeavoured to strengthen his position by cementing his alliances, and both were anxious to secure the friendship of Brittany. Its position in reference to England, giving an easy access to France, made it of the greatest importance to Edward; and the Duke, who had married Edward's fourth daughter Mary, was of course well disposed to England. But a great portion of the nobles and the mass of the people sided with the French. The Con-

---

[1] Rymer, vol. iii. p. 929.   [2] Ibid. pp. 934, 935.
[3] Walsingham, p. 313.

CHAP. X. ENGLISH ALLIANCE WITH BRITTANY. 191

stable of France, Du Guesclin, was a Breton; so also A.D. 1371.
was Olivier de Clisson, who had formerly been on the
side of the English, but now, having changed sides
had become their bitterest foe, and had well earned
his name " The Butcher." Many of the great leaders
of the "Companies," such as "Kerauloet the Breton,"
and others, were also from Brittany; Breton soldiers
were among the bravest and savagest of these marauding bands, and their successes had redounded to
the popularity of their employer, the King of France.

For a quarter of a century and more, the Kings of
England and France had fought on opposite sides in
support of the rival claimants to the duchy, and now
the latter, in order to give an odour of sanctity to
the side which he had taken up, spared no effort
to induce the Pope to canonise, as a saint, the dead
claimant, Charles of Blois. Sixty witnesses testi-
fied to the purity of his life; a hundred and fifty
to the miracles he had performed; but the Pope had
no wish to embroil himself with England, and, consequently, purity and supernatural power were obliged
to wait for their due acknowledgment. The saint's
children were thus deprived of a holy foundation to
support their claims to the duchy.

The result of these intrigues of France was to
throw the Duke more completely into Edward's
hands. He began negotiations with him on November 4th, 1371.[1] The ambassador, Sir Robert England
Neville, was instructed to propose an alliance offen- her alli-
sive and defensive against France, one of the condi- ance with
tions being the delivery to Edward of a dozen seaports and castles, Morlaix, Brest, Hennebon, and
others, till the war was ended. Edward on his part
offered to make over the castles, towns, and lordships

[1] Rymer, vol. iii. p. 927.

192   LIFE AND TIMES OF EDWARD III.   CHAP. X.

A.D. 1372. of Chisec, Melle, and Civray, in Poitou, to the Duke, as a free gift.

Negotiations were continued till the summer of 1372, and at last, on the 19th of July, a solemn treaty of alliance was signed between Edward and the Duke, by which the Duke agreed heartily to support the English King in his war with France, but at the cost of Edward. Among other conditions, it was agreed, that if Edward went personally to France, the Duke should accompany him in person, with 1,000 men-at-arms, at the wages of 160 francs a year for each man, to be paid by England; but it was also agreed, that Edward should send 300 men-at-arms and 300 bowmen to Brittany, at his own cost till they landed, after which they were to be paid by the Duke. The King also granted to the Duke and his heirs the Earldom of Richmond, which the Duke of Lancaster resigned in his favour.[1]

England and France court the alliance of Scotland.

The friendship of Scotland was another prize for which both Kings strove. King David Bruce had died on the 22nd February, 1371. He was succeeded by his nephew Robert the Second, grandson of Robert the First, whose daughter Marjory married Walter the High Steward. Walter's family name, so far as he had one, was Alan, or rather Fitz Alan, as he was descended from Alan, son of Flahald, but, according to a Scotch custom, he was called by the name of his office;[2] and hence it was changed into Steward, or, as it was written after a time, Stewart, and subsequently Stuart, and thus arose the Stuart dynasty, which ultimately succeeded to the English crown. The King of France entered

[1] Rymer, vol. iii. pp. 935, 936, 943, 955.
[2] In like manner, in England the Marshalls, and in Ireland the Butlers, were so called from their office.

Chap. X. JOHN OF GAUNT MARRIES PEDRO'S DAUGHTER. 193

into a treaty with Robert on October 28th, 1371, but it did not interfere with that existing between England and Scotland.

A.D. 1372.

Spain was, again, the greatest source of misfortune to England, and help to of France. Don Pedro's two daughters, Constance and Isabella, who had been hostages to the Black Prince for the payment of Pedro's debts, had been allowed to return to their father notwithstanding his failure to perform any of his obligations. They were at this time at Bayonne, whither they had fled on the occasion of his death. The Duke of Lancaster was a widower, and Guichard d'Angle and the other Gascon Lords suggested to him that he should marry Constance, urging as one reason for his doing so, that he would thereby become King of Castile. "My Lord," they said, "you are marriageable, and we know of a great marriage, by which you or your heir will become King of Castile, and it is a great charity to comfort and advise young girls, and especially daughters of a King; take the eldest in marriage, we advise you." It did not require much persuasion to induce the Duke to act on this advice; Constance became his wife, and his brother the Earl of Cambridge married Isabella with great pomp and feasting. Soon afterwards the two brothers went to England with their wives.[1] The Duke im-

The Spanish alliance secured by France.

Marriage of Lancaster with Constance of Castile, and of Cambridge with her sister,

[1] Froissart does not mention that the Earl of Cambridge married Pedro's daughter Isabella, but, on the contrary, he states (p. 634, Buchon's ed.) that "it was supposed that Isabel, the younger sister, would marry the Earl of Cambridge on the Duke's return to England," and I cannot find that Froissart anywhere states that the marriage took place. He also says that "about Michaelmas" the Duke talked of returning to England. Walsingham, however (p. 313), says that "in the same year (1372)

VOL. II.   O

194 LIFE AND TIMES OF EDWARD III. Chap. X.

A.D. 1372. mediately assumed the title of King of Castile in right of his wife.[1]

The effect of this marriage and assumption of regal title was of course to make Henry of Trastamare, the actual King of Castile, more intimately allied than *throws Spain into the hands of France.* before to the King of France; he immediately confirmed the offensive and defensive alliance made with him on November 26th, 1369. The fatal effects were soon seen of thus making Henry a bitterer enemy of England than he had ever been, for it enabled the King of France to make use of the Spanish fleet.

Lancaster leaves Spain. That the Duke should leave Aquitaine at so critical a period seems to have been most unwise, but he managed to gain the consent of the nobles to his departure, by alleging that he wished to inform his father of the needs of the province. It is probable that his principal object in returning to England was to get the influence over Edward into his own hands. Before embarking he appointed the Captal de Buch, the Lord of Mucident, and the Lord of Esparre, governors of all the parts of Gascony which they held; he entrusted Poitou to Louis of Harcourt and the Lord of Parthenay, while Saintonge was placed under the protection of Geoffry of Argenton and William of Montendre.

the Duke of Lancaster and the Earl of Cambridge, his brother, returned to England with two sisters, daughters of Don Pedro, formerly King of Spain, whom they afterwards married." It is unlikely that the two brothers would take the two sisters to England before they had married them, and Froissart's account is too minute and precise to leave any doubt that Lancaster's marriage took place before his departure for England. On the other hand, Walsingham's statement that Cambridge married the other sister is sufficient evidence of the fact of the marriage, and it seems probable that both marriages took place at the same time, and before their departure from Spain. [1] Walsingham, p. 313.

CHAPTER XI.

THE DISASTROUS CAMPAIGN OF 1372.

THE year 1372 opened with evil prospects for England, but the result was worse than could have been anticipated. It began with the death of two well-known warriors, whose military worth as commanders, it is true, was not of the highest order; but England had need of all her bravery, and could ill spare the services of any long-tried soldier. The first was Sir Walter de Maunay, who came to England with Queen Philippa, and whose gallantry had distinguished him in many a well-fought field; the other was Humphry Bohun, Earl of Hereford, whose second daughter Mary married John of Gaunt's eldest son Henry of Bolingbroke, afterwards Henry IV.

Numerous consultations now took place between the King and his Council as to the best course to be adopted for the recovery of Aquitaine and the defence of the coast of England.[1] It was decided that two fleets should be got ready for the invasion of France; one by way of Calais to invade Picardy, the other for the conveyance of troops to Aquitaine, which were to land at Rochelle. Great preparations were accordingly made to carry these plans into execution. At the end of the previous year, December 21st,

A.D. 1372. English prospects unpromising.

Death of Sir Walter de Maunay and the Earl of Hereford.

English plans for continuing the war.

Buchon's *Froissart*, vol. i. p. 635.

196   LIFE AND TIMES OF EDWARD III.   CHAP. XI.

A.D. 1372.

Great naval preparations.

1371, it had been proclaimed, that, whereas certain merchants had sold ships to foreigners, whereby the enemies of England were greatly helped, no such sales, openly or privately, should take place for the future.[1] On the 7th of February orders were sent to William of Latimer, the Constable of Dover and guardian of the Cinque Ports, and to the King's officer, " serving the King at arms," in every port from Northumberland round the coast to Lancaster, to seize all ships above twenty tons burthen, and to take care that they were gathered together in the harbours inside the Isle of Wight by the 1st May, and ready for foreign service.[2] But it was necessary to man the ships, and, as the poor fellows endeavoured to escape impressment and continued to follow their vocations, of which fishing was the chief, stringent commands were sent to seize all sailors in the various ports without delay.[3] On the 30th of the same month, in consequence of an alarm that the French were about to invade England, orders were given for the defence of the coast of Kent; on the 8th of June, similar precautions were taken to guard the Isle of Wight;[4] and the usual orders were issued against persons absenting themselves from their dwellings or lands on and near the coast. So great indeed was the alarm, that on the 16th of June all abbots, priors, and other ecclesiastics between the ages of sixteen and sixty were directed to be under arms, and two days afterwards the whole male population between those ages was called out, and regulations were made as to lighting beacon fires.[5] In July similar instructions were given for the defence of Kent[6] and Devonshire.

[1] Rymer, vol. iii. p. 930.   [2] Ibid p. 933.   [3] Ibid. p. 938.
[4] Ibid. pp. 942, 944.   [5] Ibid. p. 947.   [6] Ibid. p. 952.

CHAP. XI. PREPARATIONS FOR WAR. 197

It was, however, not only by getting ready to re- A.D. 1372.
ceive the attack of his enemies, and to defend his own
kingdom, that Edward prepared himself for the serious
difficulties now crowding upon him. He continued
his endeavours to strengthen his alliances, and on
January 26th, 1372, secured the neutrality of the Edward
Genoese by granting them leave to trade freely with neutrality
England, and enter her harbours with their galleys, of the
cogs, tarics and other vessels. The Genoese were in Genoese,
the habit of making a trade of hiring out their men
and their ships to other nations for warlike purposes;
but, by this treaty, they were bound not to do anything of the kind, and were forbidden to carry the
merchandise or goods of the King's enemies in their
ships.[1] The friendship of the Flemings, so ardently
desired by both people, but which the Count of and the
Flanders, from an equal distrust of his own subjects of Flan-
and of France, so jealously withheld, was also of the ders.
utmost importance to England. After long negotiations, peace was proclaimed between her and Flanders on the 28th of March.[2]

The King of France was well informed of all the The pre-
English preparations, and fortified his castles in of France
Picardy against attack; but he was unable to invade
England, being deterred probably by the measures
taken for its defence. The friendship of the King
of Castile, Henry of Trastamare, whom Lancaster's
marriage had bound firmly and closely to France,
was of the greatest moment to Charles. The Spanish
fleet was formidable; to avail himself of its assistance in order to prevent the landing of the English, now became the leading object of the King of
France.

[1] Rymer, vol. iii. p. 931.   [2] Ibid. p. 938.

198 LIFE AND TIMES OF EDWARD III. Chap. XI.

A.D. 1372.

The English prepare to invade France by Rochelle.

In accordance with the decision of Edward and his Council, the invasion of France by way of Rochelle was taken in hand. The King held many conferences with Guichard d'Angle, whom he greatly loved, and whom he had invested with the order of the Garter in the place of Sir Walter de Maunay. Edward had great confidence in Guichard, and, by his advice, made his own son-in-law John, Earl of Pembroke, Lieu-

Pembroke appointed to the command.

tenant of Aquitaine on the 20th of April; [1] soon after which Pembroke set out for Southampton to join the fleet. In accordance too with his recommendations, no great number of men were embarked; Guichard said the Earl would find 4,000 or 5,000 lances in Poitou ready to fight for him for wages, but he recommended the King to send plenty of money to pay them. The bad policy of thus sending an insufficient force to overcome any opposition to the landing of the invaders, proved in its consequences most serious. The fleet was detained at Southampton by contrary winds for fifteen days, but at length set sail about the 10th of June.

The Spanish fleet lies in wait for the English.

Then were seen the disastrous effects of having made Spain the enemy of England. The King of France, to whom every movement of the English became known, hearing of the preparations for the invasion of France, sent to the King of Castile to ask him to send his fleet to defend Rochelle. The castle was in the hands of the English, and the town was also nominally in their possession, but the citizens were entirely disaffected to their rule. The Spanish Admiral, Ambrosio Bocanegra, lost no time in responding to the summons, and his fleet, consisting of " forty great niefs and thirteen barges, well provided

[1] Rymer, vol. iii. p. 941.

CHAP. XI. ENGLISH NAVAL DEFEAT OFF ROCHELLE. 199

and castellated, as the Spanish niefs are," was soon lying at anchor before the town, waiting for the English.

A.D. 1372.

On the 22nd of June, Pembroke and his fleet appeared in sight. They were inferior to the Spaniards both in the number of ships and men, and the Spanish fleet was well armed with cross-bows, cannons, and great bars of iron and lead to cast down from their lofty decks on the smaller vessels of the English. But the English, nothing daunted, prepared for battle, and fought so valiantly, that at nightfall, although they had lost two barges, the result was still undecided. Sir John Harpenden, the governor of Rochelle, endeavoured to persuade the citizens to arm and embark in aid of the English; but the Rochellois, who were always ill-disposed towards them, excused themselves, saying, that they were not sailors, and knew nothing about fighting on the sea, but that if it were on land, they would go willingly. Four Poitevin knights then gallantly volunteered to do what the citizens had refused; at break of day they embarked in four barges full of armed men, and joined Pembroke's fleet.

Sea-fight between the English and the Spaniards.

At high tide next morning, the Spaniards raised their anchors with a noisy flourish of trumpets; then, having the wind in their favour, their gigantic ships, which dwarfed those of their enemies, bore down on the English. As soon as they had come to close quarters, the Spaniards chained their vessels to those of the English, and cast down their bars of iron, great stones, and masses of lead, on the small vessels, which lay quite under them. The English fought valiantly, but at length the Earl of Pembroke and Guichard d'Angle were taken prisoners, their fleet was utterly

Total defeat of the English.

200 LIFE AND TIMES OF EDWARD III. CHAP. XI.

A.D. 1372. defeated, and the treasure vessel was sunk in the sea, with all the money it contained.

The Spaniards take their prisoners to Spain. The next day the Spaniards, carrying their prisoners with them, set sail for Spain amid great rejoicings, and with streamers, decorated with the arms of Castile, of such a length that they trailed along the sea. It was indeed a day of triumph for the Spaniards, for the English had suffered no such defeat during the whole reign of Edward III. The Spanish fleet was delayed by contrary winds, but, after beating about at sea for a month, it arrived safely at Santander in Biscay. The prisoners were taken into the Castle and loaded with chains, according to the customs of the Spaniards. As Froissart says: " Other courtesy the Spaniards know not, they are like the Germans."[1] They were, however, soon removed to Burgos to be delivered up to the King; and on their arrival, Henry, attended by a brilliant array of knights and squires, received them with great courtesy, and soon divided them among the various castles of Castile.

The Captal arrives at Rochelle too late. The Spaniards had hardly sailed away from Rochelle, when the Captal de Buch, Sir Thomas Percy, and others, entered it with about 600 men-at-arms, and were greatly annoyed to find they were too late to assist the Earl of Pembroke.[2] The Rochellois, although they hated the English, received them well, but, as Froissart says, " they dared do nothing else."

---

[1] Buchon's ed. vol. i. p. 641.

[2] I may here point out a mistake made by that remarkably precise and accurate writer, Sir Harris Nicolas. In his *History of the British Navy*, vol. i. p. 141, he states that when Pembroke went to Rochelle, " it was besieged by the French." Of this I can find no evidence whatever, and it is evidently incorrect, as the Captal and his party could not have entered Rochelle unopposed if it had been so.

CHAP. XI. FRANCE PREPARES TO STRIKE A FATAL BLOW. 201

The Captal did not remain long at Rochelle; before his departure, however, in order to awe the citizens and prevent their surrendering the town to the French, he appointed Sir John Devereux, who had escaped from the sea fight, as seneschal, and put him in possession of the castle with 300 men-at-arms. The Captal and his companions then marched to the relief of Soubise, a strong fortress near the mouth of the Charente, which was threatened by the Bretons. The besiegers hardly waited his approach, but instantly gave up the attack, and without striking a blow, evacuated various other castles in the neighbourhood, of which they had taken possession.

A.D. 1372.

He marches to the relief of Soubise.

Many Welshmen had fled from the English rule to France, and entered her ranks to fight against the English; among them was one "Owen of Wales," who had fought at Poitiers and in Spain.[1] He soon distinguished himself, and about this time the King of France gave him the command of a fleet carrying 3,000 soldiers, and ordered him to sail from Harfleur to Guernsey. On his arrival, he landed and attacked the English forces with such success that he drove the governor into Cornet Castle, where he besieged him. The castle was well provided with artillery, and managed to resist Owen's assaults. It was while this siege was going on, that the English fleet was defeated off Rochelle. The King of France, seeing at a glance the importance of that event, and knowing that the English had now no great leader except the Captal, determined to abandon minor operations, and concentrate all his efforts to drive the English out of the South of France. It was important, however, to get possession of Rochelle; he therefore ordered Owen to give up the siege of Cornet Castle,

Singular adventures of a Welshman in the service of the King of France.

[1] Woodward's *History of Wales*, vol. ii. p. 564.

202 LIFE AND TIMES OF EDWARD III. Chap. XI.

A.D. 1372.

The Spanish fleet returns to Rochelle.

and set sail for Spain in a ship sent him for that purpose, in order to beg the King of Castile to dispatch his fleet back to Rochelle and besiege it from the sea.[1] Owen succeeded in his negotiations, and in due course of time th Spanish fleet again lay before Rochelle.

Edward makes plans to send help to the Captal, but abandons them.

When Edward heard of the defeat of the Earl of Pembroke, he perceived at once the heaviness of the blow. He therefore consulted the Duke of Lancaster, and, by his advice, determined to send the Earl of Salisbury, with 500 men-at-arms and as many archers, to defend Poitou and Saintonge. But there was now no vigour in the English councils; the King was old—in mind and body, though not in years;—he had become the slave of Alice Perrers; the Black Prince was prostrated by sickness; and there was none worthy to fill his place. The Earl of Salisbury never left the English shores; no help from England was actually sent to support the Captal; and, it was not until that valiant soldier had been taken prisoner, and Rochelle had fallen, that Edward was at length roused to exert himself.

The French act more vigorously.

The King of France displayed far more vigour. The Duke of Anjou, indeed, to whom the invasion of the Agenois was assigned, did nothing. He did not begin operations till August, and soon retired and dismissed his army.[2] But the Duke of Berri showed much more activity and skill. He was accompanied by the Constable of France, the able Bertrand Du Guesclin, who was of course the real leader of the forces under the Duke's command. The Duke of Bourbon, the Count of Alençon, the Dauphin of Auvergne, the Lord of Clisson (the Butcher), and others, also joined this division of the French army,

---

[1] Buchon's *Froissart,* vol. i. p. 640.

[2] Sismondi, vol. ii. p. 169.

CHAP. XI. SIEGE OF ST. SÉVÈRE. 203

which consisted of about 3,000 lances. They entered Poitou and took the castle of Montmorillon, killing the whole garrison; then seized Chauvigny and Lussac; after this they went to Poitiers, which, however, they did not attack, but passed on to the siege of Montcontour,[1] a strong castle six leagues from thence. After six days the garrison surrendered, on condition of their lives being spared; this condition being granted they quitted Montcontour and marched to Poitiers. When the inhabitants of that city heard of the fall of Montcontour, they were greatly alarmed, fearing it would be the next to be attacked. They therefore sent off to Rochelle to Sir John Devereux, their seneschal, begging him to come to their aid.[2] Devereux made arrangements for the safety of Rochelle during his absence, and then repaired with all speed to Poitiers accompanied by fifty lances, where he was soon joined by Sir Thomas Percy with the same number of men.

But Du Guesclin did not attack that city. The Duke of Berri had undertaken a separate expedition, and had taken a body of men to the Limousin, where he was besieging St. Sévère, a castle belonging to Sir John Devereux. Feeling that his forces were not strong enough to take it without the aid of Du Guesclin, he had written to the Constable begging he would join him. Du Guesclin at once acceded to the Duke's request, and with their united forces, amounting to about 4,000 men-at-arms, the Duke and the Constable laid siege to St. Sévère. Poitiers was thus respited.

Devereux hearing of the siege of his castle,

A.D. 1372.

The Duke de Berri and Du Guesclin enter Poitou.

Devereux and Percy march to the relief of Poitiers.

Siege of St. Sévère.

Preparations for its relief

---

[1] Buchon's *Froissart*, vol. i. p. 642.
[2] Ibid. pp. 643, 644.

204   LIFE AND TIMES OF EDWARD III.   CHAP. XL.

A.D. 1372. held a consultation with Sir Thomas Percy, at which it was agreed, that they should form a junction with the Captal, concentrate a large body of forces to attack the French, and relieve St. Sévère. The Captal had abandoned the siege of Soubise for a time, and Devereux and Percy met him while on his way towards St. Jean d'Angely. No difficulty was found, in persuading the Captal to agree to their plan. Summonses were issued, for the gathering together of the various Gascon lords who were friendly to the English; and 900 lances and 500 bowmen were soon collected on the borders of the Limousin, under the orders of the Captal.

too late. But the Captal was too late. As soon as Du Guesclin heard of the intention of the English to raise the siege of St. Sévère, he ordered an assault to be made with the utmost vigour. The ditches were full of water, but the assailants waded through, and the royal Dukes fought with as much courage as the common soldiers. The garrison little knew, that the best commander left to the English was marching to their relief, and was only ten leagues off; therefore, being hard pressed, they felt themselves obliged to *Fall of St. Sévère.* yield, and surrendered on condition of their lives being spared. Du Guesclin took immediate possession of the castle; but being a wise commander—as well as a bold, active, and gallant leader—he did not neglect to make ready to defend himself against the expected attack of the Captal. The Captal, however, having heard of the fall of the fortress, and bitterly grieved at missing his opportunity, gave up his plan of attacking the French.

The want which the English had of a great general soon again became apparent. The Captal was brave

CHAP. XI. FALL OF POITIERS. 205

enough, but not quick; another important town was **A.D. 1372.**
consequently lost to the English, by the want of
military skill and rapid action. The inhabitants of *Siege of Poitiers.*
Poitiers, like those of most towns in Aquitaine, were
divided, the greater number being adverse to the English; but the latter were in the most advantageous position, as they held possession of the city. Immediately
after the fall of St. Sévère, the French Poitevins sent
secretly to Du Guesclin, to say that if he would
come to Poitiers instantly, they would give the town
up to him. The Constable was not a man on whom
such a hint would be thrown away; he left the Royal
Dukes, with the main part of his army, to keep the
English in check, and immediately set off with 300
lances for Poitiers. They were all well mounted, and
it was needful they should be; in one day and night,
they had to march thirty leagues, through woods
and narrow lanes, to conceal themselves from the
English. If a horse fell from fatigue, they left him
and hastened on. The Mayor of Poitiers, who was
friendly to the English, had an inkling of the plot; he
therefore sent in haste to Sir Thomas Percy, to tell
him that in the city the French were five to one
against the English; that they had sent for the Constable, and that his only chance of saving the city
was to come directly with help. Sir Thomas at once
consulted the Captal, and offered to march off to
Poitiers; but the Captal feared to part with him.
" Master Thomas," he said, " you shall not leave me, *It is taken*
you are one of the chief of our body, and the one in *through the hesita-*
whom I have the greatest faith for good advice, but *tion of the Captal.*
we will send." One Jean d'Angle, a relative pro-
bably of Guichard d'Angle, was accordingly sent off
with 100 lances to save Poitiers. But he also was

206　　LIFE AND TIMES OF EDWARD III.　Chap. XI.

A.D. 1372.

too late. When he was within about a league of the city, he received the news that Du Guesclin was within the walls; and so, turning his horses' heads in the opposite direction, he rode back to the Captal.[1] The English were now utterly discouraged. No one knew what to do; no one had a plan; no one, animated with that desperate courage which often commands success, suggested a bold attack on the French army, during the absence of its able commander, Du Guesclin. On the contrary, the only arrangement they could make was, that each should go his own way; that the Poitevins should take care of themselves; that the English should form one body, the Gascons another; and that, if they saw a chance, they should meet again. "Then," as Froissart says—sarcastically, if he ever was sarcastic—"they departed one from the other *much amiably*, the Poitevins went to Thouars, the Gascons to St. Jean d'Angely, and the English to Niort."[2] Niort was occupied only by serfs, who were hostile to the English, while their absent lords were in their favour. When, therefore, the English wished to enter that town, the inhabitants closed the gates against them; but, nevertheless, the English assaulted it with complete success.

General discomfiture of the English.

They take Niort.

The Constable of France, who had remained at Poitiers, now followed up his successful capture of that city, by sending Reginald, Lord of Pons, with 300 lances, chiefly Bretons and Picards, to besiege the castle of Soubise. It was commanded by a widow lady, and, when the siege began, she sent for help to the Captal, who had gone to St. Jean d'Angely with the Gascons. The Captal, glad of an opportunity

The French attack Soubise;

[1] Buchon's *Froissart*, vol. i. p. 646.
[2] Ibid. p. 647.

CHAP. XI.   THE CAPTAL TAKEN PRISONER.   207

of again fighting, sent to Sir Thomas Percy and others, and gathered together a considerable force at St. Jean to relieve the castle. He was deceived as to the number of the besiegers, and marched from St. Jean at the head of only 200 lances; but, nevertheless, on this occasion, he managed his plans so swiftly and secretly, that he came on the besiegers before they were aware of his approach, and routed them utterly. *but are repulsed.*

In the meantime, Owen of Wales had arrived to blockade Rochelle with a Spanish fleet, consisting of forty great niefs, eight galleys, and thirteen barges, well manned and armed, under the command of Admiral Roderigo de Rosas. No attack was made on the town, for it was well known that the French party within the walls would willingly surrender, if they dared. While at anchor, Owen was informed by his spies of the siege of Soubise, and of the intention of the Captal to march to its relief; he therefore determined to endeavour to defeat the Captal's plans. He manned his thirteen barges with 400 well-armed men, rowed to the mouth of the Charente, and came to anchor opposite Soubise. He soon received news of the defeat of the French, but thought he might venture to make an attack on the Captal by night, while he was quietly encamped, unsuspecting the presence of any enemy. He landed his men, and took him by surprise. The result may be anticipated. "Why should I make a long story?" says Froissart. The Captal and Sir Thomas Percy were taken prisoners; the soldiers were all killed or captured; and the loss of the two commanders aggravated the blow to the English cause. Soubise at once surrendered; the Bretons and Poitevins revelled in triumph; and a body of 500 men attacked St. *Owen of Wales goes to join the attack on Soubise, reverses the repulse and takes the Captal and Percy prisoners,*

A.D. 1372.

208 LIFE AND TIMES OF EDWARD III. Chap. XI.

A.D. 1372.

Jean d'Angely, of which the Captal had been the commander. "No comfort from any side appeared" to the garrison, and that town also was lost to the

followed by general disasters.

English. Next fell Angoulême, Taillebourg, Saintes, and Pons, most of them surrendering without resistance. The lives of the garrisons were, however, spared, and the soldiers allowed to go safely to Bordeaux.

Owen returns to Rochelle.

Owen of Wales having taken the Captal prisoner, returned to Rochelle, but did not assault it, as he knew that it would ere long fall by treachery, and indeed by that means the city soon passed into the hands of the French. On leaving Rochelle to protect Poitiers, Sir John Devereux had left one Philip Mansel guardian of the castle. This man could neither read nor write, and the Mayor of Rochelle, Jean de Chaudrier, "subtle and crafty, and of good courage," determined to avail himself of his igno-

Its capture by means of an ingenious plot.

rance to get hold of the castle. He asked Mansel to dine with him; after dinner, he told him he had received an important letter from the King of England, and produced one sealed with the King's arms; this satisfied Jean that the Mayor's statement was true. The Mayor then called a priest, and ordered him to read the letter. The priest had received his instructions, and, forthwith, pretended to read that, preparatory to receiving their wages, Edward had ordered that the garrison of the castle should be mustered and reviewed by the Mayor in a certain open space outside the castle walls. Mansel was pleased at this, for the soldiers were clamorous for their pay. Next day the muster took place. The Mayor had filled some empty houses, just outside the castle, with a body of armed men outnumbering the garrison; and, when the soldiers were all arrayed outside the gates,

CHAP. XI. ROCHELLE GIVEN UP TO THE FRENCH. 209

these men suddenly rushed down between them and the castle, cutting off their retreat, and they were thus obliged to surrender at discretion. Rochelle by these means fell into the hands of the French on the 15th of August; but the Mayor would not give it up to the King, until he had made certain conditions with him.

A.D. 1372.

In the meanwhile, the Dukes of Berri, Bourbon, and Burgundy had kept themselves on the borders of Auvergne and the Limousin with about 2,000 lances. On hearing of the fall of Rochelle, they marched to join Du Guesclin at Poitiers, taking towns and castles on their way. They then held counsel together, as to the means which should be adopted to enable the King to obtain possession of Rochelle. They agreed to send messengers to the Mayor, to ascertain what his intentions really were. The Mayor informed them, that, if the King granted the demands of the citizens, they would become "good Frenchmen." This answer satisfied the Constable; and the Mayor of Rochelle then sent twelve of the principal citizens under safe conduct to Paris, to make terms with the King. These were, principally, that the castle should be razed to the ground; that they should not be taxed without their consent; that the town should never be handed over to the English, or any ruler but the King of France; and that the Pope should grant them absolution from their oaths to the English. After two months' consultation, the King acceded to these conditions, and sent back the messengers, loaded with jewels and rich presents for their wives. Three days after their return the destruction of the castle was begun, and the Rochellois sent to the Duke of Berri to tell him he might come and take possession

Consequences of the fall of Rochelle.

VOL. II. P

210   LIFE AND TIMES OF EDWARD III.   CHAP. XI.

A.D. 1872. of the town. The Duke sent Du Guesclin for this purpose; after receiving the oaths of the Rochellois, the Constable returned to Poitiers.

The Captal de Buch is taken to Paris as a prisoner. The King of France now ordered Owen to bring his prisoners to Paris; on their arrival, he received the Captal with great courtesy, wishing to make him his friend. The Captal offered to pay an enormous sum for his ransom; but the King knew too well his value to the English, and refused to set him free at any price. The castle of the Louvre was appointed as his prison, but his imprisonment was made as little irksome to him as possible.

The Rochellois overrun by the French. After the return of the Constable to Poitiers, he agreed with the Dukes that they should overrun the whole of the Rochellois; and they acted on this understanding, taking possession of every town and castle they approached. The only place which offered any resistance was Fontenay le Comte, in Poitou; but the garrison soon saw the impossibility of holding out, and surrendered, on condition of being allowed to go without molestation to Thouars, where all the Poitevin barons friendly to the English had shut themselves up, and which had for some time been besieged by the French.[1] This was granted them, and the Constable and the Dukes then returned to Poitiers.[2]

Siege of Thouars. Thouars was now, with the exception of Bordeaux, nearly the only place of importance remaining to the English in Aquitaine; the Constable was there-

---

[1] Although this is not stated by Froissart, it is clear that it must be the fact, as, in answer to an appeal for help from the garrison, Edward made preparations for the relief of Thouars on the 20th August.

[2] Buchon's *Froissart*, vol. i. p. 656.

CHAP. XI.   EDWARD ROUSES HIMSELF.   211

fore determined to take possession of it.   He accord- A.D. 1372.
ingly marched, at the head of 3,000 lances and 4,000
foot-soldiers, to assist in the siege.   Knowing, however, that it was well defended, his plan was to
reduce it by famine, instead of attempting to take it
by assault.

When the Barons who held the town saw what the
plan of the besiegers was, and that their numbers
increased daily, they felt, that, however they might
prolong their defence, the city, unless relieved, must
ultimately fall.   They therefore agreed with the Constable, that, unless the King of England or his
sons appeared before Thouars with a sufficient force
to hold the field against the French, on or before the
29th of September, they would enter into the allegiance of the King of France.

They accordingly sent messengers to inform King
Edward of their position, and earnestly entreated
him to come to their relief.   The King at length
roused himself, and made greater preparations for the
invasion of France, than he had before set on foot.
He told the messengers he would go in person with
all his sons; and even the Black Prince, notwithstanding his grievous sickness, declared that, although he
might die on the voyage, he would accompany his
father.[1]   Edward lost no time in making ready.   On Edward
the 20th of August, he ordered ships and sailors to relieve it.
rendezvous at Southampton with all speed, to convey Sir John Neville and others to Brittany, on
which coast he intended to land.[2]   The King himself
embarked at Sandwich.   He there received from
the Chancellor, Sir John Knyvet, the Great Seal,

[1] Buchon's *Froissart*, vol. i. p. 658.
[2] Rymer, vol. iii. p. 961.

P 2

212 LIFE AND TIMES OF EDWARD III. Chap. XI

A.D. 1372.

He embarks with the Black Prince on August 30th.

which was used for the government of the kingdom during the King's presence in England, and deposited it with the Treasurer, for safe custody, in a bag sealed with his signet; at the same time he gave another like seal to the Chancellor, to be used during his absence. This took place on the 30th of August in the "hall" or chief cabin of the King's ship, the "Grace de Dieu."[1] It had been previously arranged, that the Duke of Lancaster should invade France by Calais; but, as this plan was abandoned in consequence of the news from Thouars, all the preparations that had been made for that expedition were available without delay to aid the present purpose. The fleet consisted of 400 ships, large and small, having on board 4,000 men-at-arms and 10,000 bowmen.[2] The cost of the expedition was estimated at 900,000*l.*,[3] but the expenditure of such a sum, which would represent nearly six millions of money at this day, seems utterly incredible.

Before sailing, the King appointed his grandson, Richard, son of the Black Prince, then six and a half years old, the nominal guardian of the kingdom during his absence.[4] This ill-fated expedition never reached its destination. The fleet was five weeks at sea, beating about with contrary winds, often losing as much way in one day as it had made in three, and utterly unable to gain the land. The 30th of September arrived, while the fleet was still at sea; the King therefore ordered it to return to England, and thus ended almost the last chance which the English had of re-establishing their possession of

Disastrous failure of the expedition.

---

[1] Rymer, vol. iii. p. 962. [2] Buchon's *Froissart*, vol. i. p. 658.

[3] Walsingham, p. 315.

[4] Rot. Parl. 46 Ed. III. (m. 1.) 2; and Rymer, vol. iii. p. 962.

CHAP. XI.   DISASTROUS END OF THE CAMPAIGN.   213

the Duchy of Aquitaine. No sooner had they landed, A.D. 1372.
than the wind changed, and the people exclaimed
that "God was for the King of France."[1]

In the meanwhile, the English and Gascon barons *The siege of Thouars goes on.*
who held Niort were watching the fate of Thouars
with great anxiety. When the day of surrender had
passed, they endeavoured to persuade its garrison
to break their word, and come out and join them in
battle with the French. When a truce was granted
on promise of surrender at a certain time if no
deliverance arrived, the understanding was, that no
additional force should be added to the besiegers;
but the King of France did not, on this occasion,
consider himself bound by any such condition.
He sent "the flower of his kingdom" to join the
Constable, so that at last there were 15,000 men
at arms and 30,000 other soldiers, encamped round
Thouars, at the end of September.[2] The garrison
of Niort used every argument to persuade that of
Thouars that they were not bound by the agreement
made with the Constable; but the garrison was
well aware that to evade it would have been rank
treachery. The argument of strong battalions was *Surrender of Thouars.*
also against them; and they therefore surrendered.[3]

When Thouars was taken, the greater part of the
French army "returned to France," as Froissart expresses himself; but the Lord of Clisson besieged
Mortagne, which was saved by timely help from Niort.
During the rest of the year, there was no more
fighting in Aquitaine. The greater part of the English retired to Bordeaux, leaving garrisons in Niort,

[1] Buchon's *Froissart*, vol. i. p. 658.
[2] Ibid. p. 659.   [3] Ibid. p. 660.

214 LIFE AND TIMES OF EDWARD III. Chap. XI.

A.D. 1372. Roche-sur-Yon, Lusignan, Chizey, and Mortemer; these were almost the only fortresses in Aquitaine remaining in their hands. The French cruisers, however, did not leave England at peace, and were very active in harassing the English coast. Portsmouth suffered greatly from their attacks, and was set on fire several times.[1] The English navy had sadly declined in power, and its inefficiency became the subject of serious complaint in the next Parliament.

Brittany.   The account of the campaign of 1372 would be incomplete without a notice of what had been done in Brittany. The Duke of that province, Edward's son-in-law, had made a formal alliance with him in the course of the year;[2] but, his nobles were so generally on the side of the French, that he dared not support the English openly. Edward sent Sir John Neville with 400 men-at-arms, and as many bowmen, to St. Mahé de Fine Poterne to assist the Duke; but the Breton nobles soon convinced him, that it would be dangerous to attack the French; no fighting, therefore, took place in Brittany before the following year.

[1] Rymer, vol. iii. p. 965.
[2] Ibid. pp. 943, 948, 955, 959, 964, 968.

CHAPTER XII.

THE LOSS OF AQUITAINE.

SOON after the return of King Edward to England, Parliament again met.[1] Two days subsequently to the appointment of the child Richard as Guardian of the Kingdom, the nobles, who formed his council, had issued writs in his name for the assemblage of Parliament on the 13th of October. The King however returned before that time; Richard's power therefore ceased, and Edward ordered Parliament to assemble on the 3rd of November. "The great men and Commons," for some reason or other, did not make their appearance on that day, and Parliament was therefore prorogued till the following Friday. On its meeting in the Painted Chamber, the Chancellor, Sir John Knyvet, stated the reasons for its assemblage. " Receivers and tryers" of petitions from England, Ireland, Wales, Scotland, Gascony and other countries beyond the seas, and from " The Isles," were then appointed in the usual way; after this, the Commons departed for the day, and the King, the Prince of Wales, the Prelates, the Dukes, Earls, Barons and Bannerets adjourned to the White Chamber. Guy Bryan then made the important announcement, that the Prince had surrendered the Duchy of Aquitaine to his father.

A.D.1372.

Meeting of Parliament.

Announcement of the Prince's surrender of Aquitaine to his father.

[1] Rot. Parl. 46 Ed. III.

216   LIFE AND TIMES OF EDWARD III.   CHAP. XII.

A.D. 1372. Bryan asked the Prince if this were done with his will; to which, in the language of Northern France, he answered " *oyl.* " Parliament was then adjourned. The reason given for this act by the Prince was, that the revenues of Aquitaine were not enough to defray the expenses. But there can be no doubt that his failing health, and a feeling of despair of ever recovering possession of the province, were the causes which really actuated him.

The next day, the whole Parliament assembled in the White Chamber, when Guy Bryan gave an account of the King's unfortunate attempt to invade France ; he then stated, that the King had summoned Parliament to give him advice on this important *Grant of* matter, and to grant him a subsidy. To this request, *subsidy.* an immediate assent was given, and the subsidy was to be raised in the following manner, viz. : On each sack of wool exported, 43*s.* 4*d.* ; on every twelve score of woolfells, the same ; and on every last of leather, 4*l.*, in addition to the old customs. These duties were granted for two years ; but inasmuch as they alone would not be sufficient, Parliament granted also a fifteenth for one year. Other important matters were then considered. The first, was the complaint, that lawyers abused their privileges as Members of Parliament, by using them to promote the business of their *Lawyers* clients ; it was therefore ordered,[1] that no lawyers hav- *and She-* ing business in the King's Court should be allowed to *riffs not* *allowed* sit in Parliament, for counties. In like manner, the *to sit in* *Parlia-* Sheriffs "who are common ministers of the people, *ment.*

---

[1] " Est accorde et assentu en cest Parlement, q^e desormes null homme de ley pursuant busoignes en le Court de Roi . . . soient retournez ne acceptez chivalers des countees."—*Rot. Parl.* vol. ii. p. 310 (13). On this important matter see chap. xix. vol. i.

CHAP. XII. IMPORTANT PROCEEDINGS IN PARLIAMENT. 217

and ought to remain in their office to do right to everyone," were forbidden to sit, for counties, in Parliament; because their so doing caused them to be absent from their counties. It was also provided, that if any one belonging to either of these classes were returned to Parliament, he should receive no wages. After this, leave was given to the Knights of the Counties to depart, and to sue out writs for their wages or expenses. The citizens and burgesses were, however, ordered to remain. They assembled in a room near the White Chamber, before the Prince, the Prelates, and the Great Men, and renewed the subsidy previously granted of 2*s.* on every tun of wine, and 6*d.* on every pound of merchandise, coming into or going out of the kingdom, as a payment for the safe convoy of their ships and goods, for another year, and then departed.[1]

A.D. 1372.

Additional subsidy for safe convoy of goods.

Among the petitions presented to the King by this Parliament, was one of great importance, both in reference to its subject, and as one of the many manifestations, in this reign, of the growing power and influence of Parliament and especially of the Commons. It had reference to the Navy. Great dissatisfaction existed at its inefficiency, and the Commons consequently presented the following petition: "Also, pray the Commons, as Merchants, and Mariners of England, that twenty years since, and at all time before, the Navy of the Kingdom was in all ports and towns on the sea and rivers so noble and so plentiful, that all countries deemed and called our Lord THE KING OF THE SEA; and he and all his country were more dreaded by sea and by land

Complaints as to decline of the Navy.

[1] Rot. Parl. vol. ii. p. 310 (14 and 15).

218   LIFE AND TIMES OF EDWARD III.   CHAP. XII.

A.D. 1372. because of the said Navy; and now it is so decreased and destroyed by different causes, that in case of need there remains hardly enough to defend the country against royal power, from whence there is great danger to the whole kingdom, all the causes' of which would be too long to describe. But one cause is the greatest; the long arrest of niefs which is often made in time of war, that is, a quarter of a year or more before they go out of their ports, without taking anything for the wages of their mariners during that time, or the owners of the niefs having any guerdon for the fitting out of their niefs and their expenses. For which they pray, as a work of charity, a suitable

The King's evasive answer.

remedy." The somewhat ambiguous answer was, " That it was the King's pleasure that the Navy should be maintained and kept with the greatest ease and profit that could be." [1]

There was another petition, of so singular a nature, and so curiously illustrating the manners of the times,

Petition as to immorality of the Clergy.

that it cannot be passed over. The beneficed clergy and curates were in the habit not only of keeping concubines, but of keeping them openly, to the great scandal of the Church; and so little was thought of this gross immorality, by the Church itself, that the Ordinaries, whose duty it was to prosecute them and deprive them of their livings, often neglected to do so. A petition was therefore presented to the following effect: " Also supplicate the Commons, to the advantage of our Lord the King, and of all the kingdom, that, Whereas the beneficed gentry of the Holy Church and curates, who keep their con- cubines openly, by which they are deprivable, and are deprived, by the law of the Holy Church; if their

[1] Rot. Parl. vol. ii. p. 311.

CHAP. XII.   CONTINUED REVERSES OF THE ENGLISH.   219

Ordinaries do not make due execution within one year A.D. 1373. after the said time, the Church may be held void by the law of the land, and that he who is Patron may present. And if the Ordinary, in such case as due execution is not made, be the Patron, that the title shall accroach to our Lord the King to present to the said Benefice, and that the Bishop and the Ordinary be bound to receive the presentment in such case." [1] The compulsory celibacy of the clergy was evidently the cause of this immorality.

The course of events of the year 1373 was more Continued reverses disastrous to England than even that of the previous of the year. The total absence of military talent in the English. Duke of Lancaster or any other leader now left to the English became fatally manifest; while the cold calculating wisdom of Charles the Fifth, was as evidently conducive to the great successes of the French.

Charles had ordered the Constable to complete the conquest of Poitou early in the spring, before the time when the English were accustomed to cross the sea.[2] Accordingly, as Froissart says (although from his own statement the event happened in the early spring), "when the soft season of summer had returned, and it was good for campaigning and encamping in the fields," Du Guesclin issued from Poitiers and laid siege to Chizey. The commanders of the gar- Capture of rison, Sir Robert Miton and Martin L'Escot, feeling Chizey. that they were not strong enough to hold out against the French, sent to Niort, which was only four leagues off, for help. This was soon rendered, but was of no avail from want of skill and quick decision. The

[1] The King's answer is not entered in the Rolls. Rot. Parl. 46 Ed. III. (pp. 309–314).

[2] Sismondi, vol. xi. p. 179.

220 LIFE AND TIMES OF EDWARD III. Chap. XII.

A.D. 1373.

castle fell on the 21st of March; and all who came from Niort were either killed or taken prisoners.[1]

Poitou taken by the French.

Soon afterwards, the whole of Poitou was lost to the English. Niort fell without resistance; then Lusignan; and Castel Achard was next attacked. This was held by the wife of Guichard d'Angle, who was a prisoner in Spain with the Earl of Pembroke,[2] but he had left behind him a woman of capacity to supply his place. She sought an interview with the Constable, and persuaded him to allow her to go to the Duke of Berri at Poitiers, to negotiate for the safety of her castle. On her arrival, she melted the heart of the Duke by her supplication. "My Lord," she said, "you know that I am a lone woman, with no power of defence, and widow of a living man, if it please God, for my Lord Guichard is a prisoner in Spain." She then promised to remain neutral, if she were left in peace. The Duke granted her petition.

Mortemer net surrendered; and Du Guesclin, having driven the English as far as the Gironde, leaving no places in Poitou in their hands except Mortagne-sur-Mer, Mespin, and La Tour de Labreth, and Roche-sur-Yon on the borders of Anjou,[3] returned to Paris with the Dukes of Berri, Bourbon, and Burgundy.

Edward prepares for the defence of England and the invasion of France.

The King of England was soon made aware that he had lost Poitou, Saintonge, and Rochelle; that the French had a considerable fleet at sea, consisting of 120 large vessels, besides galleys and barges, commanded by Owen of Wales, Don Roderigo de Rosas, the Count of Narbonne, Sir John de Raix, and

---

[1] Buchon's *Froissart*, vol. i. pp. 662–665.   [2] Ibid. p. 666.

[3] "Voir est que la Roche sur Yon se tenoit encore, mais c'est sur les marches d'Anjou et du ressort d'Anjou."—Buchon's *Froissart*, vol. i. p. 666.

CHAP. XII.   THE ENGLISH AGAIN INVADE FRANCE.   221

Sir John de Vienne; and that they intended to make a descent on the shores of England. Every effort was therefore made to resist the threatened invasion. The English navy had been greatly weakened by the defeat off Rochelle, and by the oppressions of which the Commons had complained in the last Parliament. The King had therefore, in the previous autumn, reinforced it by the addition of several Genoese war galleys; of these, on the 22nd of November, he had appointed Peter de Campo Fregoso, brother of the Duke of Genoa, captain, and Sir Jacob Pronan lieutenant and sub-captain.[1] In the following January he made an arrangement for the service of 200 Genoese in his navy for one year. Means were thus taken to equip a navy for the defence of England, and also for the invasion of France. On February 8th, 1373, the King appointed William Montacute, Earl of Salisbury, captain of all the ships and barges that were about to put to sea. Salisbury agreed to serve for six months with 300 men-at-arms, consisting of himself, 20 knights, and 279 esquires, and the same number of bowmen, and having in his company the two admirals. The fleet was ordered to be ready to sail on the 1st of March.[2]

A.D. 1373.

The Earl of Salisbury was joined by Sir William Neville and Sir Philip Courtenay, with 2,000 men-at-arms, and as many bowmen, and the fleet sailed from Cornwall for the coast of Brittany. They reached St. Malo in safety, and on entering the harbour found eight large Spanish vessels at anchor, unprepared for an attack. These they immediately burned, killing all on board, and were then able to land in safety. The Bretons, suspecting that their Duke

The English fleet sails,

and lands the forces in Brittany.

¹ Rymer, vol. iii. p. 965.   ² Ibid. pp. 970, 971.

222 LIFE AND TIMES OF EDWARD III. Chap. XII.

A.D. 1373.

had given information to the English about these Spanish vessels, closed their castles and towns against him, and appealed to the King of France for help. The Duke shut himself up in Vannes, and Sir Robert Knolles, after fortifying his castle of Derval, went to Brest, which was, according to Froissart, "one of the strongest castles of the world."[1]

The King of France prepares for its defence.

The King of France, that mysterious man, who never took the field himself, nor allowed his armies to fight if they could avoid it, but who, silent and secret in his plans, contrived that his enemies should expend their force in resultless efforts, now saw, that the time had come for driving them out of their last stronghold, and destroying the power of their only remaining friend. He, therefore, ordered the Constable Du Guesclin to invade Brittany with a large force. The Duke fled to England to beg for help, and another English army was got ready to embark at the end of May.[2]

Du Guesclin enters Brittany.

Du Guesclin, accompanied by the Duke of Bourbon, the Count of Alençon, and others, advanced to Angers, where a French army of 14,000 men was gathered together. He then entered Brittany at the head of 4,000 mounted men-at-arms, proceeding first to that part of the country which was called "La Bretagne Bretonnante," and which had always been more inclined to the Duke than "La Douce Bretagne." Rennes opened its gates to him; Dinan, Vannes, Jugon, and many other towns followed its example. When Lord Salisbury and the English at St. Malo heard of the successes of the French, they sailed for Brest, in order to place their ships in greater safety, and to effect a junction with Knolles.

The English gather together at Brest.

[1] Rymer, vol. i. p. 668.   [2] Ibid. vol. iii. p. 981.

CHAP. XII. THE ENGLISH IN EXTREMITIES. 223

They had hardly left St. Malo, before Du Guesclin arrived there, with the intention of attacking them, and was much grieved at missing the chance of a battle. He had no difficulty however in taking the town, and then advanced to Hennebon, famous for its gallant defence by the Countess of Montfort. There was no Countess there now, and the French army had been swelled to the number of 20,000 men. So Hennebon surrendered. Du Guesclin did not think it advisable to attack Brest, but laid siege to Nantes.

There were now three strong places in Brittany which held out for the English—Nantes, besieged by the Constable; Brest, held by Sir Robert Knolles, from which the Earl of Salisbury had departed with his fleet when Du Guesclin marched for Nantes, but which was attacked by Olivier de Clisson on his departure; and Knolles' castle of Derval, besieged by another division of the Constable's army. La Roche-sur-Yon, on the borders of Anjou, was threatened by the Duke of Anjou; and Becherel and St. Sauveur in Normandy were also besieged by the French.[1] Derval agreed to surrender, unless relieved within forty days, and gave four hostages for the fulfilment of the agreement; Nantes submitted, on condition of being allowed to return to its allegiance to the Duke of Brittany, if he became " a good Frenchman." Roche-sur-Yon yielded to the Duke of Anjou, after waiting a month in vain for support; and Knolles, on hearing of the danger of Derval, agreed, on the 6th of July, to give up Brest to the Constable, if it were not relieved within a month. He gave hostages for his good faith, and then repaired to his castle of Derval.

Before leaving Brest, Knolles sent letters to the Earl

A.D. 1373.

Du Guesclin takes St. Malo.

and Hennebon.

Six fortresses hold out for the English.

Negotiations for their surrender.

---

[1] Buchon's *Froissart*, vol. i. p. 674.

LIFE AND TIMES OF EDWARD III. CHAP. XII.

A.D. 1373.

Salisbury ready to "keep the day" at Brest with Du Guesclin,

of Salisbury, desiring him to return thither at once. He accordingly did so, and landed with 4,000 men to "keep the day," as agreed with the Constable. Salisbury then summoned Du Guesclin, either to come to fight him, or to give up the hostages; but Du Guesclin, who was at Nantes, said that the place did not suit him, was not that which had been appointed, and that if Salisbury would come to Nantes he would fight him there. Salisbury replied in the true spirit of chivalry, saying that he had no horses, but that, if Du Guesclin would lend him some, he would give him battle wherever he pleased. The heralds went

who refuses to fight.

backwards and forwards; but it was clear that Du Guesclin did not mean to fight. He was probably under orders from the King of France not to risk a decisive battle, especially as the Dukes of Lancaster and Brittany had just landed at Calais.[1] Salisbury, therefore, after supplying Brest with men, arms, and food, re-embarked and again put to sea. The Constable then marched to Derval, to "keep his day" with Knolles. No relief had arrived, but Knolles refused to abide by the agreement that had been made in his absence; consequently, the Duke of Anjou, who had joined in the siege, cut off the heads of the four hostages, in spite of the prayers and entreaties of all the barons by whom he was surrounded. Knolles retaliated, by treating four French prisoners in the same way. But Derval did not fall; for the

Siege of Derval, which still holds out.

Duke of Anjou and the Constable were recalled from Brittany to France, to defend the kingdom against the invasion of the Duke of Lancaster.[2]

King Edward had now determined to make one more great effort to recover his French dominions,

[1] Buchon's *Froissart*, vol. i. p. 678, note.   [2] Ibid. p. 683.

CHAP. XII.   THE MAGNIFICENT INVASION.   225

being much moved to do so by the entreaties of his A.D. 1373.
son-in-law, the Duke of Brittany. The pomp, the preparations, the gorgeousness of the splendid army destined, it was hoped, to restore the English rule, were
magnificent; the result, was a failure never exceeded.

On the 12th of June Edward appointed his "dear
son John, King of Castile and Leon and Duke of
Aquitaine and Lancaster," commander of the intended expedition. A few days afterwards, a fleet
sailed from England with an army of 3,000 men-at-
arms, 6,000 bowmen, and about 2,000 other soldiers
on board, under command of Lancaster. The Duke
of Brittany, and a great array of the nobles and
barons of England accompanied him; while measures
were taken for the defence of England against invasion during their absence.[1]

The army which passed over from England, was The inva-
reinforced on its arrival, by soldiers hired from Flan- sion of
ders, Hainault, Brabant, and Germany; and by 300 France by
lances from Scotland. Six months' pay in advance Lancaster.
was given them on the arrival of the Duke. Notwith- Its dis-
standing the magnitude of the army and its admirable astrous
appointments in every way, this expedition was even failure.
more disastrous to England than the defeat of the
English fleet off Rochelle in the previous year. There
was an evident want of military genius in the Duke
of Lancaster. He had no definite plan, except to
endeavour, by laying waste the heart of the country,
to provoke the King of France to attack him and
engage in a pitched battle. But Charles had fortified
the castles against attack, and given strict orders to
his commanders to avoid a decisive engagement. The

[1] Rymer, vol. iii. pp. 977, 982, 987, 988; and Buchon's *Froissart,* vol. i. pp. 673, 678, &c.

VOL. II.   Q

226   LIFE AND TIMES OF EDWARD III.   CHAP. XII.

A.D. 1873. Duke's invasion, therefore, resulted in nothing but a marauding march through France, from north to south, with the French continually hanging on the skirts of his army, and cutting off all stragglers.

The army marches from Calais After a short sojourn at Calais, the army began its march. It proceeded in a stately manner, with flags flying, divided into three "battles." The first was that of the Marshals; the second, that of the Dukes of Lancaster and Brittany, followed by the baggage; last of all came the "battle" commanded by the Constable, Sir Edward Despencer. The soldiers never went more than two or three leagues a day, resting *through France without serious fighting.* at noon, each man keeping his rank exactly, and all joining together at night. They marched by St. Omer, Terouanne, through Artois to Arras, then to Bray on the Somme, and so into the Vermandois, the people trembling before them, and paying ransom to save their towns from fire and sword, but never fighting; then they proceeded to the Laonnais, where they had a little fighting at Ribemont. At Vaulx, near Laon, they remained three days; it was harvest time, the country was rich and full of provisions—wine and bread, beef and mutton —with which they compelled the people to supply *The French hang on the skirts of the English,* them, under threat of burning their villages. From thence they went to Soissons, about the 21st of September, keeping to the course of the rivers and fertile lands; but, they were always followed by a few hundred French lances, who kept so closely to them, that the men on each side talked and jested with each other, even the leaders joining in sarcastic sallies. "It is a fine time for flying now! why don't you fly when you have wings?" said Sir Thomas Percy, mounted on a white courser, to Amery, the son of

CHAP. XII.   THE PURPOSELESS MARCH.   **227**

the Count of Namur,[1] alluding to the universal sport A.D. 1373.
of hawking. "Sir Percy! Sir Percy!" said Amery,
riding a little out of his rank, and prancing his
courser, "you say true, flying is fine for us; and, if
I had my way, we would fly to you." "By God!"
answered Percy, "I believe you; now persuade your
companions to fly, there is plenty of game." But the
French had orders not to indulge in that kind of
sport, except at small game. At Ouchy, near Sois-   and worry
sons, Sir Walter Huet, who had been keeping watch   them by
in the English camp all night, was surprised at early   prises.
dawn, half undressed, by a full armed knight, with
whom Sir Walter, leaping on his horse, at once engaged but was quickly slain. A slight skirmish
ensued, in which the English had the advantage, but
before any large body of their men could be brought
up to the fight, the French had retreated in safety to
the woods. Even attacks of this kind, however, now
ceased, for the general instructions of the King were,
"Let them go. By burnings they will not come to
your heritage; it will weary them, and they will all
go to destruction. Although a storm and a tempest
rage together over a land, they go away and disperse
of themselves. So will it be with these English."[1]

The King of France thought it necessary, however,   The King
to hold a grand council as to the course that should   of France
be taken, for the French Barons were greatly vexed   council,
at seeing the English march through their country
ravaging and unopposed; and so, shortly after the
cruel murder of the hostages at Derval, the leaders
of the French armies were all gathered together at
Paris. The King asked their advice, and begged Du

---

[1] "À Monseigneur Aymeri de Namur, fils au Comte."—Buchon's
Froissart, vol. i. p. 681.

Q 2

228   LIFE AND TIMES OF EDWARD III.   CHAP. XII.

A.D. 1373.

Guesclin to tell him what course he would recommend. It required great persuasion to induce him to speak, before the Royal Dukes had uttered their sentiments; at last he did so, and recommended that the French should never engage with the English except at a great advantage, reminding the King of the terrible defeats of Creçy and Poitiers. Olivier de Clisson then gave the same counsel, saying that the English had had so much success that they thought they could not be conquered, and the more blood they saw flowing the more eager they were to fight. These suggestions agreed exactly with the King's views, and his brother the Duke of Anjou was no more anxious for a pitched battle than were his companions. "When they think they will find us at one part of the kingdom," said he, "we will be at the other." "At these words the King was greatly rejoiced;" and so this crafty and ignominious course was resolved on.

at which it is decided not to attack the English.

From Soissons the English marched to Epernay, to "find great pillage and great profit on the noble river Marne, of which they were lords and masters, for none opposed them;" then to Châlons-sur-Marne, and so on to Troyes.

The English march on without any apparent purpose.

The Constable and the Royal Dukes were at Troyes with 1,200 lances; but they had come to watch, and not to fight. Vain endeavours were now made by the Pope to bring about a peace. He sent Cardinals to negotiate, and the English halted for a while; but their efforts failed, and the Dukes of Lancaster and Brittany then pursued their march. It is difficult to imagine what definite object they could have had in view. If to reach Aquitaine, they certainly did not take the shortest way; if to strike a heavy blow, why did they not lay siege to Paris, or some other impor-

CHAP. XII.   THE END OF THE MARCH.   229

tant city ? But however this may be, on they went, A.D. 1373.
followed by Du Guesclin, Olivier de Clisson, and other
nobles, at the head of a splendid body of cavalry,
ready on every opportunity to cut off stragglers and
harass them; while the English were constantly
sending their heralds to offer battle, and as constantly
receiving a refusal of their proposals.

Winter was now approaching, and the country *The*
they began to traverse was bleak and barren. The *English suffer from*
Limousin, Rouergue, and the Agenois, did not supply *cold and hunger.*
them so well with food as the rich country they had
left; and they were sometimes nearly a week without
bread. In the sterile mountains of Auvergne they
fared worse; for they could get food for neither man
nor horse, and their relentlesss pursuers had increased
from one to three thousand. Their horses died in vast
numbers; more than 30,000 are said to have marched
from Calais, but it was a mere fraction of that number
that reached the journey's end alive; the army was
utterly starving, and, as Walsingham says, it was a
miserable sight to see "famous and noble soldiers,
once delicate and rich in England, without their men
or their horses, *begging their bread from door to door,
nor was there one who would give it them.*" At last,
about Christmas, after a march of 600 miles through *and at last*
France, they reached Bordeaux, a horde of miserable *reach Bordeaux*
fugitives, instead of the proud and splendid army *in utter misery.*
which had first landed. Here they passed the winter,
and here they must be left till spring returned, and
with it fresh disasters.[1]

True accounts of the failure of the expedition could *Meeting*
hardly have failed to reach England; but, instead of *of Parliament in*
allowing it to be known that the army had suffered *England,*

---

[1] Walsingham, p. 315; Buchon's *Froissart*, vol. i. pp. 677, 686.

230 LIFE AND TIMES OF EDWARD III. CHAP. XII.

A.D. 1373. such terrible disasters, the people were told of its successes; and the burning of the Spanish ships at St. Malo was magnified into a naval victory. Parliament met on the 23rd of November, and, after the usual forms had been gone through, the Chancellor, Sir John Knyvet, stated to the assembly of King, Prince, Prelates, Earls, Barons, great men, and Commons, that the King, as they knew, had sent the Duke of Lancaster " to stop the malice of his adversaries;" he then went on to say that " by their good and noble government and deeds of arms they had done great damages and destructions to the enemy over there, and also on the sea a navy of great power had held themselves well and graciously against their enemies, to the great honour, quiet, and tranquillity of our Lord the King, of the clergy, and of all others of the kingdom." Not content with this shameless suppression of the real facts, the Chancellor proceeded to say that the Duke and his army stayed among their enemies to " grieve their power;" he then asked for a further grant of money, saying, that it was the King's wish that " all manner of petitions and other business " should be put aside till this was settled. The Commons debated for five days before they agreed to the King's peremptory demands, from which it may not improbably be supposed that doubts had already arisen concerning the proper management of the war,

Fresh subsidy granted after much deliberation.

both as to expenditure and military skill. At length, however, they granted a subsidy, on the condition that the money should be spent in maintaining the war, and that no knights of shires, esquires, citizens, or burgesses, returned to Parliament, should be collectors of the tax.[1]

[1] Rot. Parl. 47 Ed. III.

Chap. XII.   THE COMMONS PRESENT THEIR PETITIONS.   231

The Commons were then allowed to present their petitions, the principal of which were, that the Great Charter and the Charter of Forests should be confirmed, the constant necessity for which shows in a striking manner the King's continual encroachments; that certain frauds in the manufacture of cloth should be prevented; that the franchises of the City of London and other cities should be confirmed; that the maintenance of the staple at Calais should be strictly enforced, the custom of merchants shipping their wools and other merchandise to other places out of the kingdom being considered a great loss to the King, to the merchandise, and to the city of Calais.   In consequence of the fact that the Statute of Labourers was not carried into effect, the Commons also petitioned that this statute should be promulgated at least four times a year.   The exactions and usurpations of the Pope in reference to ecclesiastical benefices, which the King was always resisting in his law courts, were also made the subject of great complaint; and the position of the alien priories near the coasts, by which they were more easily enabled to act as spies on England and to communicate information to France, was an evil which the Commons earnestly entreated the King to put down.[1]

In consequence of these petitions relative to the Pope's usurpations, the King sent ambassadors to him complaining of his interference with Church temporalities.   The Pope gave them no satisfactory answer; but in August of the following year it was agreed between the King and the Pope, that the latter should interfere " less " in reference to benefices.[2]

A.D. 1373.

Petitions of the Commons as to staple.

Statute of Labourers.

The Pope's usurpations.

---

[1] Rot. Parl. vol. ii. pp. 318, 319, 320.
[2] Walsingham, pp. 316, 317.

232   LIFE AND TIMES OF EDWARD III.   CHAP. XII.

A.D. 1374.

Foreign spies come to England as Oxford students;

It was by no means an unusual practice for " the King's enemies abroad" to send spies to England under various religious pretences, and, shortly before the meeting of Parliament, on the 18th of October, the King found it necessary to warn the friar preachers at Oxford, that certain enemies of England, representing themselves to be brothers of their order, had obtained admission to that city and dwelt there as if for the purpose of study, but, in reality, to act as

prohibition thereof.

spies. He therefore ordered them not to allow these wolves in sheep's clothing to remain at Oxford.[1]

Naval preparations.

The King, being again supplied with funds, began early in 1374 to prepare for collecting together an effective navy, for one more effort to save Aquitaine. Orders were given at the end of January and beginning of February for the impressment of mariners from all the eastern, northern, and southern ports, who were to be ready for service by the 1st of March.[2] Eight northern towns each furnished a new barge capable of carrying from 100 to 120 men, which was to be fully equipped and manned, and to join Admiral Neville at Sandwich by the 16th of March. Other barges were ordered to be at Plymouth on the same day. On the 12th of May, nineteen masters of ships were summoned to attend the King's Council at Westminster, for the purpose of giving information on maritime affairs; and, on the 17th of July, instructions were issued for the rendezvous of a fleet at Dartmouth and Plymouth by the 8th of September.[3]

The Duke of Lancaster was still at Bordeaux, but the Duke of Brittany had left him in February to revictual Auray, Derval, and Brest; after this, it was

---

[1] Rymer, vol. iii. p. 991.   [2] Ibid. pp. 996, 997.
[3] Ibid. pp. 998, 999, 1002, 1006.

CHAP. XII. TRUCE AGREED ON. 233

his intention to go to England with his wife. The A.D. 1874.
Duke of Anjou and Du Guesclin passed the winter at
Toulouse.

In accordance with the peculiar spirit and customs
of chivalry, it had been arranged in the previous
year, that the Duke of Lancaster and the Duke of
Anjou should meet at Toulouse, on the 10th of April,
to resume the war; but, on the 17th of March, powers
were given by the Duke of Anjou, to three persons of
his council, to postpone this meeting if they thought
fit. The meeting was accordingly put off till the
middle of August; in order, probably, that affairs
with the Count of Foix might be settled at the same
time.[1]

About the beginning of April, the Duke of Anjou
and the Constable went, at the head of 10,000 men
at arms and 30,000 foot, besides 1500 Genoese cross-
bow-men, to reduce to submission the barons on the
borders of Spain, who had always held themselves
very independent of France. Among these was
Count Gaston de Foix, who declared that he did not
know whether it was to the King of France or to the
King of England that he owed allegiance; but he
promised " to keep a day " with the Duke, at Moissac,
in the middle of August, and show himself the
stronger.

In the meantime, the legates had been incessant in The Eng-
their endeavours to bring about a cessation of arms lish send
no help to
between the Duke of Anjou and the Duke of Lancas- Aquitaine,
and Lan-
ter, and at last, a truce to continue till the end of caster returns to
August was agreed on. England.

[1] See Walsingham, p. 316 ; Rymer, vol. iii. p. 1000 ; and an
elaborate note by M. Buchon in his edition of *Froissart*, vol. i.
p. 688.

234 LIFE AND TIMES OF EDWARD III. CHAP. XII.

A.D. 1374. The Duke of Lancaster took for granted that "the day" at Moissac was thereby postponed, and, no reinforcements having arrived from home, returned to England in April.[1] It is remarkable, and almost unaccountable that no help was sent to the Duke. His disastrous position must have been known; his father had received supplies for carrying on the war; and yet all that he did was to get together ships and men, and make no use of them. The old King's infatuation for Alice Perrers continued; he had, shortly before, given her his wife's jewels;[2] and he allowed her to interfere so infamously with the administration of justice, that at last the Commons broke out into remonstrances, forbade her to attend the courts, and ordered her to absent herself from the King.

The whole of Aquitaine lost to England. The departure of the Duke of Lancaster was the signal for the defection of the whole of Aquitaine. The Duke of Anjou "kept his day" at Moissac with an army of nearly 50,000 men. Sir Thomas Felton, whom Lancaster had appointed seneschal of Bordeaux and the Bordelais in his absence, presented himself to remonstrate against Anjou's declarations that Lancaster had failed in his engagement, but his arguments were in vain; and Gaston de Foix was unable any longer to refuse his allegiance to the King of France. The Duke of Anjou then returned to Toulouse. On the 7th of September, began a campaign for the reduction of the rest of Aquitaine, and it had such success, that, before the end of the year, there was hardly a place in the hands of the English, except Bayonne and Bordeaux.[3]

[1] Buchon's *Froissart*, vol. i. p. 689.
[2] Rymer, vol. iii. p. 989.
[3] Buchon's *Froissart*, vol. i. p. 690; Walsingham, p. 317.

CHAP. XII.   DELAY IN RELIEVING BECHEREL.   235

After leaving Bordeaux, the Duke of Brittany, as already stated, went to his duchy to relieve various fortresses and raise the siege of Becherel, which had been beleaguered for more than a year. It was, however, so closely besieged by the Bretons, that he was unable to enter, or even communicate with, it; the garrison, therefore, at last agreed to surrender to the French, if they were not relieved by the 1st of November. On receiving information of this, the Duke of Brittany went immediately to England to ask for help, and Edward, who was always ready to support his son-in-law, lost no time in preparing to send troops to the relief of Becherel; but such constant delays took place, in consequence, doubtless, of the negotiations for peace, which had begun in the previous March, and had been carried on with much insincerity on the part of France,[1] that it was not until the beginning of the following year that the troops embarked. On the 23rd of August, letters of safe conduct were given, to various "persons about to go abroad in the company of the Duke of Brittany;"[2] on the 31st of the same month, similar letters were given to those who were to accompany the Earl of Cambridge. Still they did not leave England. A letter of safe conduct to the Duke of Brittany, "about to go abroad," was issued on the 30th of October; and the Earl of Cambridge was still in England on the 18th of November, on which day further orders for the assemblage of a fleet to convey him abroad were issued.[3] On the 24th of the same month the Earl of Cambridge and the Duke of Brittany were appointed the King's lieutenants throughout France;[4] but they had not left England

A.D. 1375.

Affairs of Brittany.

Edward prepares to send troops to Brittany.

---

[1] Walsingham, p. 318.
[2] Rymer, vol. iii. p. 1009.
[3] Ibid. pp. 1016, 1017.
[4] Ibid. p. 1018.

236 LIFE AND TIMES OF EDWARD III. Chap. XII.

A.D. 1375.

Unaccountable delay.

even on the 24th of December, for, on that day, orders were given by the King, to deliver up the castle of Brest to the Duke, "who is just about to go to Brittany."[1] On the 29th of December they had gone to the sea-coast, but some of the troops had not obeyed the King's directions as to going to the appointed sea-port, and they were, therefore, strictly ordered to do so within eight days.[2] At length the Duke of Brittany embarked for Calais, but apparently unaccompanied by troops. The Duke of Lancaster had gone there on the subject of the peace negotiations, and the Duke of Brittany went to meet him for the purpose, probably, of consulting him. He remained there some time; but when the Duke of Lancaster was obliged to leave that city to meet the Duke of Anjou at Bruges, the Duke of Brittany returned to England. Shortly afterwards, however, he re-embarked for France with th Earl f Cambridge, and landed at St. Mahé, in April or May, 1375.[3] On the 8th of May the King ordered prayers to be offered up for the success of those " whom we have sent to foreign parts."[4]

Surrender of Becherel.

In the meantime the day for the surrender of Becherel had long passed ; and, although " it was reported that the Duke of Brittany and the Earl of Salisbury were on the sea with 10,000 men," yet, as they did not appear, and the garrison " had held out valiantly for above fifteen months without being comforted," the castle was at length surrendered to the French.[5] Lord Latimer was Governor of Becherel

---

[1] Rymer, vol. iii. p. 1020.   [2] Ibid. p. 1021.

[3] Buchon's *Froissart*, vol. i. p. 696, note.

[4] "Quos ad partes transmarinas destinavimus."—Rymer, vol. iii. p. 1028.

[5] Buchon's *Froissart*, vol. i. p. 695.

CHAP. XII. TRUCE BETWEEN ENGLAND AND FRANCE. 237

and St. Sauveur, and the writer of a "contemporary chronicle" throws the loss of the fortress on him; "because," as he says, "when the English navy were furnished with a sufficient armed power to serve and succour the besieged, and for that purpose had received of the King our Sovereign Lord money for their wages, the said Lord Latimer hindered the same voyage, and so as well the King's town as money was lost." Lord Latimer was accused in Parliament of receiving the ransoms of places in Brittany without accounting to the King, and of other misdeeds in that country,[1] but there seems to be no foundation for this far graver charge of the chronicler.[2]

The garrison was allowed to go to St. Sauveur le Vicomte, which was still in the hands of the English, and to which Du Guesclin immediately laid siege.

When the Duke of Brittany and the Earl of Cambridge landed, they took possession of St. Mahé, then marched on to St. Pol de Léon, which surrendered to them, and afterwards laid siege to St. Brieuc. While they were thus advancing along the north of Brittany, the siege of St. Sauveur was proceeding, and its defenders were so hard pressed, and the castle so much injured by the great stones thrown by the powerful engines employed by the besiegers, that they agreed to surrender, unless relieved by the Duke of Brittany, of whose arrival and progress they had heard. The French also had received intelligence of the landing of the English, and without abandoning the siege, Du Guesclin sent Olivier de Clisson, the Count de Rohan, and the Lords of Laval and Beau-

A.D. 1375.

Siege of St. Sauveur.

Dukes of Brittany and Cambridge in Brittany.

St. Sauveur agrees to surrender unless relieved.

---

[1] Rot. Parl. 50 Ed. III. 21. [2] *Archæologia*, vol. xxii. p. 217.

238   LIFE AND TIMES OF EDWARD III.   CHAP. XII.

A.D. 1375. manoir, with 300 or 400 lances, to Lamballe to hold them in check.[1]

When the English at St. Sauveur had made terms with their besiegers, they sent information of the arrangement to the Duke of Brittany, who was then attacking St. Brieuc. He immediately held a council, at which it was decided not to abandon the siege of that city;[2] but, just at that moment, news reached him of a truce having been concluded between England and France. He had lost the mine on which he depended for the capture of the city; and was told that if he really wished to take it, he must begin another mine entirely afresh. He was also informed that Sir John Devereux was besieged in the south of Brittany.[3]

Sir John had been for some time quartered in the Isle of Quimperlé, in the south of Brittany, and had lately built a new castle about two leagues from the town, from whence he ravaged the country, and inspired such terror, that the inhabitants did not dare to journey from one town to another. Songs were sung by the young girls and children, warning people to keep away from the new castle. The *refrain* of one of these songs, quoted by Froissart,[4] was—

> Gardés vous dou Nouviau Fort,
> Vous qui allez ces allues;
> Car laiens prent son déport
> Messire Jehan d'Evrues.

On hearing of Sir John's exploits, the four Breton Lords, whom Du Guesclin had sent to Lamballe, could not refrain from marching off to attack him; and in

---

[1] Buchon's *Froissart,* vol. i. p. 696.   [2] Ibid. p. 698.
[3] Ibid. p. 699.   [4] Ibid. p. 698.

Chap. XII. THE ENGLISH BESIEGE QUIMPERLÉ. 239

like manner, when the Duke of Brittany heard of the plans of these Lords, he could not resist following them. He accordingly gave up the siege of St. Brieuc, and, accompanied by the Earl of Cambridge and other English barons, proceeded towards the new castle to attack the Bretons, who were besieging it. The Breton Lords were quite taken by surprise, and had hardly time to saddle and mount their horses. "Then," as Froissart says, "horses knew what spurs were meant for;" and it was owing only to their horses being fresh, and those of the English being tired, that they reached Quimperlé in safety.[1] The English now laid siege to that town and attacked it with such unremitting vigour, that, at last, Clisson and the other leaders agreed to surrender, unless they were relieved within eight days.

A.D. 1375.

The Duke of Brittany relieves Sir John Devereux, and then besieges Quimperlé.

In the meanwhile the negotiations for peace had been going on at Bruges; and the King of France, who had kept couriers constantly going to and fro from Paris to Brittany, and who was greatly alarmed at the progress of the English in that province, sent repeated despatches to Bruges, to tell the Duke of Anjou to hasten the conclusion of a truce. At last all was settled. Messengers went, with utmost speed, from Bruges to Quimperlé, to stop the victorious career of the English. They performed the distance in five days, and, on their arrival, found the Duke of Brittany in his tent playing at chess with the Earl of Cambridge.

The messengers were the bearers of orders to the Duke to stop all warfare instantly. The command put the Duke in a fury. He rolled his head and cried out, "Cursed be the hour when I granted

Truce concluded.

---

[1] Buchon's *Froissart*, vol. i. p. 700.

240   LIFE AND TIMES OF EDWARD III.   Chap. XII.

A.D. 1375. a truce to my enemies!" But he was obliged to obey orders, and, raising the siege, he and the English returned to St. Matthieu de Fine Poterne, where their fleet lay. The English then embarked for Eng-

The English sail home. land, and the Duke of Brittany joined his Duchess at Auray.[1]

Surrender of St. Sauveur. There can be no doubt that the siege of St. Sauveur ought to have been abandoned like the siege of Quimperlé; but Du Guesclin refused to admit that the treaty annulled the agreement which had been made by the garrison, and threatened to massacre the whole of them, if they did not surrender. Frightened by these threats, and betrayed, not improbably, by the governor, Lord Latimer,[2] they yielded, and were allowed to embark for England, whereupon Du Guesclin took possession of the fortress.

History of the negotiations for peace. It is necessary now, to relate the means by which the truce between England and France had been brought about, and to state its conditions.

The Pope had long endeavoured to put an end to the war; and, early in 1374, on the 11th of March,[3] Edward had consented to send ambassadors either to

Ambassadors sent to Calais March 11, 1374. Calais or to Bruges, to meet the Pope's nuncios relative to a treaty of peace. Bruges was the place selected, and the various intermediary negotiators met at that place; but the Duke of Lancaster remained at Calais, and the Duke of Anjou at St. Omer, until the inconvenience of sending messengers backwards and forwards from Bruges became so great, that the Dukes of Lancaster and Anjou both consented to go to that city.[4] After much negotiation, it was agreed that

---

[1] Buchon's *Froissart*, vol. i. p. 702.
[2] Contemporary Chronicle, *Archæol.* vol. xxii. p. 217.
[3] Rymer, vol. iii. p. 1000.
[4] Buchon's *Froissart*, vol. i. pp. 691, 694, 695, and 696.

CHAP. XII.   A TRUCE, BUT NOT PEACE, OBTAINED.   241

there should be a truce till the 24th of June; but, A.D. 1375.
inasmuch as the time was soon found to be too short
to settle terms of peace, the Pope issued a bull from
Avignon on the 4th of May, prolonging it till the Truce till
22nd of July.[1] Nothing, however, having been settled July,
by that time, messengers continually passed to and
fro between Edward and the Pope. Still, nothing
was concluded till the following year, for the French after which
ambassadors, guided by their crafty monarch, acted fruitless
throughout with utter insincerity. It is an interest- tions,
ing fact that Wyclif was one of the negotiators
appointed by Edward.[2]

"During the whole of this time," says Walsingham,
"the French fraudulently thought not of peace, but
of war;" and he goes on to say, that while the French
were making their preparations, the English, "who
know not prudence and forethought, but only are
excited after the manner of brute animals when they
fight, never thought of these things;" and he ends by
saying that the English were circumvented, and the
ambassadors separated without effecting a peace.[3]

On January 8th, 1375, however, negotiations were till Jan. 8,
resumed; and on that day, having previously ob- 1375.
tained the consent of Parliament, Edward appointed
three plenipotentiaries to treat for peace with France.[4]
The abbey of Bourbourg in Flanders was the place Terms of
appointed for their meeting; and on the 11th of truce
February the terms of a truce were agreed on. It February.
extended, however, only to Artois and Picardy, and
was to last only till the 22nd of April;[5] but on
February 20th, 1375, the Duke of Lancaster, the

---

[1] Rymer, vol. iii. p. 1002.   [2] Ibid. p. 1007.
[3] Walsingham, p. 318.   [4] Rymer, vol. iii. p. 1021.
[5] Ibid. p. 1022.

VOL. II.   R

242 LIFE AND TIMES OF EDWARD III. CHAP. XII.

A.D. 1375. Earl of Salisbury, and others, were appointed to negotiate for its prolongation.[1] They first met at Ghent, in order to be present at the great festivities and tournaments given by the Duke of Burgundy, which lasted for four days. When these were concluded, they all went to Bruges to consider the terms of peace. The demands made on either side were impracticable. The English demanded the restitution of all the territories they had ever conquered from France; the payment of the money due to England according to the treaty of Bretigni; and the release of the Captal. France demanded the destruction of the castle of Calais, and the repayment of the money already paid to the English.[2]

Truce to last till June 30, 1376.

It was not to be expected that these conditions could be agreed to on either side: the idea of a permanent peace was, therefore, postponed; and all that could be settled on June 27, 1375, was, that the truce should be prolonged to the last day of June in the following year.[3]

[1] Rymer, vol. iii. p. 1024.
[2] Buchon's *Froissart*, vol. i. p. 704.
[3] Rymer, vol. iii. p. 1031.

EDWARD THE BLACK PRINCE.

From his Monument in Canterbury Cathedral. (For explanation, see List of Illustrations.)

CHAPTER XIII.

PROCEEDINGS OF THE "GOOD PARLIAMENT" AND DEATH OF THE BLACK PRINCE.

THE war was now suspended, and nothing of importance took place in England, until the meeting of Parliament in the spring of 1376, after an extraordinary intermission of three years. Matters of such moment then occupied its attention, and so bold a course was taken for the promotion of the welfare of the nation, that it obtained the name of the "Good Parliament."[1] No Parliament previously held in England spoke out so boldly, or treated of such important matters, as this Parliament of the fiftieth year of Edward's reign. But its courage and its earnestness need excite no wonder. For nearly a century the nation had been by law admitted to a voice in the government of England; and so necessary did Edward deem it to ask those over whom he reigned to advise him how they should be governed, that he constantly summoned councils of special classes of persons from all parts of England, and consulted with them as to the laws relative to their particular calling. The nation thus began to feel its power, and at last the time had come for action. There was defeat and

A.D. 1376.

Meeting of Parliament.

Its importance.

---

[1] Walsingham, p. 324. "Most of our general historians have slurred over this important session."—Hallam's *Middle Ages*, vol. ii. p. 187 (edition 1841).

244 LIFE AND TIMES OF EDWARD III. CHAP. XIII.

A.D. 1376. disgrace abroad, with vast expenditure and without results; at home there was social dissatisfaction increased by an attempted interference with wages; a King enfeebled by premature age,[1] and degraded by infatuated love for a worthless woman; the heir apparent dying; the heir presumptive an infant; and treachery suspected. These circumstances were enough to rouse Parliament, and make the nation call for its interference; and Parliament responded to the call.

Lancaster's misgovernment opposed by the Black Prince. In consequence of the age and feebleness of the King, and the illness of the Black Prince, the Duke of Lancaster had now for some time past taken a prominent part in the government of the country. He had appointed to high offices, men who were devoted to him, but whose conduct, as well as his own, had become the object of grave suspicion. The Black Prince, although grievously ill, exerted himself as well as he could to oppose the Duke, and to head the popular party in demanding a reformation of State abuses. That he was the head of this party is evident from the statements of contemporary writers, and from the reversal of State policy which took place after the Prince's death. Lancaster's object was to aggrandise

---

[1] "Concerning the 'old age' of the King, so repeatedly noted in the text, it should be observed that he had at this time scarcely completed his sixty-fourth year, a period of life which would not at the present day call forth such an epithet. It may further be remarked that, on reference to Dugdale's *Baronage*, it will appear that in the middle ages the deaths of a great proportion of the English nobility, even when occasioned by natural causes (for war and pestilence had their full share), occurred under the age of forty; and that their eldest sons, though commonly the offspring of very early marriages, very frequently became wards of the Crown by reason of their minority"—i.e. when they came into possession of their family estate.—Note by Thomas Amyot, F.R.S., to the Contemporary Chronicle, *Archæol.* vol. xxii. p. 241.

CHAP. XIII.   PARLIAMENTARY STRUGGLE.   245

A.D. 1376.

himself, and to maintain the power of the Barons, in contradistinction to that of Parliament; the Black Prince, although, perhaps, unintentionally, to increase the power of the people, as represented by Parliament.

Before giving a full account of the proceedings of the Parliament which was now about to meet, it is necessary to enter a little further into the political relations between the Black Prince and the Duke of Lancaster; in order to make clear the policy pursued by each.[1]

Evidence as to enmity between the Black Prince and Duke of Lancaster:

Lancaster was greatly irritated at certain proposals of Parliament, and, as will presently be more particularly related, wished to silence the members who had made them, by force rather than by argument; his friends, however, soon convinced him that this course would be dangerous. The Reformers were supported by the Prince of Wales. On a certain occasion when the Duke was considering what course he should take relative to the charges against Lord Latimer and Richard Lyons, it is said, that he feared "the majesty of the Prince, whom he knew to favour the people and the knights."[2] When the Prince died, the Duke at once plucked up courage, and "abused

---

[1] The most important contemporary writer who relates the history of this particular period is the author of a chronicle, a translation of which exists in the Harleian Library MSS., No. 6217, and which has been reprinted in the 22nd volume of *Archæologia*. The writer, who was probably a monk of St. Alban's, is evidently imbued with a bitter hatred of the Duke of Lancaster on account of his support of Wyclif; but it is equally clear, from its marked individuality, that his Chronicle was written while the events were going on; and whatever may be the question as to his opinions and inferences, there is no reason to doubt his facts or his mirror-like reflection of the feelings of the time. See Hook's *Lives*, vol. iv. p. 332, note; and *Fasc. Ziz.* p. 523, note.   [2] *Archæologia*, vol. xxii. pp. 214, 225.

246   LIFE AND TIMES OF EDWARD III.   CHAP. XIII.

A.D. 1376. the King's simplicity ;"[1] and "the Prince being dead, the effect of the Parliament died with him."[2] It is evident therefore that there was enmity between John of Gaunt and the Prince of Wales, and that John of Gaunt feared his brother. What then

Its cause. was the cause of this enmity? There can be no doubt that the Prince embraced the popular party, and joined with those who wished to reform the wasteful expenditure of the Government, for which the Duke of Lancaster must have been to a great extent answerable; probably also, he may

Dissatisfaction with the Duke's government, have been vexed at the miserable failure of the Duke's management of the war with France. But these were hardly sufficient motives for the enmity of the Prince towards his brother, or for the fear with which the Duke regarded him ; and it seems more

and suspicion of his designs. probable, that the latter was suspected, by the Prince, of a wish to prevent his son Richard from succeeding to the throne. The proceedings of Parliament show that some of its members entertained a similar apprehension; the Duke himself complained, in the first Parliament of Richard II., that such things had been said of him as amounted to a charge of treason.[3] It is therefore tolerably clear that the Duke of Lancaster—whether justly or unjustly, it is now difficult to decide—was generally supposed to be planning an usurpation of the throne. .

Proceedings of Parliament. The course taken by Parliament, on its meeting in April 1376, must now be related.[4] It met on the 23rd, but, inasmuch as some of the Sheriffs had not returned their Briefs of Parliament, and some

---

[1] *Archæologia*, p. 240.

[2] Murimuth, edited by Thomas Hogg, London, 1846, p. 220.

[3] Rot. Parl. 1 Ric. II. 13.   [4] Ibid. vol. ii. p. 321, &c.

CHAP. XIII. PROCEEDINGS IN PARLIAMENT. 247

of the members had not arrived, the King deferred its opening until the following day; and it was therefore proclaimed in the Great Hall, that all members should be present at eight o'clock the next morning, or be fined.

On their assembling, Sir John Knyvet, the Chancellor, informed them, by command of the King, who was lying ill at Eltham, that they were summoned for three purposes. The first was, to provide for the good government of the kingdom; the second, for its defence from foreign enemies by sea and land; the third, for the carrying on of the war against France. He then said, that the King had always acted according to their advice and intended to continue to do so; and requested them to consult on the matters now brought before them, the Lords and Prelates by themselves, and the Commons by themselves in their ancient place in the Chapter House. Triers and Receivers were then appointed as usual, "The King of Castile and Leon, and Duke of Lancaster" being one of the former.[1] The Knights of the Shires refused to act without the advice of the nobles; the two divisions of Parliament therefore were ordered

A.D. 1376.

The Chancellor states the purposes for which Parliament is summoned.

---

[1] Godwin, in his Life of Chaucer, vol. iii. p. 67, states that "John of Gaunt was absent. It was while he continued abroad for the service of his country, that his adversaries opened their hostilities against him." The importance of this mistake on the part of the Duke's advocate needs no pointing out. Godwin refers to the Contemporary Chronicle, which then existed only in MS. (Harleian MSS., No. 6217), but it is evident to me that he never saw it. A single leaf of the same MS. (No. 247), of some importance, has since then been discovered. See Amyot's Preface to the Chronicle, *Arch.* vol. xxii. p. 211. Lancaster was at Bruges on the 12th of March (Rymer, vol. iii. p. 1048), but there was ample time for his return to England, after the prolongation of the truce, and before the meeting of Parliament on the 23rd of April.

248. LIFE AND TIMES OF EDWARD III. Chap. XIII.

A.D. 1376.

to report to one another what they proposed, and eleven Lords and Nobles, viz., four Bishops, three Earls, one Lord, and three Knights, were appointed to consult with the Commons.

Choice of a speaker;

The temper of the Parliament soon showed itself. "Whilst thus these nobles and knights were busy about the King's request, there arose this question among them, which of the knights should be their speaker; for they had fully resolved to deny the King's request, until certain abuses were corrected, and certain persons, who seemed to have impoverished the King and the realm and greatly blemished their fame, were examined, and their offences, according to the quality of them, punished. Careful they were, as is said, about their speaker, for they doubted certain

falls on Sir Peter de la Mare;

of the King's secretaries."[1] Sir Peter de la Mare was then chosen as speaker; and, "trusting in God, and standing together with his followers before the nobles, whereof the chief was John Duke of Lancaster, whose doings were ever contrary," he boldly

who, in the name of the Commons, demands reform.

began the attack. He said that the Commons had been oppressed by taxation, "now paying fifteenths, otherwhiles ninths and tenths," which, however, "they would take in good part, nor grieve at it, if it had been bestowed upon the King's wars, although scarcely prosperous; but it was evident neither the King nor realm had any profit thereby," and he therefore demanded that an account should be rendered of the receipts and expenditure. "When he had thus said, they having not wherewith to answer, the Judges held their peace."[2]

---

[1] Contemporary Chronicle, *Archæol.* vol. xxii. p. 213.

[2] Up to this point the quotations are from the later discovered tract.

Chap. XIII. THE DUKE OF LANCASTER ALARMED. 249

The Duke of Lancaster was now alarmed, and was disposed to try to put down his opponents by overbearing. "What, sayeth he, do these base and ignoble knights attempt? Do they think they be the Kings or Princes of the land? I think they know not what power I am of. I will therefore early in the morning appear unto them so glorious, and will show such power among them, and with such vigour I will terrify them, that neither they nor theirs shall dare henceforth to provoke me to wrath." But his "private men," whom he consulted, reminded him that "it was not unknown to him what helpes these knights have to undershore them, for they have the favour and love of the Lords, and specially of the Lord Edward Prince, your brother, who giveth them his counsel and aid effectually."[1] They reminded him also, that the Londoners were so well affected to his opponents, that they would not suffer them to be molested; and, if they were interfered with, would proceed "to attempt all extremity" against him and his friends. "With this, the Duke's guilty conscience was much troubled," and "knowing that if mention were openly made of his wicked acts he could not satisfy the people by any purgation," the next day "laying aside all vigour and stoutness of stomach, he came into the assembly of the knights, and showed himself so favourable and so mild, that he drew them all into an admiration."

The Lords and Commons then granted the King, for another three years, the like subsidy on wool, leather and woolfels, as had been granted three years before; but the Commons, apparently separating themselves from the Lords, excused themselves from

A.D. 1376.

Duke of Lancaster inclined to oppose him,

but is reminded that the Prince supports him,

and therefore refrains.

Subsidy granted.

[1] Tract No. 6217, p. 214.

250 LIFE AND TIMES OF EDWARD III. Chap. XIII.

A.D. 1376.

granting any other subsidy for the war, on account of the distresses of the times; but they promised that if the King should have any great need, they would help him to the best of their power, and "so as no other country of the world had done for their Lord in times past."[1] The Commons then proceeded to enter into the details of the reforms they demanded, and "considering the evils of the country, through so many wars and other causes, and that the officers now in the King's service are insufficient, without further assistance for so great a charge, pray that the Council be strengthened by the addition of ten or twelve Bishops, Lords, and others, to be constantly at hand, so that no business of weight should be despatched without the consent of all, nor smaller matters without that of four or six. To this request the King instantly agreed;[2] the Bishop of Winchester was one of the number chosen, but the Duke of Lancaster was not included.[3] The Commons then appeared in Parliament, protesting that they had the same good will as ever to assist the King with their lives and fortunes; but they said, that it seemed to them, that, if their said liege lord had always possessed about him faithful counsellors and good officers, he would have been so rich, he would have had no need of charging his Commons with subsidy or tallage, considering the great ransoms of the French and Scotch Kings, and of so many other prisoners; and that it appeared to be for the private advantage of some nearer the King, and of others by their collusion, that he and his kingdom were so impoverished, and the

Commons demand the addition of a continual council of ten or twelve to be added to the King's Council,

---

[1] Rot. Parl. 50 Ed. III. m. 2. 9.   [2] Ibid. 10.

[3] Lowth's *Life of Wykeham*, p. 102, note, quoting Harl. MSS. No. 247, fo. 143.

CHAP. XIII. COMMONS ACCUSE THE KING'S OFFICERS. 251

Commons so ruined. They promised, however, that if he would do speedy justice on such as should be found guilty, and take from them what law and reason permitted, with what had been already granted in Parliament, they would engage that he should be rich enough to maintain his wars for a long time without much charging his people in any manner."[1]

A.D. 1376.

and that the King's guilty officers should be punished.

The Commons next complained of the removal of the Staple from Calais, by the same advisers of the King, for their own profit and to the injury of the kingdom; of the usurious interest they had charged him; and of their buying up old debts due from the King at a low price and making him pay them the full amount.[2] They then accused certain individuals of being implicated in these crimes. Richard Lyons, a merchant of London, who was one of the Council, and farmer of the customs and subsidies, was the first whom they attacked. The principal accusation against him, in addition to these general charges, was that he had removed the staple from Calais, and had levied higher duties than were authorised by Parliament on wools and other articles of merchandise, for his own profit; and that the staple being thus removed, he and Lord Latimer "bought up all the merchandise that came into England, setting prices at their own pleasure, whereupon they made such a great scarcity in this land of things saleable, that the common sort of people could scantily live."[3] Lyons, "fearing his own skin," tried to bribe the Black Prince by sending him by the river a thousand pounds in a barrel, "as if it had been a barrel of sturgeon;" but the Prince sent it back,[4] and Lyons was con-

They make charges against Richard Lyons;

his condemnation.

---

[1] Rot. Parl. 50 Ed. III. 15.   [2] Ibid. 16.
[3] Ibid. 50 Ed. III. 17.   [4] Tract No. 6217, pp. 218, 219.

252 LIFE AND TIMES OF EDWARD III. Chap. XIII.

A.D. 1376.

Against Lord Latimer;

demned to be imprisoned during the King's will.[1] The next, was William Lord Latimer, the friend and creature of the Duke of Lancaster,[2] Chamberlain and Privy Councillor, and Governor of the Castle of Becherel and other places in Brittany. In addition to being an accomplice of Lyons, Latimer was accused of appropriating various large sums of money to his own use during the time of his command in Brittany; and of receiving bribes for the surrender of the castles of Becherel and St. Sauveur. Latimer defended him-

his condemnation.

self; but was, with the King's consent, condemned to be fined and imprisoned. He contrived, however, to obtain another hearing; and, having found sureties for his appearance on the 26th of May, was allowed to depart at liberty.[3]

Against William Ellis;

William Ellis of Great Yarmouth, Lyons' deputy there, was then charged, with extorting money from the captain of a Scotch vessel driven by a storm into the port; and also from the captain of a Prussian vessel, laden with wax, iron, and other merchandise, likewise driven by stress of weather into the port. After a most elaborate enquiry and examination of

his condemnation.

witnesses, he was condemned to fine and imprison-

Against John Peachy;

ment.[4] John Peachy, of London, was then charged with having obtained from Richard Lyons and others, for their own profit, a patent, giving him the exclusive right of selling sweet wines in London (against the ordained prohibition of the sale of which by retail the Commons had petitioned in this Parliament); and, it was added, that he had thereby been enabled

his condemnation.

to sell his wine at a higher price. He was found

---

[1] Rot. Parl. m. ii. 19.

[2] Hallam's *Middle Ages*, vol. ii. p. 188.

[3] Rot. Parl. 20–29 mn. and 4. [4] Ibid. m. 5, 31–32.

CHAP. XIII.   THE COMMONS' ACCUSATIONS.   253

guilty, fined, and imprisoned. The real crime here A.D. 1376
was the wrongful grant of the patent; but the
cause of the complaint probably was the power of
thereby raising the price of his wine.[1] Sir John *Against Sir John Nevill;*
Nevill was then accused, of having received payment
for a certain number of soldiers whom he had agreed
to collect and send to Brittany, and of sending a less
number and less efficient men; he was also called to
account for the ravaging of the country by these men
on their way to Southampton. He repelled the first
charge satisfactorily; as to the second, he declared he
was not responsible for the ill deeds of his men; the
Commons held the contrary opinion, however, and he
was therefore condemned, to make restitution and be *his condemnation;*
ousted from the offices he held.[2]

The next charge brought by the Commons was
of a still more bold and serious nature. It affected
the King's favourite, Alice Perrers, to whom he *Against Alice Perrers;*
had given the Queen's jewels, "who was too familiar
with King Edward,"[3] and who, during the Queen's
lifetime, had been "preferred in the King's love
before her."[4] This woman interfered with the course
of justice, sitting on the bench with the judges[5]
and "defending false causes everywhere by unlawful
means, to get possessions for her own use; and if in
any place she was resisted, then she went unto the
King, by whose power being presently helped, whether it were right or wrong, she had her desire."[6]
So high had she risen in the King's favour, that,
two years before, he had allowed her to ride from

[1] Rot. Parl. 50 Ed. III. 33.   [2] Ibid. 34.
[3] Continuation of Murimuth (London, 1846), p. 219.
[4] Tract No. 6217, p. 233.   [5] Walsingham, p. 320.
[6] Tract No. 6217, pp. 233, 234.

254   LIFE AND TIMES OF EDWARD III. Chap. XIII.

A.D. 1376.
—

the Tower of London through Cheapside to Smith-
field, attired as the Lady of the Sun, accompanied
by a great concourse of lords and ladies, to be pre-

her con-
demnation.

sent at a tournament which lasted seven days.[1]   The
Commons now complained that "many women pursued divers needs and quarrels in the King's Courts
by way of maintenance and for pay and sharing;"
and the King therefore ordained "that no woman
should do so for the future, and especially Alice
Perrers, and that if the said Alice should do so she
should be banished from the kingdom."[2]   Alice was
then compelled to take an oath, which was ratified
by the King, to the effect that she would never return to the King's presence.[3]

There can be no doubt that these attacks on the
King's ministers were the boldest assertions of the
right of the people to control the actions of Government that had ever taken place in English history.
It is equally certain that they were just and right-
eous.   But a heavy blow now fell on the Reformers.
Their chief supporter, without whose aid, as subsequent events too plainly showed, it would have
been extremely dangerous to attack Lancaster and
his adherents, was taken from them by death.

Death of
the Black
Prince.

On the 8th of June the Black Prince died.   His
illness had been long; it must have been a great effort
for him to have roused himself for the invasion of
France with his father three years previously; still
more, to have taken part in the attempted reformation
of the abuses and corruptions which were ruining England.   At last his strength failed; and he died in the

[1] Stow's *London*, vol. i. p. 717.
[2] Rot. Parl. m. 6, 45.
[3] Walsingham, p. 322, and Tract, p. 237.

MONUMENT OF EDWARD THE BLACK PRINCE.
IN CANTERBURY CATHEDRAL.

CHAP. XIII. DEATH OF THE BLACK PRINCE. 255

forty-sixth year of his age, in the Palace of West- A.D. 1376.
minster,[1] whither, in order to be nearer Parliament, he
had removed either from his house in Fish Street
Hill[2] or from his castle at Berkhampsted. He was
buried in Canterbury Cathedral. His will was made
only the day before his death; and it is remarkable
that he appointed the Duke of Lancaster one of his
executors. This, it must be admitted, seems to show
that he had no suspicion of him; but it is to be observed that the Bishop of Winchester, in whom the
Prince had the greatest reliance, was also one.

The Commons now felt that it was of the utmost
importance to secure the undisputed succession of the
throne to the Black Prince's son; but the Duke of The
Lancaster—if the contemporary, but somewhat preju- Duke of
diced, chronicler is to be believed[3]—took the oppor- Lancaster
attempts to
divert the

---

[1] Buchon's *Froissart*, vol. i. p. 706.

[2] "Above this lane's end (Crooked Lane) upon Fish Street
Hill, is one great house, for the most part built with stone, which
pertained, some time, to Edward the Black Prince, who was in
his lifetime lodged there. It is now (1596) altered to a common
inn, having the Black Bell for a sign."—Stow's *Survey of London*,
book ii. ch. ii. vol. i. p. 499.

[3] It must be confessed that it is doubtful whether, in this case,
the chronicler deserves credit, as his account is inconsistent with
the Rolls of Parliament. The omission from the Rolls of the Duke
of Lancaster's proposal is obviously of no importance, but the
chronicler's story is somewhat inconsistent with the Rolls. The
chronicler says that the Commons answered the Duke by saying
that "be it granted the King should depart, yet we want not an
heir, the Prince's son (now ten years old) lives, and is now living,
there is no need to labour about such matters. With these
words, the Duke confounded, herewith departed." It is hardly
possible to reconcile this with the very clear record in the Rolls
that the Commons desired the recognition of Richard as heir.
The only way of so doing is to suppose that the Commons, on reflection, thought the recognition, after the Duke's proposal, to be
requisite.

256 LIFE AND TIMES OF EDWARD III. Chap. XIII.

A.D. 1376.

succession to himself,

tunity to attempt to secure to himself the succession to the throne in the event of Richard's death, and to bring about that event by poison. The chronicler states, that " the Duke with his malefactors coming in among the knights, earnestly desired them that they, associated with the lords and barons, would deliberate who, after the death of the King and the Prince's son, ought to inherit the realm of England; furthermore, he requested that after the example of France, they would make a law that no woman should be heir of the kingdom; for he considered the old age of the King, whom death expected in the gates, and the youth of the Prince's son, whom (as it was said) he purposed to poison if he could no otherwise come by the kingdom, for if these two were taken away and such a law established, he was to be the next heir of the realm, for there was no heir male in the realm nearer than he." [1]

but the Commons demand that Richard of Bordeaux shall be recognised as heir to the throne.

Which is done.

The King was lying ill at Eltham, and his death might happen at any time. The Commons therefore petitioned the King, that " it should please him, as a great comfort to the whole kingdom, if he would summon Richard of Bordeaux, son and heir of Edward, to come before them, in order that the Lords and Commons might see and honour him, as the real heir apparent of the kingdom." The Prince was accordingly brought before them, on Wednesday, the 26th of June, when the Archbishop of Canterbury said to all present that " the said Richard, who was the true heir apparent of the kingdom, in the same way that his noble father the Prince was, ought to be held by them and all other lieges of the King in great honour and reverence." It is remarkable that this

[1] *Archæol.* vol. xxii. p. 231.

CHAP. XIII.   THE COMMONS STILL DEMAND REFORMS.   257

should have been deemed necessary, as it would seem to us, at the present day, that there could be no doubt as to the right of Richard to the throne. That it was considered essential, however, shows that the succession to the English crown was by no means clearly defined.[1] The Commons then prayed that the King would create him Prince of Wales; to which it was answered, that it did not belong to the Prelates nor to the Lords to do this in Parliament, or otherwise; but that this power belonged clearly to the King. The Prelates and Lords, therefore, promised to mediate with the King for this purpose.[2]

The death of the Black Prince produced a total change in the relative power of the two opposing parties. But, before proceeding to the events which were thus its consequence, it is necessary to conclude the account of the proceedings in Parliament.

The King was too ill to give his answer to the petitions of the Commons at Westminster, and they were therefore summoned to Eltham to receive it. One hundred and sixty petitions were presented, relating to almost every variety of subject connected with social or political life.

Three years had passed without a Parliament having been summoned; doubtless, because that of 1373 had granted a subsidy for that period; but those three years had been a period of defeat abroad and misgovernment at home. The Commons, therefore, prayed that a statute should be passed providing that a Parliament, "for the correction of errors and falsities," should be held every year; and that the Knights of the Counties should be chosen "by the common choice of the gentlemen of the said counties:" to

A.D. 1376.

Further proceedings in Parliament.

Petition that a Parliament should be held every year.

---

[1] See Appendix.   [2] Rot. Parl. vol. i. p. 380.

VOL. II.   S

258   LIFE AND TIMES OF EDWARD III.   Chap. XIII.

A.D. 1376.

which the King answered, that there were statutes to that effect, which should be duly observed.[1] They then petitioned, that " those who put on new taxes by their demesne authority for their own profit, accroaching to themselves Royal Power, without leave of Parliament, should suffer judgment of life, of members, and of forfeiture."[2]   Another petition, with somewhat of the same object, was to the effect, that no officers or members of the King's Council who have been, or should be, found guilty of any act against their allegiance, or contrary to their oath of office, should be pardoned; that they should be duly punished, and that they should never again be allowed to be councillors or officers of the King.   To this the King curtly answered, that he would act according to his own will as seemed good to him.[3]   The Duke of Lancaster was probably beginning to regain his influence.   A petition, almost to the same effect, had been presented earlier in the session, to which, however, was added, as a reason, that if any such person were restored to his office he would " grieve and destroy " those who had been the cause of his dismissal; the answer also was somewhat different.   The King had then replied that " the charges should be shown to

That corrupt officers should be punished.

King's unsatisfactory answer, caused by Lancaster's influence after the Prince's death.

---

[1] Rot. Parl. 50 Ed. III. No. cxxviii.

[2] Ibid. cxxxiii.   This petition shows an important advance in the civil freedom of the people.   Those who originally held in *demesne* were the mere serfs or villeins who held their land at the mere will of the owners or Lords of the Demesnes, and could be lawfully taxed at will.   Nothing was more common than for cities and towns holding in free burgage, to protest against being taxed as if they were in *demesne*.   But the tenants in *demesne* had now become tenants by certain right, and were gradually advancing to tenure as copyholders of manors.

[3] Ibid. 53 Ed. III. No. cxxx.

Chap. XIII. THE ABUSES OF THE COURT OF ROME. 259

the King and his Council; and, if seemeth to them that the defaults deserve such judgment, the King, by the advice of his Council, will make such judgment as shall seem to him best in such a case."[1] This was before the Duke had acquired any influence.

The Pope's usurpations were another matter that occupied much of the time of the Parliament; and, as the Bishop of Winchester was regarded with " special affection and singular delight "[2] by the Black Prince, it is probable that the Prince and his friends acted in this matter by his advice. No less than twelve petitions had relation to this grievance. They were made with unusual solemnity, begging the King to give "good consideration" to them, and saying, that the remedy of the grievance would be " the most profitable for him and his kingdom that was ever made." The King was then prayed " to think and rethink" how his progenitors and other great men of the land had founded the churches, and given them great possessions, amounting to one-third of the kingdom; and " to think" how they had " peaceable possession to grant, to whom they pleased, the churches and benefices, in like manner, as the King St. Edward gave the Bishopric of Worcester to St. Wolstan;" also, how, " by grant of the King, confirmed by the Court of Rome," the cathedrals had free election of their prelates; and " so long as these good customs prevailed the kingdom was prosperous, but, since they had been perverted into simony and covetousness, the land was full of adversity." The petition then went on to say, " Also, it is to think about, that no man who loves God and the Holy Church, the King and

A.D. 1376.

Commons petition against the Pope's usurpations,

especially against his appointment to benefices and dignities in the Church.

[1] Rot. Parl. 53 Ed. III. No. xiv.
[2] Clause in the pardon granted to Wykeham by Richard II.

s 2

260   LIFE AND TIMES OF EDWARD III. CHAP. XIII.

A.D. 1376. kingdom of England, has not reason to think, to grieve, and to weep that the Court of Rome, which ought to be the fountain, root, and source of holiness, and destruction of covetousness and simony, has so subtly, by little and little, by process of time and by sufferance, drawn to himself the collation to bishoprics and other dignities, and of every bishopric and other benefices which he gives he wishes to have the tax." Further, that the persons appointed by the Pope to these preferments live in the " sinful city of Avignon ;" and put out their benefices to farm ; that thus, aliens " who have never seen and never will see their parishes" are in possession of them ; that consequently " the Holy Church is more destroyed by such bad Christians than by all the Jews and Saracens of the world ;" and that " God has given his sheep to our Lord the Pope to feed and not to shear."

Enormous sums received by the Pope. The magnitude of the Pope's receipts from these sources, and the consequent drain on England, are shown by a statement, in one of the petitions,[1] that the Pope's collector lived in a great palace in London, with clerks or officers, as if it were for the receipts of a Prince or a Duke; and they also said that, "when the Pope wanted money for his wars in Lombardy and elsewhere, *or for the ransom of his French friends taken prisoners by the English,* he demanded a subsidy from the English clergy."[2]

The King declares he is proceeding against the Pope. The whole of the petitions relative to these grievances well deserve perusal; but it would occupy too much space here to enter into further details, and it is necessary only to give the King's answer, which was to the effect that he had beforetimes ordained

Rot. Parl. 50 Ed. III. No. xlv. xlvi.   [2] Ibid. No. xlviii.

CHAP. XIII.   COMMERCIAL LEGISLATION.   261

sufficient remedies, that he was "pursuing" them
before the Pope, and that he had "perfect will" to
follow them up to the end.[1]

In consequence of the priories and other religious
houses, which were subject to foreign houses (priories
alien as they were called), being filled with Frenchmen
who acted as spies, the Commons also petitioned, that,
so long as the war lasted, all Frenchmen should be
banished the kingdom; but no action was taken for
this purpose.[2]

Other petitions were presented relative to trade
and commerce. The salmon and other Thames fish
having been injured by " Trynks " and other engines
put in the river, which destroyed the fry—or rather
retained it, as it was given to the pigs to eat—it was
prayed that none such should be allowed between
London and the sea; that no salmon should be taken
between Gravesend and the bridge at Henley-on-
Thames during kipper time, that is between the 6th of
January and the 3rd of May; and that no nets, except
with large meshes, should be allowed in the river; and
they ended by praying the King to make these orders
for three years, so that people might buy as good a
salmon for two shillings as they then bought for ten.[3]
Protection of the fish in the Brent, a branch of the
Thames, was also demanded;[4] and in both of these
cases it was ordered that the law should be put in
force.

The impediments to the free navigation of the
Thames were also a subject of complaint. New locks
and weirs had been put up, and tolls demanded, at the

A.D. 1376.

Petition against the filling of priories alien with foreigners.

Petitions as to trade and commerce.

Salmon fishery in Thames.

Navigation of the Thames

---

[1] Rot. Parl. 50 Ed. III. No. xliv. Nos. 94 to 103. See also
xv. xvii. xl. xlv. l. lii. lxi. lxv.
[2] Ibid. No. lxix.   [3] Ibid. No. v.   [4] Ibid. No. vi.

262 LIFE AND TIMES OF EDWARD III. Chap. XIII.

A.D. 1376. various bridges, such as Staines, Windsor, and Maiden-head (Maydehethe), and a new lock at Hampton (Hamelden), at which accidents often happened; the Commons therefore prayed that this grievance should be remedied. As to the locks and weirs, it was ordered, that a former statute should be put in force; as to the tolls, the petitioners were told to appeal to the Court of Chancery, and found their writs on their ancient franchises.[1]

Herring fishery. The herring fishery and trade, always of the greatest importance and fostered with the utmost care,[2] had been interfered with at Yarmouth to such an extent, that the Commons alleged that the Yarmouth people themselves could witness that two herrings were sold for 1*d.*;[3] and they prayed, therefore, that a certain charter, which had been granted to Yarmouth and which caused this dearness by interfering with the trade, should be revoked. This was done, but it was restored in the following reign.

Harbours choked with sand. The driving of fish stakes in the harbours, which caused sand to accumulate and the harbours to be choked up,[4] was another matter for which a remedy was prayed and granted.

Petition against usurious foreign money-lenders dwelling in London. Various other important commercial matters were also brought before the King. Foreign money-lenders, who were mostly Lombards, and who lent money at what was considered usurious interest, were petitioned against, and the King was asked to banish them.[5] He was also petitioned by the Mayor, Aldermen, and Commons of the city of London, to forbid foreigners from dwelling in the city or acting as

---

[1] Rot. Parl. 50 Ed. III. No. lxxv.   [2] Ibid. No. xxv.
[3] *Archæol.* vol. xxii. p. 238.   [4] Rot. Parl. 50 Ed. III. No. xix.
[5] Ibid. No. vii.

CHAP. XIII.   EXPORT OF YARN PROHIBITED.   263

brokers and buying and selling by retail, which they
alleged to be against their ancient franchises.   To this
the King answered, that, if they would put the city
under good government, for the future no foreigner
should be allowed to dwell, act as broker, or sell by
retail in London or the suburbs, save and except the
merchants of the Hanse Towns.[1]   It was also a
matter of complaint that the franchises of cities
and towns in general were invaded.   In answer to the
prayer of the Commons for a remedy of these grievances, those who had charters or liberties were
ordered to show them in the Court of Chancery, and
it was promised that right should be done them by
advice of the Great Council.[2]

In another matter, the King wisely resisted a petition of the Commons, viz. that the export of corn
might be forbidden, because of its dearness, which
was alleged to be a consequence of its exportation.
His answer, which was singularly contrary to the
spirit of the times, was, " Let the King's lieges be free
to carry it for their profit wherever it shall seem them
best."[3]   Another petition, however, involving similar
principles, was answered in a contrary spirit.   The
merchants of Wiltshire, Bristol, Somerset, Gloucester,
Dorset, and elsewhere, complained of the manufacture of woollen yarn, and of its export to Normandy
and Lombardy for its manufacture into cloths.   The
reasons alleged for ordering this to be forbidden were,
that the King lost the export duty on the manufactured cloth, and that so many people were employed
in the making of this yarn that the labourers became
insolent (*la plus fols du corps*) and would not gather in

Margin notes:
A.D. 1376.

King answers that the City must first be put under good government.

Against general invasion of franchises.

Against export of corn which King rejects.

Petition against export of yarn, because of its raising wages by giving employment.

---

[1] Rot. Parl. 50 Ed. III. No. lxxxiv.   [2] Ibid. No. viii.
[3] Ibid. No. xcvii.

264 LIFE AND TIMES OF EDWARD III. CHAP.XIII.

A.D. 1376.

King grants the petition.

the harvests. The King at once granted the petition, because it affected his own pocket; thus acting against all the recognised principles of political economy, as now usually received. A trade, which was evidently of great importance in furnishing employment for large numbers of people, was discouraged because it raised the price of labour; and, also, because the price of the English manufactured cloths would require to be lowered, in order to compete with the cloths manufactured abroad with yarn exported from England.

Struggle between labourers and employers.

Petitions against refractory labourers who want higher

This proceeding arose out of the struggle between labourers and employers, which was so marked and interesting a feature of the reign, and was an especial subject of consideration in this Parliament. The Statute of Labourers was continually evaded; and the Commons now complained, that when the masters offered to pay their labourers according to the wages laid down in the statute, they fled to other places; from county to county, from hundred to hundred, from town to town, to places unknown to their masters; and, what was worse, that they obtained immediate employment at the places to which they fled, which set so bad an example, that masters did not dare challenge or displease their servants, but were obliged to give them what they asked. They then went on to attribute all sorts of evils to this struggle of the labourers for fair wages; such as that they became beggars, and staff-strikers, and sturdy rogues; and the Commons prayed, that no sustenance or alms should be given them, whether in boroughs or in the country, under heavy penalties; that they should be sent to the nearest gaol, till they were willing to return to their own country, and serve their neighbours according to law; that any one who harboured

Chap. XIII.   NO CHANGE MADE IN THE LAW.   265

any such runaway servant should be liable to a pen- A.D.1376.
alty of £10; and, that any runaway, who had committed such offence three times, should be imprisoned
for a year, and find surety for his good behaviour
before release.   The Commons then went on to pray,
that no artificer should keep any labourer or servant
of any town as apprentice, or in the service of his
art "so long that there remain none to till the
ground;"[1] under penalty of £10 to the King, and
100s. to the party complaining.

No change was made in the law in consequence of but no
this petition, nor indeed was any needed, for the only made in
defect of the existing law was, that it could not be the law.
put in force; but, it was ordered, that " the statutes
and ordinances already made, should be held and kept
in all their points, and duly put in execution."[2]

These are the principal matters which occupied the
time of this important Parliament.

---

[1] " ꝙ nulle de la dite Ville ad mestre de laborer de mayntenir la
coulterre de la terre."
[2] Rot. Parl. 50 Ed. III. No. lvii. and lviii.

266   LIFE AND TIMES OF EDWARD III. Chap. XIV.

CHAPTER XIV.

COUNTER REVOLUTION CONSEQUENT ON THE DEATH OF THE BLACK PRINCE.

A.D. 1376.

Changes consequent on the death of the Black Prince.

THE changes produced by the death of the Black Prince, which began almost immediately after the dismissal of Parliament in the beginning of July,[1] must now be related.

The Duke of Lancaster was foiled in his endeavours to meddle with the succession to the throne; but it was no difficult matter for him to wreak his vengeance on his opponents. He lost no time in so doing.

Lancaster returns to power;

He immediately resumed the government of the kingdom, and retained it until the King's death.[2]

he imprisons De la Mare;

His first victim was Peter de la Mare, the Speaker of the last Parliament, whom he sent to prison at Nottingham.[3]

restores Lord Latimer.

Lord Latimer was restored to favour, and other obnoxious persons were brought back to the Court.

Alice Perrers returns.

Alice Perrers returned to the company of the King.[4] She belonged to the Duke's party, and without doubt was enabled, by her influence over the infatuated old King, to support the Duke in the counter-revolution which had now begun.

Mortimer, Earl of March, got rid of.

Mortimer, Earl of March, was another enemy to be got rid of. He was the husband of Philippa,

---

[1] Lowth, *Life of Wykeham*, p. 111. [2] Walsingham, p. 322.

[3] Ibid. p. 321; but at Newark, according to Chronicle, *Arch.* vol. xxii. p. 243. [4] Walsingham, p. 322.

MONUMENT OF WILLIAM OF WYKEHAM, BISHOP OF WINCHESTER.

IN WINCHESTER CATHEDRAL

Chap. XIV.   WILLIAM OF WYKEHAM.   267

daughter of Lionel, Duke of Clarence, from whom A.D. 1376.
Edward the Fourth descended; he was guilty of the
unpardonable crime of being married to one whose
child would be nearer to the throne than Lancaster,
unless the latter should succeed in his efforts to
exclude succession through females; moreover he
was the patron of De la Mare. The Duke ordered
him, as Earl Marshal, to go to Calais, to examine
the state of the castle; but the Earl, knowing
that the Duke " had an old and great hatred against
him, for the which he supposed this honey was not
drink unto him without gall," and suspecting, therefore, that the Duke's only object was to get him out
of the way, refused to go, and " gave the rod of his
marshalship unto the Duke." [1]

Another opponent to be punished was William of Lan-
Wykeham, Bishop of Winchester, a man honoured caster's
attack on
to this day, as one among the Englishmen who have William of
Wykeham,
conferred lasting benefits on their country. So re- Bishop of
Winches-
spected was he by his contemporaries, that the ter.
Duke's attack on him was described as " seeking a
knot in a rush." [2] He was born in 1324, of humble
parents, and his first appearance in public history is
as Secretary to Nicholas Uvedale, Constable of Winchester Castle. Uvedale made him known to the
King when he was about twenty-three years old.
After a few years he rose to be the King's surveyor,
and superintendent of his great works at Windsor;
and at last, after years of varied activity, became
Bishop of Winchester and Lord High Chancellor of
England.

It would be out of place here to write a biography Account of
Wyke-
of this Bishop, whom Lancaster hated because he ham's life.

---

[1] Chronicle, p. 246.   [2] Chronicle in *Arch.* vol. x.

268   LIFE AND TIMES OF EDWARD III. CHAP. XIV.

A.D. 1376. feared him; but, in order to appreciate his power and greatness, it is necessary to relate a few details of his life.

Nothing is positively known about Wykeham, from the time of his introduction to the King until his appointment on May 20th, 1356, as clerk of all the King's works, in his manors of Henley and Geshamsted. He seems, while holding this appointment, to have had the care of the King's eight dogs, for the keep of which he was allowed sixpence a day, and

His skill in architecture. twopence a day for a boy to attend them.[1] He rose quickly in the King's favour, and his extraordinary skill in architecture so soon displayed itself, that, five months afterwards, he was appointed surveyor of the King's works at Windsor, where he was employed in making great additions to the castle, and had 360 masons impressed from different counties at work under him. "He now reigned at Court," says Froissart, "everything being done by him and nothing

Enters Holy Orders, but this does not interfere with his employment as King's architect. without him." It is probable that he entered into Holy Orders in 1352, but his first preferment was in 1357. This, however, did not interfere with his architectural employments; in 1369, he was appointed chief warden and surveyor of the King's castles at Windsor, Leeds, Dover, and Hadlam, which were to be put in a state of defence against apprehended attacks. From this time, honours and offices were heaped upon him. He attended the King at Calais in 1360, on the ratification of the treaty of Bretigni; soon afterwards, he was chief of the Privy Council and Governor of the Great Council; and, in

His further promotion October, 1366, was appointed Bishop of Winchester.

---

[1] Pell's *Records*, vol. iii. p. 163, as quoted by Foss, *Lives of Judges*, vol. iv. p. 115.

CHAP. XIV.   CHARGES AGAINST WYKEHAM.   269

Before he was consecrated, however, he became Lord High Chancellor of England. He was removed from this office in 1371 on the remonstrance of the Commons.

It was supposed by the Bishop's enemies that this was the Duke of Lancaster's doing, and was the cause of enmity between them. For this, however, there seems to be no foundation. There is no evidence that the Duke had anything to do with the Commons' petition; and, so far from there being, at that time, any enmity between them, the Duke constituted him his attorney in 1375, during his absence at the Congress at Bruges. It is much more probable, that Lancaster bore enmity against Wykeham for the part he took in the Parliament of 1376; and, inasmuch as the Duke commenced proceedings against the Bishop immediately after the death of the Prince of Wales, there can be no doubt that it was the Prince's death, which first gave the Duke power to make his attack. The Bishop was in no way disgraced by his dismissal from the Chancellorship, but continued in favour both with the King and the Commons. The former appointed him one of the four Bishops, who attended the Great Council at Winchester in 1372;[1] and, in the following year, the Commons named him as one of the Lords, with whom they prayed to have a conference relative to a subsidy to be granted to the King.[2] The part which he took in the "good Parliament" has already been related, and it now remains to give an account of the Duke's proceedings against him.

The charges brought against the Bishop were, that he had mismanaged the King's revenues, which was

A.D. 1376, and appointment as Bishop of Winchester.

Supposed cause of enmity between Wykeham and Lancaster.

Lancaster's charges against Wykeham

---

[1] Louth, p. 59.   [2] Rot. Parl. 47 Ed. III. (m.i.) 5.

270 LIFE AND TIMES OF EDWARD III. Chap. XIV.

A.D. 1376. the very charge, brought by the Commons against the King's council, besides which, the Bishop was not the Treasurer of England; that he had ordered certain of the King's captains in the French wars to be fined; and that, by the ill-feeling he had thus created, he turned them into leaders of freebooting "Companies." It is needless to examine the other charges brought against the Bishop; they are all equally frivolous and vexatious, and, in none of them, is the Bishop accused of acting for his own benefit. Lancaster, however, had now undisputed power, and the Bishop was deprived of his temporalities and forbidden to come within twenty miles of the Court. The temporalities were granted to Richard Prince of Wales on

Wykeham is condemned. the 15th of March following,[1] and the Bishop was especially exempted from the general pardon granted by the King in the year of his Jubilee;[2] but, as the temporalities were restored to the Bishop three months after they were taken away,[3] and the Bishop was fully pardoned at the beginning of the next reign, but little weight need be attached to his condemnation under the influence of Lancaster.

Lancaster was now all powerful. The King was in his dotage, ruled over at Eltham by that heartless wanton, Alice Perrers, who robbed his dead body as soon as life had departed from him, and the Duke had everything his own way.

[1] Rymer, vol. iii. p. 1075.   [2] Stat. 50 Ed. III. c. 3.
[3] Rymer, vol. iii. p. 1079.

CHAP. XV. NEGOTIATIONS FOR PEACE. 271

CHAPTER XV.

**PROCEEDINGS IN PARLIAMENT UNDER RICHARD PRINCE OF WALES.
WYCLIF AND THE DUKE OF LANCASTER—THE KING'S DEATH.**

THE history of the relations between England and
France has now to be resumed. The truce made on
June 27th, 1375, as already related,[1] was to last till

A.D. 1376.

Negotiations for prolongation of peace.

[1] Froissart's account of these negotiations for peace is somewhat confused. He states (p. 705) that the truce was to last till April the 1st, 1376, whereas it is clear from the treaty published in Rymer (vol. iii. p. 1030), dated June 27th, 1375, that it was to last till the last day of June, 1376. He then goes on to say (p. 707) that according to agreement the plenipotentiaries met again on All Saints (November 1st), but that nothing was done; that ("environ le quaréme") about Lent (of course 1376), which may be considered to mean about the end of February or the beginning of March, a secret treaty was made between the English and French, which was to be taken for approval to their respective kings, and the negotiators were to return to Montreuil-sur-mer, and that in the meantime, apparently, the truce was pro-longed to the 1st of May (!). He proceeds to say that they did return, that Geoffry Chaucer, Guichard d'Angle, and Richard Stury were the English representatives, that they talked a great deal about the marriage of Prince Richard with the daughter of the King of France, and that the truce was prolonged to June 24th. He (p. 708) adds that certain French nobles were sent " to *these* talkings and secret treaties at Montreuil," that the Earl of Salisbury, Guichard d'Angle, the Bishop of Hereford, and the Bishop of St. David's went to Calais on the part of England, and that the Archbishop of Ravenna and the Bishop of Carpentras went backwards and forwards from one to another, but that in consequence of the French demanding the dismantling of Calais, negotiations were broken off and war renewed. He then (p. 708) goes on to say that when the Duke of Brittany, who was at Bruges with his

272   LIFE AND TIMES OF EDWARD III.   Chap. XV.

A.D. 1376. the end of June 1376, but it was agreed that the Commissioners should meet again at Bruges on the previous 15th of September.[1]

The meeting apparently did not take place, for on October 10th, 1375, power was given by the King of England to the Duke of Lancaster to treat for peace. Nothing, however, resulted, and England prepared for a renewal of the war. Early in January, 1376, preparations were made for the defence of the kingdom;[2] but, in consequence of the Pope's continual efforts to bring about a peace, negotiations were recommenced, and, on the 18th of February, the King of

cousin, the Earl of Flanders, heard of the failure of the negotiations, and the legates had returned to Bruges, he wrote to Guichard d'Angle at Calais to beg him to come to him at Bruges with 100 men, as he wished to return to England. This was done, and the Duke was conducted to Calais.

This is all very difficult to reconcile with the documents in Rymer, and it appears to me that the treaty at Montreuil, at the beginning of March 1376, mentioned by Froissart, by which he says the truce was prolonged to May 1st, refers to the treaty published in Rymer (vol. iii. p. 1048) dated March 12th, 1376, by which the truce was prolonged till April 1st, 1377, and that the negotiations between Calais and Montreuil, which Froissart relates as if they were a continuation of the previous negotiations at Montreuil, were those which were renewed on April 26th, 1377 (Rymer, p. 1077), and which were interrupted by the death of King Edward.

I have therefore taken Rymer as my authority.

There is an unanswerable argument in favour of the view that the meeting at Calais and Montreuil was in 1377 and not in 1376, as Froissart states, and that is that Froissart relates that the Bishop of St. David's was one of the negotiators, and he describes him as Chancellor. He did not receive his appointment as Chancellor till January 11th, 1377 (Rot. Claus. 50 Ed. III. p. 2. m. 27), as quoted in Foss' *Lives of the Judges*, vol. iii. p. 326.

---

[1] Rymer, vol. iii. p. 1034.   [2] Ibid. p. 1045–6.

CHAP. XV.   TRUCE PROLONGED.   273

France appointed the Dukes of Burgundy and Anjou to treat with the Duke of Lancaster. Geoffry Chaucer, our first great poet, accompanied Lancaster as one of the English commissioners.[1] On the 12th of March it was agreed, that the truce should be prolonged till April 1st, 1377. After signing the treaty, the Duke of Lancaster returned to England to be present at the meeting of "the Good Parliament" on the 23rd of April.

A.D. 1376.

Prolonged till April 1st, 1377.

On the following Christmas Day, the King, having somewhat recovered his health, held a grand feast at the Palace at Westminster. His grandson, the young Prince Richard, who had been created Earl of Chester and Prince of Wales during the sitting of Parliament,[2] was present, and was "carried before him." On this occasion, the King formally invested him with the succession to the throne, and made all the Prelates, Barons, Knights and officers of the various cities and ports who were present on this important occasion, swear that they held him as their future King. Edward had evidently roused himself for this ceremony. His health improved and his waning life flickered up for a moment; but he soon relapsed, and retired to Havering-atte-bower, in Essex. His end was approaching, and he never again appeared in public.[3]

The King holds a grand Christmas feast in honour of his grandson.

The Londoners were anxious to do their part in showing their regard for their future King, the son of their favourite, and, in accordance with the quaint and merry spirit of the times, determined to express it by a mummery on horseback. "On the Sunday

The Londoners entertain the young Prince of Wales with strange mummeries.

[1] See Buchon's *Froissart*, vol. i. p. 707.
[2] Walsingham, p. 321; and Rot. Parl. 51 Ed. III. (m. 9) 1.
[3] Buchon's *Froissart*, vol. i. p. 707.

VOL. II.   T

274   LIFE AND TIMES OF EDWARD III.   CHAP. XV.

A.D. 1376. before Candlemas (1st February), in the night, 130 citizens, disguised and well horsed, in a mummery with sound of trumpets, large trumpets, horns, shalms, and other minstrels, and innumerable torchlights of wax, rode from Newgate through Cheap, over the Bridge[1] through Southwark; and so went on to Kennington, besides Lambeth, where the young Prince remained with his mother, and the Duke of Lancaster his uncle, the Earls of Cambridge, Hertford, Warwick, and Suffolk, with divers other Lords. In the first rank did ride forty-eight in the likeness and habit of esquires, two and two together, clothed in red coats and gowns of Say or Sandall with comely vizors on their faces. After them came riding forty-eight knights in the same livery of colour and stuff. Then followed one richly arrayed like an Emperor, and after him at some distance, one stately attired like a Pope, whom followed twenty-four Cardinals, and after them eight or ten with black vizors not amiable, as if they had been legates from some foreign Princes. These maskers, after they had entered the Manor of Kennington, alighted from their horses and entered the hall on foot, which done, the Prince, his mother, and the Lords came out of the Chamber into the Hall, whom the said mummers did salute, showing by a pair of dice on the table their desire to play with the Prince, which they so handled that the Prince did always win when he cast them. Then the mummers set to the Prince three jewels one after another, which were a bowl of gold, a cup of gold, and a ring of gold, which the Prince won at three casts. Then they set to the Prince's mother, the Duke, the Earls, and the

[1] London Bridge was then the only bridge over the Thames till Windsor.

CHAP. XV.   MEETING OF PARLIAMENT.   275

other Lords, to every one a ring of gold, which they did also win. After which they were feasted and the music sounded, the Prince and the Lords danced on one part with the mummers who did also dance. Which jollitry being ended, they were again made to drink and then departed in order as they came."[1]

On the 27th January, Parliament again met, Richard Prince of Wales being present and taking the place of the King, in accordance with his instructions,[2] as expressed in a letter to the Parliament, which was read to the members. Notwithstanding the decision come to in 1371, that no ecclesiastics should hold high offices of State, the Bishop of St. David's was now the Lord Chancellor, and opened Parliament. He had been appointed, on the 11th of January, by the Duke of Lancaster, in pursuance of his policy of reversing the proceedings of the Parliaments which had opposed him. His predecessor being a layman, had omitted the usual form of addressing Parliament in the form of a sermon; but the present Chancellor, being a priest, revived the practice, and preached a most elaborate sermon on the occasion. He took for his text, " Ye suffer fools gladly seeing that ye yourselves are wise," and applied it in the oddest manner, for he said, " And as you are wise and I am a fool, I suppose you want to hear me."[3] He then said that the King's health was nearly restored. If it were so, he must soon have relapsed; for, on the 22nd of February, he was lying "too ill" at Shene, whither

A.D. 1376.

Meeting of Parliament attended by the Prince of Wales.

[1] Harleian Tracts, 247, as quoted in Stow's *Survey of London*, Strype's edition, vol. i. p. 303.

[2] Rymer, vol. iii. p. 1070.

[3] Rot. Parl. 51 Ed. III. (m. 9) 4.
"Et pur tant q̃ vous estes sages et je fouls
j'entenk q̃ vous avez desir de moy oier."

T 2

276 LIFE AND TIMES OF EDWARD III. Chap. XV.

A.D. 1377. he had removed from Havering, and whither, according to custom, the Chancellor and principal officers of Government went to report to him the proceedings of Parliament,[1] before the Commons presented their petitions.

Parliament reverses the proceedings of its predecessor.

The proceedings in this Parliament were most remarkable, but may be easily accounted for by the fact of the Duke of Lancaster's return to power.[2] He had contrived to influence the elections, so that those who had opposed him in the last Parliament were not again elected, with the exception of twelve, " whom he could not remove, for that the counties where they were would not elect any other."[3] The Lords, who were appointed to confer with the Commons, were all " either bound unto him for his benefits, or for other familiar causes expected his help."[4] Under these circumstances, it is not to be wondered at that this Parliament entirely reversed the proceedings of its predecessor. During its session, the Commons prayed that Lord Latimer, the Duke's especial friend, should be pardoned; the King, acting of course under the Duke's influence, at once granted the petition.[5] When the session was ended, and answers had been given to all the petitions, Sir Thomas Hungerford, the Speaker, prayed that this being the Jubilee year, or celebration of the King having sat on the throne for fifty years, he would be pleased to pardon certain persons, who, as he alleged, had been unjustly condemned in the former

Latimer pardoned.

---

[1] Rot. Parl. 51 Ed. III. (22).
[2] Walsingham, p. 323.
[3] Contemporary Chron. *Arch.* vol. xxii. p. 250.
[4] Ibid., p. 251; and Rot. Parl. 51 Ed. III. (m. 8) 18.
[5] Rot. Parl. 51 Ed. III. 75 (No. lviii.).

Chap. XV. THE DUKE OF LANCASTER USURPS POWER. 277

Parliament. The King asked whether pardon was A.D. 1377.
asked for all such persons, to which Hungerford
answered that all were included in the petition, and
he was then ordered to specify each case in writing
distinctly. Seven bills were accordingly prepared relative to Richard Lyons, Alice Perrers, Adam de
Bury, John Peach, and William Ellis; also as to John
of Leicester, Walter Sporier, and Hugh Fastolf whose
previous condemnation is not recorded. Sir John de
Nevill, who had been condemned, was omitted for
some unexplained cause. These Bills having been
presented after Parliament was ended, nothing could
be done;[1] but yet, Alice Perrers immediately returned to the King's company, accompanied by her
daughter. The fact of this being the Jubilee year Jubilee
may have had some influence on Parliament in re- year.
questing these pardons, and if so there would be
some excuse for its inconsistency, but it is much
more probable that its proceedings were influenced
entirely by the Duke of Lancaster. A general pardon General
of all minor offences, and a release from the pay- pardon,
ment of various feudal fines, was granted in com- Bishop
memoration of this jubilee year. The Duke of Lan- excepted.
caster being now at the head of the government, it
need be no matter of surprise, that he contrived to
get his friends included in it; nor that the Bishop of
Winchester, against whom he had a particular hatred,
should be specially excepted, notwithstanding that
the prelates and clergy of the province of Canterbury
petitioned in his favour.[2] The Bishop's temporalities
were, however, restored to him in the following June,

[1] Rot. Parl. 51 Ed. III. (m. 1) 87.
[2] Ibid. No. 1 (m. 7) 23, and (m. 2) 85; and Stat. 50 Ed. III.
c. 3.

278   LIFE AND TIMES OF EDWARD III.   CHAP. XV.

A.D. 1377. in consideration of his having undertaken to fit out three ships of war for the defence of the kingdom,[1] and, as already stated, in the beginning of the following reign, when the Duke of Lancaster's influence had declined, he was fully pardoned and restored to honour.

There were other matters of importance and interest brought before the Parliament. The first was, of course, the question of supplies.

The Chancellor informed the Parliament that the truce having nearly expired, the King of France was making ready for renewal of the war, and the King therefore requested its advice, and a further grant of

Poll tax granted. money. In answer to this request, the Commons granted a tax " hitherto unheard of,"[2] and which was evidently the precursor of the tax which produced such serious consequences in the following reign. It was a poll tax of 4d. a head on all persons, male or female, over fourteen years of age, with the singular exception of all real beggars.[3] The Commons then prayed the King, that he would appoint two Earls and two Barons, as guardians and treasurers of this and of the subsidy formerly granted; that they should be sworn in their presence that the subsidies should be spent in the war, and in no other way; and that the Lord High Treasurer should have nothing to do with them. The Commons were evidently anxious to pre-

---

[1] Rymer, vol. iii. p. 1079; and Lowth, p. 146.

[2] Walsingham, p. 323.

[3] Rot. Parl. 51 Ed. III. (19). Walsingham (p. 323) says that this tax was to be levied on the laity, but that "from all members of religious orders of either sex, and from all ecclesiastics having preferments, twelve-pence; and from those not having preferments, four-pence; except the Brothers of the four orders of Mendicants."

CHAP. XV.   FISHERIES AND NAVIGATION.   279

vent the recurrence of the evil practices, which had   A.D. 1377.
been brought before the last Parliament; but, owing
probably to the domination of the Duke of Lancaster,
they were singularly fickle in this their just determination, and when it came to be decided how much these
four treasurers should be paid yearly, they drew back
from their purpose, and prayed that the money might
be given to the High Treasurer.[1]

The other matters which came under the con-   General
sideration of this Parliament, were those which, at   business
this period, were almost invariably brought forward.   ment.
The proceedings as usual began with a petition for the
observance of the Charter of the Forests, and complaints that the boundaries of the forests were en-
larged. Then, the appointment of foreigners to bene-   The
fices, and the rapacity of the Pope's collectors, were   Pope's
again remonstrated against. The protection of fisheries   tions.
and the removal of impediments to river navigation,   and navi-
were also the subjects of petitions. With regard to the   gation.
former, it was prayed, that a patent, giving one Reginald Newport leave to put kidells and trynks in the
Thames and Medway, to the great injury of salmon and
other fish, should be withdrawn; and that the use of a
new and horrible instrument, called a Wondyrchoun,
should be forbidden. This it was said, was made
after the manner of a drag for oysters; was beyond
measure long; the meshes of the net so small
that no fish could get through them; that there
was a long and thick iron attached to it, which
" dragged along the ground so heavily, that the fertile
slime and flowers of the earth below the water were
destroyed by it, as was also the spat of the oysters,
mussels, and other fish on which the great fish lived

[1] Rot. Parl. 51 Ed. III. (21).

280   LIFE AND TIMES OF EDWARD III.   Chap. XV.

A.D. 1377.

and were nourished;" and it was added, that, by this instrument, the fishermen took so many fish that they fed their pigs on them,[1] and "fattened them beyond measure." With regard to the impediments to river navigation, the erection of mills, as having this effect, was considered an especial grievance. It was complained that the navigation of the waters between St. Ives and Huntingdon was stopped by the erection of three mills. The King's answer to this was, that there was already a law to prevent such things,[2] and that it should be put in force. The navigation of the Severn, too, was alleged to be stopped, and floods caused by the erection of Gors,[3] —whatever that may mean. It was also prayed that deodand should not be granted in cases where the death of a person was caused by falling out of a ship, the deodand in such case being the forfeiture of the ship. It was alleged that this heavy penalty discouraged the building of ships. The King granted the petition as regarded ships on the sea; but, as to those on fresh water, he said he would do as he pleased.[4] The forfeiture, as a deodand, or gift to God, to be applied for masses for the souls of those perishing suddenly, or to other pious purposes, of any chattel which was the immediate and accidental occasion of the death of any reasonable creature, is of very ancient origin, and may be clearly traced in the laws of Moses; but the custom, which, as Blackstone says, is repugnant to the feelings of mankind, is now entirely obsolete.[5]

Deodands in case of death caused by falling out of a ship.

---

[1] Rot. Parl. No. xxxiii. (50).   [2] Ibid. No. i. (m. 3) 67.

[3] Ibid. 72.   [4] Rot. Parl. No. i. (m. 3) 78.

[5] See Stephen's *Blackstone* (1842), vol. ii. p. 565. Deodands were abolished in 1846 by stat. 9 and 10 Vic. c. 62.

CHAP. XV. PROTEST AGAINST ARBITRARY TAXATION. 281

Another matter of importance, as showing the growing power of Parliament, and the determination of its members that their authority should not be disregarded, was brought before the King. He had imposed certain aids and charges on the nation, and had levied duties on exports without consent of Parliament, and of this the members seriously complained. The King, or rather the Duke of Lancaster, with a greater wisdom than that shown by Charles I. when the levying of ship-money was objected to, returned a gracious and apologetic answer to this complaint. With regard to the first, he said he had never willingly thus laid on charges without great need and for the good of the kingdom; with reference to the second, that there was a statute relative to it, which he was willing should be put in force.

During the session of this Parliament, events of importance relative to the power of the Duke of Lancaster, but of still greater importance as bearing on the dawn of the Reformation, took place. John Wyclif, the first English Reformer, "the father of English prose," and whose writings contributed more than those of any other writer to the Great Reformation of the Church of England, and its severance from the Church of Rome a century and a half later, was born about the year 1324,[1] a few

A.D. 1377.

Protest against taxes being levied without consent of Parliament.

Wyclif.

Sketch of his life.

---

[1] "It is not by his translation of the Bible, remarkable as that work is, that Wyclif can be judged as a writer. It is in his original tracts that the exquisite pathos, the keen delicate irony, the manly passion of his short nervous sentences, fairly overmasters the weakness of the unformed language, and gives us English which cannot be read without a feeling of its beauty to this hour."—*Fasciculi Zizaniorum Magistri Johannis Wyclif cum Tritico.* Edited by the Rev. W. W. Shirley, M.A., London, 1858. Introduction, p. xlv.

282 LIFE AND TIMES OF EDWARD III. Chap. XV.

A.D. 1377. years before the beginning of this reign. When about 36 years of age, he was appointed Warden or Master of Baliol Hall, as it was then called. At that time, he distinguished himself, by taking the part of the University of Oxford, against the encroachments of the Mendicants or Begging Friars. In consequence of the opposition of the University to the schemes of these Friars, they had stirred up the scholars to sedition; and had taken every opportunity of seducing them from the colleges into their convents, insomuch that people were afraid of sending their children to the University, lest they should be kidnapped by them. By these means, the number of the students had been reduced from 30,000 to 6,000. "Freres," says Wyclif, "drawen children fro Christ's Religion into their private Order by hypocrisie, lesings and steling. . . . And so they stelen children fro fader and moder."[1] Wyclif was the great opponent of these Friars. His next appearance was in 1366, in defence of the King of England against the Pope's demands for arrears in the payment of tribute money granted by King John.[2] In 1368 he published his "Theory of Dominion," (De Dominio Divino), the preface to which work is considered[3] to be "the true epoch of the beginning of the Reformation." In 1372, he began to attack the abuses of Christianity, declaring, in his lectures, that "the true spirit of Christianity seemed to be wholly

[1] Lewis's *Life of Wyclif*, p. 7.

[2] See an interesting account of Wiclif's proceedings, and the curious and characteristic opinions delivered by seven barons at a solemn debate in the King's council on the subject.—Milman's *Latin Christianity*, vol. viii. p. 168.

[3] Fasciculi Zizaniorum, p. xl.

Chap. XV. JOHN WYCLIF. 283

lost, and had degenerated into shows and ceremonies," A.D. 1377.
and that "the greater and more necessary articles
of faith, and all genuine and rational knowledge of
religion had generally given place to fabulous legends,
. . . which in this respect only differed from those of
the ancient heathen poets, in that they were more
incredible and less elegant." [1] Wyclif here appears
most unmistakably as a precursor of the Reformation.

Two years afterwards, in 1374, he, together with
Simon Sudbury, Bishop of London, accompanied the
Duke of Lancaster on his mission to Bruges to treat His mis-
for peace with France. It was also the object of the sion to Bruges.
embassy to treat with the Pope, as to the cessation
of his meddling with the appointments to benefices.
The result of the embassy was not satisfactory, and
contributed not a little to the overthrow of Lancaster
by the "Good Parliament." [2] Independently of the
failure of the peace negotiations, the struggle with
the Pope ended rather in his favour than in that of
England. The Pope's object was to nullify, if possible, the Statute of Provisors, and, to some extent,
he succeeded. The Pope agreed to desist from
making reservations; but the King undertook to
make no more appointments by writ of Quare Im-
pedit, that is, to take no legal proceedings to establish
his right to present to a living, which was impeded
or obstructed by some one else, appointed probably
by the Pope. On Wyclif's return to England, after
nearly two years' absence, impressed with the ambition, covetousness, and faithlessness of the Pope, he
attacked him in his public lectures; styling him

[1] Lewis's *Life of Wyclif*, p. 22.
[2] See Hook's *Lives of the Archbishops of Canterbury*, vol. iv.
pp. 253, 254.

284   LIFE AND TIMES OF EDWARD III.   CHAP. XV.

A.D. 1377. "Antichrist, the proud worldly priest of Rome, and the most cursed of clippers and purse-kervers." [1] These and other attacks on the Pope naturally excited him against Wyclif, and in the spring of 1377, he issued bulls, commanding the Archbishop of Canterbury and the Bishop of London, to renew the proceedings against him which had been begun in February. [2]

Wyclif's friendship with Lancaster,

It was shortly before Wyclif's embassy to Bruges that he became a friend of the Duke of Lancaster, to whom at this time he dedicated some of his works. [3] This alliance between an ascetic priest of deep piety and irreproachable morals, and an ambitious and somewhat dissolute noble, is not otherwise intelligible than as viewed in connexion with Lancaster's friendship for Chaucer. Thus considered, it may fairly be explained by attributing to the Duke a mind, capable of appreciating, and indeed deeply loving, energy and intellect, but not untinged by a consciousness that men possessed of these qualities might be useful to him, especially in his opposition to the clergy. This

who defends him against the Bishops.

may well be considered the key to the Duke's defence of Wyclif against the attacks of the Church, among the leaders of which was the Duke's own opponent, William of Wykeham, Bishop of Winchester.

The Bishops demand that the Bishop of Winchester shall be restored to his temporalities.

The Bishop of Winchester, having been deprived of his temporalities, was not summoned, to attend the Parliament which met at the end of January 1377, nor to Convocation, which met for the purpose of granting a subsidy on the 3rd of February. Simon Sudbury, Archbishop of Canterbury, was a friend of Lancaster,

---

[1] Lewis's *Life of Wyclif*, pp. 38–7.

[2] Ibid. p. 49; and Fas. Zizan. p. xxviii.; and Lowth, p. 140 (note 7).   [3] Ibid. p. 20.

CHAP. XV.   PROCEEDINGS AGAINST WYCLIF.   285

and was afraid to summon Wykeham for fear of of- A.D. 1377.
fending the Duke; but, in consequence of the spirited
remonstrances of William Courtenay, Bishop of London, and afterwards Archbishop of Canterbury, Archbishop Sudbury was obliged to yield.[1] Wykeham,
took his seat in Convocation, consequently, between
the 14th and 18th of February.[2] Before the conclusion Proceed-
of its session, the Bishop of London summoned ings
against
Wyclif to appear before him to answer a charge of Wyclif,
heresy. Wyclif, as already stated, had lectured against
the Pope, and also in favour of the supremacy of
Kings and other temporal over spiritual rulers.[3]
This was reason enough why the Bishops should
attack him; and Walsingham[4] displays all the bitterness of a monk against a man who dared to attack
established doctrines. " Quidam Borealis," a certain
Northman, he terms him, and then details the horrible
heresies which he says Wyclif promulgated. But
there was another cause for the enmity of the ecclesiastics. This was, as we have already seen, Wyclif's
intimate connexion with the Duke of Lancaster. The
Duke had taken him into his house, the Savoy Palace
in the Strand,[5] as an inmate, for the purpose of
availing himself of his services in curbing the power
of the Church.

Wyclif's heresies, however, were not made the
subject of accusation against him in this first trial.
" How entirely," says Mr. Shirley, " the meaning of
this prosecution was political, may be gathered from
the total omission in the articles of accusation of all

[1] Hook's *Lives of the Archbishops of Canterbury*, vol. iv.
p. 328.
[2] Lowth, p. 138.   [3] Lewis's *Life*, pp. 46–9.
[4] P. 324.   [5] Hook's *Lives*, vol. iv. p. 329.

286　LIFE AND TIMES OF EDWARD III.　Chap. XV.

A.D. 1377.
caused mainly by his friendship with Lancaster.

matters not bearing on the question of the hour. Wyclif had long ago been accused of heresy on the subject of the Incarnation, but this was not mentioned; his doctrine of the imperishability of matter had been actually condemned by Archbishop Langham, but it was not alluded to; he had been accused of reviving the necessitarian tenets of Bradwardine, but neither were these touched upon. The object of the prosecution was to proclaim to the world that society was endangered by the political principles which John of Gaunt was putting in practice against the Church." [1]

Wyclif appears before the Bishops.

On the 23rd of February, Wyclif answered the summons and appeared before his judges in St. Paul's. He was supported and accompanied by his friend the Duke of Lancaster, and also by the newly appointed Earl Marshal, Lord Percy. It is also stated that "four Doctors of Divinity, one of every order of the begging friars" came with him by order of the Duke of Lancaster; [2] but this can hardly have been with Wyclif's consent, as Wyclif was a great opponent of that order. St. Paul's Church—not the gigantic, but somewhat pagan structure of the present day, but the noble Gothic Church destroyed by fire in 1666— was filled and crowded, before Wyclif arrived at the Western entrance. Prelates and nobles had assembled at an early hour, and were transacting some preliminary business, when a shout was heard, and a tumultuous mob rushed in through the side doors. It was announced that Wyclif had arrived; but so great was the crowd that it was hardly possible for him to enter, and Lord Percy was obliged to order his men to clear

[1] Fas. Ziz., p. 27.
[2] Stow's *Chronicle*, p. 273; and *Arch.* vol. xxii. p. 255.

Chap. XV. WYCLIF'S TRIAL. 287

the way. This necessary exercise of authority of- A.D. 1377.
fended the Bishop of London, and caused a wrangle between him and the Duke of Lancaster. At last, however, Wyclif and his friends arrived in the Lady
Chapel; the Duke, the Prelates and other nobles took
their seats, leaving Wyclif standing. Percy ordered
a seat to be given him, saying, "He hath much to
answer, he hath need of a better seat." The Bishop
was naturally offended at this improper interference,
and declared that so long as Wyclif was on his trial
he was bound to stand. A fierce contention between Lancaster
the Bishop and the Duke then began, the Duke defends
him vio-
"turning red with rage because he could not prevail;" lently.
but the Bishop kept his temper. The Duke swore he
would pull down the pride of the Bishop of London
and of all the Bishops in England; and then, taunting
the Bishop with his pride of birth, said, "Thou trustest
in thy parents who can profit thee nothing, for
they shall have enough to do to defend themselves."
The Bishop answered calmly, "I trust not in my
parents, nor in the life of any man, but in God, in
whom I ought to trust." The Duke could then restrain himself no longer, and muttered that he would
rather drag the Bishop out of the Church by the
hair of his head, than hear such things. The Lon- A riot
doners overheard this threat and rose to defend their ensues and
Lancaster
Bishop. It is evident, that, from the very first, the escapes
with diffi-
Londoners took the part of the Bishop against the culty from
Duke, and that the trial excited their most passionate the fury of
the mob.
interest. It is somewhat difficult to account for this.
Wyclif belonged to the party of the people, for he
inveighed against the abuses of the Church and the
tyranny of the Pope; no reason, therefore, can be
assigned for the multitude regarding him with any

288   LIFE AND TIMES OF EDWARD III.   Chap. XV.

A.D. 1377. feeling but that of approbation. On the other hand, John of Gaunt was a proud feudal lord, known as the defender of abuses, and suspected of being an enemy of Richard of Bordeaux, the son of the nation's favourite, the Black Prince.

Another reason is alleged,[1] viz. that the people had become aware that the Duke had proposed in Parliament that there should no more be a Mayor of London, but that a Captain should be appointed in his stead, and that the preservation of order should be entrusted to the Earl Marshal. It is, however, most probable that this proposal was made after, and in consequence of the riot at St. Paul's, instead of before that occurrence.[2]

The assembly in St. Paul's broke up in disorder; and the Duke had evidently lost ground in popular favour. The next day this became still more evident. Lord Fitzwalter, the hereditary Constable of Castle Baynard and Banner-Bearer of London, came into the city with Guy de Brian, the member who announced the Black Prince's resignation of Aquitaine to Parliament in 1372. The citizens were in a very excitable state, and suspecting the motives of their coming, were about to fall upon them and beat them ; but Fitzwalter soon convinced the citizens that he

---

[1] Contemporary Chronicle, p. 259.

[2] The trial began soon after nine o'clock in the morning. "After the ninth hour, John aforenamed was brought forth," &c. (Contemporary Chronicle, p. 257), but it must soon have ended, unless there is a confusion as to days, for the Chronicler goes on to say (p. 259), " Their fury was the more increased, *for that the same day before noon*, in the Parliament of Westminster," the Duke made the proposals in question. On the other hand, Stow (p. 273) says, " Their furie was the more increased, *for that the day before*," &c. &c.

CHAP. XV. LANCASTER'S ARMS REVERSED BY THE MOB. 289

was on their side. He managed to induce them to attack the Marshal's inn or house, and release a prisoner confined there. The mob then proceeded to search for the Marshal himself, but they could not find him, for he and the Duke had gone to dine with one John of Ypres, a Flemish merchant, in St. Thomas Apostle. The people of course were not aware of this, and hoping to find them both at the Duke's Palace, The Savoy, rushed thither. On their way they met an unfortunate priest, who began to abuse them, telling them that Sir Peter de la Mare, who, they thought, was imprisoned in Lord Percy's inn, was a traitor, and worthy to be hanged long ago.[1] Infuriated by this language they attacked the priest and beat him so savagely, that he died soon afterwards. By this time the Bishop of London had heard of the riot, and hastened to quell it. This he succeeded in doing, and the people contented themselves with hanging up the Duke's arms reversed in the principal streets, as a sign of his being a traitor.

In the meantime the Duke had been warned of the disturbance, while he was at dinner, and seeing the urgency of the occasion, he jumped up in such haste, that he hurt both his legs. Disregarding the pain, and refusing the wine offered him by his attendants, he and Lord Percy fled without delay, and took refuge with the Princess of Wales at Kennington.[2] The Princess, who

A.D. 1377.

---

[1] Contemporary Chronicle, p. 262.

[2] The Chronicler (p. 262) says, "Entering the Thames they never stinted rowing until they came to a house near the manor of Kennington." It is not easy now to understand how the Duke could get to Kennington by water unless indeed the manor then reached the river. Dr. Hook, in his Life of Archbishop Courtenay,

VOL. II.   U

290   LIFE AND TIMES OF EDWARD III.   CHAP. XV.

A.D. 1377. doubtless, as the widow of the Black Prince, had great influence with the Londoners, endeavoured to pacify the citizens, and sent Sir Aubrey de Vere, Sir Simon Burley, and Sir Lewis Clifford to persuade them to be quiet. They answered that for her sake they would do what she commanded, but they told the Knights that they would not be content until the Bishop of Winchester and Sir Peter de la Mare had had a fair trial, and they insinuated that the Duke was a traitor.

No further proceedings were taken against Wyclif during Edward's reign. The Pope, at the instance of the Bishops, issued bulls ordering him to be again put on his trial, but nothing more was done for some time, and it was not long after these events that Edward died.

Death of Edward. That event took place on the 21st of June, at his palace at Shene in the sixty-sixth year of his age, and fiftieth of his reign. He was deserted by all, even by Alice Perrers, who fled from him after robbing him of his finger rings. "Amongst a thousand there was only present at that time a certain priest."[1]

Such was the sad end of a monarch who began his life with manly opposition to a profligate guardian, who throughout his manhood was conspicuous for courage and warlike capacity, but whose sad end, clouded with defeat abroad and shame at home, came when all that had given glory to his life and splendour to his reign had departed from him.

says that it was *Kingston* to which they rowed, but this is an evident error, for Stow (p. 274) says, "besides Lambeth."

[1] Contemporary Chronicle, p. 282.

MONUMENT OF KING EDWARD THE THIRD,
IN WESTMINSTER ABBEY.

CHAPTER XVI.

CONCLUDING REMARKS.

THE reign of the King whose history has been related in these pages may, not unaptly, be considered to represent, in the political life of the English nation, that period in the life of man when he first arrives at manhood, begins to feel his strength, and dares to use it. Since the reign of King John and his unsuccessful struggle with the Barons, the people, by that continued opposition to attempted irresponsible power which culminated in the establishment of a representative system of Government, had been forging constitutional weapons for future use, and slowly learning their possible application. But it was not until this reign that they availed themselves of this knowledge, and turned it to practical account.

It was then that Parliament first dared to exercise its lawful power of opposing Government, and, by asserting and enforcing its right so to do, compelled the King to desist from illegal tyranny. But it went still further, and called his advisers and officers to account. Representative government had existed for nearly seventy years, but when Edward came to the throne Parliament was unconscious of what it could accomplish. Mortimer and the Queen were ruling England without a shadow of legal right, and, indeed,

*292 LIFE AND TIMES OF EDWARD III. Chap. XVI.

Contrast between the beginning and end of the reign.

in direct opposition to the decision of the legislature. Guardians of the young King had been appointed by Parliament to govern the kingdom, and although he was not one of them, Mortimer had usurped all power in the State. His measures often disgusted the whole nation, but yet Parliament dared not raise its voice against him. So far indeed was it from so doing, that many of the nobles, when summoned to attend, instead of all assembling together in full conclave to charge Mortimer with his crimes, absented themselves from its meetings, and the Commons were so totally inert as to be almost unmentioned in the history of the period. It was the young King's own determination and courage, backed up by that of such of the nobles as were ready to follow when a leader came, that enabled him to free himself from the shackles that bound both him and his people.

What was the action of the nation, as represented by Parliament, under analogous circumstances, at the end of the reign? Excessive and illegal taxation, misappropriation of revenue, oppressive practices which had ruined the navy, interference with the administration of justice, and other like grievances, were then being endured by the people. John of Gaunt, availing himself of the King's senile imbecility and sensual weakness, had usurped the functions of government, much as Mortimer had done in the beginning of the reign, and had thrust his own subservient creatures into many of the great offices of State. No sooner did Parliament meet than it began a struggle with the Government which almost exactly prefigured those of the present day. It chose a speaker in direct opposition to the noble, who, if terms may be used which were not then literally applicable, might be

CHAP. XVI. CONCLUDING REMARKS. 293

called the Prime Minister. Not content with thus entering into a direct conflict with this powerful noble, Parliament, and now chiefly the Commons, then proceeded to impeach the ministers, and succeeded in bringing about their condemnation.

The part taken by the Black Prince at this conjuncture is very remarkable. With characteristic courage and spirit he roused himself from a bed of sickness to lead the opposition. It was the bright dying flame of the expiring lamp of life which shot up for a moment and then was quenched. The impulse under which he acted must have been deep and powerful. Was it a clear though late insight into the wisdom of rulers governing justly? or, a mistrust of his brother's motives? In either case he thereby gave a great impulse to the growing power of Parliament. His death was a serious blow to the nation's welfare, for, no sooner had it occurred, than the legislature, by a retrograde course, reversed all that it had previously done. Had he lived, he might, in all probability, have averted the evils arising from popular violence which soon followed the death of his father.

The Black Prince in Parliament.

The conduct of John of Gaunt is somewhat difficult to understand. On the one hand, as a supporter of Wyclif and his new and bold theological doctrines, he must be considered an earnest and sincere Reformer; and, as the friend and patron of Chaucer, a man of cultivated and enlightened understanding. On the other, as the defender of the King's corrupt ministers, and the opponent of Parliamentary government, he showed the spirit of a selfish tyrant. The total reversal of policy, which, after the death of the Black Prince, he was enabled to effect, and the pardon of the

Character of John of Gaunt.

294 LIFE AND TIMES OF EDWARD III. CHAP. XVI.

impeached ministers which he compelled the King to grant, furnish ample evidence of the conflicting principles on which he and his brother acted. Be this, however, as it may, the proceedings of this last Parliament of Edward's reign clearly showed its increased power. This new-born vigour and influence of the nation's representatives sprang, as has always been the case under similar circumstances, from the necessities of the King. His foreign wars, which he carried on with an extravagance which was as reckless as the wars themselves were selfish and abortive, demanded almost unlimited supplies of money. The King found by experience that he could not raise supplies without consent of Parliament. To obtain these he was forced to listen and yield to its demands, and thus, unwillingly, increase its power.

Popular power sprang for royal need.

Another prominent fact to be noticed in this reign is, that in it began that downfall of the supreme influence of mere personal strength and skill in the use of arms which came to pass when these became opposed to the inventions of human ingenuity. The introduction of gunpowder and the decline of chivalry were contemporaneous, and they were accompanied by the growth of Parliamentary power and the birth of English literature—and thus as mind progressed, brute force receded. The Norman knights, mounted on mail-clad horses and equipped in armour hardly penetrable by arrows shot from long bows and cross bows, which, though terrible when used against the less perfectly defended foot-soldiers, rebounded harmless from their panoply of steel, could be successfully encountered only by men of their own degree similarly equipped and equally well armed. By the advantage in battle which this gave them they had been able

Decline of chivalry.

CONCLUDING REMARKS.

for centuries to sweep before them, like chaff before the wind, the half-armed multitudes of the mass of the people, and keep them in subjection. Thus, to select one instance among many from the present reign, when multitudes of infuriated peasants rushed in thousands to attack Meaux, a handful of knights in armour was able to defeat them at once and with ease, and to slaughter them like sheep. Yet, under specially favourable circumstances, even such despised villeins, when well commanded, were sometimes able to baffle the skill and courage of well-appointed knights, and thus the furious and successful onslaught of the Welshmen on the French nobles at Crécy was a heavy blow to the prestige of chivalry. But its greatest enemy was gunpowder, and the first puff of smoke from the cannon's mouth was as certain a precursor of its fall, as the first discharge of a modern rifle was of that of the hitherto received principles of military tactics. Nor is the decline of chivalry to be mourned, for, however noble were some of the feelings and actions associated with it, its general characteristic was a total disregard of all but the vanity and pride of its own order. Any idea of the general welfare of a nation was then unknown. The castles in which the nobles lived were strongholds in which, before the use of gunpowder in war, they lived secure from attack by oppressed serfs, and from which, when they pleased, they could issue to ravage with impunity the lands of the defenceless tillers of the soil, and the houses of the unwarlike traders. Their sport was battle in the time of war, and warlike diversions in time of peace.

The character of the times in which he lived deeply impressed itself on that of the King himself, and is

296. LIFE AND TIMES OF EDWARD III. Chap. XVI.

strikingly manifested in the purposeless character of much of his war with France. It was the venturesomeness of war, its stirring strife and magnificent pomp that delighted him—as it has delighted barbarians in all times. Possessed of a fine person, "having a god-like face," as an old chronicler says,[1] he loved, like his prototype Alexander, to display himself surrounded by a gorgeous array of thousands of splendidly attired followers at the Court of the Emperor, or of the King of France, or, clad in singular but magnificent apparel, at feasts and festivities such as those which followed the establishment of the Order of the Garter. Courage he possessed in an eminent degree, combined, however, with no small amount of chivalrous rashness. His fight with Ribaumont at Calais is ample evidence that he possessed both qualities. A manly love of confronting danger then induced him to fight hand-to-hand as an unknown knight, regardless of the consequences which might have followed from his death, as king and leader of his army. His conduct admits only of the discreditable excuse that such hand-to-hand fights on foot between two mail-clad warriors must have ended more often in exhaustion from fatigue than in death from wounds. Of his personal character in other respects but few traces remain, and some of them are not such as to excite much admiration. Conjugal fidelity at that time was not considered a necessary virtue in sovereigns, and certainly was not practised by Edward III. In this matter it is but fair to judge him by the habits of the times, but his disgraceful subjec-

---

[1] "Vultum habens deo similem, quia tanta gracia in eo relucebat." Contin. Adam Murimuth, 226, and Knighton, col. 2630.

CHAP. XVI.   CONCLUDING REMARKS.   297

tion in his old age to a worthless woman was the
natural sequel to a licentious life, and deeply stains
the conclusion of his reign. That he was unscrupu-
lously despotic is clear enough from the facts mentioned in the course of this history, and that he was
cruel and revengeful is far from doubtful when his *and cruelty.*
conduct to the burgesses of Calais is considered; for
he either intended to put them to death in revenge
for their courageous defence, or else, with cat-like
wantonness, cruelly disregarding their misery, tor-
tured them with the fear of a punishment he never
intended to inflict. Manly courage and personal
energy are the chief noble qualities that can be assigned to him. He had, besides, the questionable
virtue of indomitable will. The commercial pro- *Com-*
sperity of the nation during his reign was great, and *mercial prosperity.*
he deserves credit for laying the foundations of Eng-
lish manufacturing industry by his encouragement
of Flemish weavers ; but the progress made must be
attributed to causes arising, unintentionally on his
part, from the advantages of increased foreign inter-
course, and from the concessions he was compelled
to make to his subjects, in order to obtain the means
of gratifying his warlike passions and his love for
inordinate splendour, rather than to a wise foresight
directing the policy of his reign.

It would be unjust to withhold admiration from *Verdict.*
the military and naval glories in which he took a
prominent part, or from the gallantry which he and
the Black Prince invariably displayed in the midst
of danger ; but, in awarding this due meed of praise,
let us not be dazzled, by the splendour of the victories they gained, into a blind forgetfulness of their
vanity, or into an unreflecting admiration of two

298 LIFE AND TIMES OF EDWARD III. CHAP. XVI.

men, who, though possessed of qualities particularly qualified to excite the admiration of unthinking hero-worshippers, have but little claim to the commendation of the wise and thoughtful.

APPENDIX.

(See page 256.)

The following note on the English succession has been kindly communicated to me by Miss Cooper, Authoress of "The History of America," and other works.

THE ENGLISH SUCCESSION.

THE right of succession to the English crown was one of the most disputed questions in our early history. So unsettled was this point, that after the death of the Black Prince it needed a special Act of Parliament to declare his only son, Richard, inheritor of his claim to the crown. From the time of William the Conqueror, indeed, there were always several persons who, as far as "right divine"—that is to say, right by direct descent—went, had greater claims than the actual wearer of the crown. But it is from the reign of Edward the Third that we may date those numerous factions that not only supported various pretenders in England, but asserted the legal rights of French, Spanish, and Portugese princes to the English throne. So late as the reign of James the First their arguments were so powerful as to deprive James of all feeling of security, and prompt him to imprison Arabella Stuart in the Tower for no other crime than that of marrying a descendant of the youngest sister of Henry the Eighth, possessing a claim to the crown by the will of the last named monarch.

Queen Elizabeth imprisoned for life Catherine Grey, for the same cause.[1]

Mary the First was jealous of Elizabeth's claim, and those of the house of Grey.

[1] In 1562, the claims of Catherine Grey to the succession were urged by a lawyer named John Hales, whose pamphlet, filling the Queen with such a fury of suspicion, created what was called the "Halesian Tempest."

300 APPENDIX.

Edward the Sixth died too young for controversy.

Henry the Eighth sent Margaret Douglas to the Tower lest she should "impedite the succession." [1]

Henry the Seventh put the Earl of Warwick to death from jealousy of his more legitimate descent from John of Gaunt.

The Wars of the Roses sprang from the rival claims.

Henry the Fifth died too young to be troubled by this question.

Henry the Fourth reigned by a disputed right.

Richard the Second was considered by many to have usurped the rights of his uncle, John of Gaunt.

The Sons of Edward the Third.

Two died in infancy, leaving—

1. EDWARD THE BLACK PRINCE (died before his father).
2. LIONEL, DUKE OF CLARENCE (died before his father).
3. JOHN OF GAUNT, DUKE OF LANCASTER.
4. EDMUND, EARL OF CAMBRIDGE (made Duke of York by Richard the Second).
5. THOMAS, EARL OF BUCKINGHAM (made Duke of Gloucester by Richard the Second).

The Black Prince left one son, viz.: Richard the Second.

"On the death of the Black Prince there wanted not divers learned and wise men in England that were of opinion that John of Gaunt, Duke of Lancaster, eldest son then living of the said King Edward, should have succeeded his father, *jure propinquitatis*, before Richard, that was but nephew and one degree further off than he; but the old King was so extremely affectionate unto his eldest son, the Black Prince Edward, newly dead, that he would not hear of any to succeed him, but only Richard, the said Prince's son. Wherefore, he presently called a Parliament, which was the last that ever he held, and therein caused his said nephew Richard to be declared heir apparent."—PARSONS.

Though no obstacle was opposed to the King's will, yet the fact of the Black Prince exacting a promise from his father and brothers that his son should succeed to the crown in case of his own death before that of Edward the Third[2] shows how uncertain was the question. Richard was well aware that many thought his uncle's title better than his own, and this was the chief cause of his hatred of the Lancaster family.

---

[1] See Statutes of Henry the Eighth.   [2] See Froissart.

APPENDIX. 301

Thus the great controversy was whether a younger son was not nearer to the King than a grandson. From the Conquest, hereditary succession had been as much disregarded as in the Saxon times. Thus Henry the First had been preferred to William, the son of his elder brother, and King John before his nephew Arthur. As Richard the Second had no children, the question of succession was again mooted. Again the pretensions of John of Gaunt were set aside, and the grandson of King Edward's second son declared heir presumptive.

The Second Son of Edward the Third was

Lionel, Duke of Clarence. He had one daughter, Philippa. This Philippa married Edward Mortimer, Earl of March. She had one son, Roger Mortimer, Earl of March.

Roger Mortimer declared heir by Richard the Second.

From him descended the house of York, which, according to priority of birth, had the first claim.

But then came the arguments in favour of Lancaster:

1. The greater right of a son over a grandchild.
2. Henry of Lancaster traced his descent from Edward the Third entirely by the male line, while Roger Mortimer claimed his from his mother. And though the Salic law did not prevail in England, the Salic prejudice did, and furnished strong arguments and real supporters of the house of Lancaster. And the arguments in favour of Lancaster prevailed over those of York, otherwise Roger Mortimer would have been king at the downfall of Richard.

It is therefore worthy of remark, though well known, that if we appeal to the favorite reason of the English for any departure from established rule, viz. that of *precedent*, (for without a " precedent " we are almost afraid to move,) we shall find that the kings of England up to Charles the First furnished the strongest arguments against hereditary succession and " right divine." But it is from the reign of Edward the Third that this question takes its serious aspect, and it was owing to this controversy that not a king sat with confidence on his throne from the time of Edward the Third to James the First. The descendants of the three wives of John of Gaunt were a constant terror to the reigning family, and by their marriages with foreign princes became

302 APPENDIX.

the centres of plots and intrigues that filled our sovereigns with gnawing suspicions, prompting them to most of their worst deeds of injustice and cruelty.

John of Gaunt

Married, first, his cousin Blanche, daughter of Henry, Duke of Lancaster, and it was through her that he obtained his title of Lancaster.

NOTE. The titles of men by right of their wives, appear, at this time, to have been more readily admitted than titles inherited from their mothers.

Children of John of Gaunt by Blanche.

1. Philippa, married John the First of Portugal.
2. Elizabeth, married to John Holland, Duke of Exeter.
3. Henry Bolingbroke.

Children of Henry Bolingbroke. (Henry the Fourth.)

1. Henry the Fifth.
2. Thomas, Duke of Clarence.
3. John, Duke of Bedford.
4. Humphrey, Duke of Gloucester.

Only child of Henry the Fifth.

Henry the Sixth.

Only child of Henry the Sixth.

1. Prince Edward (in him the line of Henry the Fifth ends.)

The other three sons of Henry Bolingbroke either died without children or they were slain in the civil wars.

So the representative of John of Gaunt was Philippa the eldest daughter, and it was from her that the house of Portugal claimed the crown of England.

But John of Gaunt married a second wife, viz. Constance, daughter and heiress of Peter the Cruel, and by her right he claimed for himself the crown of Castile.

Child of John of Gaunt and Constance.

Catherine, who married Henry, King of Castile.

APPENDIX. 303

From her descended the Infanta, daughter of Philip the Second[1] of Spain, who claimed the crown of England.

John of Gaunt married a third wife, viz. Catherine Swinford.

Children of John of Gaunt and Catherine Swinford.

Three sons and one daughter. Of these, two sons died without leaving any children. There survived

John, Earl of Somerset.

Children of John, Earl of Somerset.

John, Duke of Somerset.
Edmund, the second Duke of Somerset.

Child of John, Duke of Somerset.

One daughter, viz. Margaret, married the Earl of Richmond and became mother of Henry the Seventh.

The children of Edmund, the second Duke of Somerset, being all slain in the civil war, Margaret was the sole representative of the male line of Lancaster.

But as the children of Catherine Swinford were born before marriage and only legitimatised by Act of Parliament, the House of Spain refused to acknowledge them.

The descendants of each of these wives had a strong party, and Henry the Seventh claimed the crown not by right of his wife, Elizabeth of York, but by his own right as heir of the house of Lancaster by the male line.

---

[1] Philip the Second of Spain was descended by his mother from the first wife of John of Gaunt, and by his father from the second wife. Mary the First of England was the representative of the House of York. Their marriage was the legitimate union of the Houses of York and Lancaster, and a child of Philip and Mary would have had a greater claim to the English crown than any sovereign since Edward the Third.

INDEX.

ABS

ABSENTEEISM, evils of, in Ireland, ii. 9. Edward III.'s laws against, 11

Achard, Castel, taken by the French, ii. 220. Saved by the lady of, 220

Acts of Parliament, mode of promulgation of, i. 77, 78

Adrian IV., Pope, his bull authorising the English invasion of Ireland, ii. 3

Agace, Gobin, points out to Edward III. a ford over the Somme, i. 251, 252. The King's reward to him, 252, 253

Agenois, the Lord of Montpezat's castle of, taken by and from the French, i. 41

Agenois, withheld from England by Charles IV., i. 42. Conduct of the French seneschal of, 72. Various towns of, besieged by Philip VI., 127. Towns of, taken by the English under the Earl of Derby, 240. Invaded by the French, under the Duke of Anjou, ii. 172

Agnes, Black, her defence of the castle of Dunbar, i. 190

Agworth, Sir Thomas d', placed in command in Brittany, i. 243. Commands the English in Brittany, 274. His defeat of a French force under Charles of Blois, 274, 275. Relieves Roche Derien, 275. His death, i. 334

Agworth, Sir N. d', engages in the French expedition against Pedro the Cruel, ii. 111

Aiguillon, Castle of, taken by the Earl of Derby, i. 242. Reinforced by the Earl of Derby, 243. Escape of John of Norwich into, 244. Besieged by the Duke of Normandy, 244, 271. The siege raised, 272. Taken by the French, ii. 173

Airaines, Edward III. at, i. 250. His hasty retreat from, 251

ANG

Albret, Lord of, joins the Black Prince on his expedition into Spain, ii. 123, 124. At the battle of Navarrete, 131. Gained over by the King of France, 141. Marries Margaret of Bourbon, 141. Opposes the Prince of Wales's hearth-tax, 142. His defiance of the Prince, 143

Alençon, Count of, watches the English on the frontiers of Aquitaine, i. 44. Attacks and captures Saintes, 45. Which is restored to England, 47. Commands an army at Boulogne, 125. Joins an expedition into Brittany, 198. Joins Philip VI. against Edward III., 249. At Crécy, 259. Slain, 260. Disgraced for his flight at Poitiers, ii. 20. One of the King's hostages, 58. Joins the Duke of Berri in Poitou, ii. 202. Accompanies the Constable into Brittany, ii. 222

Alfonso IV., King of Aragon, agrees to suppress letters of marque, i. 61

Alfonso XI., King of Aragon, makes an alliance with Edward III., i. 187

Ambrecicourt, Eustace d', begins the battle of Poitiers, i. 389. Taken prisoner by the French, 389. Released in the fight, 391

Amiens, meeting of Edward III. and Philip VI. at, i. 28, 29. Defeat of the citizens of, by Harcourt, 250. Flight of Philip VI. to, after the battle of Crécy, 261

Angely, St. Jean d', recaptured from the English by the French, i. 329. Taken by the French, ii. 208

Angers, an army collected by the Duke of Normandy at, i. 215

Angle, Guichard d', favoured by Edward III., ii. 198. Taken prisoner by the Spaniards, 199. His widow saves his castle, 220

Angoulême, the nobility of, roused by the Duke of Normandy, i. 241.

VOL. II. X

306 INDEX.

ANJ

Taken by the Earl of Derby, 242. Besieged by the Duke of Normandy, and abandoned by the English, 243, 244. Rent-charge on, given to Charles the Bad, 356. Returned to John II. of France, 356. The English army gathered at, ii. 158. Taken by the French, 208

Anjou, House of, origin and kings of the, i. 1

Anjou, Duke of, one of the hostages for the King of France in England, ii. 58. Breaks his parole, 90. His return demanded, but without effect, 99. Restrained from fighting the English, 105. Advises the King of France to send an army to support the King of Castile, 124. His hatred of England, 136, 137. Commands an army against the English, 171. Transfers the command to Du Guesclin, 172. Accomplishes nothing, and breaks up his army, 202. Takes Roche-sur-Yon, 223. His treatment of his hostages, 224. Recalled to defend France in the north, 224. His advice as to the mode of treating the English, 224. Marches to reduce Gaston de Foix, 233, 234

Annan, surprise of Edward Balliol's camp at, i. 58

Antwerp, Edward III. at, i. 132, 134

Aquitaine, Lord Montacute appointed seneschal in, i. 35. Occupied by the French under Charles of Valois, 41. The whole of, except Agenois, restored by France to Edward II., 42. Interference of Philip VI. in the affairs of, 72. Edward's preparations for its defence, 73. Determination of Philip to wrest it from England, and of Edward to keep it, 94. A fleet provided to protect, 112. Events in Aquitaine during Edward III.'s invasion of France, 271. Given up to Edward III., ii. 55. Edward the Black Prince created Duke of, 68. Departure of the Black Prince for his duchy, 87. The kingdom of Aquitaine a thorn in the side of France, 98, 99. Unpopularity of the Prince of Wales's hearth-tax, 142. Local warfare in the duchy, in 1371, 186. Invaded by Henry of Trastamare, 136. Pillaged by the " Companies," 139. Declared confiscated by the Parliament of Paris, 171. The Duke of Lancaster left in charge of, by the Black Prince, 179. Losses of the

ART

English in, 203–209. The duchy surrendered by the Black Prince to his father, 215. No help sent to the duchy, 233. Lost to England, 234

Aragon, kingdom of, after the defeat of the Moors, i. 322

Arche, Pont de l', burnt by Edward III., i. 247

Archery, practice of, commended by the King, ii. 85

Armagnac, Count of, advises the people of Toulouse not to attack the English and Gascons, i. 366. Collects an army to meet them, but retires into the city, 368. Detached by Charles V. from the English, ii. 142. Opposes the Prince of Wales's hearth-tax, 142. His defiance of the Prince, 143.

Armourers, dispute with the, i. 364.

Army, the first recorded as clothed in uniform, i. 120

Arques, visit of Edward III. to, i. 142

Arrows, prices of, i. 187

Artevelde, James van, history of, i. 109. Enters into an alliance with England, 110. Negotiations for an alliance between England and Ghent opened with, 123. His statesmanlike views, 124. Advises Edward III. to assume the title of King of France, 124. His grandfather put to death by the Count of Flanders, 124, 125. Driven by Count Louis to Cadsand, 125. Causes the Flemings to expel Count Louis from Flanders, 134. Brings Flanders and Brabant into close commercial union, 156. Thrown into prison, but released, 205. Conference of Edward III. with him in Flanders, 232. His wise rule of his country, 233. His enemy, Gerard Denys, 234. Murdered by him, 235. His character, 235

Artois, Robert, Count of, his influence over the conduct of Edward III., i. 95. History of him and of his country, 100, 101. His claim to the earldom decided against him, 102, 103. His escape to Brussels, 103. Resorts to sorcery to harm Philip VI., 104. And flies to England, 105. Proclamation of Philip VI. against all persons harbouring him, 105. Friendship of Edward III. for him, 106. Joins Edward III. at Mechlin, 150. Defeated by the French at St. Omer, 177. At the English court, 197. Goes to Brittany with the expedition under the Earl of Northampton, 207. His expedition to Brittany,

INDEX.

307

ART

212. Takes Vannes, 213. His wound and death, 214

Artois, ravaged by Edward III., i. 361. Raid of the Duke of Lancaster in, ii. 46, 48. Ravaged by Sir Robert Knolles, 174

Arundel, Richard, Earl of, commands the English army in Scotland, i. 129. At the battle of Crécy, 255, 260. Sent on an embassy into Flanders, 277. At the battle of " L'Espagnols-sur-Mer," 325

Athole, Earl of, concludes a treaty of peace with Edward III., i. 70. Appointed governor of Scotland, 70. Murdered, 70

Aubenton, pillaged by the Count of Hainault, i. 173

Auberoche, taken by the Earl of Derby, i. 240. Besieged by Lille Jourdain, and relieved by the Earl of Derby, 241, 242

Audeneham, Marshal Arnoul d', his command at Poitiers, i. 386. Taken prisoner, 389

Audley, Hugh de, created Earl of Gloucester, i. 111

Audley, James, his gallant exploits at Poitiers, i. 390. His interview with the Prince of Wales, 394. Retires from his command in Poitou, ii. 158, 159

Auray, given up to John de Montfort, i. 196. Besieged by Charles of Blois, 211, 212. Battle of, ii. 104

Austria, Duke of, enters into an alliance with Edward III. against France, i. 147

Auvergne, plundered by the Prince of Wales, i. 378

Auvergne, Dauphin of, joins the Duke of Berri in Poitou, ii. 202

Avignon, the " Babylonish Captivity " of the Popes at, i. 66, 137. March of the " Companies " to, who obtained money and absolution from the Pope, ii. 111

Avignonet, sacked and burnt by the English and Gascons, i. 366

BACHE, ANTONY, lends a large sum to the King, i. 170

Bacon, the brigand leader, i. 291. Takes the castle of Comborn, 291. And rewarded by Philip VI., 292

Balliol, Edward, afterwards King of

BEA

Scotland, joins Edward in his march against the Scots, i. 12. Sent back to France for a time, 12. Returns to England and joins Lord Beaumont in a descent on Scotland, 54, 55. His rapid successes, 56. Defeats the Scottish army, and is crowned King at Scone, 56, 57. His army surprised, and he is compelled to fly into England, 58. Determination of Edward III. to march to his help, 59. Defeat of the Bruce party at Halidon Hill, 63. Balliol reseated on the throne, 65. Gives up all Scotland south of the Forth to Edward III., 65. Alienates his subjects, and causes the rise of the Bruce party again, 66. Again flies to Berwick, 67. Joined by Edward III. and overruns the country, 68, 69. Appointed by Edward constable of the army, 69. His insecure hold of his dominions, 189. Not recognised by the Scots as king, 401. Surrenders all his rights to King Edward, 407. Resides as a private gentleman in England, and charged with poaching, 407. His death, ii. 97

Bamborough, Sir Richard, governor of the castle of Ploërmel, i. 333. In the battle of the Thirty, and killed, 333, 334

Bardi, Lombards, or Longobardi, the, in London, i. 15. Lend money to Edward III., 15, 28. Their failure, 15. Forthcoming history of the, 16, note *

Barfleur, taken by the King, Edward III., i. 245

Barons, band themselves together against Mortimer, i. 25. Their charges against him, 25. Baffled by him, 26

Baseille, St., taken by the Earl of Derby, i. 242

Basset, Lord, sent to confer with the garrison of Calais, i. 285

Batefol, Sir Thomas de, his treachery, ii. 173, Struck dead by the Captal de Buch, 173

Bayonne, called upon to supply ships of war, i. 113. Earl of Derby lands at, with an army, 239

Beauchamp, Earl, sent to relieve St. Jean d'Angely, i. 331. Retreat followed by the French, who are defeated, 331, 332

---

* Just published. M. Firenze, " Coi Tipi di M. Cellini, E. C."

x 2

308 INDEX.

BEA

Beauchamp, John, of Warwick, appointed governor of Calais, i. 405

Beaumanoir, Robert de, his adventures, i. 333. Gets up the Battle of Thirty, i. 333

Beaumanoir, Lord of, his parley with John of Chandos, ii. 104

Beaumont, Lord, his residence in France, i. 54. Joins Edward Balliol in a descent on Scotland, 54, 55. At the meeting of Edward's allies at Halle, 137. His desertion from Edward III. to the French, 236

Beauvais, destruction of the abbey of, i. 250

Becherel, relieved by the Duke of Brittany, ii. 235. Surrendered to the French, 236

Belleperche, the English besieged in, ii. 170. Evacuated by them, 171

Benedict XII, Pope, his endeavours to prevent war between England and France, i. 71. Sends ambassadors to Edward III. to make peace, 126. Makes advances to the Emperor of Germany, 138. His quarrel with Germany and the Emperor, 140. His remonstrance with Edward III. as to his alliance with the Emperor, 145, 149, 158. Threatens the Emperor with renewed excommunication, 148. Excommunicates all Flanders, 156. Endeavours to dissuade Edward from continuing the war with France, 169. Places Flanders under an interdict, 174. His death, 204

Benevolence, a, granted by the merchants to Edward III., i. 67, 68

Bentley, Sir Walter, appointed commander-in-chief in Brittany, i. 334

Bereford, Sir Simon, sent to the Tower, i. 36. And executed, 39

Bergerac, taken by the Earl of Derby, i. 240, and note

Berkeley Castle, murder of Edward II. in, i. 19

Berkeley, Thomas de, his trial for being implicated in the murder of Edward II., i. 39, 40.

Berri, Duke of, commands an army against the English, ii. 171. Takes Linoges, 173. His activity and skill, 202. Enters Poitou, 203. And takes the castle of Montmorillon, 203. Seizes Chauvigny and Lussac, 203. Takes St. Sévère, 203, 204. Grants the request of the Lady of Castel Achard, ii. 220. See Charles V., Edward III.

BOU

Berri, plundered by the Prince of Wales, i. 378.

Bertrand, Cardinal, his visit to Edward III., i. 126, 128.

Berwick-on-Tweed, offered by Edward Balliol to be given up to Edward III., i. 57. Garrisoned by the Bruce party, 60. Former conflicts for its possession, 60. The Scots besieged in, by Edward III., 61. Surrender of the town, and Edward's endeavours to promote its commerce, 64. Taken by the Scots, 362. Town, but not the citadel, taken by Earl Douglas, 405. Journey of Edward III. to its relief, 405

Bidaus, i. 365

Biscay, province of, handed over to the Black Prince, ii. 119.

Black Death, breaking out of the, in England, i. 302. Its origin and course, 302, 303. Its contagious character and symptoms, 303. Extent of the mortality in England, 304, 305. Its effects in various parts of Europe, 306. Return of the plague to England and France, ii. 67.

Black Prince. See Edward the Black Prince

Blanche of Bourbon, married to Pedro the Cruel, ii. 107. Murdered by her husband, 108

Blanche of Lancaster, her marriage to John of Gaunt, ii. 42.

Blanche Tache, Godemar du Fay, defeated by Edward III. at, i. 252

Blois, Charles, Count of, joins Philip VI. against Edward III., i. 249. Elected President of the States General, ii. 20. See Charles, Count of Blois

Boccaccio, his account of the Black Death in Italy, i. 307

Bohun, William de, created Earl of Northampton, i. 111.

Bois-de-Vincennes, treaty of peace of, i. 45

Bolton, John, anecdote of, at Rennes, ii. 17, 18

Bordeaux, Lord Derby takes up his quarters at, i. 240, 242. The Earl of Lancaster at, 273. Landing of the Black Prince at, 362, 365. Arrival of the Prince of Wales with the captive King of France at, 397

Boucicault, Lord of, taken prisoner by the English, i. 331. Defeated in an attack on the English, 380. Retires into Romorantin, which is taken, 380,

INDEX. 309

BOU

381. His parley with Chandos, 381. Made marshal of France, and joins Du Guesclin in Normandy, ii. 102

Boulogne, burnt by Edward III., i. 248

Bourbon, Duke of, joins an expedition into Brittany, i. 198. Placed in defence of Languedoc, 240. Attempts to negotiate a peace between France and England, 355. Sent to destroy the "Great Company," ii. 64. But his army utterly routed by them, 65. He and his son wounded, and die shortly after, 66.

Bourbon, Duke of, sent to relieve Belleperche, ii. 170

Bourbon, Duke of, joins the Duke of Berri, ii. 202. Their successes, 203 –209. Accompanies Du Guesclin into Britta'ny, 222

Bourdeille, siege of, ii. 158

Bourg la Reine, burnt by Edward III., i. 248

Bourges, suburbs of, burnt by the Prince of Wales, i. 379.

Bovines, besieged by the Flemings, i. 249.

Bows and Arrows, prices of, i. 187, 189

Brabant, joins England against France, i. 107. Establishment of a staple in, 108.

Brabant, Duke of, enormous sum promised to him for his alliance, i. 117. Arrangement of Edward III. with him, 119. His fears of offending the King of France, 136. Obtains commercial privileges from Edward, 136. Wavers as to joining England against France, 148. But joins Edward at Mechlin, 150. Makes an important treaty with Edward, 153. Empowered to carry on the war during Edward's absence, 157. Edward's endeavours to secure the Duke's alliance, 228. Offers his daughter in marriage to the young Count of Flanders, 277. Obtains the marriage of his daughter with the Count, 335.

Brabant, brought into close commercial union with Flanders, i. 56

Brabanters, alliance of Edward III. with the, i. 107. Allowed to buy wool in England, 115

Brandenburg, Margrave of, joins Edward III. at Mechlin, i. 150

Brest, taken by John of Montfort, i. 195. Fortified by Sir Robert Knolles, ii. 222. Strength of the castle of, 222. The English gather together at, 222. Agree to surrender if not

BRU

relieved, 223. Landing of Salisbury at, 224

Breteuil, besieged and taken by the King of France, i. 377

Bretigni, peace of, ii. 55. Conditions of the treaty, 55, 56, 59. Found to be null and void, 61, 62

Brie, separation of, from Navarre, i. 356

Brieuc, St., besieged by the English, ii. 237

Brigands in France, i. 291. Their warfare against the English, 291. Brigands on the English side, 292

Brittany, history of the dispute as to the succession to the duchy of, i. 194. The principal places surrender to John of Montfort, 195, 196. His claims set aside by Philip VI., 196. Montfort's journey to England, where he obtains help, 197, 198. But taken prisoner in Nantes, 199. Review of events in Brittany after the capture of Nantes, 209. Opening of the campaign of 1342, 209. Siege of Hennebon, 211. Various towns taken by the French, 211, 212. Operations of the English, 212, et seq. Return of De Montfort to his duchy, 232. The war of 1345 in, 242. Events in, in 1346, 274. The war in, since 1347, 331. The Battle of Thirty, 331. Defeat of the party of Charles of Blois by the English and adherents of the Countess of Montfort, 334. March of the Duke of Lancaster to recover the duchy for young De Montfort, 374. The war between Charles of Blois and the Duke of Lancaster, ii. 17. Settlement of the affairs of, 59, 105. State of the duchy after the peace of Bretigni, 103. War between the rival claimants, 104. Battle of Auray, 104. An alliance with Brittany courted both by England and France, 190. The alliance with England cemented, 191. Conditions of the treaty, 192. Affairs of, in 1372, 214. Landing of an English expedition in, 221. Entry of Du Guesclin with a French army, 222. Its affairs in 1375, 235. March of the Duke of Brittany and the Earl of Cambridge, 237

Broye, La, Edward III. at the castle of, i. 253

Bruce, Edward, Earl of Carrick, invited by the native chiefs to Ireland, ii. 10. Where he is crowned king, 10. His death, 11.

Bruges, endeavours of Count Louis to

310 INDEX.

BUC

detach it from Ypres and Ghent, i. 316

Buch, Captal de (Jean de Grailly), sent to reconnoitre the French position at Poitiers, i. 384. His title of Captal, 384, *note*. Accompanies the Prince of Wales to England, 398. Joins Gaston de Foix in his crusade against the Pagans of Prussia, ii. 33. Aids the Royalists at Meaux, and exterminates the Jacques, 33. Defeated and taken prisoner at Cocherel, 102. Joins the Black Prince on his excursion into Spain, 123, 124. At the battle of Navarrete, 130. Joins the English at Angoulême, 158. Saves La Linde from the French, 173. Relieves Soubise, 201. Abandons the siege of Soubise for a time, 204. Marches to the relief of St. Sévère, but too late, 204. His bravery, but want of rapidity, 205. Sends Jean d'Angle to Poitiers, but too late, 205, 206. Routs the French besiegers of Soubise, 207. But afterwards taken prisoner by Owen of Wales, 207. His town of St. Jean d'Angely taken by the French, 208. Taken prisoner to Paris, 210.

Bullock, Sir William, his capture at the castle of Perth, i. 191

Burgage tenure applied to Berwick, i. 64

Burgh, De, family of the, defies Edward III., and renounce their allegiance to England, ii. 11

Burghersh, William de, Constable of Dover, brings over the Princess Philippa of Hainault, i. 22. Ordered to "arrest" ships for the King, 128

Burghersh, Bartholomew de, states to Parliament the failure of the King's efforts to make peace with France, i. 353

Burgundy, extent of the kingdom of, i. 97. March of Edward III. through, ii. 51. Devastated by the "Great Company," 63

Burgundy, Duke of, joins an expedition into Brittany, i. 198. Makes a treaty with Edward III., ii. 51. His defeat of the Navarrese under Louis of Navarre, 103. Ordered to attack the Duke of Lancaster, but retreats without fighting, 163. Placed in command of the army of reserve, 172.

Butchers, knavery of the, in England, ii. 77

CAM

CADSAND, Van Artevelde driven by Count Louis to, i. 125. Battle of, 125

Caen, besieged and taken by Edward III., i. 245

Calais, first idea of Edward III. of seizing, i. 246, 247. His march to, 263. His arrival before the town, 264. Summons it to surrender, 265. His preparations for a long siege, 265. His town of Newtown the Bold, 265. All persons unable to defend the town expelled by the governor, 267. Progress of the siege, 279. A tower built by the English to command the harbour, 280. Great distress of the garrison, 281. Preparations of King Philip to relieve it, 281, 282. Advance of the French army under the King, 282, 283. Who soon after retreats, 285. Surrender of the town to the English, 285, 286. Story of the six burgesses, 286, 287. Preparations of King Philip to recover it, 288. Attempt to obtain possession of it by treachery, 317. The French defeated and made prisoners by Edward III., 317–320. Foreign adventurers in the pay of the English at, ii. 46. Dispersion of them, 48. King John brought from England to Calais, 57. Removal of the staple from London to Calais, 75, 77. Special privileges granted to the town, 77

Callet, Guillaume, chief of the Jacquerie, ii. 31

Calverley, Sir Hugh de, joins John of Montfort at Auray, ii. 104. Agrees to accompany the expedition against Pedro the Cruel conditionally, 110. Summoned by the Prince of Wales to return from Spain, 120. Sent to bring Charles the Bad to his senses, 123. Defeated by the Spaniards, 126. At the battle of Navarrete, 131. Joins the English at Angoulême, 158.

Cambrai, siege of, i. 150. Siege given up, 152

Cambridge, Prince Edmund created Earl of, ii. 87. His marriage with Margaret of Flanders prevented by the Pope, 99. Goes to Brittany against the French, 157. Marches to Angoulême, 158. Married to Isabella of Castile, 193. Embarks for France, 236. In Brittany, 237. Besieges St. Brieuc, 237. Relieves Quimferlé castle, 239. Returns to England, 240

INDEX.

311

CAN

Cannon, first used in warfare, i. 174. Date of the earliest cannon in existence, 175. Asserted use of, at Crécy, 256. Used at the siege of Calais, 280

Capital, struggle between labour and, i. 5

Carcassonne, attacked and plundered by the English and Gascons, under the Prince of Wales, i. 367

Carantan, Edward III. at, i. 245

Carhaix, taken by the Earl of Northampton, i. 243

Carinthia, Duke of, enters into an alliance with Edward III. against France, i. 147

Carlisle, gathering of the Scottish army at, i. 13

Cassel, battle of, i. 27

Castile, kingdom of, after the defeat of the Moors, i. 322. Bloodless revolution in, ii. 113]

Castle Rising, imprisonment of Queen Isabella at, i. 40. Imprisonment and death of Queen Isabella at, ii. 42

Castro, Fernand de, the only friend of Pedro the Cruel, ii. 113. Joins the King in his journey to the Black Prince, 114

Cerda, De la, family claims of, to the throne of Navarre, i. 323.

Cerda, Charles de la, appointed to command a Spanish fleet for attacking England, i. 323, 324

Cervolles, Arnaud de, the Archpriest, his ravages in Provence, ii. 24. Killed by the Germans, 106

Champagne, separation of, from Navarre, i. 356. The "Companies" driven out of, ii. 40. Ravaged by Sir Robert Knolles, 174

Champerty in law, meaning of, i. 347, note

Chancery, Court of, establishment of the, in London, i. 233

Chandos, John of, his feats of valour, i. 151. At the battle of Crécy, 255. At the battle of "L'Espagnols-sur-Mer," 325. His parley with the defenders of Romorantin, 381. Keeps near the Prince of Wales in the battle, 393. Made Edward III.'s lieutenant in France, ii. 63. Sent to aid John of Montfort, in Brittany, 104. His parley with the Lord of Beaumanoir, 104. Enormous ransom paid for his prisoner, Bertrand du Guesclin, 109. Refuses to join the invaders of Pedro the Cruel's do-

CHA

minions, 111. Sent to negotiate with the King of Navarre, 119. And with Gaston de Foix, 121. Tries to dissuade the Prince of Wales from his enterprise, 121. Joins the Prince on his expedition, 124. At the battle of Navarre, 130, 131. His advice disregarded by the Prince of Wales, 143. And goes to St. Sauveur, 143. Returns at the Prince's request, 146. Takes up his headquarters at Montauban, 146. Becomes seneschal of Poitou, 159, 165. Invites the Earl of Pembroke to join him in a foray, but the Earl refuses, 159. Appealed to, by Pembroke, for help, which he gives him, 160. His death, 164–166. Grief of the Poitevins at the event, 168.

Channel Islands, fortified, i. 71. Invaded by the French, 114. Thomas Ferrars appointed governor of the, 115. Theobald Russel appointed governor of the, 117.

Chantonceaux, siege and capture of the castle of, i. 198.

Chargny, Geoffry de, carries the oriflamme at Poitiers, where he is killed, i. 392.

Charlemagne, extent of his empire, i. 95

Charles of Spain, i. 356, Created Constable of France, and has the counties of Champagne and Brie given to him, 356. Marries Margaret of Blois, 356. Murdered by the King of Navarre, 357.

Charles II., the Bad, King of Navarre, his possessions in Normandy, 355. Affianced to Joan, daughter of John II. of France, 355. Cause of his quarrel with John, 356. Married to the Princess Joan, 356. Jealousy between him and Charles of Spain, 356. Resides at Evreux, 357. Murders Charles of Spain, 357. Flees to Avignon, 358. Negotiates with the English for an alliance, 358. His offers to Edward III., 358. Settlement of the plans for an invasion of France by him and Edward, 359. Charles's supposed visit to England, 359, note. Raises troops and lands them at Cherbourg, i. 361. Waits in vain for the promised assistance from England, 361. And makes a hollow treaty with the King of France, 361. Resists the payment of the Salt Tax in Normandy, 371. Bloody revenge of King John, 372. Charles sent to

312 INDEX.

CHA

prison, 372. Proposal in the States General to release him, ii. 26. Delivered from prison by Marcel, 27. And enters Paris, 27. Resolves to recover his castles, 28. Appointed captain-general of Paris, 34. Agrees to betray Marcel to the Duke of Normandy, 34, 35. Compelled to retire from the city, 36. But offered by Marcel to be proclaimed King of France, 37. Makes a treaty with Edward III. and joins his brother at Nantes, 38. Lays waste the country, 38. But is gained over by the Duke of Normandy, 40. Declares war against the Duke of Normandy, 50. Brings his quarrel with France to a conclusion, 105. Promises to permit the passage of the English and Gascons to Spain, 119. Terms agreed upon, 119. His treachery to both Henry and Pedro, 120. Defeated, 123. Compelled to accompany the Prince of Wales's army across the Pyrenees, 124, 125. Escapes from the English, 125. Offers terms of alliance with England, which are refused by the Prince of Wales, 178, 179.

Charles the Bald, extent of his kingdom, i. 96

Charles IV., King of France, his efforts to compel Edward II. to do him homage, i. 41. Concludes peace with England, 42. His death, 43

Charles V., King of France (see also Charles, Duke of Normandy), ascends the throne, ii. 92. Sanctions his brother's breach of parole, 100. Breaks the treaty with England, 100. But wishes to settle France before beginning war with England, 101. Successes of his commanders, Du Guesclin and Boucicault, 103. But loss of Du Guesclin at Auray, and settlement of the affairs of Brittany, 105. Brings his quarrel with Navarre to a conclusion, 105. His sister Blanche murdered by Pedro the Cruel, 108. Charles and the Pope support Henry of Trastamare as a rival to the throne of Pedro the Cruel, 108. Charles's arrangements for the war in Spain, 109. Places the army under the command of Du Guesclin, 190. His complaints of the ravages of the "Companies," 140. Keeps up an appearance of friendship with England but prepares for war, 140, 141. Courts the friendship of the

CHA

Gascon nobles, 141. Summons the Prince of Wales to appear at Paris, 144. The Prince's answer, 145. Charles sends ambassadors to Edward III., 147. But declares war against England, 148, 150. Wrests Ponthieu from the English, 150. Enters into a treaty with the King of Scotland, 153. Plans the invasion of England, 161. But gives up the proposed invasion, 162. Orders only desultory warfare to be carried on, 169, 170. Makes great preparations for war, 171. Sets on foot two armies, 171. Their successes, 172, 173. Ravages of Knolles in the north and up to the gates of Paris, 174, 175. Charles makes alliances with Scotland and Spain, 192, 194. His preparations for war, 197. His activity and vigour, 202. Successes of his commanders, 203–209. Value of his calculating wisdom to the French, 219. Has a considerable fleet at sea, 220, 221. His secret policy, 222. Concludes a truce with England, 238, 240. Accounts of the negotiations for peace, 271.

Charles of Bohemia, nominated Emperor by the Pope, i. 248. Refused entrance into Aix-la-Chapelle, 248. Offers his services to the King of France, 249. At the battle of Crécy, 261. Elected Emperor of Germany, 292

Charles of Blois, his marriage with Jeanne of Penthièvre, i. 195. Appeals to King Philip against John of Montfort, 196. And obtains judgment against him, 196. Takes possession of the duchy, 198. And makes John of Montfort prisoner, 199. Opening of the campaign of 1342, 209. Capture of Rennes, 210. Siege of Hennebon, 210, 211. Besieges and takes Auray and Vannes, 211, 212. Collects a force at Nantes, and is besieged by Edward III., 214. Relieved by the Duke of Normandy, 215. Truce concluded, 216. Defeated by Sir T. d'Agworth, 274. Attacks, but is repulsed at, Roche Derien, 275. Taken prisoner and sent to the Tower of London, 276, 333. The war carried on by his wife, 276, 333. His daughter Margaret married to Charles of Spain, 356. Breaks his treaty with John of Montfort, and goes to war, ii. 103, 104.

INDEX. 313

CHA

Killed at the battle of Auray, 104, 105. Penthièvre settled on his widow, 105

Charles of Valois, occupies Aquitaine, and conquers the greater part of Guienne, i. 41, 42

Charles the Dauphin (afterwards Charles V.) holds his court at Rouen, i. 372. Bloody revenge of his father on the King of Navarre and other Norman nobles, 372. His command at Poitiers, 385. Discomfited in the battles, 390. His flight from the field, 391. Assumes the government during the captivity of his father, 397. *See* Charles V. Cares for nothing but extravagance and luxury, ii. 19, 23. Resists the proposed reforms of the States General, 21. Summons the States of the Langue d'Oc, 22. But resists their measures of reform also, 22. His efforts for the release of the King from captivity, 22. Returns to Paris, but alarmed by a threatened revolution, 23. Agrees to the demands of the States General, 26. Opposes the government of the Thirty-six, 26. But compelled again to yield, 27. Shuts himself up in the Louvre, 28. Meets the people, and makes charges against the Thirty-six, 28. Marcel's refutation, and commencement of a revolution, 29. Escape of the Duke under the protection of Marcel, 29. Presides over a meeting of the States of Champagne, 30. Prepares for the siege of Paris, 31. Begins the siege, 34. Withdraws from Paris, 36. His answer to Marcel, 36. Death of Marcel, and return of the Duke to Paris, 38. Takes the " Companies " into pay, 38. Rejects his father's treaty with England with scorn, 39. Besieges Melun, and brings forward Bertrand du Guesclin, 40. Gains over the King of Navarre, 40. Rejects terms of peace offered by England, 43. Shuts himself up in Paris, on the invasion of Edward III., 49. His policy of inaction, 50, 54. War declared against him by the King of Navarre, 50. March of the English up to the gates of Paris, 54. His rejection of Edward's offers, 54. His alarm and offers of peace, 55. Conclusion of the treaty of Bretigni, 55. Ascends the throne as Charles V., 92. *See* Charles V.

CLE

Chartres, made the headquarters of King John, i. 378

Château Neuf-sur-Charente, captured by the Earl of Lancaster, i. 273

Chaucer, notice of, and of his works, ii. 73

" Chaumont, The Hermit of," his attack on the English, and defeat, i. 382. Defends the castle of Romorantin, which is taken, 381, 382

Chauveau, Renaud, Bishop of Châlons, urges his King to refuse the terms offered by the Prince of Wales at Poitiers, i. 388. Killed, 393

Chauvigny, seized by the Duke of Berri, ii. 203

Cherbourg, Edward III. at, i. 245. Landing of the King of Navarre at, 361. Meeting of the Duke of Lancaster with Philip of Navarre and Godfrey of Harcourt at, 374. Their retreat into, from the French, 375

Chivalry, decline of, in the reign of Edward III., ii. 294

Chizey, besieged and taken by Du Guesclin, ii. 219

Cinque Ports, injury done by the French fleet to the, i. 144. Their rights and duties, 163. Ships promised by them to aid the King, 164. Tenure on which they were originally held of the King, 205

Clarence, Lionel, Duke of, birth of, i. 143. Left by his father guardian of the kingdom, 232, 238. At the tournament at Windsor, 296. Goes with his father to invade France, 361. Marries Elizabeth de Burgh, ii. 15. Goes to quell the Irish, 15. His straits in Ireland, 15. Accompanies his father to France, 47. Created Duke of Clarence, 86. Death of his wife, 97. Recommended as king of Scotland, 98. His visit to Paris on his way to Italy, 140

Clement V., Pope, his removal from Rome to Lyons and Avignon, i. 137

Clement VI., Pope, his mission (when Abbot of Fécamp) from Philip VI. to Edward III., i. 27. Ascends the pontifical throne, 204. Vainly endeavours to make peace between England and France, 204. Fails to induce the Flemings to submit to their Count, 204. Commissioners sent from England and France relative to peace, 220, 221. Resistance in England to the Pope's " provisors," 221, 222. The Pope's Bulls prohibi-

314 INDEX.

CLE

ted in England, 222. His vain attempts to prevent a renewal of the war, 230. His efforts to make peace, and grasp power in England, 237. His quarrel with the Emperor, 248. Whom he curses, and nominates another king of the Romans, 248. Mediates between England and France, 289. His death, 352

Clergy, their extravagance in dress, i. 296. Petition against their holding high secular offices, ii. 183. Petition to Parliament as to the immorality of their lives, 218

Clermont, John of, Marshal, his command at Poitiers, i. 386. Killed, 389

Clermont, Robert de, Marshal of Normandy, murder of, ii. 29

Clinton, William de, brings over Philippa of Hainault, i. 22

Clisson, Amaury de, sent by the Countess of Montfort to England for help, i. 200. Success of his mission, 202. Arrives with help at Hennebon, 211. Joins Sir W. de Maunay, and defeats Louis of Spain, 212, 213

Clisson, Garnier de, his death, i. 195

Clisson, Olivier de, gives up Roche Periou to John de Montfort, i. 196. Executed by Philip VI., 223

Clisson, Olivier de (son of the last), joins the Prince of Wales on his expedition into Spain, ii. 123. At the battle of Navarrete, 131. Won over to the King of France, 141. Opposes the Prince of Wales's hearth-tax, 142. His title of "The Butcher," 191. Joins the Duke of Berri in Poitou, 202. Obtains Mortagne, 213. His advice as to the mode of dealing with the English, 228. Sent to hold the English in check, 237

Cloud, St., burnt by Edward III., i. 248

Clynton, William de, created Earl of Huntingdon, i. 109

Cobham, Earl of, sent on an embassy to the Flemings, i. 277

Coblentz, meeting of the Emperor and Edward III. at, i. 141

Cocherel, battle of, ii. 102

Cognac, the Black Prince's forces collected at, ii. 172

Coins, regulations as to taking, out of the kingdom, ii. 79, 80

Comborn, Castle of, seized by the brigand Bacon, i. 291

Commerce, progress of, in the reign of Edward III., i. 2, 3. His commercial parliament summoned, 4. High es-

COM

teem in which merchants were held at this time, 4. The first negotiation for international law, 60, 61. Efforts of Edward III. to promote the trade of Berwick, 64. Arrangements made, and laws passed, for the regulation of commerce, 76. Law for promoting freedom of commerce, 78. Charter of Edward III. to foreign merchants, 79, 80. Interference of pirates with trade, 80, 81. The principal places of trade at this time, 81, 82. The King's legislation contrary to the true principles of commerce, 90. Wool staples, 91, 92. Alliances and commercial treaties made by the King with foreign powers, 108, 109. Interference of Parliament with trade, 338, 339; ii.73, 80, 81. Petitions of the Commons as to trade and commerce, 261. The commercial prosperity of England during Edward III.'s reign, 297

Commissions, Royal, summoned by the King, i. 4, 5

Commons, House of, their remonstrance against the King's wasteful expenditure, i. 3. Growing importance of the Commons in Parliament, 160. Openly declare themselves the representatives of the electors, and demand reform of abuses, 161, 162. Separation of the Commons from the Lords, 219. Members paid by their constituents, 220. Counsel the King to resistance to the Pope, 221. Grant the King two-fifteenths for the war, 266. Their complaints of illegal oppressions, 267. Petition the King against taxation without their consent, 314. Mode of electing the Commons, 351. Mode of proceeding in Parliament, ii. 86. Their petition to the King as to the staple, 231. And as to the Statute of Labourers, 231. Elect a Speaker, who demands reforms, 248. Their complaints and demands, 250, 251. Obtain the recognition of Richard of Bordeaux as heir to the throne, 256. Petition against usurpations of the Pope, 259. General business of the Parliament of 1377, 278, et seq.

Companies, Free, formation of, in France, ii. 19, 24. Called into Paris by Marcel, 34. Encountered by the Parisians, who are routed, 36. Taken into pay by the King of Navarre and Duke of Normandy, 38. Efforts made to ex-

INDEX.

315

CON

tinguish them, 39, 40. Again begin their devastations, 63. The "Great Company," 63. Their defeat of the Duke of Bourbon, 65. Prepare to attack the Pope, 66. Who buys them off, 66. Ordered by Edward III. to be suppressed, but without effect, 100. Their immense numbers in 1365, 106. Their services secured for the expedition to Spain, 106, 110. Their march to Avignon, 111. And to Spain, 111. Their return to France, 113. Summoned by the Black Prince to return from Spain, 120. Reach the Prince, after having defeated the Seneschal of Toulouse, 122. Demand their pay from the Black Prince, who is unable to satisfy them, 139. Pillage Aquitaine in consequence, 139. Join the English standard, 158. *See* Edward the Black Prince

Conches, burnt by the Duke of Lancaster, i. 375

Conflans, Lord of, Marshal of Champagne, murdered, ii. 29

Constance of Castile, her journey with her father to Bordeaux, ii. 114. Her marriage with John of Gaunt, 114. Hostage in the hands of the Black Prince, 119. Married to the Duke of Lancaster, 193

Copland, the Knight, takes David II. prisoner, i. 271. Gives up his prisoner, and receives a pension, 271. Saves the castle of Berwick, 405

Corfe Castle, Edward II. said to be alive in, i. 31, 33

Corn, export of, supported by the King, ii. 263

Cornwall, John of Eltham created earl of, i. 24. Appointed regent of the kingdom during the King's absence in France, 28. Proposal to marry him to one of the daughters of Philip VI., 30. Left in command of the army in Scotland, 73. His death, 73

Corvara, Peter de, anti-pope, his death and confession, i. 138

Council, the Great, formation of the, i. 50; ii. 85

Council, Privy, or King's Council, establishment of the, i. 49. Members of the, 50

Coucy, Ingelram de, ii. 91. Marries the Princess Isabella, 92.

Courtenay, Sir Philip, joins an expedition to Brittany, ii. 221.

Cows, export of, forbidden, ii. 77

Craon, Lord of, defeated by the English,

DAV

and shut up in Romorantin, i. 380. Which is taken, 381, 382.

Crécy, chosen by Edward III. as his battle-field, i. 254. Complete defeat of the French at, 261. Number and rank of the slain, 262. Consequences of the battle, 263.

Croquard the Brigand, on the English side, i. 292. His depredations, 292. Rallies the English at the battle of Thirty, 334.

Crotoy, town of, taken by the English, i. 253

Crotoye, battle of, i. 280

Crusade, a joint, proposed by Philip VI. to Edward III., i. 52. Causes which put a stop to it, 53

Currency, law as to the debasement of the, i. 81. Gold and silver forbidden to be carried out of the kingdom, 82. Very little gold currency at this time, 82. Leopards and nobles coined, 82, 83. Endeavour of Edward III. to establish an international currency, 83. Value of money in the fourteenth compared with that of the nineteenth century, 126, *note*

Curry, Walter, his capture of Edinburgh Castle, i. 192

DAVID II., King of Scotland, feasted by the Lord Mayor of London, i. 4. Betrothed to the Princess Joan of England, 19. His accession to the throne, 31. His army defeated by Edward Balliol, who is crowned king, 56, 57. Escapes to France, 57. His competitor, Balliol, driven into England, 58. Preparations of David's party for the defence of Scotland, 30. Defeat of his party at Halidon Hill, 63. His residence at the court of France, 65. Plottings of the French in his favour, 65, 66. Rise of his party again, 66. But Scotland overrun by Edward III. and Balliol, 69. Who compel the Bruce party to submit, 70. Commissioners appointed by Edward III. to treat with David, 72. Invades England with an army, 269. Lays the country waste, and halts at Nevill's Cross, 269. Defeated and taken prisoner by the English, 270, 271. Confined in the Tower, 271. Failure of negotiations for his release, 403, 404. Renewal of the negotiations, 409. Set at liberty, 410. Conditions of the treaty, 410. Disinherits Robert

316 INDEX.

DEN

the Steward, but subsequently reconciled to him, 410. Death of his enemy, Edward Balliol, ii. 97. Proposes the Duke of Clarence as his successor, 98.

Denys, Gerard, his enmity to Van Artevelde, i. 234. Whom he murders, 235

Derby, Henry of Lancaster created earl of, i. 111. Left in pawn by the King, 178. Challenges the "Flower of Chivalry" to run three courses with him, 190, 191. Appointed English commander in Gascony, 231. Embarks for Gascony, 232. His campaign in Guienne and Gascony, 239. Lands at Bayonne, 239. Takes Bergerac, 239, 240. Captures several smaller towns, 240. And returns to Bordeaux, 240. Relieves Auberoche with 900 men, 242. And takes various towns in the South, 242. Goes into winter quarters at Bordeaux, 242. Becomes Earl of Lancaster, 232, *note*. Not yet Duke of Lancaster, Joins the King at the battle of "L'Espagnols-sur-Mer," 325. *See also* Lancaster

Derval, castle of, fortified, ii. 222. Defended by Knolles, 224

Despencer, Monsieur Hugh le, takes the town of Crotoy, i. 253

Devereux, Sir John, his operations in the Limousin, ii. 189. Appointed seneschal of Rochelle, 201. Relieves Poitiers, 203. His castle of St. Sévère taken by the Duke of Berri, 203. Leaves Rochelle in the hands of Philip Mansel, 208. Who is cheated in delivering up the castle, 208. Besieged in Quimperlé, but relieved, 239.

"Dieu et mon Droit," the motto first used, i. 156

Dinan opens its gates to Du Guesclin, ii. 222.

Doublet, Colin, sent by Charles the Bad on an embassy to Edward III., i. 358

Douglas, Sir James, his death, i. 55

Douglas, James, killed, i. 70

Douglas, Sir Archibald, joins the attack on Edward Balliol's camp at Annan, i. 58. Leads an army to the relief of the Scots in Berwick, 62. Defeated by Edward III. at Halidon Hill, 63. Defeated by the English, 70. Wounded at a joust, 190

Douglas, Sir William, Knight of Lid-

EDW

desdale, advises his countrymen not to invade England, i. 268. Defeated by the English at Nevill's Cross, 269, 270. Taken prisoner, 270. Set at liberty by Edward III., 403. Murdered by Earl Douglas, 403

Douglas, William Earl, with John II. of France before Breteuil, i. 377. Returns from France, and clears parts of Scotland from the English invaders, 402. Murders his kinsman, 403. Commences Border warfare, 404. Takes the town of Berwick, but not the citadel, 405. Makes a truce with the Earl of Northampton, and joins the French service, 409

Drapers, regulations for the trade of, ii. 82

Dress, extravagance in, of both clergy and laity, i. 296, 297. Regulations as to, ii. 83

Dunbar, besieged by the English, i. 189. The castle defended by the Countess, Black Agnes, 190

Dupplin Moor, battle of, i. 56

Durfort, Aymeric de, expelled by the French seneschal of Agenois, i. 72

EATING, law relative to, passed, i. 83, 84

Eclipse of the Sun in 1339, i. 191

Edinburgh, taken from the English by the Scots, i. 177, 192

Edward II., King of England, his character contrasted with that of his son, i. 1. His imprisonment and deposition, 7. His humiliation and consent to resign, 8. Murdered in Berkeley Castle, 19. Punishment of his murderers, 39, 40. History of his dispute with the King of France, 41

EDWARD III., King of England, his Angevin descent, i. 1.

— contrasted with his father, i. 1

— evil influences under which he ascended the throne, i. 2

— characteristics of his reign, i. 2

— his claim to the title of "the Father of English Commerce," i. 3, 76

— his birth and accession, i. 6

— deposition of his father, i. 7

— guardians appointed to watch over his interests, i. 9

— threat of King Robert Bruce to invade England, i. 11

— Edward prepares to defend England, and marches to the North against the Scots, i. 11

INDEX. 317

EDW

EDWARD III.—*continued*

— his fortification of York, i. 11

— summons Edward Balliol to join him, i. 12

— joined by his Flemish allies at York, i. 12

— hastens to meet the Scots, i. 13

— but fails to bring them to battle, i. 14

— borrows money from the Bardi and the Hanseatic League, i. 15, 16

— sudden departure of the Scots, i. 16, 17

— dismisses his army, and summons a colloquy at Lincoln, i. 17

— makes overtures of peace to the Scots, i. 17

— concludes a treaty with Scotland, i. 18

— murder of his father, i. 19

— his marriage with Philippa of Hainault, i. 21

— pedigree of his relationship to the Princess, i. 21, *note*

— lays claim to the throne of France, i. 23, 43

— examination of his claim, i. 23

— summoned by Philip VI. to do homage, i. 26, 43

— agrees to do homage, but secretly protests that he does not renounce his claim to the French throne, 28

— goes to France and does homage under protest, i. 28, 29, 44

— his oath, i. 30

— his return to England, and proposals for connecting the royal families of England and France by marriage, i. 30

— execution of his uncle, the Earl of Kent, i. 33

— birth of his son, the Black Prince, i. 34

— his seizure and imprisonment of Mortimer, i. 35, 36

— who is executed, i. 39

— imprisonment of his mother, i. 40

— history of the disputes with France, i. 41

— Edward does homage to Charles IV. for the duchies of Aquitaine and Ponthieu, i. 42

— his preparations for war with France, i. 44, 45

— granted a subsidy by Parliament, but peace suddenly made, i. 45

— his secret journey to France, and settlement of the form of homage to Philip VI., 47

— his establishment of order, and the

EDW

EDWARD III.—*continued*

supremacy of the law in his kingdom, i. 49

— machinery of government, i. 49, 50

— the King turns his attention to the turbulent state of his kingdom, i. 51

— accepts the proposal of Philip VI. to join him in a crusade, i. 52

— but prevented from carrying out his wishes, i. 53

— forbids Beaumont and Edward Balliol to march troops through England against the Scots, i. 55

— considers whether he should recognise Edward Balliol as king, i. 57

— homage offered to be paid him by Balliol, i. 57

— summons Parliament to consider Scottish affairs, i. 58

— prepares to march against the Scots, i. 59

— charges the Scots with breaking the peace, i. 59, 60

— goes to Newcastle, and writes justifications of his proceedings, i, 60

— takes measures to protect commerce during war, i. 60, 61

— besieges Berwick, and defeats the Scots at Halidon Hill, i. 61–63

— surrender of Berwick, and endeavours of Edward to promote its commerce, i. 64

— the whole of Scotland south of the Forth given up to him, i. 65

— his attention divided between Scotland and France, i. 65

— flight of Balliol and rise of the Bruce party again, i. 66, 67

— increase of the animosity of Philip VI. against him, i. 67

— again sets out for Scotland to help Balliol, i. 67

— a "benevolence" granted him by merchants, i. 67, 68

— overruns Scotland, and leaves Balliol constable of the army, i. 69

— agrees to a truce with Scotland, i. 69

— returns to Scotland, and compels the Bruce party to submit to him, i. 69, 70

— his return to England, and preparations to defend his kingdom against a threatened invasion of the French, i. 70, 71

— concludes a temporary truce with Scotland at the wish of the Pope, i. 71

— returns to Scotland, and appoints Commissioners to treat with France and Bruce, i. 72

318   INDEX.

EDW

Edward III.—*continued*
— his preparations for the treachery of Philip VI., i. 72, 73
— summons a parliament at Nottingham, i. 73
— preparations of the King of France for invading England, i. 73
— again returns to Scotland on the death of his brother, the Earl of Cornwall, i. 73
— his preparations for defending his kingdom, i. 74
— claims dominion over the sea, i. 74
— leaves Scotland to defend England, i. 75
— sketch of the laws relative to social and commercial life passed during the early years of his reign, i. 76
— his legislation contrary to the true principles of commerce, i. 90
— his preparations for war with France, i. 93
— causes of the war, i. 93, 94
— makes foreign alliances, i. 95
— account of these allies, i. 100
— endeavours of the King of France to goad Edward into war, i. 105
— his friendship for Robert, Count of Artois, i. 105, 106
— his alliance with the Flemings and Brabanters, i. 106–108
— and with James Van Artevelde, i. 109
— his alliance also with the Count of Gueldres, i. 110
— his inconsistent prohibition of the export of wool, i. 111
— creates his eldest son Duke of Cornwall, i. 111
— and confers other dignities on his friends, i. 111
— his preparations for war and against invasion, i. 112
— appoints admirals and builds ships, i. 112, 113
— continues to offer peace, and makes ready for war, i. 114
— goes to the North to resist the Scots, i. 114
— makes alliances with Hainault, Gueldres, and Juliers, i. 115
— writes to Bayonne to say that the King of France disdains peace, i. 116
— enormous expenses of his preparations, i. 116, 117
— returns to London, and makes arrangements to resist invasion, i. 117.
— subsidy granted to him in the shape of wool, i. 117
— his difficulty in selling it, i. 118.

EDW

Edward III.—*continued*
— his arrangements with the Duke of Brabant, i. 119
— makes an alliance with the Emperor of Germany, i. 119
— asks for supplies, and explains the cause of his war with France, i. 120
— renews negotiations for peace, i. 121.
— calls himself "King of France," i. 122
— opens negotiations for an alliance with Ghent, i. 123
— advised by Van Artevelde to assume the title of King of France, i. 126
— Count Louis's troops defeated at Cadsand, i. 125
— arrival of two Cardinals to treat for peace with France, i. 126
— at their request Edward postpones his invasion of France, i. 127
— continues his preparations on the return of the Cardinals, i. 128
— his plan of attack of France, i. 128.
— revokes his promise to the Cardinals, i. 129
— and sails from England for Flanders, i. 130
— determines to invade France from the north, i. 132
— his difficult position at Antwerp, i. 134
— his allies hang back, i. 135
— his difficulties for money, i. 135
— grants commercial privileges to the Duke of Brabant, i. 136
— meeting of his allies at Halle, i. 136, 137
— opens negotiations with the Emperor of Germany, i. 137–139
— meets the Emperor at Coblentz, i.141
— makes an alliance with the Emperor, and is created vicar-general of the empire, i. 142
— birth of his son Lionel, i. 143
— opens negotiations with the Flemings and with their Count, i. 143
— ravages of the French fleet on the English coast, i. 144
— the Pope remonstrates with Edward, i. 145
— sends ambassadors to treat for peace with France, i. 145
— measures of his son at home for carrying on the war, i. 146
— Edward concludes an alliance with the Dukes of Austria, Styria, and Carinthia, i. 147
— his want of money, and expedients resorted to to obtain it, i. 147.

INDEX. 319

EDW

EDWARD III.—*continued*
— the Emperor persuaded by Philip to break with Edward, i. 147
— wavering of the Duke of Brabant, i. 148
— Edward still unwillingly treats for peace, i. 149
— waits for the arrival of his allies, i. 149
— their arrival at Mechlin, i. 150
— Edward's defiance of the King of France, i. 150
— besieges Cambrai, i. 150, 151
— but gives up the siege and invades France, i. 152
— offers battle to Philip, who fixes the day, i. 152
— but the campaign ends without fighting, i. 153
— Edward's own account of the campaign, i. 153
— makes an important treaty with the Duke of Brabant, i. 153
— quarters his arms with those of France, i. 156
— allies himself with the Flemings, and treats with Count Louis, i. 156
— obtains leave from his creditors to return to England, i. 157
— his preparations for the invasion of France in the following year, i. 157
— his constant negotiations for peace, i. 158
— which are finally broken off, i. 158
— returns to England, i 159
— an aid to carry on the war granted by Parliament, i. 163
— ships promised by the Cinque Ports and other coast towns, i. 164
— explains his calling himself King of France, i. 165
— supplies for two years, and redress of grievances granted, i. 166
— statute relative to the King's assumption of the title of King of France, i. 168, 169
— endeavours of the Pope to dissuade him from continuing the war with France, i. 169
— raises more money by loans, i. 170
— and sets sail for Flanders, i. 171
— and defeats the French fleet with immense loss, i. 172, 173
— birth of his son, John of Gaunt, i. 173
— arranges a plan of a fresh campaign, and writes urgently to England for supplies, i. 175
— subsidy granted by Parliament, and remitted to him at Bruges, i. 175

EDW

EDWARD III.—*continued*
— lays siege to Tournai, i. 176
— his offers to Philip, and Philip's answer, i. 176, 177
— harassed by want of money, and makes offers of peace, i. 177
— defeat of his ally, Robert of Artois, i. 177
— concludes a truce with the French for nine months, i. 178
— and "steals away" with the Queen to England, i. 178
— his punishment of the Constable of the Tower, and of other officers, i. 179
— his quarrel with Archbishop Stratford, i. 179–184
— his treachery to Parliament, i. 185
— prepares for the renewal of the war with Scotland, i. 186
— negotiates for peace with France, but prepares for war, i. 187
— orders a fleet to be collected, and a supply of bows and arrows to be got together, i. 187, 188
— his further negotiations for peace, i. 188
— war with Scotland, i. 189, 190
— death of the Regent of Scotland, and appointment of Robert the Steward to be governor, i. 191
— loss of Perth and Stirling, i. 191, 192
— the King's advance to the North, i. 192
— loss of Edinburgh, i. 192
— concludes a truce with the Scots for six months, which is afterwards extended to two years, 193
— returns to England, i. 193
— origin of his fresh war with France, i. 194
— gives help to John of Montfort on condition of acknowledging him as King of France, i. 197
— error of Froissart as to Edward and the Countess of Salisbury, i. 200–202, *note*
— orders forces to be sent to Brittany, i. 202
— treats for peace with France, but does not relax his preparations for war, i. 203.
— summons a naval Parliament, i. 203
— endeavours of Clement VI. to make peace between England and France, i. 204.
— arranges his troops, i. 255
— estimate of the numbers of his army, i. 256

320INDEX.

EDW

EDWARD III.—*continued*
— his exact position, i. 256
— progress of the battles, i. 258–260
— utter defeat of the French, i. 261
— Edward's reception of his son after the battle, i. 262
— renewed fighting the next day, and further defeat of the French, i. 262
— Edward's march to Calais, i. 263
— Edward's continuation of his preparations for war, i. 205
— becomes weary of negotiation, and tells the Pope he is going to invade France, i. 207
— sets sail for Brittany, i. 208
— lands at Vannes, and lays siege to it, i. 214
— but leaves it and goes round to Rennes, i. 215
— besieges Nantes, and returns to Vannes, i. 215
— where he gathers all his forces, i. 215
— conclusion of a truce between the armies, i. 216
— Edward returns to England, i. 217
— meets Parliament on the question of peace or war, 220
— sends commissioners to the Pope relative to peace, i. 220
— his resistance to Papal aggression, i. 220
— his defence of the Church of England, i. 222
— failure of negotiations for peace with France, i. 223
— his objects in his repeated invasions of France, i. 223
— proclaims a Round Table at Windsor, i. 224
— the truce broken by Philip, i. 225
— Edward's preparations for the war, i. 226
— Return of his crown from Germany, i. 227
— his negotiations for peace, i. 228
— attempts to gain the alliance of the Duke of Brabant, i. 228
— his arrangements for the defence of Gascony, and for the attack of France in Brittany, i. 231
  instructs the Earl of Northampton to defy Philip VI., i. 231
— provides for the invasion of France in two places, i. 232
— goes to Flanders to try its fidelity, and takes his eldest son with him, i. 232
— proposes to make. his son Edward Duke of Flanders, i. 234

EDW

EDWARD III.—*continued*
—returns to England, i. 235
— deputations from various towns to him, i. 235
— desertion of the Lord of Beaumont, i. 236
—death of his brother-in-law, the Count of Hainault, i. 236
— prepares actively for war, and provides for its cost, i. 236, 237
— his rejection of the Pope's proposals for peace, i. 237
— his preparations for the defence of England, i. 238
— sails with his son for Normandy, i. 238, 244
— successes of the Earl of Derby, i. 239–242
— knights his son on his landing, i. 244
— his progress through Normandy, i. 245
— towns taken by him, i. 245
— besieges and takes Caen, i. 245, 246
— gives the town up to pillage, i. 246
— marches towards the Seine, but unable to cross it, i. 247
— takes Louviers, and marches close to Paris, i. 247
— ravages the country, i. 247
— large army collected by the King of France at St. Denis, i. 249
— Edward's dangerous position, i. 249
— retreats over the Seine, i. 250
— his discipline, i. 250
— tries to find means of passing the Somme, i. 250
— rests at Oisemont, i. 251
— defeats Godemar du Fay and crosses the Somme at Blanche Tache, i. 252, 253.
— rests at La Broye, i. 253
— and chooses Crécy as his battle-field, i. 254
— number and cost of his forces in Normandy and before Calais, i. 264, *note*
— summons Calais in vain to surrender, i. 265
— prepares for a long siege, i. 265.
— invasion of England by the Scots, who are defeated at Nevill's Cross, i. 268–271
— the King joined by the Queen, i. 271
— events in Aquitaine, i. 271–273
— events in Brittany, i. 274
— plans of Philip for the relief of Calais, i. 276, 277
— sends ambassadors to court the alli-

INDEX.
321

EDW

Edward III.—*continued*
ance of the Flemings, and offers his daughter Isabella in marriage to their young Count, i. 277
— his interview with the Count at St. Vinox, i. 278
— escape of the Count to France without performing his promise to marry Isabella, i. 279
— progress of the siege, i. 280
— cannon used by him, i. 280
— builds a tower to command the harbour, i. 280
— preparations of the French for the relief of the beleaguered town, i. 281, 282
— march of the French, under their King, on the town, i. 282, 283.
— offer of Philip to fight Edward single-handed, i. 284
— surrender of Càlais, i. 285–287
— story of the six burgesses, i. 286, 287
— enters the city, and orders all the inhabitants to quit the town, i. 288
— preparations of Philip to recover Calais, i. 288
— concludes a truce with the French, and returns with the Queen to England, i. 288, 289
— his expostulation with the Virgin, i. 289
— henceforth takes a less active part in war than his son, i. 290
— renewal of the truce with France from time to time, i. 291
— prosperity of his kingdom, i. 292
— offered the Imperial crown, but refuses it, i. 292, 293
— his fondness for tournaments and hawking, i. 293, 296
— his establishment of the Order of the Garter, i. 295, 296, 298
— his plays, i. 297
— domestic legislation, i. 300
— visitation of the Black Death, i. 303, *et seq.*
— prolongs the truce again, i. 313, 314
— petition of Parliament against taxation without their consent, i. 314
— attempt to convert the truce into a permanent peace, i. 315, 316
— endeavours of Count Louis of Flanders to detach Ypres and Ghent from their English alliance, i. 316
— loss of St. Jean d'Angely, i. 329–332
— renewal of the truce with France, i. 333
— hostility of the Count of Flanders,

EDW

Edward III.—*continued*
and increasing goodwill of the Flemings, i. 335
— renewal of the war with France, i. 352
— failure of efforts to make peace, i. 352, 354
— war subsidy granted by the King to him, i. 353
— negotiations for an alliance with Navarre, i. 358
— settlement of the alliance, and consequent plans for the invasion of France, i. 359
— invades the north of France, and ravages Artois and Picardy, i. 361
— returns to England to resist the Scots, i. 362
— the Prince of Wales's campaign in the South of France, i. 365–369
— alliance between Edward and Philip of Navarre and Godfrey of Harcourt, i. 373
— goes to Calais with his son, and defeats an attempt to take the town, i. 317
— — fighting and "raging like a wild boar" at the castle gate, i. 319
— takes the French prisoners, i. 319, 320
— his treatment of his prisoners, i. 320
— his return to England, i. 320
— prepares for war, but renews the truce, i. 321
— death of Philip VI., and accession of his son, John II., i. 321
— sets sail with his sons, and defeats a great Spanish fleet in the Channel, i. 325–327
— obtains from his people the title of "King of the Sea," i. 328
— mutual recriminations of Edward and the King of France, i. 328, 329
— purchases the castle of Guisnes, i. 329
— demands a subsidy from the clergy, on account of French preparations for invading England, i. 329
— commencement of the war, i. 329
— the battle of Poitiers gained by his son, i. 392
— and the King of France taken prisoner, and brought to England, i. 392–399
— Edward's meeting with the captive King, i. 399
— to whom he assigns the palace of the Savoy as a residence, i. 400
— his treatment of the Scottish people, i. 402, 403

VOL. II.   Y

322 INDEX.

EDW

EDWARD III.—continued

— negotiations for the release of King David, i. 403, 404
— Edward's journey to the relief of Berwick-on-Tweed, i. 405
— which he accomplishes, and then prepares for the subjugation of Scotland, i. 407
— surrender of all his rights by Balliol, i. 407
— Edward's advance into Scotland, i. 408
— his ignominious retreat, and arrival in London, i. 409
— promises to govern Scotland according to her ancient laws, i. 409
— truce concluded between England and Scotland, i. 410
— sets King David II. at liberty, and adopts a policy of conciliation towards the Scots, i. 410, 411
— his ordinances for the reformation of Ireland, ii. 11
— defied by the De Burghs, ii. 11
— Edward's Irish policy, ii. 12
— induced by the settlers to revoke his resumption of lands in Ireland, ii. 13
— his strong measures against Ireland, ii. 14
— sends his son Lionel to Ireland, ii. 15
— his treaty with King John of France, ii. 39
— his second invasion of France, ii. 40, 41
— death of his mother, and marriage of his son John of Gaunt, ii. 42
— failure of negotiations for peace with France, ii. 42, 43
— his preparations for war, ii. 43
— takes hawks and hounds with him to France, ii. 44
— his measures for the safety of England, ii. 44, 45
— foreign adventurers flock to him at Calais to join his standard, ii. 46
— his embarkation, and number of his troops, ii. 46, 47
— joined by the Duke of Lancaster, ii. 48
— disperses the adventurers at Calais, ii. 48
— sufferings of his army from want of food and bad weather, ii. 49
— his arrival before Rheims, ii. 50
— abandons Rheims, and marches through Burgundy, ii. 51
— makes a treaty with the Duke of Burgundy, ii. 51

EDW

EDWARD III.—continued

— marches on Paris, ii. 54
— determines to march through France, and return to besiege Paris in the autumn, ii. 54
— concludes the peace of Bretigni, ii. 55
— terms of the treaty, ii. 55, 56
— Edward returns to England, ii. 57
— goes to Boulogne and embarks for England, ii. 59
— unstable nature of the peace with France, ii. 61
— the treaty of Bretigni null and void, ii. 62, 63
— restores the Priories Aliens in England, ii. 67
— marriage of his son, the Black Prince, whom he creates Duke of Aquitaine, ii. 68
— domestic legislation from 1362 to 1364, ii. 70–86
— his inability to speak English, ii. 72
— jubilee on the occasion of his attaining the fiftieth year of his reign, ii. 86
— honours conferred by him on his sons, ii. 86, 87
— his hunting parties, ii. 87
— departure of his eldest son for Aquitaine, ii. 87
— return of King John to captivity and death, ii. 91, 92
— resistance to the usurpations of the Pope, ii. 94–96
— his son Lionel proposed as king of Scotland, ii. 98
— unfriendly relations with France, ii. 98
— marriage of his son Edmund with Margaret of Flanders prevented by the Pope, ii. 99
— orders his lieutenants in France to put down the "Companies," ii. 100
— the treaty with France broken by Charles V., ii. 101
— sends John of Montfort aid in Brittany, ii. 104
— his treaty with Pedro the Cruel, ii. 109
— endeavours in vain to prevent the English in Aquitaine from joining the expedition against Pedro, ii. 111–114
— agrees to support Pedro by force of arms, ii. 117.
— decline of English rule in France, and declaration of war by the King of France, ii. 134
— prospective view of the conclusion of Edward's reign, ii. 134
— endeavours of the King of France to blind Edward as to his intentions, ii. 146

INDEX. 323

EDW

EDWARD III.—*continued*
— but Edward prepares for war, ii. 147, 149
— war declared by France, ii. 148
— capture of Ponthieu by France, ii. 150
— increase in the King's preparations, ii. 151
— resumes the title of King of France, ii. 151
— subsidy granted by Parliament, ii. 152
— he extends the truce with Scotland, ii. 152
— and tries in vain to make an alliance with Flanders, ii. 154
— his alliances, and those of France, ii. 155
— commencement of the war, ii. 155
— proposed invasion of England by the King of France, ii. 161
— Edward summons a special Parliament, ii. 161, 162
— sends the Duke of Lancaster to invade France, ii. 162
— desultory warfare in that country, ii. 162–169, 170
— orders the Prince of Wales to give up the hearth-tax, ii. 169
— and sends over the Duke of Lancaster to Aquitaine, ii. 170, 172
— return of the Black Prince to England in broken health, ii. 172
— Edward, eldest son of the Black Prince, his death, ii. 179
— he prepares to renew the war, and summons a Parliament, ii. 181
— the war not carried on with vigour, ii. 181
— influence of Alice Perrers over him, ii. 182, 202, 234
— cements his alliance with Brittany, ii. 191
— marriage of his sons, ii. 193
— unpromising aspect of English affairs, ii. 195
— his plans for continuing the war, ii. 195
— no longer any vigour in his councils, ii. 202
— general discomfiture of the English in France, ii. 206–209
— sails with the Black Prince to the relief of Thouars, but returns without landing, ii. 211–213
— the Duchy of Aquitaine surrendered to him by his son, ii. 215
— his evasive answer to the complaints as to the decline of the navy, ii. 218
— continued reverses of the English in France, ii. 219

EDW

EDWARD III.—*continued*
— prepares for the defence of England and invasion of France, ii. 220
— six fortresses only remaining to him in France, ii. 223
— sends the Dukes of Lancaster and Brittany to invade France on the north, ii. 224
— utter failure of the expedition, ii. 225–229
— proceedings of Parliament in 1373, ii. 230–232
— Edward's preparations for making the fleet effective, ii. 232
— sends no help to the Duke of Lancaster, and loses Aquitaine, ii. 233, 234
— his mistress ordered by the Commons to absent herself from him, ii. 234
— sends troops to Brittany, ii. 235
— concludes a truce with France, ii. 238, 240
— his illness at Eltham, ii. 247, 256
— the negotiations for peace, ii. 271, *note*
— holds a grand Christmas feast in honour of his grandson, the Prince of Wales, ii. 273
— retires to Havering-atte-Bower, ii. 273
— his death, ii. 290
— characteristics of his reign, ii. 291
— contrast between the beginning and end of the reign, ii. 292
— review of Edward's character, ii. 295
EDWARD THE BLACK PRINCE, his birth, i. 34. Sent to Nottingham for safety, 71. Created duke of Cornwall, 111. Meets the ambassadors from the Pope, 127. Appointed guardian of the kingdom during the absence of the King, 130. Provides for the defence of the kingdom, 132. His measures at home for carrying on the war with France, 146. Proposal to marry him to the daughter of the Duke of Brabant, 147. Left again guardian of the kingdom, 171. His first campaign, 194. Left again guardian of the kingdom, 208. His preparations for continuing the war with France, 216, 217. Created Prince of Wales, 219. Proposal of his father to marry him to a daughter of the Duke of Brabant, 229. Accompanies his father to the Continent, 232. Proposal of his father to make him Duke of Flanders, 234. Gathers together an army in Wales, 236.

Y 2

324 INDEX.

EDW

Sails again with his father for Normandy, 238. Knighted by his father, 244. Has command of the first division at Crécy, 255. His conduct in the battle, 260. Story of his adoption of the plume of feathers, and the motto of 'Ich dien,' 261, *note*. His meeting with his father after the battle, 262. Returns with his parents to England, 289. Takes a more active part henceforth than his father in war, 290. Accompanies his father to Calais, 317. Joins his father in the battle of "L'Espagnols-sur-Mer," 325. His bravery, 326, 327. His army for the invasion of France in 1355, 359. Sails from England, 360. Lands at Bordeaux, 362, 365. No definite purpose in his invasion, 362. Arrangements for his expedition, 363, 364. Receives full power to act in the King's name, 364, 365. Opening of the campaign, 365. His army designated by Froissart as robbers, 366, 367. His progress and return with plunder, 366–368. Retires to Bordeaux, 369. His campaign of 1356, 377. Ravages the central parts of France, 378. Reaches Bourges, 379. Takes Vierzon, 379. Retreats towards Bordeaux, 379. Besieges and takes Romorantin on his way, 380–382. Followed by the French and their king, 383. Finds the French in advance of him, and is compelled to fight, 384. Preparations of the French for battle, 385. Edward's preparations and order of battle, 386, 387. Attempt of the Cardinal Perigord to prevent the battle, 387. Edward's terms rejected by the French, 388. His conduct in the battle, 390. Panic and flight of the French, 391. The King of France taken prisoner on the field, 392. Marches with his prisoners to Bordeaux, 396, 397. His account of the battle, in a letter to the Lord Mayor of London, 396, *note*. His reception in London, 399. Accompanies his father on his second campaign, ii. 47. Conducts King John back to France, 57. His marriage to the Fair Maid of Kent, 68. Created duke of Aquitaine, 68. But not made absolute sovereign of that country, 69. Embarks for his new dominions, 69, 87. Sends De Montfort aid in Brittany, 104. Gives his stepdaughter in

ELA

marriage to De Montfort, 105. His hospitality to the dethroned Pedro the Cruel, 115. Advised not to help Pedro, 115. But declares he is bound in honour to do so, 116. King Edward agrees to support Pedro, 117. The Prince's arrangements with Pedro, 119. Summons Calverley and the "Companies" from Spain, 120. Preparations in England to support him, 122. Marches for Spain, 122, 123. Birth of his son Richard, 123. Gaston de Foix pays him his respects at Dax, 123. His friends flock around him, 123. Crosses the Pyrenees, 124. And musters his troops at Pampeluna, 124. Receives a letter from Henry of Trastamare, 125. Sends forward Felton to reconnoitre, 125. Takes Salvatierra, 125. Advances, but cannot bring on a battle, 128. Marches to Navarrete, which he makes his headquarters, 128. Defeats the Spaniards there, 129–132. Dangers of his armies at Crécy, at Poitiers, and at Navarrete, 132, 133. His illness at Valladolid, 135. Returns to Aquitaine, 136. Unable to pay the "Companies" what is due to them, 132. Tells them to ravage France, 140. Unpopularity of his hearth-tax, 142. Extravagance of his court at Bordeaux, 143. His indignation at the conduct of the King of France, 145. His failing health, 145, 147. Recalls John of Chandos from St. Sauveur, 146. Ordered by his father to give up the hearth-tax, 169. Makes ready for war, 172. Joined by the Duke of Lancaster, 172. Collects his forces at Cognac, 172. Retakes Limoges, 176. His brutal massacre of the inhabitants, 177. Refuses terms of alliance with the King of Navarre, 178. Returns to Bordeaux, 179. Death of his eldest son Edward, 179. Returns to England with his wife and son Richard, 179. Joins his father to relieve Thouars, 211. But returns without landing in France, 212. Opposes his brother Lancaster's misgovernment, 44. Enmity between the brothers, 245. His death, 253. His last will and burialplace, 255. Review of his part in Parliament, 293

Eland, Sir William, governor of Nottingham Castle, gives up Mortimer to the King, i. 36

INDEX. 325

ELE

Eleanor, the Princess, sister of Edward III., proposal to marry her to the eldest son of Philip VI., i. 30. Married to the Count of Gueldres, 110

Ellis, William, trial and condemnation of, ii. 252. Pardoned, 277

Eltham, meeting of Parliament at, i. 45

Emeric de Pavia, governor of Calais for Edward III., attempt to bribe him to betray his trust, i. 317

England, foreign wars of, in the reign of Edward III., i. 2. Its commercial and social progress at this period, 2, 3. Its relations with Ireland, 5. Ravages of the Scots in the northern counties, 13–16. State of the kingdom in 1331, 51. Order established by Edward III., 51. Threatened invasion by the French, 70, 71. Preparations of Philip VI., 73. Period of extravagance in dress and food, 83, 84. Enormous expenses of the proposed war, 116. Arrangements to resist invasion, 117. Commencement of the war, 131. Preparations against invasion, 132, 133. Anxiety of the Normans to invade and again conquer England, 144. Impoverishment of the country by the war with France, 161. Dangerous state of the country, 162. Causes of the unpopularity of the war, 164. Ravages of the Scots in the North, 177, 268. Conclusion of a truce with France, 289. General character of the reign after the taking of Calais, 290. Domestic affairs, 290. Prosperity of the country, 290. Sports and pastimes of the people at this time, 293. Hawking, 293. The spoils of France spread over the country, 294. Tournaments forbidden without leave, 294, 295. Extravagance in dress of both clergy and laity, 296, 297. Popularity of plays, 297. Legislation for keeping the peace of the nation, and administration of justice, 300. Breaking out of the "Black Death," 302. Extent of the mortality, 304. The most eminent victims, 306. Effects of the superstition engendered by the plague on the treatment of the Jews, 308. Fall in the value of land in consequence, 309. Disputes between employers and workmen, 309–312. Attempt to convert the truce into a permanent peace, 315. Renewal of the truce, 321. Domestic events between 1352

EVR

and 1355, 336. Laws against forestallers and regrators, 336, 337. Interference of Parliament in trade, 338–341. Trade with Scotland forbidden, 341. Causes of the enmity of the Irish to England, 342. Marriages between English and Irish illegal, 343. Laws relating to purveyors, 344. Statute of Treasons, 345. And of Provisors, 346. Mode of making laws, and constitution of Parliament, 350, 351. Renewal of the war with France, 352. State of England after the battle of Poitiers, ii. 41. Preparations for war with France, 43. And measures taken for the protection of England during the King's absence, 44, 45. England invaded by the French, 51. Who are driven back, 52. Active measures taken to prevent a recurrence of invasion, 52, 53. Return of the plague, 67. Important domestic legislation in 1362–1364, 70–86. The English language ordered to be used in courts of law, 70. French the language of the upper classes, 71. Regulations as to persons passing in or out of the country, 79. History of the resistance to the usurpations of the Pope in England, 92 *et seq.* War declared against England by France, 148. The English bishops preach against France, 156. An invasion of England planned by the King of France, 161. Given up, 162. Results of the campaign of 1379, 180. An invasion threatened by the French, 221

English language used in courts of law, i. 3; ii. 70

"Espagnols-sur-Mer," battle of, i. 325–327

Estaples taken by Edward III., i. 263

Ettrick, forest of, given to Lord Montacute, i. 35

Eu and Guisnes, Raoul, Count of, taken prisoner at Caen, i. 328. Suspected by the King of France of treason, and afterwards put to death, 328, 329

Europe, Western, origin, extent, and mutual relations of the kingdoms of, i. 95

Evreux, residence of Charles the Bad at, i. 357. Refuses to open its gates to John II. of France, 358. Besieged and taken by King John, 377. Philip of Navarre establishes himself at, ii. 25

326 INDEX.

FAM

"FAMOSUS LIBELLUS," the, of Edward III., i. 182

Fauquemont, Lord of, at the meeting of Edward's allies at Halle, i. 137. Joins Edward III. at Mechlin, 150

Felton, Sir Thomas, accompanies Chandos on a mission to Pampeluna, ii. 119. Tries in vain to dissuade the Prince from his invasion of Spain, 121. Sent forward to Navarrete to reconnoitre, 125. His death, 127. Saves La Linde, 173

Ferrars, Thomas, appointed governor of the Channel Islands, i. 115

Fife, Duncan, Earl of, his trial and pardon, i. 402, 403

Fifteenth, a, granted to the King for two years, i. 166

Fish, salt, interference of Parliament in the trade in, i. 339 ; ii. 81

Flagellants, rise of the order of the, i. 307. Their origin and spread, 308. Their discipline, 308

Flanders, territories into which it was divided, i. 123

Flavigny taken by assault by Edward III., ii. 51

Fleet, Edward III.'s, in 1336, i. 112. His admirals at home and in Aquitaine, 112. Mode of providing ships of war at this time, 113. The King's own ships, 113, 114. Ships ordered to be "arrested" by Edward, 128. His fleet accompanies him to Flanders, 130. Destroys the French fleet at Sluys, 172, 173. The fleet collected for a new campaign in France, 187. Its defeat of a great Spanish fleet in the Channel, 324-327. The fleet for conveying the Black Prince to France, on his first expedition, 363. A great fleet prepared for the invasion of France, ii. 196

Fleet, English, decline of the strength of the, ii. 215, 221. Preparations for making it effective, 232

Fleet, French, its damage to English seaports, i. 144. Destroyed at Sluys, 172, 173. Strength of the, of Charles V., ii. 221

Fleet, Spanish, sent to invade England, i. 324. Defeated by Edward III. in person, 325-327

Flemings, brought over to join Edward III. against the Scots, i. 12. Their quarrel with the English at York, 12. Their rebellion against their Count, Louis I., 26. Defeated with great slaughter by the French, 27. Woollen

FRA

weavers introduced into England by William the Conqueror, and by Edward III., 86, 87. Their friendship sacrificed by Edward I., 86. Towns in which they settled, 87. Importance to Edward III. of an alliance with the Flemings, 106. Edward III.'s negotiations with them and with their Count, 143. Flanders and Brabant brought into close commercial union, 156. Excommunicated by the Pope, 156. Endeavours of Philip VI. to gain over the Flemings, 174. Flanders placed under an interdict, 174. Vain endeavours of Clement VI. to induce the Flemings to submit to their Count, 204. Attempts made to detach them from their English alliance, 229. Visit of Edward III. to them, 233. Quarrel between the inhabitants of the large and small towns, 233. Besiege Bovines, and advance to Gravelines, 249. Their alliance courted both by the English and French, 277. Insist upon their Count marrying Isabella of England, 277, 278. But he refuses, and escapes to France, 278, 279. The Flemings adhere more firmly to Edward III., and put an army on the French frontier, 279. Ravage the country, and refuse an alliance with France, 279. Attacked by the French at Cassel, but defeat them, 282. State of their affairs in 1349, 316. Tumults caused by their Count, 317. Compelled to agree to the marriage of their Count with a daughter of the Duke of Brabant, 335. Increase of their goodwill to England, 335. Remain friendly with England, ii. 154-197. See Artevelde, Van ; Edward III.

Foix, Gaston de, joins the Captal de Buch in a crusade against the pagans of Prussia, ii. 33. Aids in putting down the Jacquerie, 33. Absent from the parliament of Gascon nobles at Bordeaux, 116. Compelled to do homage to the King of England, 116, 117. Refuses the "Companies" passage through Foix, 121. Pays his respects to the Prince of Wales, 123. War between him and France, ii. 233. Gives in his allegiance to France, 234

Fontenay le Comte, surrenders to the French, ii. 210

Forestallers, laws against, i. 336, 337

France, wars of England with, in the

INDEX. 327

FRA

reign of Edward III., i. 2, 6. Peace concluded between Charles IV. of, and Edward III., 23, 42. Claims of Edward to the throne of, 23. The claim examined, 23. Edward summoned by the King of France to do homage, 26. History of the disputes between England and France, i. 41. Treaty of peace concluded, 45. Increasing hostility of the King of France, 93. Causes of the war, 93, 94. History of France as a kingdom, 96. Its foundation and feudal dependencies, 98. Mutual aid given by France and Scotland, 114. Edward III.'s preparations for war, 112–120. Negotiations for peace, 121. Edward III. styles himself "King of France," 122. Commencement of the war with England, 131. Edward's invasion of, 152. End of the campaign without fighting, 157. Preparations of England for invasion the following year, 157. Successes of the Earl of Derby in the South, 239–242. Ravages of Edward III. through Normandy and near Paris, 245–247. Battle of Crécy, 261. Consequences of the battle, 263. Ravages of the Flemings in 1347, 279. Conclusion of a truce between England and France, 289. The country infested by brigands, 291. Who keep up warfare against the English, 291. Wretched state of the country in consequence, 292. Effect of the Black Death on prices in, 312. Negotiations relative to the truce and to a permanent peace with England, 313, 315. Prolongation of the truce, 314. Struggle of the French to regain Calais, 317–321. Renewal of the truce between the countries, 321. Connection between France and Navarre, 321. Outbreak of hostilities with England, 329. Renewal of the war, and France again invaded by the English, 352, 354. A truce agreed to, 354. Preparations for war, 355. History of the quarrels between France and Navarre, 355. Invasion of France by the English in both the North and South, 362, 365. No definite purpose in the invasion, 362. The Prince of Wales's invasion for the sake of plunder and fighting only, 362, 363. Towns plundered and burnt, 366, 367. Others pay ransoms to avoid being plundered, 368. The States General

FRA

called together, 369. Golden opportunity lost on this occasion to France, 370. The Langue d'oc and Langue d'oil, 370. The central parts of the country ravaged by the Prince of Wales, 378. The King and his youngest son taken prisoners to England, 397. The government assumed by the Duke of Normandy, 397. A truce for two years concluded, 397. State of France after the battle of Poitiers, ii. 17, 19. Non-observance of the two years' truce, 17. Reassembling of the States-General, 19. Oppressions of the feudal lords in raising money for their ransom from the English, 23. Origin of the term *Jacques bon homme*, 24. Oppression of the peasants by the nobles and by the disbanded soldiers, 24. The "Free Companies," 19, 24. The government of the Thirty-six, 26. Opposition of the Duke of Normandy to their decrees, 26. Release of the King of Navarre, who, joined by his brother Philip, ravages the country, 28. Commencment of a revolution under Marcel, 29–31. The Jacquerie, its origin and progress, 31. Death of Marcel, and end of the revolution, 38. Debasement of the coinage by the Duke of Normandy, 38. Confusion and wretchedness of the country, 38, 39. The treaty of King John with England rejected by the people with scorn, 39. Efforts made to drive out the "Companies," 39, 40. Preparations of war with England, 43. Raid of the Duke of Lancaster in Artois and Picardy, 46, 48. March of Edward III. and his army, 48. Edward at Rheims, and in Burgundy, 50, 51. His march on Paris, 54. Condition of the country at this time, 54, 66, 67. His march towards Brittany, 55. Conclusion of the treaty of Bretigni, 55. And release of the King of France, 58, 59. End of the first great epoch of the war, 59. The peace on an unstable foundation, 61. The treaty of Bretigni null and void, 61, 62. Return of the ceded castles, 62, 63. The "Companies" again begin their devastations, 63. Return of the plague, 67. And wretchedness of the kingdom, 90. Return of the King to captivity, 91. Death of King John in London, 92. Unfriendly relations of England and France, 98. Events in France invol-

328 INDEX.

FRA

ving English interest, after the death of King John, 100. The treaty of peace broken by Charles V., 100, 101. Successes of Bertrand du Guesclin and Boucicault in Normandy, 102, 103. War declared against England, 148. The French clergy preach against England, 150. The North ravaged by the Duke of Lancaster, 164. Skirmishes between the French and English, 165–169. But no great battles, which the French are ordered to avoid, 169, 170. Commencement of a regular campaign, 172. Successes of the French, 172, 173. Ravages of Knolles in the North, 174. Desultory warfare in the South, 188. Brittany joins with England, 192. But Scotland and Castile join with France, 192, 194. English preparations for the invasion of France, 196. General discomfiture of the English, 205, 206. Consequences of the fall of Rochelle, 209. Further successes of the French, 210–214, 219, et seq. Invasion of the Dukes of Lancaster and Brittany in the North, 224, 225. Its disastrous failure, 225

Frankfort, quarrel of the States General of, with the Pope, i. 140

Fraser, Sir Simon, joins the attack on Edward Balliol's camp at Annan, i. 58

French language used by the upper classes in England, ii. 71

G ALEAZZO VISCONTI, Lord of Milan, releases John II. of France from captivity, ii. 57

Garencières, Eugene de, carries bribes to Scotland, i. 404. Accompanies Douglas in his Border warfare, 404

Garter, Order of the, established, i. 295, 296, 298

Gascons, their covetousness, i. 398

Gascony, preparations of Edward III. in, i. 72. Request of, for English soldiers, i. 230. Embarkation of the Earl of Derby for, 232. Bands of brigands in, 292.

Gaunt, John of, his birth and birth-place, i. 173. Joins his father at the battle of "L'Espagnols-sur-Mer," 325. Goes with his father to invade France, 361. His marriage to Blanche of Lancaster, ii. 42. Accompanies his father to France, 47. Created Duke of Lancaster, 87. His marriage with Constance of Castile, 114.

GER

Joins his brother in his expedition into Spain, 123, 124. Attacked by the Spaniards, 127. At the battle of Navarrete, 130, 131. Sent to command the troops at Calais and Guisnes, 151. Sent to invade France, 162. Ravages the country round Calais, 162. Face to face with the Duke of Burgundy, who departs without fighting, 163. Returns to Calais, 164. Ravages the North of France, and returns to England, 164. Sent by his father to Aquitaine, 170. Joins the Prince of Wales against the French, 172. Left by his brother to take charge of Aquitaine, 179. One of the leaders of the feudal party in England, 182. Retakes Montpaon, 187, 188. Returns to Bordeaux, 188. And makes love to Constance of Castile, 188. Marries her, 193. And assumes the title of King of Castile, 194. Leaves Aquitaine, 194. His invasion of France in the North, ii. 224. His disastrous march to Bordeaux, 224–229. No help sent to him from England, and he returns home, 233, 234. Goes to Calais, 236. His misgovernment opposed by the Black Prince, 244. Enmity between the brothers, 245. Apprehensions of Parliament of his designs, 246. Inclined to oppose the Commons, 249. Attempts to divert the course of the succession to the throne, 255, 256. His evil influence after the death of the Black Prince, 258. His acts on his return to power, 266. His friendship for Wyclif, 284. Whom he defends violently, 287. Escapes with difficulty from a mob, 287. Review of his character, 293

Genoa, the mercenary sailors of, and their ravages on the English coast, i. 144. Genoese crossbowmen at the battle of Crécy, 258. Their retreat, 259. Their soldiers fight as mercenaries on both sides, 322. Their neutrality secured by Edward III., ii. 197. Genoese in the English fleet, 221

Geoffrey de Chargny, his attempt to obtain possession of Calais by bribery, i. 317. Defeated and taken prisoner by Edward III., 320

Germain, St., burnt by Edward III., i. 248

Germans, defeated at Poitiers by the English, i. 391

Germany, origin of, i. 99. And of the

INDEX.

329

GHE

empire of, 99. Its resistance to the claims of the Pope over, 140. Determination of the Diet, and States General of Frankfort, 140'

Ghent, negotiations opened by Edward III. for an alliance with, i. 123. Endeavours of Count Louis to detach it from Ypres and Bruges, 316. Disturbances in the city caused by Louis, 317

Girald de Barri (Giraldus Cambrensis), appointed companion and adviser to Prince John, ii. 6. Advises castles to be built in Ireland for the protection of the English settlers, 6

Giscar, Mont, sacked and burnt by the Black Prince, i. 366

Gloucester, Hugh de Audley created earl of, i. 111

Godemar du Fay, defeated by Edward III. at Blanche Tache, i. 252, 253. Accused by Philip VI. with having been the cause of his misfortunes, 276

Goldsmiths, interference of Parliament with the trade of, ii. 81

Government, machinery of, in the reigns of Edward I., II., and III., i. 49

Gower, John, his works, ii. 73

Gravelines, advance of the Flemings to, i. 249

Greek fire used at the defence of Breteuil, i. 377. Employed against Romorantin, 382

Gregory XI., Pope, tries to arrange a peace between England and France, ii. 190. Complaint of Parliament of his usurpations, 231. Edward III. comes to an agreement with him, 231

Griffiths, the Welsh brigand captain, ii. 24

Gueldres and Zutphen, Count of, his marriage with the Princess Eleanor, i. 110. His alliance with Edward III., 110. Makes an alliance with Edward III., 115. At the meeting of Edward's allies at Halle, 137.

Gueldres and Zutphen, Count Raynald of, sent by Edward III. to negotiate with Count Louis of Flanders, i. 143. Joins Edward III. with his army, 150. His friendship with England, ii. 155.

Guesclin, Bertrand du, in Rennes, ii. 17. Rise of, 40. His campaign in Normandy, 102. His defeat of the Captal de Buch, at Cocherel, 102, 103. Made Earl of Longueville, 103. Assists in defeating the Navarrese,

GUI

103. Taken prisoner at Auray, 105. Amount of his ransom, 109. Placed in command of the army sent against Pedro the Cruel, 109. Secures the services of the "Companies" for the expedition, 110. His march with the "Companies" to Avignon, and his difficulties with the Pope there, 111. Reaches Barcelona, 112. And Calaharra and Burgos, where Henry of Trastamare is crowned, 113. Returns to France, 114. Joins the reigning King of Castile with troops to oppose the Black Prince, 123, 124. At the battle of Navarrete, 130. Where he is taken prisoner, 130. Engaged with the Duke of Anjou, 137. Again ransomed, and joins Henry of Trastamare in Spain, 137. Defeats Don Pedro at Montiel, 138. Joins the Duke of Anjou at Toulouse, 172. And appointed commander of the French forces, 172. Appointed Constable of France, ii. 175. Compels Usson to yield, 189, 190. His activity, 202. Joins the Duke of Berri, and enters Poitou, 202, 203. Takes the Castle of Montmorillon, 203. With the Duke, takes St. Sévère, 203. Sets off to besiege Poitiers, 205. Goes to Rochelle to receive the town for the King of France, 210. Besieges and takes Thouars, 210–213. Completes the conquest of Poitou, 219, 220. Enters Brittany with an army, 222. Takes St. Malo and Hennebon, 222, 223. And besieges Nantes, 223. Summoned by the Earl of Salisbury to fight, which he refuses to do, 224. Besieges Derval, 224. Recalled to defend the North of France, 224. His views as to the mode of dealing with the English, 228. Goes to reduce the Count of Foix, ii. 233. Besieges St. Sauveur, 237. Sends forces to hold the English in check, 237.

Guienne, the greater part conquered by Charles of Valois, i. 42. Aggressions of Philip VI. in, 127. Great part of, taken by the French, 177

Guillon, encampment of Edward III. at, ii. 51

Guines, Count of, sent by Philip VI. to assist Normandy, i. 245. Taken prisoner by the English at Caen, 245, 246

Guisnes, Castle of, sold to the English, i. 329

330   INDEX.

GUN

Gunpowder, use of, the downfall of chivalry, ii. 291
Guy de Nesle, opposes the advance of the English to St. Jean d'Angely, i. 331. Defeated and taken prisoner, 331
Guzman, Leonora de, murder of, by Pedro the Cruel, ii. 107

HAINAULT, William, Count of, his daughter Philippa married to Edward III., i. 21, 22. Agrees to protect commerce during war, 61. Makes an alliance with Edward III., 115. His death, 137
Hainault, Count of (son of the preceding), at the meeting of Edward's allies at Halle, i. 137. Joins Edward against Cambria, 150. But refuses to invade France, 151, 152. His towns pillaged by the French, 173. The Duke of Normandy sent by France to punish Hainault, 174. His death, 236
Hainault, Sir John of, at the meeting of Edward's allies at Halle, i. 137. Joins Edward III. with his Flemings at York, 12. Sum ordered to be paid to him for his services, 176. Joins the French, 249, 257. At Crécy, 257. Advises Philip to retreat, 259
Halidon Hill, battle of, i. 63.
Halle, meeting of Edward's allies at, i. 136
Hannekin, his intrepidity, i. 325
Hanseatic League, the, i. 16. Lend money to Edward III., 16.
Harbours, choked with sand, remedies of the Commons for, ii. 262.
Harcourt, Count of, resists the payment of the salt tax, i. 371, 372. Put to death by the King of France, 372
Harcourt, Geoffrey of, persuades Edward III. to invade Normandy, i. 244. Advises Edward to be merciful to the people of Caen, 246. Defeats the citizens of Amiens, 250. At the battle of Crécy, 255
Harcourt, Godfrey of, refuses to go to Rouen, i. 372. The King's treachery to his brother, who is murdered, 372. Sends his defiance to the King, 373. Goes to England, and enters into an alliance with Edward III., 373. Makes homage to Edward for the fiefs he held in Cotentin, 374. Joins the expedition of the Duke of Lancaster, 374. Escapes from before the French. 375, His death, ii. 22

HER

Haspre, pillaged by the French, i. 173
Hatfield, in Yorkshire, residence of King Edward Balliol at, i. 407
Hawking, fondness of Edward III. for, i. 293. Export of hawks forbidden, ii. 76
Hennebon, surrender of the castle of, to John of Montfort, i. 196. Put into a state of defence by the Countess of Montfort, 199. Her gallant defence of it, 210. The siege abandoned, 211. The siege resumed, but again abandoned, 212. Taken by Du Guesclin, ii. 223
Henry of Trastamare, with John II. of France at the siege of Breteuil, i. 377. Supported by Charles V. as a rival to Pedro the Cruel, ii. 108. Encouraged also by the Pope, 108. March of the French army to Spain, 111. Henry meets them at Barcelona, 112. Proclaimed King and crowned, 113. Sends a letter to the Black Prince, 125. Surprises the English, 126. Whom he defeats in small bodies, 127. Advised to reduce the English by famine, 127. But he determines to fight, 127. Marches to Najera, 129. Defeated at the battle of Navarrete, 129–132. His bravery, 132. Flees into France, 132. Goes to Toulouse, 136. And invades Aquitaine, but returns when the Prince of Wales comes back, 137. Received well in Castile, and marches on Toledo, 137. Defeats Pedro at Montiel, 138. Death of Pedro, 139. Confirms his alliance with France, 194, 197
Henry II., King of England, his invasion of Ireland, ii. 3, 4. Pretext for his invasion, 3. Goes with Earl Strongbow and a large army, 4. Grants the land to his barons, 5. Fears lest the Norman lords of Ireland should become independent of him, 6
Henry III., King of England, his oppression of the Irish, ii. 8
Hereford, Humphry Bohun, Earl of, at the battle of Crécy, i. 255. At the battle of " L'Espagnols-sur-Mer," 325. Appointed the King's lieutenant at Calais, ii. 151. His death, 195
Herring fishery, remedies of the Commons for abuses in the, ii. 262
Herring trade, interference of Parliament in the, i. 338
Herz, visit of Edward III. to, i. 142

INDEX.   331

HIG

Higden, Ralph, his English, ii. 71, *note*
Holland, Robert Lord, murdered, i. 25
Homage, oath of, made by Edward III. to the King of France, i. 28
Horses, export of, forbidden, ii. 77
Huntingdon, William de Clynton created Earl of, i. 111
Hurdles, or fascines, used in war, i. 364

INGHAM, Sir Oliver de, sent to the Tower, i. 36, 37. Edward's seneschal in Gascony, 72
Innocent VI., Pope, his negotiations for peace between England and France, i. 352, 354. Preparations of the " Great Company " to attack him at Avignon, ii. 66. He buys them off, 66
International law, beginning of, i. 60, 61
Ireland, relations between England and, i. 5. Disturbances in, 50. Explanation of the enmity between English and Irish, 342 Marriages between English and Irish forbidden, 343. Mischievous character of the English rule in, ii. 1. Sketch of the history of the conquest of, 1. Rule of the Normans in England, and of the English in Scotland, compared with that of the English in Ireland, 2. Political divisions of Ireland at the time of the invasion of Henry II., 3. Pretext for the invasion, 3. Offers of the King of Leinster to the King of England, 3, 4. Henry II.'s invasion, 4. Henry grants lands to his barons, who seize it by force of arms, 5. The first Viceroy, 5. Henry's son, John, invested with the dominion over Ireland, 5. Encouragement of the enmity between the English and Irish, 6. Murder of the Viceroy, 6. Castles built for the protection of the settlers, 6. The Irish forbidden to bear arms, 6. Endeavours of the English settlers to become independent, 7. The Viceroys suspected by their English masters, 7. King John goes to Ireland to make war on his own Viceroy, 7. And makes rules for the defence of the country against the Irish, 7. Appointments of native Irish to cathedral preferments forbidden, 8. Resistance of the Irish septs to the English rule, 8. Division of the country into liberties and

JEA

counties, 8, 9. Evils of absenteeism, 9. Adoption of Irish habits by the settlers, who are forbidden to do so, 9, 10. Encouragement of the native Irish to resistance, 10. Edward Bruce crowned King of Ireland, 10. His death, 11. Ordinances of Edward III. for the reformation of the country, 11. Laws against absenteeism, 11. The King set at defiance by the De Burghs, 11. Successes of the Irish, 11. Policy of Edward III., 12. His division of the settlers into " English by birth " and " English by blood," 12–15. The settler Lords refuse to attend a Parliament in Dublin, 13. And induce the King to revoke his resumption of lands, 13. Edward's strong measures against the Irish, 14. The settlers forbidden to leave the country, 14. The election of " mere Irish " to any post in the dominions forbidden, 15. The Duke of Clarence sent to Ireland, 15. The Statute of Kilkenny, 15, 16. General results of the policy of England to Ireland, 16.
Iron, export of, forbidden, i. 342
Isabella of France, Queen of Edward II., her dowry after the deposition of her husband, i. 6, 7. Causes of her unpopularity, 19. Joins Mortimer at Nottingham, 35. Where he is made prisoner, 36. Her subsequent imprisonment at Castle Rising, 40. Her death, ii. 42
Isabella, daughter of Edward III., offer to marry her to the Count of Flanders, i. 277. Married to Ingelram de Coucy, ii. 92
Isabella of Castile, her marriage with Edmund, Duke of York, ii. 114, 193. Hostage in the hands of the Black Prince, 119. Returns to Spain, 193.
Issoudun, unsuccessfully attacked by the Prince of Wales, i. 379
Italy, effects of the Black Death in, i. 307

JACQUERIE, origin of the term, ii. 24, 31. Its progress, 31. Marcel sends the Jacques assistance, 32. Their attack on, and massacre at, Meaux, 32, 33.
Jean d'Angely, St., captured by the Earl of Lancaster, i. 273
Jeanne of Penthièvre, her marriage with Charles of Blois, i. 195. Carries on

332 INDEX.

JER

the war with the English during her husband's imprisonment, 276

Jersey taken by the French, i. 163

Jewel, John, at the battle of Cocherel, ii. 102

Jews, massacre of the, i. 308

Joan, daughter of Edward II., betrothed to David, afterwards King of Scotland, i. 19. Her negotiations for the release of her husband, 403

Joan, daughter of Edward III., accompanies her parents on a journey in Germany, i. 141. Her death from the Black Plague at Bordeaux, 306

Joan, daughter of John II. of France, affianced to Charles the Bad of Navarre, i. 355. Married to Charles, 356

Joan, Fair Maid of Kent, her husbands, ii. 68. Her marriage with the Black Prince, 68

John, afterwards King of England, invested by his father with the dominion over Ireland, ii. 5. Returns to England, 6. Goes to Ireland, and makes war on his own viceroy, 7. And makes rules for the defence of Ireland against the Irish, 7

John II., King of France (see also John, Duke of Normandy), entertained by the Lord Mayor of London, i. 4. Ascends the throne, 321. Incites Spain to attack England by sea, 324. Total defeat of the Spaniards, 325–327. Puts the Count of Eu to death, 328. Mutual recriminations of the Kings of France and England, 328. Preparations for renewing the war, 329. John begins the war, 329. Takes St. Jean d'Angely, 332. Renewal of the truce with England, 333. His troops defeated in Brittany, 334. Gives his consent to the marriage of the Count of Flanders, 335. Renewal of the war with England, 352. Offers Charles the Bad, of Navarre, his daughter Joan in marriage, 355. His treachery to Charles after the marriage, and consequent quarrel between the two sovereigns, 356. Murder of the Constable Charles of Spain by Charles the Bad, 357. Makes war against Navarre, 358. Arrangements of England and Navarre as to an invasion of France, 359. Makes a hollow treaty with the King of Navarre, 361. Invasion of France in the north by Edward III., 362. And by the Black Prince

JOH

at Bordeaux, 362–365. Opening of the campaign by the English and Gascons in the South, 365. Reasons of King John's inability to send an army to resist the Prince of Wales in the South, 369. His bloody revenge on the King of Navarre, and other Norman nobles, 372. Pursues the English and their allies to l'Aigle, 375. But finds they have escaped, 375. Besieges and takes Evreux and Breteuil, 377. Hastens to Paris and Chartres to defend his kingdom against the Prince of Wales, 378. Orders his army to follow the English in their retreat to the South, 382. Crosses the Vienne, 383. Immense numbers of his army, 383. Finds himself in advance of the English, near Poitiers, 384. His preparations for battle, 384, 385. Ranges his men in order of battle, 386. Attempt of the Cardinal De Perigord to make peace, 387. But the French refuse the terms offered by the Prince, 388. Defeat of his army and flight of the Princes, 391. Taken prisoner, 392. Brought to the Prince of Wales, 395. The Prince's courtesy to the King, 395. Taken to Bordeaux, 397. His residence there, 397. Taken to England, 398. His reception in London, and residence at the Savoy Palace, 399, 400. His life and death there, 400. His treaty with Edward III. rejected by his subjects, ii. 39. His treatment in England, 41. Amount of his ransom, 56. Returns to France, 57. Released by Galeazzo Visconti, 57. Ceremonies of his release, 58, 59. His career of expenditure, 90. His son, the Duke of Anjou, breaks his parole, 90. King John returns to England in consequence, 91. His hospitable reception, 91, 92. His death in London, 92.

John, King of Bohemia, i. 148. Persuades the Emperor to break with the King of England, 148. Joins Philip VI. against Edward III., 249, 257. Slain at Crécy, 260, 261.

John, son of John II. of France, at the battle of Poitiers, i. 385. His flight from the field, 391.

John III., Duke of Brittany, his death, i. 195

John, Duke of Normandy (afterwards John II. of France), sent to punish Hainault and Flanders, i. 174. Com-

INDEX. 333

JOH

mands an expedition into Brittany, 198. Collects an army at Angers, 215. And marches to Nantes to assist Charles of Blois, 215. Commands in Touraine, Vienne, Haut Vienne, and Angoumois, 240. His visits to various towns, 241. Affects to despise the English, 242. An immense army placed under his command, 243. Besieges Angoulême, 243. And also Aiguillon, 244, 271. Raises the siege, 272. Gives Sir W. Maunay a safe conduct to Paris, 273. Insists upon Sir W. Maunay being set free, 274. Attacks the Flemings at Cassel, but defeated by them, 282. Becomes King of France, 321. *See* John II.

John of Norwich, besieged by the Duke of Normandy in Angoulême, i. 243. Withdraws his troops to Aiguillon, 243, 244.

John de Vienne, Governor of Calais, refuses to surrender the town to Edward III., i. 265. His preparations for defence, 267. His expulsion of all persons unable to assist in defence of the town, 267. His letter to his master describing the misery of the garrison, 281. Surrenders the town to the English, 285.

John XXII., Pope, his endeavours to prevent war between England and France, i. 66. His belief in sorcery and magic, 103.

Jousts forbidden, i. 51

Jubilee on the King attaining the fiftieth year of his reign, ii. 86

Judges, endeavours of armed men to overawe the, i. 51. Seized on the highway, 51

Jugon, opens its gates to Du Guesclin. ii. 222

Julien, St. Louis de, takes St. Savin, ii. 165

Juliers, Margrave of, at the meeting of Edward's allies at Halle, i. 137. Sent by Edward on a mission to the Emperor, 140, 141. Joins Edward with his forces, 150. Advises Edward III. not to accept the offered Imperial Crown, 293. His friendship with Edward, ii. 155

Jurors, Grand, punishment provided for, i. 300

Justice, provision of Parliament against delay in, i. 167

Justices of the Peace, appointed, i. 302

L'AI

KEITH, SIR WILLIAM, forces his way into Berwick, i. 62

Kenilworth Castle, imprisonment of Edward II. at, i. 7

Kent, Earl of, uncle of Edward III., one of the guardians of the King, i. 10. His unsuccessful attempt to make peace between England and Scotland, 10. Falls a victim to the ambition of Mortimer, 24, 26. Mode in which it was accomplished, 31–33. Punishment of his murderers, 38, 39. Besieged by Charles of Valois, in the castle of La Réole, 42

Kerauloet "the Breton" helps to take St. Savin, ii. 165

Kilkenny, Statute of, passed, ii. 15. Provisions of the, 15

King, power of Parliament to depose a, i. 7, *note*

Kinghorn, landing of Edward Balliol at, i. 55

Knights, men having forty pounds a year ordered to take up the military order of, i. 68

Knolles, Sir Robert, joins the Duke of Lancaster at Cherbourg, i. 374. His ravages in Normandy, ii. 24. Aids John of Montfort in Brittany, 104. Invades Picardy, 172. His operations, 174, 175. Unwilling obedience of his leaders, 175. Retires to Derval, 176. Fortifies Derval, and retires to Brest, 222. Returns to Derval, 223. The Duke of Anjou's treatment of Knolles' hostages, and Knolles' retaliation, 224

Knyvet, Sir John, his misstatements to Parliament, ii. 230. States to Parliament the purposes for which it is summoned, 247

LABOUR, struggle between capital and, i. 5

Labourers, Statute of, petition of the Commons as to the, ii. 231. Struggle between labourers and employers, 264

Lacy, Hugh de, first viceroy of Ireland, ii. 5. Dismissed from office, but reinstated, 6. Murdered, 6

Lacy, Hugh de (son of the preceding), his oppression of the English colonists in Ireland, ii. 7. Whom he encounters in battle at Thurles, 7. Driven by King John before him, 7

L'Aigle, murder of Charles of Spain at, i. 357. Retreat of the Duke of Lan-

INDEX.

334

LAN

caster and his allies to, and their escape from, 375

Lancaster, John of Gaunt, Duke of. *See* Gaunt, John of

Lancaster, Thomas, Earl of, reversal of the proceedings against, i. 8

Lancaster, Henry, Earl of, knights his cousin, Edward III., i. 6. Has custody of Edward II. at Kenilworth, 7. Obtains a reversal of the proceedings against his brother Thomas, 8. Appointed guardian of Edward III., 9. Joins the barons against Mortimer, 25. His protection of a murderer, 25. Joins the King in seizing Mortimer at Nottingham, 35

Lancaster, Henry, Earl (afterwards Duke of), appointed to the command of the army during the absence of the King in Scotland, i. 72. Created Earl of Derby, 111. Advances to the relief of Aiguillon, 272. Refuses a truce to the Duke of Normandy, 272. Takes several French towns, and returns to England, 273. Joins the King with a force at Calais, 280. Defends the approaches to Calais against the King of France, 283. Sent to France to make peace, but fails, 353, 355. Negotiates for an alliance with Navarre, 358. His expedition to Brittany to support the Countess of Montfort, 359. Goes with the King to invade France, 361. Marches through Normandy into Brittany, 374. Joins Philip of Navarre, and marches as far as Verneuil, 374, 375. Retreats from before the French, 375. Goes into Cherbourg, 375. Resumes the campaign in Brittany, 376. His war with Charles of Blois, in Brittany, ii. 17. Lays siege to Rennes, 17. Ordered to raise the siege, 18, 19. His vow, 18. Marriage of his daughter Blanche to John of Gaunt, 42. Keeps the foreign adventurers at Calais in order, 46. His raid in Artois and Picardy, 46. Joins the King, 48. Conducts King John back to France, 57. His death from the plague, 67

Lands in mortmain, in what they consisted, ii. 185, *note*

Languedoc, defended by the Duke of Bourbon, i. 240

Langue d'oc and Langue d'oil, the two divisions of France, difference in the governments of the, i. 370

LON

Latimer, Lord, surrenders Becherel to the French, ii. 236, 237. Charges against him, 237. Charges of the Commons against him, 252. His condemnation, 252. Restored by the Duke of Lancaster, 266. Pardoned, 276

Law, courts of, the English language first used in, i. 3

Laws, mode of making, in the time of Edward III., i. 350

Lawyers, certain, excluded from Parliament by implication, i. 346, 347

Lecoq, Robert, Bishop of Laon, in the States General, ii. 20, 25. Notice of him, 20. His speech setting forth the grievances of the people, 25

Leopards in gold, coined, i. 82, 83

Lewis of Bavaria. *See* Louis.

Libourne taken by the Earl of Derby, i. 240. Treaty of, ii. 119, 120

Liddesdale, Knight of, bring the Scots help from France, i. 191. Advises the Scots not to invade England, 268. Set at liberty by Edward III., 403. *See also* Douglas

Lille, taken by the Earl of Derby, i. 240

Lille Jourdain, Count of, his defence of Perigord, the Limousin, and Saintonge, i. 239. Loses Bergerac, 239. Retreats to La Reole, 239. His campaign against the English, 241. Besieges them in Auberoche, but fails, 241, 242

Limoges, the nobility of, roused by the Duke of Normandy, i. 241. Taken by the Duke of Berri, ii. 173. The Prince of Wales retakes it, 176. His brutal massacre of the inhabitants, 177. Courage of the three knights, 177, 178

Limousin, the, defended by the Count of Lille Jourdain, i. 239. Plundered by the Prince of Wales, 378. Sir John Devereux's operations in the, ii. 189

Lincoln, colloquy summoned by Edward III. at, i. 17

Linde, La, saved by the Captal de Buch and Sir Thomas Felton, ii. 173

Lô, St., Edward III. at, i 245

Lombards, or Longobardi. *See* Bardi

London, tournaments in, i. 44. Persons forbidden to enter the city or suburbs armed, 51, 52. The city put into a state of defence; a threatened invasion of the French, 71. The Lord Mayor thrown into prison, 179. Establishment of the Court of Chan-

INDEX. 335

cery in London, 233. Burialplace of the victims of the Black Death in, 305. Entrance of the Prince of Wales and his royal prisoners into, 399, 400. State of the city in 1357, ii. 42. Reception of the French prisoners, 60. Regulations of Parliament as to the trade of, in fish, 82. Petition of the Commons against foreign usurers in, 262. Entertainment given to Richard, Prince of Wales, 273. Riot respecting Wyclif, 287–289

Longland, his ' Piers Ploughman,' ii. 73

Lorraine, Duke of, joins Philip VI. against Edward III., i. 249.

Louis of Bavaria, Emperor of Germany, his quarrel with Clement V., i. 137. Makes ineffectual advances to Benedict XII., 138. Throws himself into the arms of England, 138. His alliance with Edward III., 119. His proposal of an alliance with France, 139. Meets Edward III. at Coblentz, 141. Makes him his Vicar-General of the Empire, 142. Evil deeds charged against him by the Pope, 145. Persuaded by Philip VI. to break with England, 147, 148. His quarrel with the Pope, 248. Cursed by the Pope, and another Emperor nominated, 248, 249. His death, 294.

Louis of Spain, i. 209. Appointed marshal of France and to the command of the army in Brittany, 209. Besieges Hennebon, 210. Gives up the siege, 211. Ravages the country, but defeated by Sir Walter de Maunay, 212. His ravages in Lower Brittany, 212. Defeated and pursued by De Maunay and De Clisson, 212.

Louis, son of John. II. of France, at the battle of Poitiers, i. 385. His flight from the field, 391.

Louis of Navarre, his defeat by the Duke of Burgundy, ii. 103

Louis I., Count of Flanders, his treatment of the Flemings, i. 26. Driven by them to Ghent, 26. His part taken by Philip VI. of France, 26, 27. Who defeats the Flemings at Cassel, 27. Marriage of his daughter with Edmund, son of Edward III., prevented by the Pope, ii. 99. Bound to France, 154

Louis, Count of Flanders. *See* Flanders.

Louis, Count of Flanders, seizes English merchants and their property, i. 74.

Notice of him and of his tyranny, 106, 407. Sides with France against England, 123. Puts Van Artevelde's grandfather to death, 124, 125. Compels Van Artevelde to fly from Bruges, 125. Driven out of Flanders by the people, 134. Negotiations of Edward III. with him, 143. Ambassadors sent from Edward III. to him, 156. Endeavours of the Pope to induce the Flemings to submit to Louis, 204. State of his dominions in 1345, 234. Joins Philip III. against Edward III., 249. At the battle of Crécy, 259. Slain, 260

Louis le Mâle, Count of Flanders, succeeds his father, i. 277. Offers of the King of England and Duke of Brabant to form an alliance with him, 277. Refuses to marry the daughter of Edward III., 278. Kept under guard, but escapes to France, 278, 279. Reconciled to his subjects by Edward III., 316. His subsequent perfidy to the weavers, whom he massacres, 317. Allows a Spanish fleet, for the invasion of England, to assemble at Sluys, 324. His increasing hostility to England, 335. His marriage with a daughter of the Duke of Brabant, 335

Louviers taken by Edward III., i. 247

Louvre, the Duke of Normandy shuts himself up in the, 29. Murder of the King's officers in the, 29. Escape of the Duke, 29. Seized and fortified by ·Marcel, 30, 31. The Captal de Buch imprisoned in the, ii. 210

Lussac, seized by the Duke of Berri, ii. 203

Lyons, Richard, charges of the Commons against, ii. 251. Condemned, 251. Pardoned, 277

Lyons, the Papal court at, i. 137

MACMURRAGH, Dermod, King of Leinster, calls in the English into Ireland, ii. 3. Gives his daughter in marriage to Earl Strongbow, 4. His death, 4

Malestroit, truce of, i. 216

Maillart, Jean, his quarrel with Marcel, ii. 37. Whom he kills, 38

Maintenance in law, meaning of, i. 347, *note*

Majorca, King of, makes an alliance with Edward III., i. 187. Enters Spain with the Black Prince, ii.

336 INDEX.

MAL

Malo, St., taken by the Earl of Salisbury, ii. 221. And by the Constable Du Guesclin, 222

Man, Isle of, given by Edward III. to Lord Montacute, i. 35

Mansel, Philip, governor of Rochelle, cheated into giving up the castle to the French, ii. 208

Mar, Donald Earl of, appointed regent of Scotland, i. 56. Defeated by Edward Balliol at Dupplin Moor, 56

Marcel, Etienne, his character, ii. 20. In the States General, 20, 25. Delivers the King of Navarre from prison, 27. And demands the return of the King's possessions from France, 27, 28. His exertions to fortify Paris, 28. Refutes the charges of the Duke of Normandy, 29. Obtains the assistance of the King of Navarre, 30. His mistakes, 30. Seizes and fortifies the Louvre, 30, 31. Sends assistance to the Jacques, 32. Who are defeated at Meaux, 33. Breaks with the Duke of Normandy and the nobles, and obtains the appointment of Captain-General of Paris for the King of Navarre, 34. Calls in the help of the "Companies," and loses the confidence of the people, 34. Siege of Paris by the Duke of Normandy, 34. Entreats the Duke to return to the city, 36. His final scheme, 36, 37. And death, 38

March, Mortimer, Earl of, got rid of by the Duke of Lancaster, ii. 266

March, Patrick, Earl of, conducts an army against Edward Balliol, i. 56. His army melts away, 57. Submits to Edward III., 64

Marche, John of Bourbon, Count de la, placed in nominal command of the army for the invasion of Castile, ii. 109

Mare, Peter de la, chosen speaker of the Commons, ii. 248. Imprisoned by the Duke of Lancaster, 266

Marriages, causes of, in the middle ages, i. 22. Between English and Irish forbidden, i. 343

Maunay, Sir Walter de, his arrival in England, i. 22. Defeats De Rickenburg's soldiers at Cadsand, 125. Ordered to watch the French ships in the Channel, 126. His feats of valour, 151. Sent with an army to Brittany, to support Montfort, 201, *note.* His relief of the castle of Hennebon, 211. His bold advice to the

MON

Earl of Derby, 239, 242. Obtains a safe conduct to Calais, 273. Taken prisoner at Orleans, 274. Threat of King Philip to put him to death, 274. Released, and receives presents from Philip, 274. Joins Edward III. at Calais, 274. Sent to treat with the garrison of Calais, 285. Brings the six burgesses to King Edward, 286. Counsels mercy to them, 286, 287. Commands the attack on the French who attempt to take Calais, 319, 320. Appointed to lay the King's wishes before Parliament, 405. Sent to negotiate a truce with France, ii. 42. Has custody of the King of France at Calais, 57. His advice to Lancaster, 164. His death, 195

Maunay, Olivier de, anecdote of, at Rennes, ii. 17, 18

Mautravers, John, his trial and execution, i. 39

Meaux, seized by the Duke of Normandy, ii. 31. Attacked by the Jacques, 32. But defended by Gaston de Foix, 33. Who, with the Captal de Buch, massacres the Jacques at Meaux, 33

Mechlin, visit of Edward III. to, i. 142

Meissen, or Misnia, Margrave of, joins Edward III. against France, i. 150

Melun, siege of, by the Duke of Normandy, ii. 40

Menteith, John Graham, Earl of, his trial and execution, i. 402

Meulan, taken by Du Guesclin, ii. 102

Money. *See* Currency

Montacute, Lord, his plan for the seizure of Mortimer, i. 35. The King's requitement of his services, 35. Helps to seize Mortimer, 36. Accompanies the King on his secret visit to the King of France, 47. Created earl of Salisbury, 111. *See* Salisbury

Montauban, ravaged by Henry of Trastamare, ii. 136

Montcontour, taken by Sir Thomas Percy, ii. 189. Surrenders to the Duke of Berri and Du Guesclin, ii. 203

Montebourg, Edward III. at, i. 245

Montfort, John of, measures of John III. of Brittany to exclude him from the succession to the duchy, i. 195. His plans for taking possession of the duchy, 195. Takes Brest, 195. Summoned to Paris, by King Philip, 196. Who decides against his claims, 196. Escapes to Nantes, 196. And goes to England, and secures help from

INDEX.

337

MON

Edward, 197. Created earl of Richmond, 198. Active measures of the King of France and Charles of Blois to take possession of his duchy, 198. Returns and is taken prisoner at Nantes, 199. In which they succeed, and make Montfort prisoner, 199. Heroic efforts of his Countess, 199. Escapes from prison, and does homage to Edward III. for Brittany, 231. His death, 242

Montfort, John of (son of the preceding), joins the expedition of the Duke of Lancaster, i. 374. Who is appointed to the command in Brittany, 375. War between him and Charles of Blois, ii. 104. Defeats Charles at Auray, 104, 105. Settles the affairs of his duchy, 105. Marries the step-daughter of the Black Prince, 105

Montfort, John, Duke of Brittany, shuts himself up in Vannes, ii. 222

Montfort, John de, invades France in the North, ii. 224. Failure of the expedition, 225

Montfort, John of, relieves Becherel, ii. 235. Goes to Calais, and returns to England, 236. Embarks for France, 236. In Brittany, 237. Besieges St. Brieuc, 238. Attacks the besiegers of Quimperlé, and relieves the garrison, 239. Conclusion of a truce, 239. Goes to Auray, 240.

Montfort, Countess of, her loss of her husband, i. 199. Her heroism, 199. Puts the castle of Rennes in a state of defence, 199. And retires to the castle of Hennebon, 199. Sends Amaury de Clisson to England for Edward's promised help, 200. Her promises to Edward, 200, 201. Success of De Clisson, 202. Her gallant defence of Hennebon, 210, 211. Help arrives from England, 211. Takes part in the siege of Vannes, 213. Expedition of the Duke of Lancaster to Brittany, to support her claims, 359

Montiel, battle of, ii. 138

Montjoie, burnt by Edward III., i. 248

Montmorillon, castle of, taken by the Duke of Berri and Du Guesclin, and the garrison put to death, ii. 203

Montpaon, castle of, retaken by the Duke of Lancaster, ii. 187

Montpaon, William de, his treachery, ii. 187

Montpezat, Lord, loses but recovers his castle of Agenois, i. 42

NAN

Montsegur, taken by the Earl of Derby, i. 242

Moray, Thomas Randolph, Earl of, leads a Scottish army into the North of England, i. 13. Refuses to fight the English, and finally escapes, 14–16

Moray, Randolph, Earl of (second son of the last), attacks Edward Balliol at Annan, i. 58. Appointed one of the regents of the kingdom, 67. Taken prisoner by the English, 70. Commands the right wing at Nevill's Cross, 270

Moray, Sir Andrew, of Bothwell, his career, i. 66. Slays the Earl of Athole, 70. His death, 191

Morbecque, Denis de, takes John II. prisoner at Poitiers, i. 392. His reward, 397

Mortain, rent charge on, given to Charles the Bad, i. 356

Mortemer taken by the French, ii. 220

Mortimer, Roger, Earl of March, indemnified from the consequences of his treason, i. 8. Not named one of the guardians of Edward III., 9. His adulterous life with Queen Isabella, 9, 19. His arrogance and usurpation of power, 9. The treaty of peace with Scotland supposed to be his work, 19. His insolence at the Parliament of Salisbury, 24. Beginning of the struggle between him and the Barons, 24. Made earl of the Marches of Wales, 24. The Barons banded against him, 25. Their charges, 25, Mortimer baffles their designs, 26. Mode in which he accomplishes the ruin of the Earl of Kent, 31–33. His boundless arrogance, 33. Called by his son the "Knight of Folly," 33. Resolution of the King to free himself from Mortimer, 35. Who is made prisoner, and sent to the Tower, 35, 36. Charges brought against him at his trial, 37, 38. Condemned to death, 38. And executed, 39

Murage, foreign merchants exempted from, i. 79

NAMUR, Count of, defeated by the Scots, i. 69. But generously sent over the Border, 69. Joins Edward III. at the siege of Cambrai, 150. But refuses to invade France, 151, 152

Nantes, surrendered to Charles of Blois,

VOL. II.

Z

338 INDEX.

NAR

199. Besieged by Edward III., 215. Taken by Du Guesclin, ii. 102. Besieged by Du Guesclin, 223. Surrenders, 223

Narbonne, plundered and burnt by the Prince of Wales, i. 368

Nasco, Count of, taken prisoner at Poitiers, i. 391

Navarre, kingdom of, after the defeat of the Moors, i. 323. Connection between it and France, 323. History of the quarrel between France and, 355, 356. Jealousy between Spain and, 386. Charles of Spain murdered by Charles of Navarre, 357. Quarrel between France and Navarre brought to a conclusion, 105

Navarrete, battle of, ii. 135

Navy: the navy put into order by the King, i. 227. Petition to Parliament as to the decline of the navy, ii. 215. Petition to Parliament as to the state of the navy, 184. Preparations for forming an effective one, 232

Neuf Châtel d'Aury, sacked and burnt by the English and Gascons, i. 367

Nevill, Sir John, his trial and condemnation, ii. 253. Sent to relieve Thouars, 211. Sent to Brittany, but does nothing, 214

Neville, Ralph de, sent by Edward III. to Scotland by Balliol, i. 402

Neville, Sir Robert, his mission to Brittany, ii. 191

Neville, Sir William, joins an expedition to Brittany, ii. 221

Nevill's Cross, battle of, i. 269–271

Newtown the Bold, Edward III.'s town of, i. 265.

Nido, Count of, taken prisoner at Poitiers, i. 391.

Niort, shuts its gates against the English, ii. 206. Taken by the French, 220

Nobility, short duration of life of the, in the middle ages, i. 22; ii. 244, note

Nobles in gold, coined, i. 82, 83

Norfolk, Thomas Plantagenet, Earl of, ordered to lead an army against the Scots, i. 11

Normandy, proposed invasion of England by the Normans, i. 142, 246. Edward III.'s punishment of the Normans in consequence, 246. Resistance to the salt-tax in, 371, 372. The King's bloody revenge on the Norman nobles, 372. March of the

OYE

Duke of Lancaster through Normandy to Brittany, 374. Ravaged by Godfrey of Harcourt and Philip of Navarre, ii. 22. Ravaged by the "Companies," 24. Affairs of Normandy from 1361 to 1364, 101. Successes of Du Guesclin, 102, 103

Normans, their anxiety to invade England, i. 144. Their rule in England contrasted with that of the English in Ireland, ii 2

Northampton, William de Bohun, created Earl of, i. 111. Commands an expedition to Brittany, 206. Appointed King's lieutenant in Brittany, 207. Ordered to defy the King of France, 231. Embarks for Brittany, 232. Commands in Brittany for the young Montfort, 242. Returns to England, and joins the King on his expedition to Normandy, 243. His division at the battle of Crécy, 255, 260. Sent on an embassy into Flanders, 277. Defeats the French fleet at Crotoye, 280. At the battle of L'Espagnols-sur-Mer, 325. Left as King Edward's lieutenant in Scotland, 409. Makes a truce with Earl Douglas, 409

Norwich, Sir John, appointed admiral, i. 74

Norwich, Norman woollen manufactures of, i. 86

Nottingham, meeting of Parliament at, i. 73

OMER, ST., defeat of Robert of Artois at, i. 177

O'Neills, the, their successes in East Ulster, ii. 11

Oriflamme, the, displayed at Poitiers, i. 385

Orleans, a large French army assembled at, i. 243

Orleans, Duke of, his command at Poitiers, i. 385. Disgraced for his flight at Poitiers, ii. 20. One of King John's hostages, 58

Owen of Wales, his adventures, ii, 201. Blockades Rochelle with a Spanish fleet, 207. Joins the French in their attack on Soubise, and takes the Captal de Buch and Sir Thomas Percy prisoners, 207. Returns to Rochelle, 208

Oxford, foreign spies at, as students, prohibited, ii. 282

Oyer and Terminer, commission of, instituted, i. 301

INDEX.

339

PAD

PADILLA, MARIA DE, becomes the mistress of Pedro the Cruel, ii. 107
Paris, Edward III.'s ravages of the country near, i. 248. Alarm of the people of, 248. Measures of the States General for protecting the city, ii. 20. The citizens compel the Duke of Normandy to yield to their demands, 23. Marcel's measures for the defence of the capital, 28. Crowding of the peasants into the city, 23. The revolution under Marcel, 29. Who causes the execution of royal officers, 29. Marcel seizes the Louvre, 30. The Duke of Normandy's preparations for besieging the city, 31. The King of Navarre appointed captain-general of the city, 34. The "Companies" called in by Marcel, 34. The city besieged by the Duke of Normandy, 34. Treachery of the King of Navarre, 35. Encounter between the citizens and the "Companies," 36. Marcel's plot for delivering up the city to the King of Navarre, 37. Death of Marcel, and return of the Duke of Normandy, 38. Conspiracy to give up the city to the King of Navarre, 50. Ravages of Sir Robert Knolles up to the gates of the city, 175.
Parliament, influence of, in government, in the reign of Edward III., i. 3. The first parliamentary struggle recorded, 3. Special business of Parliament, 5. A commercial parliament summoned, 4. A parliament of men from seaport towns summoned, 4. Power of Parliament to depose a sovereign, 7, note. Its reversal of the proceedings against Thomas, Earl of Lancaster, 8. Its indemnification of the supporters of Queen Isabella and the Mortimers, 8. Colloquy at Lincoln in 1328, 17. Meeting at York, 18. At New Sarum, 24. At Westminster, 28. Meeting of a packed Parliament at Winchester, 32. At Westminster, 37. Its condemnation of Mortimer to death, 38. Matters of importance settled by this Parliament, 40. Meeting of Parliament at Eltham, 45. Members of Parliament forbidden to enter London armed, 51, 52. Regulation for the prevention of any disturbance of Parliament, 52. Constitution of the Parliaments of this period, 53. Meeting of Parliament at York, 58, 59.

PAR

At Nottingham, 73. Mode of promulgating the Statutes of the Realm, or Acts of Parliament, 77, 78. Proceedings of Parliament during the King's absence in France, 160. Growing importance of the Commons, 160. Proposed aid to the King for the war, 161. Reform of abuses demanded by the Commons 161, 162. The aid granted for the war, 163. Proceedings of the Parliament of March 1340, 165. Statute relative to the King's assumption of the title of King of France, 168, 169. Growing power of Parliament at this time, 169. Supplies refused without redress of grievances, 185. The demands granted by the King, but treacherously revoked, 185. Statute as to the privilege of Peers passed, 286. A naval Parliament summoned at Westminster, 203. Meeting to consider the question of peace or war, 219. Constitution of Parliament at this time, 219. Division of the two houses, 219. Meeting with the King in the White Chamber, 220. Its jealousy of the Pope's interference, 220, 221. Its agreement to the renewal of the war with France, 225. Meeting in 1346, 266. Grants the King an aid of two-fifteenths, 266. Legislation for keeping the peace of the nation, and for the administration of justice, 300. Petition to the King against taxation without their consent, 314. Domestic legislation between 1352 and 1355, 336. Certain lawyers excluded from Parliament, 346, 347, 350. Mode of making laws at this time, 350. And of summoning Parliament, 351. Statement of the King's Chamberlain, De Burghersh, of the failure of efforts to make peace with France, 353. War subsidy granted to the King, 353. Statements of the Chief Justice and Sir W. de Maunay to Parliament, 405. Subsidy granted to the King, 406. Important domestic legislation, ii. 70–86. Practice of Parliament at this period, 85, 86. Proceedings in Parliament as to the usurpations of the Pope, 93–96. Measures of Parliament for meeting the war with France, 151, 152. Grants a subsidy to the King, 152. Summoned in 1371, 181. Reasons for requiring a subsidy stated by William of Wykeham, 181. The

z 2

340 INDEX.

·PAU

first Parliamentary struggle, 182, 183. Meeting of Parliament in 1372, 215. Guy Bryan's important announcement, 215, 216. Grants subsidies to the King, 216, 217. Lawyers and sheriffs excluded from Parliament, 216, 217. Complaints of the decline of the navy, 217. Petition as to the immorality of the clergy, 218. Meeting in 1373, 230. Fresh subsidy granted, 230. Business transacted, 230–232. Proceedings of the "Good Parliament," 243, 246. Grants a subsidy to the King, 249. Punishes various guilty persons, 251 *et seq.* Its further proceedings, 257. Proceedings of the Parliament under Richard Prince of Wales, 272. The Prince of Wales attends the meeting of Parliament, 275. Reverses the proceedings of the preceding Parliament, 276. General business of the session, 278 *et seq.* Increase of the power of Parliament during the reign of Edward III., 291

Paul's, St., in London, meeting of the Confederate Barons at, i. 25

Pavage, i. 79. Foreign merchants exempted from, i. 79

Peace, keepers (afterwards justices) of the, appointed, i. 40, 51. Peace, keepers of the, appointed, 301. Origin of the office of, 301, *note.* When called justices of the peace, 302

Peachy, John, his trial and condemnation, ii. 252. Pardoned, 277

Pedro the Cruel, King of Castile, his murders, ii. 107. Marries Blanche of Bourbon, but intrigues with Maria de Padilla, 107. Allies himself with the Mahommedan kings of Granada, 108. Refuses to answer the summons of the Pope, 108. Who supports a rival to his throne, 108. France disposed to attack him as England's ally, 109. His treaty with Edward III., 109. Arrangement of France for war against him, 109. March of Du Guesclin against him, 111, 112. And coronation of Henry of Trastamare, 113. Pedro flees to Seville, 114. Reaches Coruna and Bayonne, 114. Goes to Bordeaux to meet the Prince of Wales, 115. Unwillingness of the Gascons to help him, 115. His promises of payment to them, 116, 118, 119. His promises to the Prince of Wales, 119. His cruelty

PER

after the battle of Navarrete, 132. Neglects to pay his debts, 133. Marches to the relief of Toledo, 138. Defeated at Montiel, 138. Killed by his brother Henry, 139

Peebles, county and town of, given by Edward III. to Lord Montacute, i. 35

Peers, statute as to the privilege of, passed, i. 186

Pembroke, Earl of, takes the command in Bergerac, i. 240. Defeats the French fleet at Crotoye, 280. Goes to meet the French in Brittany, ii. 157. Marches to Angoulême, 158. Refuses to join Chandos, 159. Surprised by the French, and obtains help from Chandos, 160. Appointed to the command of the expedition to France, 198. Totally defeated at sea by the Spaniards, 199. Taken prisoner, 199

Percy, Lord Henry, appointed guardian of the Northern Marches, i. 55. Ordered to prevent the passage of Balliol's troops, 55. Sent by Edward III. to Scotland with Balliol, 402

Percy, Sir Thomas, departs from Chandos, ii. 165. Who is killed, 167. Appointed seneschal of Ponthieu, 170. Takes Montcontour, and the garrison put to death, 189. Aids in relieving the garrison of Poitiers, 203. Prevented from defending the town, 206. Joins the Captal de Buch, and relieves Soubise, 207. But afterwards taken prisoner by Owen of Wales, 207

Perigord, defended by the Count of Lille Jourdain, i. 239. Towns of, taken by the Earl of Derby, 240. Ravaged by the English, ii. 158.

Perigord, Cardinal de, attempts to prevent the battle of Poitiers, i. 387

Perion, Roche, castle of, given up by Olivier de Clisson to John de Montfort, i. 196

Perrers, Alice, her influence over Edward III., ii. 182–202. Ordered by the Commons to absent herself from the King, 234. Charges of the Commons against her, 253. Her condemnation, 253. Returns to the King, 266, 277. Robs him of his finger-rings after his death, 290

Perucchi, the bankers, i. 15. Lend money to Edward III., 15. Forthcoming history of the (now published), 16, *note*

INDEX. 341

Peter, Cardinal, his arrival in England, i. 126–128

Philip VI. (of Valois), King of France, his claim to the throne of France, i. 23. Summons Edward III. to do homage, 26, 27. Meeting of the two kings at Amiens, 29. Homage done by Edward under protest, 29, 30, 44. Proposal of Edward to join the two houses in marriage, 30. Philip sends ambassadors to Edward about his homage, 31, 43. Agrees to suppress letters of marque, 61. His secret support of the Scots against Balliol and Edward III., 65. Increase of his animosity against Edward, 67, 70, 71. Keeps up an interference with Scotland, 72. Causes of his war with England, 94. His encroachments in Aquitaine, 94. Causes of his personal ill-feeling against Edward III., 101. His belief in sorcery, 103, 105. His proclamation as to Robert, Count of Artois, 105. Continues his aggressions in Guienne, 127, 131. Commencement of the war with England, 131. His arrangements to invade England, 132, 133. His efforts to injure England, 143. Ambassadors sent by Edward to him to treat for peace, 145. Persuades the Emperor to break with England, 148. Beginning of the war with England, 150. Edward's invasion of France, 152. Philip declines battle, and ends the campaign, 153. His tactics during Edward's absence from the Continent, 164. Defeat of his fleet by Edward III. off Sluys, 172, 173. Offends the Count of Hainault, 173. Sends his son, John of Normandy, to punish the Hainaulters and Flemings, 174. Tournai besieged by Edward, 176. Philip's answer to Edward's challenge, 177. Desires to bring the war to a conclusion, 177, 178. And concludes a truce, 178. Breaks up the alliance between the Emperor and Edward III., 188. Assists the Scots with five ships, 191. Summons John de Montfort to Paris, 196. And gives judgment against him, 197. Failure of negotiations with England for peace, 223. Philip's execution of Olivier de Clisson, 223. Object of Edward III. in his repeated invasions of France, 223, 224. Breaks the truce, and recommences the war, 225. His pre-

parations for the renewal of war, 243. Landing of Edward III. in Normandy, which he ravages, 244, 245. Philip sends the Counts of Guisnes and Tancarville to Normandy, 245. Progress of Edward III. through Normandy to the gates of Paris, 245–248. Philip's alarm, 248. Collects a large army at St. Denis, 249. And follows the English leisurely, 250, 251. Fails to catch them in a trap, 254. Gives battle to the English at Crécy, 254. His carelessness, 255. His arrangements for the battle, 257. Progress of the fight, 258–261. Utterly defeated by the English, 261. Mounts a horse, and retreats to Amiens, 261. His town of Calais besieged by Edward III., 265. Orders his son, the Duke of Normandy, to join him, 273. Several towns taken by the English in Aquitaine, 273. Threatens to put Sir Walter de Maunay to death, 274. But subsequently sets him free, 274. His conduct after the battle of Crécy, 276. Goes to Paris, 276. His plans for the relief of Calais, 276. Escape of the young Count of Flanders from Flanders to France, 278, 279. Rejection of Philip's offers by the Flemings, 279. His preparations for the relief of Calais, 281. Marches to Arras, 282. His son defeated by the Flemings, 282. His march on Calais, 282. Challenges Edward III. to single combat, 284, 285. And retreats from before Calais, 285. Surrender of the city to the English, 285–287. His preparations for recovering it, 288. Concludes a truce with the English, 289. Attempt to convert the truce into a permanent peace, 315, 316. Endeavour of the French to take Calais by bribery, 317–320. Preparations for war, but renewal of the truce, 321. Philip's death, 321

Philip of Navarre, refuses to accept an invitation to Rouen, i. 372. Where his brother King Charles is treacherously taken prisoner, 372. Sends his defiance to King John, 373. Goes to England, and allies with Edward III., 373. Joins the Duke of Lancaster at Cherbourg, 374. Marches with the Duke, but escapes from before the French, 374, 375. Ravages Normandy, ii. 22. Resumes the offensive and establishes himself at Evreux, 25. Joins his brother, who is re-

342 INDEX.

PHI

leased from prison, and ravages the country nearly up to Paris, 28. Left by his brother in charge of part of Normandy, 101. His death, 101.

Philip, son of John II. of France, at the battle of Poitiers, i. 385. Behind his father in the battle, advising him what to do, 392. Taken prisoner with his father, 395. Conveyed to England, 397. His treatment in England, ii. 41

Philippa of Hainault, her marriage with Edward III., i. 21. Pedigree of her relationship to the King, 21, *note*. Her reception in England, 22. Accompanies her husband to Herenthals, 141. Birth of her son, Lionel, 143. Birth of her son, John of Gaunt, 173. Said to have been present at the battle of Nevill's Cross, 269. Joins the King at Calais, 271. Accompanies the King to meet the young Count of Flanders, 279. Intercedes for the lives of the burgesses of Calais, 287. Returns with the King to England, 298. Her death, ii. 162

Picard, Sir Henry de, Lord Mayor of London, his banquet to the Kings of England, France, and Cyprus, i. 4; ii. 22

Picardy ravaged by Edward III., i. 361. Raid of the Duke of Lancaster in, ii. 46, 48. Ravaged by Sir Robert Knolles, 174

Pierre, Eustache de St., the burgess of Calais, story of, i. 286

Piracy, in the beginning of the fourteenth century, i. 80, 81. The pirates of France and England, 81

Plague, the. *See* Black Death

Plays, popularity of the performance of, 297

Poissy, Edward III. at, i. 247

Poitiers, the nobility of, roused by the Duke of Normandy, i. 241. Taken by the Earl of Lancaster, 273. Position of the French and English near, 384. Commencement of the great battle, 389. Complete defeat of the French, and flight of the Princes, i. 391. The King of France taken prisoner, 392. Losses on either side, 392. Alarm of the city at the approach of Du Guesclin, ii. 203. Relieved by Devereux and Percy, 203. Besieged and taken by Du Guesclin, 203

Poitou, bands of brigands in, i. 292. Invaded by the Duke of Berri and

QUI

Du Guesclin, ii. 203. The conquest of, completed by Du Guesclin, 219, 220

Pontage, i. 79. Foreign merchants exempted from, 79

Pol de Leon, St., surrenders to the English, ii. 237

Poll tax granted, ii. 278

Pons taken by the French, ii. 206

Pons, Reginald, Lord of, sent to attack Soubise, ii. 206. But routed by the Captal de Buch, 207

Pont-Audemer refuses to open its gates to John II. of France, i. 358. Besieged by him, 375. The siege raised, 375. Surrenders, ii. 22

Ponthieu captured by the French, ii. 150, 151

Popes, resistance of Parliament and the clergy to the encroachments of the, i. 5. The mere creatures of France, 137. Their court at Lyons and Avignon, 66, 137. Quarrel with the Emperor and Germany, 137–140. History of resistance to the usurpations of the, in England, ii. 92, *et seq.* Petition of the Commons against the usurpations of the, 260, 277. Enormous sums received by them, 260

Ports, lists of, from which supplies are demanded, i. 205, *note*, 226, *note*

Portsmouth burned and pillaged by the French, ii. 129, 208; ii. 162

Portugal, kingdom of, after the defeat of the Moors, i. 322

Præmunire, statute of, passed, ii. 94

Prices, combinations to raise or abate, forbidden by law, i. 337

Priories, Aliens, restored by Edward III., ii. 67. Revenues of, seized in England by the King, 152. Petitions of the Commons against filling them with foreigners, 261

Provence ravaged by the "Companies," ii. 24

Provisors, Statute of, passed, i. 346. Nature of the usurpation forbidden by the statutes, ii. 92. Proceedings in Parliament, 92, 93

Purveyors, confirmation of the laws against, i. 40, 168, 344. The name changed to buyer, 344

QUESNOY, besieged by the French, i. 174. Cannon first used at this siege, 174.

Quimperlé besieged by the Bretons, but relieved by the Duke of Brittany, ii. 239

INDEX. 343

RAM

RAMSAY, Sir William, killed at a joust, i. 191

Randolph, Earl of Moray, fails to restore certain estates according to treaty, i. 54. His death, 55.

Ravenspur, Edward Balliol's embarkation at, i. 55

Reformation, dawn of the, in England, i. 5

Regrators, laws against, i. 336, 337

Rennes given up to John of Montfort, i. 195. Captured by De Blois, 210. Besieged by the Earl of Salisbury, 214. Besieged by the Duke of Lancaster, ii. 17. Incident during the siege, 17, 18. The siege raised, 18. Opens its gates to Du Guesclin, 222

Rent of houses, regulated by Parliament, i. 341

Renty, Oudard de, taken prisoner in Calais, i. 318, 319

Réole, La, castle of, besieged by Charles of Valois, i. 42. The Count of Lille Jourdain retires to, 240. Besieged and taken by the Earl of Derby, 242.

Revolution in France in 1358, ii. 29

Reynolds, Walter, Archbishop of Canterbury, crowns Edward III., i. 6. His sermon in Westminster Abbey, 7.

Rheims, march of Edward III. to, ii. 50. Abandoned by him, 51

Ribaumont, Eustace de, brings a challenge from Philip VI. to Edward III., i. 284. His fight with Edward III. at Calais, 320. Where he is taken prisoner, 320. The King's treatment of him, 320. Reconnoitres the English position at Poitiers, 385. His report to his King, 385, 386

Richard, Prince (afterwards Richard II.), his descent, ii. 97. His birth, 122. Made guardian of the kingdom, 212. Recognised as heir to the throne, 256. Grand Christmas feast held by the King in Richard's honour, 273. Entertainment given to him by the Londoners, 273. Attends Parliament, 275

Rickenburg, Guy de, placed in command of the garrison of Cadsand, i. 125. His troops defeated by Sir Walter Maunay, 125. Taken prisoner, 125

Robert (Bruce), I., King of Scotland, his formal defiance of Edward III., i. 10. His preparations for invading England, 11. March of Edward against him, 11. Bruce sends his nephew, the Earl of Moray, to ravage the North of England, 13. His ill-

ROO

ness, 13. Concludes a peace with England, 18. His death, 31

Robert II., King of Scotland, makes a treaty with the King of France, ii. 153. Enters an alliance with France, 192, 193.

Robert of Namur, Sir, his ravages round Calais, ii. 162. Drives back the French, 163.

Robert, the Steward of Scotland, appointed one of the regents of Scotland, i. 67. Concludes a treaty with Edward III., 70. Appointed sole governor by the Scots, 191. Defeated at Nevill's Cross, 270. Escapes from the field, 271. Made guardian of Scotland, 401. His supporter, Lord Douglas, 402. Disinherited by David II., but restored subsequently, 410

Roche de Rien, taken by the Earl of Northampton, i. 243.

Roche Derien, the French under Charles of Blois defeated at, i. 275

Rochelle, prays the King of France not to be handed over to England, ii. 64. Refuses to help the English fleet, 199. Return of a Spanish fleet to, 202. And fall of the town, 202. Blockaded by a Spanish fleet, ii. 207. Captured by the French by an ingenious plot, 208. The castle razed, and the town handed over to the French, 209, 210.

Rochellois, the, overrun by the French, ii. 210

Roche-sur-Yon, surrender of, to the English, ii. 158. Yields to the Duke of Anjou, 223.

Roger, Peter (afterwards Pope Clement VI.), his mission from Philip VI. to Edward III., i. 27

Rokeby, Thomas de, knighted by Edward III., i. 14

Romans, their sumptuary laws, i. 83, note. Their introduction of the woollen manufacture into England, 85

Romans, King of the, first adoption of the title of, i. 99

Rome, Church of, opposition to the doctrines of the, i. 5

Romorantin, skirmish of French and English near, i. 380. Siege and capture of, by the Prince of Wales, 380–382

Roncesvalles, pass of, ii. 124

Roos, John de, appointed admiral, i. 112. Captures two Flemish ships with Scots and treasure, 116

344 INDEX.

ROS

Rosas, Admiral Rodrigo de, blockades Rochelle with a Spanish fleet, ii. 207

Rouen, the bridges over the Seine broken down at, i. 247

Round Table, a, at Windsor, i. 224, 225, *note*

Roxburgh, threatened by the Scots, i. 362.

Russel, Theobald, appointed governor of the Isle of Wight and the Channel Islands, i. 117.

SAARBRUCK, Count of, taken prisoner at Poitiers, i. 391

Sagebran, Henry, the monk, his interview with Robert of Artois, i. 104

Saintes, filled with soldiers by the English, i. 44. Taken by the Count of Alençon, 45. Taken by the French, ii. 208

Saintonge, defended by the Count of Lille Jourdain, i. 239. Bands of brigands in, 292

Salisbury, meeting of Parliament at, i. 22. Mortimer's insolence at, 24.

Salisbury, William de Montacute created earl of, i. 111. Created admiral of the fleet, 112. His siege of Dunbar, 189. Raises the siege, 190. Joins an expedition to Brittany, 213. Ordered to go to Poitou, but does not leave England, ii. 202. Appointed admiral of the fleet, 221. Sails and lands the forces in Brittany, 221. Sails for Brest, 222. But leaves, 223. Lands at Brest, and challenges Du Guesclin, 224.

Salisbury, Countess of, Froissart's error as to the, and the King, i. 200–202, *note*. Story of her and the establishment of the Order of the Garter, 299.

Salmon fishery, regulations of the, in the Thames, ii. 261, 277.

Salt tax, oppression of the, in France, 371, 372. Resisted in Normandy, 371, 372

Salvatierra taken by the Prince of Wales, ii. 125

Sarum, New, meeting of Parliament at, i. 22

Sauveterre, captured by the Earl of Lancaster, i. 273

Sauveur, St., besieged by Du Guesclin, ii. 237. Agrees to surrender unless relieved, 237. Surrendered, 240.

Savin, St., attempt of Chandos to retake it, ii. 165

Savoy Palace, residence of King John

SCO

of France and his son in the, i. 400. His life and death there, 400

Say, Sir Geoffrey, appointed admiral, i. 74

Scone, great stone of, brought to London, i. 19. Refusal of the Londoners to return it to Scotland, 19

Scotland, wars between England and, in the reign of Edward III., i. 2. First war of Edward III. with, 13–16. Conclusion of peace with England, 18. Abandonment of Edward III.'s claims over Scotland, 18. Beginning of the war again between England and Scotland, 54. Invasion of Scotland by Edward Balliol, 54, 55. Who defeats David's army, and is crowned king at Scone, 56, 57. But is surprised by Bruce's companions, and compelled to fly into England, 58. Preparations of Edward III. for war with Scotland, 59. Siege of the Scots in Berwick, 61. And defeat of Douglas at Halidon Hill, 63. Balliol reseated on the throne, 65. The whole of Scotland south of the Forth given up to Edward III., 65. Flight of Balliol again, and rise of the Bruce party, 66, 67. The kingdom overrun by Edward and Balliol, 68, 69. Edward returns to England, and agrees to a truce, 69. He again invades Scotland, 69. Submission of the Bruce party to Edward, 70. Conclusion of a temporary truce, 71. Return of Edward to Scotland, 73. Leaves for England, 75. Mutual aid given by France and Scotland, 114. Siege of Stirling by the Scots, 114. The Earl of Arundel in command of the English army in Scotland, 129. Preparations of Edward III. for renewal of the war with Scotland, 186, 189. Events from Edward's departure till the truce with France, 189. Frightful sufferings of Scotland from the miseries of war, 192. Trade with Scotland forbidden by English law, 341. Death of Balliol, and intrigues as to David's successor, ii. 97, 98. Origin of the Stuart dynasty in Scotland, 192

Scots, an army of the, invade England, and ravage the North, i. 13, 14. Their rapid movements and little impediment, 13. Encamp on the Wear, but will not be brought to battle, 14. Disappear, but are found again, 15. Finally escape, 16. Com-

INDEX. 345

SEA

clusion of peace between England and Scotland, 18, 19. Stirling besieged by the Scots, 114. Two Flemish ships and a number of Scots taken by the English, 116. Ravages of the Scots in the North of England, 177. Their defence of Dunbar, 189, 190. Death of their Regent, 191. Their capture of the castle of Perth, 191. Of Stirling, 192. And of Edinburgh, 192. Conclusion of a truce for two years with the English, 193. Their invasion of England in 1346, 268. Plunder and lay waste the country, 269. The defeat at Nevill's Cross, 270, 271. Take Berwick, and about to attack Roxburgh, 362. Retreat of Edward, and conclusion of a truce, 409, 410. King David set free, and returns to Scotland, 410. A policy of conciliation adopted by Edward III., 411. Events in Scotland after the battle of Nevill's Cross, 401. Balliol not recognised as king, 401. Edward III.'s treatment of the people, 402, 403. Negotiations for the release of King David, 403. Their failure, and commencement of border warfare, 404. Attack of Douglas on Berwick-on-Tweed, 405. Relief of Berwick by King Edward, 407. Who prepares for the subjugation of Scotland, 407. Advance of the English, and retreat of the Scots, laying the country waste, 408. The truce with the Scots extended by Edward III., 153. Enter into an alliance with Charles V. of France, 192, 193

Sea, Edward III. claims dominion over the, i. 74

Selkirk, forest of, given to Lord Montacute, i. 35

Sessions, Quarter, establishment of, i. 302

Seton, son of the Governor of Berwick, given to Edward III. as hostage, i. 62. Hung before the town, 62

Seton, Sir John, conduct of, at Noyon, ii. 174

Sévère, St., castle of, taken by the Duke of Berri and Du Guesclin, ii. 203

Shareshull, Sir William, Chief Justice, his statement to Parliament, i. 405

Sheep, exportation of English, forbidden, but some smuggled into Spain, i. 87

Sheppey, Isle of, threatened invasion of the, i. 133.

STA

Sheriffs, abuses of the, i. 162. Provision of Parliament against their oppressions, 166. Excluded from the representation of counties, 348

Silver, law as to the exportation of, and debasement of the currency, i. 81

Sluys, sea-fight off, i. 172. An immense Spanish fleet allowed by the Count of Flanders to assemble in the harbour of, 324.

Soldiers, first clothed in uniform, i. 120. Rate of payment to, 206. Payments made by grants of wool, 206

Soubise, relieved by the Captal de Buch, ii. 201 The siege abandoned for a time, 204. Besieged by the French, who are routed by the Captal de Buch, 207

Southampton, regulations for, in danger of French invasion, i. 134. Pillaged and burnt by the French, 144

Spain, war with, in the reign of Edward III., i. 2. English sheep smuggled into, 87. Involved in the war between England and France, 322. History of the Peninsula, 322. Sends a powerful fleet under De la Cerda, to invade England 324. Employment of the "Companies" in, ii. 106. The campaign of 1365-6 in, 107. March of the invaders to Barcelona, 112. And to Castile, 113. March of the Black Prince for, 122, 123. Defeat of an English fleet by a Spanish one, 199

Speaker, a, chosen by the Commons, ii. 248, 249. His demands, 248

Spies, foreign, forbidden at Oxford, ii. 232

Stanhope Park, encampment of the Scots, under the Earl of Moray, in, i. 15

Staple, Statute of the, i. 340. Staples established at certain places, 341. Proposed removal of the wool staple from London to Calais, ii. 74. Petition of the Commons as to the staple, 231. Formation and organisation of wool staples, 91. Places at which staples were appointed, 91, 92. Passing of the Statute of the Staple, 92. Establishment of a staple in Brabant, 108

States General called together by John II. of France, i. 369. Their grant of unpopular taxes, 371. Assembling of the, ii. 19. Proposals of reform submitted by them, 21. But resisted by the Duke of Normandy, 21. The States persuaded to disperse, 21.

346 INDEX.

STA

Meet again, 25. Reforms demanded by them consented to by the Duke of Normandy, 25, 26. Compel the Duke to submit to their Committee of Thirty-six, 26, 27. The Duke's charges against the Thirty-six, 28. Reject King John's treaty with England, 39

States General of the Langue d'oc, meeting of the, ii. 22. Their reforms resisted by the Duke of Normandy, 22

Statutes of the Realm, mode of promulgation of the, i. 77, 78

Stephen's St., completion of the chapel of, at Westminster, i. 315

Stirling, siege of, by the Scots, i. 114. Captured from the English, 192

Stratford, John, Bishop of Winchester, obtains the consent of Edward II. to resign his throne, i. 7, 8. Created Lord Chancellor, 47. Accompanies the King on his secret journey to France, 47. Meets the cardinal ambassadors from the Pope, 127. His account given to the Parliament of the campaign in Flanders, 160. Resigns his office of Chancellor, but reinstated by the King, 170, 171. Again resigns, 171. The King's quarrel with him, 179–184

Stratford, Robert, Bishop of Chichester, appointed Chancellor, i. 171

Strongbow, Earl (Richard Fitzgilbert, Earl of Pembroke), goes to Ireland to assist Dermod MacMurragh, ii. 4. Marries Dermod's daughter, and claims the kingdom of Leinster, 4. Opposed by the King of Ireland, whom he subdues, 4. Returns to England; accompanies Henry II. to Ireland with an army, 4

Styria, Duke of, enters into an alliance with Edward III. against France, i. 147

Succession, note by Miss Cooper on the succession to the English crown, ii. 299

Suffolk, Robert de Ufford, created Earl of, i. 111. Appointed Admiral, 112. At the battle of "L'Espagnols-sur-mer," 325. At the battle of Poitiers, 393. Leads the way to Bordeaux, 396

Sumptuary laws of Edward III., i. 83. Those of the Romans, 83, *note*

TAILLEBOURG, taken by the French, ii. 208

TRA

Tancarville, Count of, sent by Philip VI. to assist Normandy against the English, i. 245. Taken prisoner at Caen, 245, 246

Talleyrand, Cardinal of, his endeavours to promote peace, i. 397

Taxes, levied on particular classes, i. 68. Arbitrary taxation for providing ships of war, 113. A fifteenth granted to the King for two years, 166. Labourers exempted from taxation, 166. Petition of Parliament against taxation without their consent, 314; ii. 281. Subsidy granted to the King in 1371, 185. Poll-tax granted, 278.

Tello, Don, surprises the English, ii. 126, 127. His flight at Navarrete, 131, 132

Thames, the salmon fishery of the, ii. 261, 277. Regulations as to the navigation of the, 261, 277

Thanet, Isle of, put into a state of defence, i. 117

Thirty, battle of, i. 333

Thomas of Woodstock, appointed Guardian of the kingdom, ii. 47

Thouars, besieged by the Constable Du Guesclin, ii. 210. Preparations of Edward III. to relieve it, 211. Failure of the expedition, 212. The city surrenders to Du Guesclin, 213

Thurles, battle of, ii. 7

Toledo, besieged by Henry of Trastamare, ii. 137

Tonnerre, taken by assault by Edward III., ii. 51

Toulouse, a large French army assembled at, i. 243. Threatened by the Black Prince, 366. Some French troops defeated by him before, 368

Tournai, besieged by Edward III., i. 176. Its distress, 178

Tournaments forbidden, i. 51, 294. Edward III.'s Round Table at Windsor, 224. Fondness of the Court for, 293. Irregularities at them, 295

Tours, the nobility of, roused by the Duke of Normandy, i. 241.

Tower of London, the Constable of, thrown into prison, i. 179. David II. of Scotland confined in the, 271. Charles of Blois imprisoned in, 276

Trade, special parliaments assembled to discuss questions of, i. 4, and *note*. Regulations of the Parliament of Westminster (1330), 40. Interference of Parliament with, ii. 73–80. trade in corn allowed, 263

INDEX. 347

TRA

Traylbaston, courts of, establishment of, i. 301. Abolished, 302.

Treason, High, Statute defining the crime of, passed, i. 345

Troyes, Bishop of, drives the "Companies" out of Champagne, ii. 40

Tyne, crossed by the Scots, i. 13

UFFORD, ROBERT DE, created Earl of Suffolk, i. 111. *See* Suffolk

Ufford, Sir Robert, Viceroy of Ireland, his Irish policy, ii. 8. His severity, 14. His death, 14

Ulster, John de Courcy, Earl of, becomes an independent ruler, and defeats the Viceroy of Ireland, ii. 7

Urban V., Pope, supports Henry of Trastamare as a rival to the throne of Pedro the Cruel, ii. 108. His part in the payment of the expedition against Pedro, 111. His death, 190. Notice of him, 190

Urban VI., Pope, resistance of Parliament to his claims, ii. 94. Revives his claim of an annual subsidy, 95. Rejection of the Pope's demand, and settlement of the question, 95, 96. Prevents the marriage of the Earl of Cambridge with Margaret of Flanders, 99

Urdiales, Castro de, handed over to the Black Prince, ii. 119

Usmaris, Nicholas, appointed vice-admiral of the fleet of Aquitaine, i. 112. Ordered to destroy all French ships in port, 114

Usson, taken by Sir John Devereux, ii. 189. And retaken by Du Guesclin, 190

Usury, petition of the Commons against, ii. 263

VALOGNES, taken by Edward III., i. 245

Vannes submits to John of Montfort, i. 196. Taken by Charles of Blois, 212. But besieged and captured by the English, 213. Retaken by the French, 214. The English forces gathered before the town, 215. Opens its gates to Du Guesclin, ii. 222

Vega, Garcilasso de la, murdered by Pedro the Cruel, ii. 107

Vernon burnt by the English, i. 247

Viceroy of Ireland, the first, ii. 5

Vierzon, taken and occupied by the

WOO

Prince of Wales, i. 379. Cruelty of the English to the garrison, 380

Ville Franche taken by the Duke of Normandy, i. 243. Retaken by the Earl of Derby, 243

Vital, St., Cardinal of, endeavours to make peace, i. 397

WAGES, disputes as to, i. 309. The King's proclamation, 309. The Statute of Labourers passed, 311. Petitions of Parliament against labourers who require higher wages, ii. 264. But no change made in the law, 265

Wales, castles of, ordered to be put into a state of defence, i. 117

War, great engines of, made for the campaign against the Scots, i. 59. Courtesy in warfare in the middle ages, 151. Unpopularity of the war with France, 164

Warwick, Earl of, at the battle of Crécy, i. 255. Commands a fleet in the Channel, 280. At the battle of Poitiers, 393. Searches for King John, 394. Leads the way to Bordeaux, 396

Wear, meeting of the English and Scots on either side of the, i. 14

Weights and measures, enforcement of uniformity of, i. 168

Westminster Abbey, coronation of Edward III. in, i. 6. Completion of the chapel of St. Stephen at, 315

Wight, Isle of, fortified, i. 71. Attacked by the French, 74. Theobald Russel appointed governor of, 117

Winchelsea, landing of the French at, ii. 51. Who are driven into the sea, 52

Winchester, meeting of a Parliament packed by Mortimer at, i. 32. Roman woollen manufactories at, 85. Walls of, ordered to be repaired, 134

Winchester, Statute of, Provisions of the, i. 300

Windsor, Edward III.'s Round Table at, i. 224

Windsor Castle, account of the building of the Round Tower of, i. 413–415

Wine-trade, interference of Parliament in the, i. 338. Punishment for selling corrupt wines, 40

Wool manufactures, increase of the, in the reign of Edward III., i. 3. Encouragement given to Flemish weavers to settle in England, 4. Efforts of

348 INDEX.

WOR

Edward III. to promote the manufacture, 85–87. History of the trade in England, 85. Act compelling the English to wear English-made clothes only, 88. Exportation of wool by the King, 89. Exports of wool permitted, but the King to be first served in buying and selling, 90. The Brabanters allowed to buy wool in England, 115. Subsidy granted to the King in the shape of wool, 117. His difficulty in selling it, 118. The wool granted to Edward fails to arrive, 135. Wool ordered to be taken anywhere, 135. An aid of 30,000 sacks of wool granted to the King, 163. Regulations as to the sale of cloth, 340. Statute of the Staple, 340, 341. Unwise interference of Parliament with the price of, ii. 74. Wool allowed to be exported, but not woollen goods, 75. Export of yarn prohibited, 263, 264

Workmen, dispute between employers and, i. 309. The King's proclamation as to, 309. The Statute of Labourers passed, 311

Worsted manufactures of Norfolk, i. 86

Wyclif, John, his work on the Black Plague, i. 306. His first appearance as an opponent of the Pope, ii. 96, 97. His opposition to the appointment of

YPR

ecclesiastics to great offices of state, 182.

Wyclif, William, his opposition to the doctrines of the Church of Rome, i. 5. One of the negotiators of peace with France, ii. 241. Notice of him and his works, 281. His trial, 265

Wykeham, William of, Bishop of Winchester, his statement to Parliament of the reasons for requiring a subsidy, ii. 181. Attacked by the Duke of Lancaster, 267. Account of him, 267, 268. Causes of the enmity of the Duke, 269. Condemned, 270

Wyther, Sir Thomas, his murder of Lord Holland, i. 25

YORK, Edward III. at, i. 11. Fortified by order of the King, 11. Quarrel between the English and Flemings in the city, 12. Meeting of Parliament at, to discuss peace with Scotland, 18. Marriage of Edward III. and the Princess Philippa at, 22.

York, House of, origin of the, ii. 97

Yorkshire, Roman woollen manufactories in, i. 85

Ypres, its alliance with Edward III., i. 316. Endeavours of Count Louis to detach it from Bruges, 316

THE END.

CPSIA information can be obtained
at www.ICGtesting.com
Printed in the USA
BVHW082045200622
640215BV00001B/178